Lost in the Snow

Lost in the Snow

TRACY CAROL TAYLOR

PRINCE OF PAGES, INC.
ARLINGTON

Prince of Pages, Inc.
Carlin Springs Road.
Arlington, VA 22203
www.princeofpages.com

ISBN: 978-1-949252-37-8
Editing and Cover Art by: Lauren Gonzales
Editor: Samantha Johnson
Distributed by IngramSpark

Contents

Lost in the Snow

by

Tracy Carol Taylor

Chapter 1

Anyone who's ever said that winters in New York were wonderful, have never had to drive in them. The towering cold icy city spread around her as she pushed her car forward a few measly inches. She seethed as she had to stop again...for the third time... in the same two block stretch. It was bleak and snowy and the dark indigo clouds visible over the highway and the sprawling energetic city hid the moon from view. She turned up the radio and sighed deeply to calm herself. It would get better once she was out of the city, or so she kept telling herself. She watched almost hypnotized by the rhythm of the wiper blades as they pushed snow from her windshield. Finally, she exited the main highway, heading into more open road. Unfortunately, neither the road nor the weather got any better.

The road was lit only by Jessie's headlights, and she still struggled to see what was ahead of her. Just shy of a blizzard, snow was falling in a tumultuous flurry, and was caking the windshield in a layer of powder. This was not the *ideal* weather to be driving in. She should have just waited until the weather was better, but it had been a long trip already. She just wanted to go home and sleep in her own bed. But now she just hoped that she could make it home before the storm worsened.

She was only going about 15 miles an hour, yet she was gripping the wheel just to keep the car under control. The long stretch of hardened tar was slick with ice and buried underneath a foot of snow. She'd been driving for hours; turning left, then right, only to make a U-turn when the GPS rerouted her. The strain from staring only made it worse and gave her a throbbing headache. Aggravated, she let out a groan of frustration.

"Stupid GPS! Where the hell am I?" *Jessie griped. Sliding to a stop on the side of the road, she slammed her right fist into the padded headrest repeatedly.* "Dammit," *She hissed.*

Jessie rubbed her eyes with the heels of her hands and then squinted at the GPS screen on her phone. She put the car in reverse and swung it wide on the empty upstate road and shifted into drive. She peeled away down the dark road and faster than she could react, in a blink, a large buck bounded across the road. The young woman instinctively jerked the wheel. She was careening on slick ice, and her tires were gliding out of control. There was a loud bang, blinding pain, and then the feeling of weightlessness. She was thrown back into the seat as the car collided with guard rail. The deer bounded over the rail and fled. Its white tail and proud antlers vanishing into the trees at the other side of the road.

Chapter 2

"Ugh," Jessie groaned. She cracked open an eye and squinted against the glare.

The sun was shining, and it bathed her in the radiant yellow glow of day. The birds were singing, happily unfettered, but she felt slow and stiff. The bright and nearly blinding sun caused her to blink. She screwed her eyes shut tight again. Then she remembered... antlers. *Antlers?* She opened her eyes ignoring the stabbing pain from the light of day filtering in from the windows. Windows she didn't recognize. She attempted to shoot up and snarled in agony collapsing back into the bed. A soft bed that wasn't hers.

"Where am I? What happened? Whose place is this?" Her mind ran in frantic circles.

Every inch of her was quivering in pain; her fresh wounds pulled and wanted to open. It was unbearable. Her body was stiff, and every movement felt like a knife had slowly carved its way across her skin. Her face felt swollen, and her mouth felt dry and stuffed with cotton. Jessie's headache was excruciating, worse than any migraine or hangover that she'd ever had before.

It was as if someone was trying to hammer spikes into concrete behind her eye, especially her left one. She lifted her arm, slowly that time, to the left side of her head just above her ear to find the source. She winced and let out a small cry and snapped her hand away.

"What happened to me?" The raspiness caused her to cough; searing pain shot through her stomach, and she had to refrain from clutching at her side.

"Shit!" She sucked air from between her teeth in a pained hiss and made the slow uncomfortable shuffling and slinking effort to move. She lifted her shirt, wincing and gasping and glanced down.

A *bandage?* It was wrapped around her midsection and surrounded by a sea of black and purple that disappeared into the waistband of her thick flannel pajama bottoms. These weren't her clothes. "Where was I going? How did I get here? Whose clothes are these?" She stayed stationary, except for the stiff swivel of her still aching head scanning the room. This was not the four-star hotel that she had been in yesterday, nor was it her room back home in New York. "Where..." She shifted her eyes nervously, "...am I?"

There were three doors: the one that was ajar

was empty, this she knew was a closet. The second one, she assumed led to the rest of the building she was in. The third hopefully led to a bathroom. *Ok, check the locks.* The room itself wasn't large, but it seemed like a massive undertaking to get up and cross it. However, she had to get up. She had to get moving. She felt her pulse quicken, but she stilled it, breathing deeply despite the tightness to her chest. She threw her legs over the side of the bed and stood up. First hurdle averted, she didn't crumple to the floor, but the world swam and spun perilously, and she hunched over tightly gripping her damaged midsection tenderly. She braced herself, took a few deep breaths, and crossed to the door she assumed led outside. It took her a few tries to actually reach the doorknob. Things were blurry as she moved, and she was seeing doubles.

Why can't I remember... the head injury, she realized. She reached up to touch it again, and felt...dried blood flake away to stick to her fingers? Her arms were riddled with small scratches and dark purple blue bruises even against her brown skin and her hands were shaking. There were the sore itchy beginnings of scab on her knuckles. She silently cheered in relief when the doorknob turned. It was unlocked. "Yes! It's unlocked!!"

"Time to see who owns this house." The injured woman stopped before she opened the door. *Need a weapon. Just in case.*

Jessie cursed under her breath as she scanned the room. She settled for the lamp on the bedside table. She yanked the cord out of the socket and hefted it by the bar that held the bulb and lampshade. It was heavy and solid, so she could smash it against someone's head if she needed. It would have to do. Moving got easier and her head was starting to clear. Slowly, she tiptoed on bare feet out of the room. She didn't bother closing the door for fear it would click or make some noise.

Ahead of her, she could see stairs. So, this place was apparently two stories. Jessie's mind raced with possible scenarios for engaging the enemy, but it was hard to think straight with this raging headache. All of a sudden, the glorious aroma of a home cooked meal interrupted her thoughts, lured her down the stairs, and toward the kitchen. When she turned the corner, she saw a man cooking over the stove dressed in nothing but a pair of red flannel pajama bottoms. Jessie and her instinct to hit him was dumbfounded, and she stood there gawking at him with raised eyebrows.

"Whoa," She mouthed to herself.

He had athletically, chiseled features with whispering peach skin and dark brown hair. The lack of a shirt gave her full view of his broad shoulders and muscular upper body. He had a couple of old scars down the left side of his chest that only seemed to add to his attractiveness. Jessie also saw a black and white elk's head logo tattooed opposite to his scars.

Jessie grimaced in pain as she remembered, THE DEER. Her eyes widened and a single memory shot forward. But it was only for a second before it was gone again. Disappearing into her foggy memory. She gathered herself and stood up straight, clearing her throat to get his attention before he caught her staring straight at him. When he turned his head towards her, Jessie's breath caught. Her eyes connected with his soft brown ones.

Well, she's awake, and carrying a lamp. Must be scared. Probably thinks I'm a kidnapper. Smile, make her feel at ease. He offered her a smile.

"Bonjour, comment vous sentez-vous aujourd' hui?" He asked, as he stirred the pancake mix. *No sudden movements. Take it nice and slow. Allow your prey to come to you. Prey can spook easily and will fight if backed into a corner.*

Jessie blinked and her back straightened. She did not expect to hear him speak French. "What?"

"Ah, American?" He chuckled, "I said, good morning, how are you feeling today?" He doled the pancake batter into the frying pan and the smell of the butter and frying batter made Jessie's stomach not only groan, but snarl.

"Is there a reason why you are holding a lamp?" He questioned her. His left eyebrow arched in curiosity.

Jessie held the lamp ready to defend herself. "Tell me where I am," She demanded. "Now." He just frowned at her and gave her such a look that Jessie added the word. "Please."

The man nodded. He was pleased by her "attitude" adjustment, and he wiped his hands on his apron.

"Of course, you must be confused with the bashing you took." He addressed the injured woman, who was glaring at him and still brandishing the lamp like a club. The man turned down the eye of the stove and turned to face her. "You were in an accident de voiture."

Jessie continued to stare at him and did not lower her impromptu weapon. She was desperately trying to remember her basic French from College, but with this massive headache it was hard to think.

"Avez-vous...de...l'aspirine?" Jessie asked, finally remembering some French.

"You speak some French?"

Jessie noted that this man was bilingual, and he seemed to flow from French to English easily. Jessie decided to stick with English.

"Not really, just the basics. I flunked French."

"I do have l'aspirine. It is in cabinet over there." He pointed and Jessie glanced to her right. "You were in bad accident," René turned back to the stove and flipped the pancake with a quick flick of the sizzling skillet. His thick French accent flowed like silk, and he spoke. "There was a huge snowstorm last night. I am surprised that you were dumb enough to be out in it."

Jessie took offense to his insult, and she prepared to stare him down.

"Hey!"

But their eyes met and neither of them broke eye contact for a few seconds. When he realized that he was staring at her, René turned his attention back to cooking. Jessie felt her face warm and turned her head as well.

"Would you like eggs et Bacon too?" He offered her.

"I'm sorry, but I don't like eggs." Jessie reluctantly lowered the lamp, placed it on the counter, and took a cautious slow step towards the cabinet with the pain killers.

"Really?" He raised an eyebrow at her and shrugged. "More for me then." With the tension broken and him fairly confident he was not about to be smashed in the head with a light fixture, he turned from the stove and fished out eggs and bacon from the refrigerator.

Jessie watched as he added fresh herbs, grated cheese, and a diced onion to his eggs as he whisked. She examined the bottle of aspirin. She tried to sit down in the chair but moved wrong and yelped. She clutched her side and winced in pain. The muffled sound caught his attention and he turned to her again. The man ran a hand along his side in a helpful pantomime before asking,

"Does it still hurt?"

"A little." Jessie admitted still holding her side tenderly.

"Let me see." He walked over to her and gently lifted the side of her pajama shirt.

Jessie froze. Her cheeks felt heated, and she

could feel her pulse quickening. She also felt silly. *Oh, good grief, keep it together Jessie.*

"Well, it's uh," He paused, and took a good look at the wound. It was healing nicely, but she was going to have deep scar. "It's going to be fine. Just don't overexert yourself." He dropped her shirt. Looking up, their eyes met, and he smiled at her.

"Uh, thanks," She whispered, looking down at him.

"Oh, pardon me." He held out his hand. "Je m'appelle René Voclain."

Jessie shook his hand and gave him a nice grin. "I'm Jessie. Jessica Tyler. Thank you for...uh...saving me?" She went back to stool and sat down without hurting herself.

"You have no idea what happened yesterday, do you?" René asked, as he scrambled his eggs and then took them off the stove.

"Not really, but I've narrowed it down to either a bear fight or skydiving gone wrong." She joked, but the flaring pain of her muscles when she laughed made her stop.

René shook his head and then began cooking the bacon. "There was no fight, you got caught in a raging snowstorm and wrapped your car around a tree."

Jessie groaned and rubbed small circles into her temples. "Are you sure I wasn't Deer Boxing? Because I feel punched."

René chuckled. *Interesting choice of words.* "John said you had concussion. The coussin gonflable..."

"Airbag?" she questioned, wondering if that was the right word. *Concussion? That explains my mashed potato memory.* Jessie felt a bit woozy and lightheaded. "Do you have a phone? I need to call home."

"Bien sur, madame. On the wall behind me." He tossed his head back to indicate the direction, as he turned his bacon over.

As she dialed Erik, she took the time to look around the kitchen. It was a small chef's kitchen, with two wall ovens on the back wall. Natural oak cabinets with the same brass handles she had seen in the bathroom earlier. Beautiful slate stone countertops, a farmer's sink, and cozy kitchen island with an attached breakfast bar, that she had been sitting at. René opened one of the top cabinets and Jessie saw lots of spices.

"You must really enjoy cooking." Jessie gave a small smile, as her senses wept for joy at the aroma of a delicious meal. *Maple bacon with cinnamon for sure.*

"I do. Alright so, no eggs for you, but how do you feel about sausage and hash browns? Or maybe some scrapple then?"

"Sausage and hash browns sound great, but what's scrapple?" Jessie narrowed her brow, but that was a mistake. Her head still hurt. She gently pinched the bridge of her nose to ease away the pain.

"Well, it's-" René had begun to explain, but then the phone picked up. Jessie held up a finger to let him know.

"Hello? Erik?" Jessie turned her attention away from Rene.

"Dio mio! Jessie! Are you okay? Where are you?" Came the very worried Italian tenor voice.

"I'm fine Erik, quit yelling." Jessie held the phone away from her ear.

"Girl, where are you? You went missing. I called the hotel, but they said that you left, and you didn't come back. I called the police, but they said you had to be missing for 24 hours." Erik reported. "Besides that, they were busy with all the road accidents yesterday. Please tell me that you weren't out in that blizzard."

"Afraid so. I didn't plan to be." Jessie chuckled

lightly and leaned against the wall. "I actually had an accident of my own."

"Did you get hurt? Tell me where you are." Erik pulled a pen and small notebook out of the breast pocket of his hand tailored suit. "I'll send a car for you."

Jessie pulled the phone away from her ear and looked over at René. "René, where are we?"

"My house." He replied, as he pulled out two more slices of bread.

"Which street, smart ass?" She deadpanned.

"Hanowa Island, Ontario, Canada." René pushed the button down for the toast, and then went back to see about his sausages.

"Canada?!" Jessie whisper screamed at him.

"What's wrong Jessie?" Erik questioned. "Where are you?"

"Apparently I'm in Ontario, Canada." Jessie put the phone on speaker, so that she wouldn't have to relay the whole conversation. "With what I now know to be a very French Canadian." She rubbed her hands over her face.

"Wow, you were really lost last night, weren't you?" Erik commented.

"You have no idea. I was in Syracuse for a book signing and I was driving down Highway 81. How the hell did I end up in Canada?" Jessie blew out a deep breath. "I don't know."

"If I had to guess," René interjected, while he set the plates out. "I would say you missed the Southern Exit to New York and ended up taking the Northern Exit sending you towards Canada, and then you accidently drove across the lake. You are very lucky that the ice held. But then your car was small."

Ok, that sounds logical. Jessie reasoned, but she still had a few more questions. "Hey René, where is my car? All I remember is swerving to miss a deer, skidding across the ice, and then...." Jessie drew a complete blank. "How did I get here?"

"Well, last night you crashed your car into a tree," René explained, as he recalled last night. "The boys and I were playing poker, when Sarah started barking up a storm and scratching the door to be let out. We thought she had to go, so we opened the door, and that's when we saw the fire."

"Fire?!" Both Erik and Jessie's eyes flew open wide, and their mouths fell open.

"I was on fire?!" Jessie repeated. Shock and disbelief colored her face.

"Not you, the car. You were lying in the snow a few feet from your car. A good thing to or you would have been toast." René continued to fill them in about last night, as he laid out napkins and silverware on the table.

"So, you guys brought me back here?" Jessie asked him, her mind still trying to process the information and fill in the blanks.

"Oui." René nodded at her as he finished setting the table. "Jack towed what was left of your car back to town."

"In a snowstorm?" Jessie started rubbing her temples again.

"Jack has a four-wheel drive snow truck," he said. "It was no trouble really. He just jacked it up and towed it away."

"Did you at least take her to a doctor?" Erik asked.

"I didn't have to. John was here. He looked her over. He said that she would be fine. That she only had a concussion, a few scrapes, and bruises, and that a day or two of rest would do her good."

"Oh bene." Erik smiled to himself. "I'm glad."

"Although, he normally prefers his patients walking on four legs and being covered in fur." René tried to hide his mischievous smile.

Jessie's face twisted with confusion. "What?"

"What kind of practice does John specialize in?"

Erik shook his head silently laughing. He already knew the answer.

"He's a veterinarian," René told them, nonchalantly.

"You let a vet look me over?" Jessie's eyes exploded with shock, and she shouted at René. "I could have been dying!"

"It's the best we could do in a blizzard." René gave her a small shrug. "Besides, a doctor is a doctor."

"Well, at least you are safe." Erik sighed with relief. "Now, Jessie do yourself a favor and stay gone."

"Say what now?" Jessie cocked her head to the side, as if she had misheard him, and her eyebrows shot up.

"Since you went missing so dramatically, both you and your books are trending. They are selling like hotcakes again."

"Lovely," Jessie gave him a sarcastic grin and she rolled her eyes. "Now what was that about staying gone?" Jessie stared at the phone and concentrated her attention on him.

"Samantha, your publisher, thinks this mini-vacation of yours is the perfect cover story. The media has been devouring your disappearance."

"Please stop feeding the paparazzi dogs." Jessie

again pinched the bridge of her nose. The headache wasn't getting any better.

"Since the search is confined only to America, no one has been able to find your body or your car. You've just vanished."

"Why not just tell them that I was alien abducted." Jessie joked.

"Hm." Erik reflected, with his hand to his chin.

"Erik don't." Jessie warned him. Her small smile dropping into a frown.

"Well, if you want to know what I think…" Erik began, with a positive tone.

"Erik…don't start. I know exactly what you're thinking." Jessie sighed, and she turned back towards the phone.

"Look Jessie, you haven't had a vacation in years," Erik told her, and he placed a hand on his hip as he spoke to her. "Not a real one anyway."

"I don't have time for a vacation right now. I have a book that I have to finish and a new one to start. Not to mention the book signings and interviews I have lined up." Jessie crossed hers, uncrossed her arms, and waved her right arm out, as she got more frustrated with each word.

"Those are not until March," Erik coolly reminded her.

"Erik, just send a car up here to get me!" She shouted at him. "I have work to do!"

"I can't!" Erik shouted right back. He wasn't fazed at all by her outbursts. He was used to them.

"Why not?" She protested.

"For your information, there's a huge winter storm going on. All the flights in and out of New York are grounded right now." Erik reminded her, as he put away his pen and notebook. "It will be at least a week before I could even get a helicopter up there for you."

"Now you're just making excuses." She rubbed her forehead in irritation and paced in a small circle.

"Don't blame me. Blame the weather." Erik insisted, with a snicker.

Jessie could literally here the smugness and the teasing grin in her friend's voice, now that the relief that she was okay was fading.

"You know what Canada is like in the winter. Besides, consider yourself officially on bed rest."

"What? Why? I'm fine." Jessie lied. Her bravado was in opposition to her actual condition. A condition that was getting worse with her agitated state.

"You're not fine. You're injured. You have a concussion, and you need to heal."

"Actually, I don't," Jessie still insisted, even though her headache was a constant reminder of her true condition. "But that's not the point. I need-"

"Well, there you go," Erik's cheery voice interrupted. "Take the week off and have a look around."

"Well, to be honest..." René said, coming over to stand beside Jessie. "If it is a normal winter here, you might not get her back till the end of the month. And if it's really bad, then she might be here until the end of March."

"March!" Jessie exclaimed. "I can't be stuck here for five months!" Jessie's temperature was rising, and she was pacing back and forth in a much larger area. "It's not even December yet."

"Well, since you're stuck up there anyway, it'll give you time to write that book, you get so easily distracted here." Erik nonchalantly looked at his watch.

"No, I don't." Jessie bristled and her back stiffened at the reproach.

"Yes, you do. The night clubs, the parties, the theater premieres, and Angelo's." Eric droned on, as if telling an age-old story. The injured writer seethed in irritation, and she knew that Erik was counting on his fingers as he made this list of her flaws. "Then I end up scolding you, and then you pull all-nighters till it makes you sick just to meet your deadlines. You go on energy drink and caffeine benders until you're done, and then you go on liquor benders with the girls…"

"Erik, It's my life. I like to have fun." Jessie threw her hands up into the air. Then brought them down, crossed them, and waved her left hand outward. "Now just send a car up here to get me! I have work to do!" Jessie insisted angrily. "You can just leave me here."

"Yes, I can." Erik replied placidly. He removed his cellphone from his pocket and quickly entered his pin with his thumb. He looked over Jessie's schedule on his phone. He knew his employer well. Then he started reading over the weather conditions for Ontario, Canada on his weather app. "The blizzard has closed the roads and shut the airports down up there as well. So, I won't be sending a car or a helicopter for you."

"Erik!"

"You don't need to worry about things here," he told her assuredly. "I will take care of everything for you, even your virtual fish." Erik deleted a few of Jessie's scheduled 'distractions' from her calendar.

"You have virtual fish?" René scoffed at her. Then he looked her up and down with a smirk, trying to judge what type of woman would keep virtual fish.

"Shut up!" Jessie sneered at René. "They are very relaxing and easy to keep." Jessie asserted and counted out each point on her fingers. "No feeding, no changing the water, and they don't die on you."

"Remind me to take you fishing someday and I will introduce you to some real fish," René offered, with a tickled grin.

"That's a wonderful idea." Erik beamed.

"What is?" René asked, wondering what he had just done.

"Erik, don't you dare," Jessie warned her assistant.

"René, can I trust you with my girl?" Erik asked René seriously.

"Pourquoi?" René raised an eyebrow in concern. *What is he thinking?*

"Because I'm asking you to take good care of her for the next few months."

Jessie saw René's back bristle to this idea. *He doesn't want me here anymore than I want to be here.*

"Months?! Oh, now wait a minute." René stood taller, and he objected to this turn of events. "I'm a mountain ranger not a wildness hotel. Being a good Samaritan for a few days is one thing. But a host to a foreign exchange...ragazza"

"I'll pay you $5,000 a week." Erik told him flat out.

"Erik!" Jessie complained.

"Jessie, One, you were in a car accident. Two, the severity of your injuries demands rest. Three, the roads and airports are closed on **both** sides of the border. So, until further notice, you are trapped there whether you like it or not." Erik defended his position with facts and logic.

"He has a point." Rene just shrugged, as he conceded to Erik's logical deductions. "But again, I'm not a hotel. And I don't need your money."

"You're turning down $5000 a week." Jessie stared at him in awe. "What are you stupid?"

Rene narrowed his eyes on her. "Some of us aren't driven by the pursuit of material things. Some of us just enjoy the grandeur, peace, and quiet that God has given us. And I wasn't the one out driving in a blizzard." He smirked at Jessie. "Stupid."

Jessie narrowed her eyes on him for that insult, but then she blew him off. "So do the bums living on park benches." Jessie scoffed and rolled her eyes.

René just shook his head at her. "Greedy American know-it-all. Too busy chasing money to appreciate real life."

"What do you know of life?" Jessie furrowed her brow at him. "You live all by yourself alone in the woods. You're two steps shy of a serial killer. In fact, where did I put that lamp?"

Rene sneered at her. "At least you'd get breakfast before you die."

"Speaking of which," Erik interrupted their tiff. "In the morning, Jessie likes apple oatmeal and orange juice. She hates coffee and eggs…" Erik began relaying information.

"So, she has told me. Is there anything else I need to know? Does she have any food allergies?" Rene snickered sarcastically. *I don't believe this.* He shook his head in frustration. *Wait, why the hell am I agreeing to this? I didn't agree to this.*

"Hello, I'm right here." Jessie fumed and waved a hand at the phone. "I'm not a child that you're dropping off at day camp."

"No, other than eggs, octopus, snails, or frogs' legs, she'll eat about anything," Erik revealed, with humor in his voice.

"Erik!" Jessie shouted angrily. "Erik! You can't do this to me!" Jessie hollered at him. "This is mutiny!"

"Technically captain, I'm marooning you." Erik corrected her. "And since I'm not the one stuck in Canada, yes I can."

Jessie could hear the amusement in his voice. "So, help me...when I get back...I'm going to kill you!"

Again, Erik ignored her ranting. "René, try to have her back to me by March. She has two book signings then, and a television interview in April."

"I will be glad to get rid of her sooner, if the weather lets up." René reassured him.

"Alright then, Buon Natale, Felice Anno Nuovo, and I'll see you on St. Patrick's Day. Addio Jessie."

"Erik! Erik!" Jessie shouted, as the beeping of a disconnected phone filled her ears. "Erik! That bastard!" Jessie ground her teeth and tightened her fists as she growled to herself. "That asshole! Why do I even keep him around? I just call myself..." Jessie searched her pockets for her cellphone, but then realized that she was still wearing Rene's pajamas.

"Rene, did you happen to see my cellphone out there?"

"No." Rene shook his head. "But I did see a melted lump of green and black."

"Damn, so my wallet died too." Jessie blew a disgusted breath. *So, no wallet and no phone. I might as well be homeless.* Jessie snickered to herself. *Maybe I should look for a park bench.*

"So, was that your husband, your brother, or your boyfriend?" René quirked an eyebrow.

"Why would you think that?" Jessie looked at him, taken aback a bit.

"He cares for you," René answered honestly. "And he seems very supportive."

"You noticed, huh?" Jessie's anger bled from her as fast as it had risen. "Well, you're wrong on all three counts. Erik is my personal assistant."

"And what does he assist you with?" He asked, standing beside her.

"Writing. I'm an author." Jessie leaned against the counter.

"Are you famous?" René' asked, genuinely interested in her.

Jessica snorted. "I used to think I was, but you've never heard of me. So no."

"Sorry, madame. Not everyone can be Shakespeare."

"What do you do spring through fall, when you're

not stuck in this house?" Jessie took quick glances around.

"I'm a forest ranger. I keep an eye on the trees, the animals, and their numbers. I look out for fires and in the summer months I'm a tour guide on the nature trails."

"Is winter really that long here?" Jessie's shoulders dropped, as she complained.

"It depends. Sometimes winter starts in October and doesn't end until April. It can also very cold. Now and then, it could drop to -20 degrees Celsius."

"I don't know how cold that is, I'm used to Fahrenheit." Jessie confessed, as she tried to remember the conversion rate from math class.

"Ah, right." René's brow furrowed as he did the math in his head. "It's probably about -5 degrees Fahrenheit."

"Oh, I'm going to die here," Jessie groaned. Her body shivered just thinking about temperatures so low.

"You can't die, Erik will miss you," René reminded her with a teasing grin.

"Miss me?" Jessie scoffed. "Bah, he'll be on vacation too. No more 'Erik, I need this done. Erik, schedule this for me.' Keeping up with me ain't easy. But there is just so much to do, and he knows how to get it all done." Jessie confessed, and then she gave a deep sigh. "I really do need him. I don't think I'd be as successful as I am without him."

"Then you should tell him that from time to time." René turned back towards the breakfast bar. "Now come and get your breakfast. It is getting cold."

Jessie finally hung up the still beeping phone, sat down, and looked down at her plate. "This looks good."

"Not to brag, but I'm a damn good cook." Erik winked at her.

Jessie's stomach growled and begged her to sit down and eat. She made a bacon sandwich and scarfed down the sausage. The crisp sweet maple bacon and honey smoked pork tantalized every tastebud she had with their sweet savory flavor.

"Mmmm, this really is good." She smiled happily.

"It is even better when you stop to taste it." René watched her eat. *I am surprised by her lack of table manners for a city girl.* René buttered his toast and took a bite.

Jessie just raised an eyebrow at him. "What do you do for fun?" She asked, as she wiped her mouth with her left knuckle.

"Hunting, fishing, climbing...." René informed her, and he handed her a napkin.

"That's it? I really am going to die here," Jessie complained, imaging days and days of boredom.

"City girl." René took a sip of his coffee. "You should learn to stop and take it slow once in a while."

"Take it slow?" She playfully rolled her eyes. "There's a reason why they call it a New York minute."

"I can see this is going to be a long six months for you," He cut up his sausage into smaller bites and then ate two sections.

"Look, no offense, but I can't stay here. I need to get back to my life." Jessie told him and then took another big bite of her bacon sandwich.

"Well, the only way down is by snowmobile or dog sled."

"Do you have one?" Jessie's eyebrows shot up with hope.

"No, my Titan is broken, and I do not see poor Sarah pulling you all the way to town." René neatly scooped up and ate his perfectly seasoned scrambled eggs. "You could walk, but it is a twenty-klick hike, and it is supposed to snow again tonight."

"Twelve miles?!" Jessie gaped. "Why do you live so far from town?"

"Twenty-klicks really isn't that far, if you are driving. But with three feet of snow out there..."

"I'm stuck here." Jessie groaned and dropped her head into her hands.

"Well, like Erik said, just think of this as a vacation." René shrugged at her.

Jessie sighed and looked out of the window at the height of the snow. *Twelve miles isn't that far.*

"What do you usually do on your vacations?" René asked her.

"I don't take vacations. My job allows me to travel all the time anyway, so I never need to." Jessie rested her chin against her fist and just looked at René.

The odd French ranger looked back at her. He grinned and met her stare. His deep brown eyes twinkled with delight at how happy the food had made her, and his smile was contagious. He took up his coffee and shoved his hair out of his face. He made the sloppy bed head look good. His dark brassy brown hair was a bit long, but he wore it well in a scruffy roguish way.

"So, I guess this will be a working holiday for

you." René drank his coffee. "What kind of book are you supposed to be writing? Jessie?"

It was only then that Jessie realized she had been staring at him stupidly and he had said something. "Sorry, Sorry," She shoveled more food into her mouth and didn't meet his eyes again. She swallowed her mouthful and then said, "I'm still a little out of it. What were you saying?"

"Le Livre?" He put his coffee cup down. "What kind of book will you write?" He looked at her intently.

"I don't know." Jessie stopped eating, sat up, and sighed again. "I'm out of ideas."

"Hm, how about a wilderness survival guide." René suggested in all seriousness, and then he gave her a bit of cheesy smirk.

Jessie was caught off guard by this bit of humor, but then she rolled her eyes at him. "Tais-toi."

After breakfast, René cleaned up and washed the dishes.

"Do you live alone?" Jessie asked, still sitting at the breakfast bar.

"For the most part, yes." René rinsed off a dish and set it aside to dry. "It's just Sarah and me. But I do go out and hang with the guys. We go hunting, or rock climbing, and we play poker."

"I haven't met Sarah yet." She looked around for the dog he mentioned earlier.

René whistled and a big Native American Indian dog appeared from around the corner. The dog came to René and sat in front of him. René smiled and patted her head. Jessie stood up from the bar and crouched to the floor.

"How adorable," She cooed, as she scratched the dog's grey and white belly. She looked part wolf with her pointed ears and sharp amber eyes.

"Sarah, Jessie. Jessie, Sarah," René introduced. Sarah jumped up on Jessie and started sniffing her as she wagged her tail.

"Hi, Sarah." Jessie smiled at her. "Thanks for sharing your home with me." The dog barked and panted with her tongue hanging out.

"That means you're welcome." He pulled Sarah down away from Jessie and let her return to her spot by the fireplace.

Jessie winced as she got up from the floor. *Damn, forgot about my stomach wound.* She wandered into the living room and sat down in the recliner. It was so cozy, and she felt herself relax into it.

Finished with the dishes, René followed Jessie into the living room.

"Comfortable?" He asked, a mischievous idea coming to mind. "That chair was my mother's favorite chair," René faked a sad sigh and he looked away as if reminiscing.

"What happened to her?" Jessie couldn't help but wonder.

"She died," René said, "Sitting in that chair actually."

"What?!" Jessie jumped out of the chair like it had bitten her. René's straight face broke into a laughing grin. However, Jessie was not as amused. "Why didn't you tell me that before I sat down," She whispered, horrified.

"Calm down, I was only kidding." René waved off her fear. "My mother is alive and lives up north in Charleston." His roguish smile grew wider as she settled back down in the chair. "Maybe you could use this as inspiration for a horror novel."

"If I do it will be about a novelist who kills her kidnapper." Jessie huffed at him, as she curled up in the chair.

René's smile faded when he noticed that Jessie was falling asleep. He took an oversized throw blanket of Iroquois design to cover her up with.

Even though she'd only been up an hour or two, the doctor had said that she should rest. As he covered her up, René stopped to look at her. Despite her stubborn, fiery attitude, he couldn't deny that she was attractive. Then he decided to check on her wounds. He gently lifted sections of her shirt to check on her scars.

Jessica Tyler was a cinnamon skinned pear-shaped beauty, with curly red cascading auburn hair and Florence brown eyes. Aside from the tattoo on her backside, that he had seen last night, she also had another bite mark on her right leg. René wondered what bit her. Jessie was not a petite person by any means, but not obese either. Just full bodied with nicely curved hips. And speaking of big bones, that pirate tattoo on her backside was awesome. It was a skull and crossed bones with a pirate hat, a single rose in its mouth, and two up crossed swords behind them. He wondered where and why she had gotten it. Lastly, he checked her left side. The wound had healed, but it would leave a nasty scar.

"Well, for a writer, it will be just another story to tell." He mused.

After making sure she was tucked in, he quietly

took Sarah out for her morning walk while Jessie slept.

Chapter 3

When Jessie woke up, she groaned, rubbed the crust from her eyes, and scanned the room. The house was strangely quiet.

"René?" Jessie looked around. Seeing and hearing no one, she got up and investigated the kitchen. Nothing. No René and no Sarah. "René?!" She called a little louder, thinking that he must be upstairs.

But there was no response. There was, however, a note taped to a lamp.

Jessie, I had to go to work. I should be back by 5pm before the weather gets bad. There's supposed to be another snowstorm tonight. There's food in the fridge, feel free to help yourself. There's also cable TV. You could watch a movie, and the library is upstairs just opposite the bedroom, should you feel like starting on that book of yours. René.

"How is he getting around in this snow if his Titan is broken?" Jessie scanned the living room. "Did he take the snowshoes or was I just dreaming?"

Jessie stretched again. Her muscles were taunt and aching, and she felt a little chilly. She looked around. The living room and the dining room were open and spacious and there were four large picture windows that faced both the front yard and backyard. He had three soft brown leathers sofas, each easily seating four people each. He had box seats with storage in them under each window. Decorative wooden coffee tables that looked handmade and a large tv.

Around the room were pictures of animals that looked like he had taken them himself, blew them up, and framed them. He had two fishing poles on the wall facing the backyard and she wondered if they were just for decoration. She also spotted two sets of skis piled up in a corner. Rene's home was strong, warm, and cozy, nothing like hers at all.

Jessie was a minimalist. Most likely a trait she picked up from her Army days. Her place was a two-bedroom, two-bathroom penthouse condo. Her living room, dining room, and kitchen were all open concept. She only owned two weeks' worth of clothes, for each season. She had no TV, but a professional's laptop. Tables, beds, chairs, and kitchen things, she didn't worry too much about. It was only her and Erik. Compared to René's home, hers was cold and barren, like no one was living there.

Slowly shuffling over to the skis, she stared at the space. Had there been snowshoes here?

"Must have been. He's a ranger. There's no way he'd be walking through snow this deep, just to make his rounds."

Jessie stretched her neck and felt is pop as the muscles twisted. She rolled her shoulders and yawned again. The silence was a little unnerving. Her world was never this quiet. Then she looked over at Rene's TV.

"Guess, I'll just watch a movie."

By the time Rene' and Sarah made it back home it was dark, and the snow had been falling harder. The wind had also picked up and it did not make things any easier. Its icy grip trying to rip the warmth from his body. The temperature was dropping. The wind was pushing against them as if to blow them back into the woods, and it was getting harder to see with the snow falling into his eyes. René opened the door and led Sarah inside. Sarah barked happily, rushed inside, and quickly went to stand in front of the fireplace.

Rene' decided to check on his houseguest. He

found Jessie lying on the couch where he had left her. She didn't look good. She was shaking.

"She must be cold." René rushed to create a fire in the fireplace and then he returned to her side. Sarah shook the cold from her body and then laid down in front of the fire. René was more concerned for Jessie. "Why didn't she make a fire if she was cold?" René checked her forehead and found her to be burning up. René looked at Jessie's left arm; it seemed to be developing an unusual skin rash. "Jessie," He called to her, seriously worried by her condition.

"Ugh, too bright." Jessie whispered, with a dry harsh voice. Her whole body shook with exhaustion. "I'm so cold."

"Crap, I have got to warm you up."

René picked up Jessie and carried her upstairs. He laid her on the guest bed, went to the bathroom, and turned on the water. Then he came back to Jessie, but she was already asleep.

"Come on Jessie," René made her stand up. "Wake up, we need to get you undressed." Jessie didn't answer. She just slept on. "Aw, bon sang."

René quickly removed her clothing and bridal carried her to the guest bathroom. He slid her into the lukewarm water and turned off the facet. René then ran to the kitchen, got some ibuprofen, and took it upstairs to the bathroom.

"Here Jessie, take this." He opened the bottle, took out one, and forced it into her mouth. "Alright, drink this." He lifted a cup of water to her lips, but she didn't drink.

"Come on Jessie. Jessie?" He blew an exasperated breath. *Guess, I have no other choice.*

René took a swig of water and forced the water down her throat. Jessie swallowed, then she reached up, pulled his head towards hers, and kissed him. It was a sweet kiss. Very gentle and...affectionate. She gave him a small smile, and then her arm dropped back into the tub. At first René was stunned, her eyes were still closed, but she was moving around, and that was a good sign. He pulled back and licked his lips. *Well, that was interesting.* Knowing that she wouldn't drown, he went downstairs to make a phone call.

"John, viens vite!" René told him hurriedly. "Jessie has a fever. She's burning up."

"What?" John gaped. "What the hell ye two bin doing over thare? She should be in kip resting. She had a concussion."

"I know. She was resting. She was shaking with cold when I got home." René informed him, as he gripped the phone tightly. Stress, worry, and strain shown in his voice. "Just get here as quickly as you can. I know it's snowing, and I wouldn't ask, but I don't know if I've done enough to help her."

"Don't worry. I'll be thare in twenty, but git ready for a night guest cause I'm nae driving back."

"You got it. Beef and Beer is on me."

After the phone call, René went back upstairs to check on Jessie. He sat down to wait, and rested his chin against his right hand, as he watched over Jessie. Twenty minutes passed slowly, but René practically flew down the stairs when he heard the doorbell ring. He opened the door and the blizzard tried to force its way into the house. The temperature difference between his warm house and the blizzard's freezing temperatures was immense. He quickly shut the door to keep the warm air inside.

"Tis a wee bit of a snell. It's fair jeelit ootside." John complained about the weather and the fact that he probably wouldn't be able to find his Titan snowmobile tomorrow, as he took off his hat and coat and hung them up.

"John, Dieu merci." René shook his hand. He was exceedingly grateful that his old friend had come, and in such weather too. "She's upstairs in the guest bathroom."

"Soaking in lukewarm water?" John inquired.

"Yes." René nodded. "With a cold compress on her forehead."

"For how lang?" John headed over to the stairs.

"Must be at a least twenty minutes now." René followed behind him. "I just need you to look her over and tell me that she won't die."

When René started to follow John upstairs, John placed a hand on his chest and held him back.

"Did ye start dinner lad?"

"No, not yet."

"Then do so." John continued up the stairs. "Thare is nothing else that ye kin do for her right now."

As René made John's favorite of barbequed round steak strips over rice, John looked Jessie over. He had taken her out of the bath and dried her off. He checked her arms, her legs, and her torso, but he didn't see any other bleeding wounds. The cut that she had gotten from the car wreck had reopened deeper than before and was bleeding again. He decided to sew up her side just in case, and then treated her other scratches. He was placing bandages on her when Jessie finally woke up.

Jessie looked at him and tried to focus her bleary eyes. She stirred and realized that she was naked. She tried to wet her mouth by swallowing so that she could speak. In the meantime, her eyes focused enough to tell that this man was not René. *Ah, he must be John. The vet.*

John had curly tomato red hair, light blue eyes filled with knowledge, and freckles on his face and neck, that she could only assume continued to his shoulders. He was tall, wide-boned, and just as handsome as René. If only he were a real doctor and not a veterinarian.

"Aw, not you again." Jessie groaned and tried to sit up.

John chuckled at her. "Crakin' to see ye again too, lassie."

Did he mean personally or physically? She eyed him but decided to give him a pass for helping her.

"What happened?" She forced herself to swallow. "Where's René?"

"Ye should be resting." John scolded her, his thick Scottish accent coming through more and more. "Ye had a concussion."

"I did rest. Ask René." Jessie protested. Again, the pain in her side radiated through her body as she spoke to John. It felt like someone tearing at her skin with steel wool. Jessie reached over to feel of the bandage that covered her stiches. "He must have taken Sarah out while I slept, because when I woke up, they were both gone."

John smacked her hand away from the bandage. "Do nae make excuses." John packed up his medical kit. "Yer body needs the rest, nae the stress and strain." He stood up and prepared to leave. "I suggest that ye git dressed, René is making dinner."

"Yes, doctor." Jessie watched John leave, and as he closed the door, she slowly got up to get dressed.

Downstairs, John talked with René, as he set the table for dinner.

"How is she?" René asked, his eyes wide with concern.

"She's alright." John took a seat at the dining room table. "She just needs to rest." He gave René a pointed look.

"Okay," René promised, and he sighed with a small smile.

John just shook his head. "Take the young lass some chicken soup and hot tea with honey." John prescribed, seriously. "And make sure ya keep her hydrated."

René nodded. "Sure thing, John." Then he returned to the kitchen to make some soup.

Knock, Knock.

Jessie looked to the door. "Come in." She groaned. She really didn't feel like talking.

The door opened and René stood there holding a tray of soup and hot tea. Jessie squinted at him.

"Erik?"

"How are you feeling?" Rene's gentle French voice inquired.

"Ugh." Jessie groaned and hid under the covers. Not Erik. "I'm not hungry."

"I do not care if you're not hungry." René walked over to the nightstand and placed the tray down. "John said you need to eat to keep up your strength." René sat on the bed and pulled her covers down. He looked her over. "You look horrible."

"And you're an ass." Jessie pulled the covers away from him. "Go away."

"Not until you eat your dinner...please." Rene's harsh voice softened with concern.

"I'm not hungry." Jessie's dry throat whispered harshly at him.

René leaned forward and felt of her head. "You're still hot."

"Thanks. You look good too." Jessie allowed herself a tiny giggle for that one.

René leaned back and scoffed at her. "Delirious too, I see."

"Go away." Jessie frowned.

"Eat your soup or I'll force feed you."

"Fine." Jessie groaned and she slowly sat up.

René took the bowl of soup and held it up to her. He dipped the spoon, taking a small portion of soup and blew on it. Then he presented it to her. She looked at him and rolled her eyes, but then leaned forward and tasted the soup. He watched her as her eyebrows shot up.

"That's good."

"I'm glad." Rene's stern look softened into a nice smile. "Now eat up."

Jessie took the bowl and chowed down on the soup. The hot delicious broth warmed her whole body and seemed to clear her nasal and throat passageways. The tenderness of the chicken was moist and yummy, and the natural salt rehydrated her. The nicely cut chunks of celery, carrots, onions, and garlic were filling, but not too harsh on the stomach. Jessie gave Rene' a big smile as she gave the bowl back to him. *He was right. He's a damn good cook.*

"Thank you."

"That's a good girl." He smiled softly at her. "Now get some sleep."

Jessie didn't argue. She sighed contently and snuggled back down under the covers. René left the tea but took the bowl back with him. He turned off the light and returned to the kitchen.

After feeding Jessie, René put fresh sheets on his bed for John, and then pulled out an extra pillow and blanket from the hall closet for himself.

John said his goodnights and retired. He pulled his pajama bottoms out of his overnight bag and put them on. As he did, he thought about his wife Michelle. She had been upset that he had to go out on an emergency call. But it couldn't be helped. He was the closest doctor, even if he was only a Vet. John pulled his cellphone out of his pants pocket and called his wife. He let her know that he was okay and that his patient would live. He blew her a kiss and wished her goodnight. Then he too went to bed.

"It's just you and me tonight, Sarah." He smiled, petted his dog, and turned on the TV.

By the time René was ready for bed, He decided to check on Jessie one last time. He found Jessie fast asleep. She was sleeping with one arm hanging off the bed, and the covers pushed down. René gently replaced her arm back onto the bed and covered her up again. He smiled at her as he watched her sleep...in his pajamas.

Why am I doing this? Because she was in a car accident and needs your help. No. Why am I letting her stay? For five thousand a week? No. It's not the money. Then why?

René shook his head free from these thoughts, and then he went back downstairs and got comfortable on the couch. Sarah joined him and slept on the floor beside him. René sighed heavily and he drifted off to sleep.

Chapter 4

When René got back from walking his dog, he took off his hat and coat and hung them up. He sat down and took off his boots. The amount of snow that fell off them and onto the floor made it apparent that he should have come in through the mudroom. Sarah shook the cold wet snow from her body and René got hit with tiny snowballs.

"Hey, easy girl." He gave her a stern look as he petted Sarah, and they headed for the living room.

He shook his head when he found Jessie coiled up on the couch, in his robe, covered by blankets, watching TV. He chuckled. *She looks like a turtle.* He also noticed that she was shivering.

"Why didn't you make a fire, if you are cold?"

"Because I don't know how." Came the answer from under the blankets. "My place has central heating. I've never had to use a fireplace before."

René got up and walked over to the fireplace. "Well, come here and I'll show you. We can't have you catching a fever again."

Jessie threw off the blankets but kept on the robe. She got up off the couch and went over to watch what he was doing.

"First, you need to make sure the damper is open. Otherwise, you will smoke up the house," He instructed. "Then take two small pieces of firewood and put them on the grate. Crumble up some newspaper and place it between the logs for tinder. Now cover the tinder with kindling."

"That seems easy enough, but why would I do it if I have you?" She smiled cheekily.

"Fille de la ville." René rolled his eyes.

"Nature boy," She retorted. Then she thought about Erik and wondered if he knew how to make a fire. *Of course, he does. Erik knows everything.*

"Now put on two more pieces of firewood on top of the kindling. Arrange them like this so that there is proper air flow. A good fire needs to be able to breath."

"Don't we all?" She quipped. "Now you light it?"

"Yes, now we light it." René lit the tender and tended it.

Soon René had a roaring fire going and Sarah barked her gratitude as she too shook off the cold of the afternoon's snow from her bones and sat in front of the fireplace.

René got up off his knees. "Okay, you sit and get warm, and I am going to take a shower. Then I will get started on making us dinner."

"I feel like I should be making you dinner for saving me." Jessie wondered back over to the couch. "You've helped me so much already."

"Do you know how cook?" He asked, realizing that he knew almost nothing about her.

"Well, no." She confessed with a wry grin.

"Wow, you do not know how to do anything, do you?" He teased her from the foot of the stairs.

"Oh whatever." She playfully sneered and threw a pillow at him, still wrapped up in his robe.

René headed up the stairs. "I'll be right back."

Jessie stuck her tongue out at him as he walked away. Then she relaxed back onto the couch as the fire from the fireplace chased away the cold and warmed the whole house.

"This is so much better." Jessie told Sarah.

Sarah just looked at Jessie and wagged her tail, as she sat with her back to the fire and got warm. Jessie stretched out and yawned. That fire felt really good. She had gotten cramps curled up and huddled over to keep warm. But in twenty minutes, that fireplace had the whole house feeling warm and cozy. Now good and warm, Jessie's tightened muscles that had shivered with cold, were now warm and relaxed and tired. Jessie's breathing slowed and she closed her weary and heavy-laden eyes. Jessie was asleep again by the time René came back downstairs. He gently woke her and asked...

"What do you want for dinner?"

She glanced up at him, his slightly damp hair was falling in his face. He reached up and tucked it back. Something about knowing he was just naked under a stream of water had her heating up, and she couldn't blame it on the fire. She shifted her body and pulled the blankets over her tighter.

"Hm..." She mumbled sleepily.

"Dinner?"

"Um, peanut butter and uh...jelly?" Jessie rolled over and turned away from him.

"What?" René leaned back and stared at her. "Is that what you eat at home?"

"TV dinners or takeout." Jessie answered him honestly.

"Well, we're not doing that." René walked back to the kitchen. He checked the fridge taking inventory of what he had. "Alright, you can have either chicken, beef, or fish."

"What about beef stew?" She mumbled, from under his thick robe, "That's nice and warm."

René walked back into the living room and stood

over Jessie. "Good idea, come on get up." He gave her a gentle tug.

Jessie looked over her shoulder at him and groaned. "What for?"

"You are going to help me make dinner." He told her. "I am going to teach you to cook."

"Just call me when you're done." She groused trying to get some more rest.

"Oh no, come on, into the kitchen, or I will take that robe off you and put out the fire." He teasingly threatened her, and he pulled on his robe.

"You wouldn't." She looked up at him. He looked serious. "So, you'll just take this robe off me?" She challenged, and tauntingly looked up at him. He quirked an eyebrow and leaned down, placed his hands on the arms of the chair, caging her in. *Oh crap.* The defiant look quickly fell from her face, and she sucked in a shallow breath while her cheeks tinted.

"You heard me. So, what's it going to be?" They were locked in a staring test of will when Sarah barked, they both snapped their heads towards Sarah and Jessie cleared her throat. René stood up and backed away.

"I'll be in the kitchen," he said, and walked back

towards the kitchen. He was standing at the breakfast bar waiting on her. "Jessie."

"Ok, Ok, I'm coming." She responded and blew out a breath.

Jessie got up, decided to take the robe off so it wouldn't get dirty, and followed him into the kitchen. She watched as he pulled out a large stock pot, potatoes, carrots, beef cubes, celery, tomatoes, and onions. Then René handed her a knife.

"Wash all the veggies and then start peeling the potatoes. I'll start cutting up the beef." René ordered, as he pulled the beef from the refrigerator.

Jessie washed the vegetables and then she started peeling potatoes, while she watched as René expertly chopped up the beef into smaller chunks. René then heated vegetable oil into a large stock pot where he added the beef chunks, seasoned salt, and the chopped onions. Rene' looked over at Jessie to see how she was coming with the potatoes. His eyebrows arched in surprise. Jessie was peeling the potatoes with expert precision. Each peel was thinly sliced, and the potato had barely any waste to it.

"Where did you learn to peel potatoes like that?"

Rene' covered the meat to let it cook. "Even my brother Jules leaves his potatoes full of nicks and bits of peel."

"I was in the Army." Jessie told him, as she gently kept the pressure on the knife and the peel. "KP duty gave me hours of practice."

Rene' knit his brow at her in puzzlement. "I though KP duty was a punishment."

"No, it's rotational, like CQ duty. Everybody has to pull it." Jessie stopped peeling potatoes, turned, and looked at him. "What are you implying?" She asked, as she gave him a side glance.

Rene' shook his head and put his hands up in surrender fashion. "Nothing. I was just wondering."

"Hmm." Jessie gave him another sideward glance and then went back to peeling the potatoes.

Rene' chuckled to himself but went back to his simmering beef.

"Now, we put the heat on medium-high, and when it begins to smoke slightly, add the beef and make sure it's brown all the way through. Now, add the salt and pepper as the beef browns." René continued his lecture on how to properly make beef stew, as his hands expertly performed each task. She couldn't help but just stare in amazement.

"Okay, now that's it browned..." He trailed off,

looking for something, "You want to take the beef out with a slotted spoon, ah there it is," he grabbed it from the drawer, "So that all of the fat drains, then you just set it aside. Once you've done that, sauté the onions for about 5 minutes, turn the heat down to medium-low, add the flour, and cook it for 2 minutes. Oh, and make sure to stir it often."

The handsome man's smile lit up as the kitchen began to fill with the smell of sizzling oil crushed garlic and searing meat.

"Classic beef stew. It's such a good thing for cold weather. It can be so rich and filling. You know, you can make your own stock for it. I've done it before, and it makes the stew taste so much better. It makes the stew real velvety, and you can balance the salt to just how you like it. Soon this place will smell just like grandmother's house." It was only then that he dumped the last of the butchered roast.

Jessie stopped watching at him and went back to chopping vegetables for the stew.

"Non. Non." René shook his head. He plopped a lid on the big skillet with the meat and in an instant, he was right behind her. "When chopping the carrots. Make sure to slice them round so that they can simmer evenly. He stepped behind her, leaned lightly against her, and took her hands in his. He positioned them on the knife correctly and guided her hands. "You do like this, like a cat paw. If you chop straight down, then you can get a rhythm going. Like this. He guided her hands up and down in a steady chopping and she could feel the warm presence of him right behind her looking over her shoulder at the cutting board. "Yes, just like that. Be sure to pay attention to what you are doing, or you might cut your fingers. Keep your left hand moving back as you push the vegetable forward to cut it. Alright, after you've done all of that, we can add it to the hot water to start the broth's about, I want to say maybe two, three centimeters, above the beef. Cover the large stock pot and turn the heat to low and let it simmer for a few hours and you're done."

"Yeah, I got it." Jessie swallowed, as he nodded, stepped away, and returned to the stove.

"I like using really big chunks." René smiled at Jessie. "They're hearty and filling. I haven't made beef stew in a while. This is going to be great. I just need some wine."

"Wine? Really?" Jessie couldn't help but feel...amazed.

"What? It's secret ingredient." René noticed

Jessie's face and continued his explanation. "For the beef." Then he shook a warning finger at her. "Don't tell anyone."

"Like whom, the polar bears." Jessie joked.

"There are no polar bears this far south." René informed her, as he doled out a good portion of wine into the pot.

"I like watching you cook." Jessie admitted. She watched him intently. "It's just like a cooking show, or those Japanese restaurants where you get to watch the chef make your dinner right in front of you."

René gave her a wry grin for her wisecrack but kept on stirring.

"You're amazing." Jessie praised him. "How do you keep track of all that?"

"All what? Cooking isn't that hard." René told her. "You just have to concentrate on what you're doing. Do one thing at a time and keep your kitchen clean."

"No wonder I never learned." Jessie stretched and rolled a kink out of her neck. "It's too much work."

"Work?" He laughed at her. "No, I love cooking. I find that cooking is a very enjoyable pastime with delicious benefits." René wiped his hands on a dish towel and left the kitchen. "Do you want to watch a movie while we wait?"

"Sure." Jessie shrugged yes, and they walked to the living room and sat down on the couch.

By the time the ending credits rolled the smell of cooking beef and stock had filtered all the way from the kitchen to the second floor. René and Jessie returned to the kitchen and René continued the cooking lesson.

"Alright, time to put the veggies in." René instructed Jessie and watched her pour in the sliced and chopped onions, carrots, potatoes, and celery. He smiled at her and then continued. "Now we add some parsley, bay leaves, thyme, a bit of rosemary, and black pepper. Then we cover it and let it simmer for thirty minutes." The Frenchman handed her a large wooden spoon and pushed her gently towards the pot. "No more watching from the sidelines. You're need to stir it, so it doesn't burn or stick to the pot." He pantomimed big stirring motions and urged Jessie on.

It feels odd having him just there. Watching me and instructing me like this. Usually, I'm annoyed at having people stand over me like this. I've never had much love for cooking or the kitchen anyway.

Wonder why since I love to eat. But having someone who clearly loves what he does... makes it almost fun. Cooking isn't hard to do. She smirked to herself. *With handsome help.* Still lost in her thoughts, it was a while before she noticed that he was right next to her again. His shoulder brushing hers as he dipped his own much smaller spoon into the pot.

"Now this is best part. We have a small taste! To see if we want to add any more seasonings." He offered the spoon to Jessie, and she obediently opened her mouth. She nearly squealed in pleasure. It was scrumptious.

"Mmmmm, this is so good." Jessie's smile was so big, that her face was glowing.

René noticed her smile and it made him smile too. He loved having someone to cook for. Sure, he had cooked for friends and family before, but cooking for her and seeing the smile on her face was...elating.

"Good. I'm glad, because I'm starving," Rene' left Jessie stirring the stew and stealing spoonsful of stew, while he went to set the dinner table. "Turn off the stove." He requested, as he placed the plates.

"OK." Jessie turned off the stove and carried the

stock pot to the table. She set it down on a big square ceramic trivet.

In ten minutes, they were both enjoying a hearty beef stew on a very cold winter's night. René picked up Jessie's bowl and served her first. Then he settled into the chair across from her. He spooned a heaping, steaming spoonful into his mouth and nodded in approval.

"Congratulations, Jessie, now you know how to make beef stew." He looked over to her and saluted her with his spoon.

Jessie's smile lit the room as she blushed under the praise he offered. "Thanks." She chuckled. "That was actually quiet fun." Jessie lifted her spoon, dove in, and chowed down. Moans of satisfaction and gratefulness escaped her while she ate.

Rene' just sat back and watched her for a while. *She does love to eat.* "Well, since I made dinner," René lifted the spoon to his mouth, and ate his well-cooked meal. "You get to do the dishes."

"Hey, I helped," She pointed out, and now she looked up at him, "I did the veggies."

"Then I will help you wash the dishes," He offered with a smile.

When dinner was done, Jessie cleared the table and René cleaned up his kitchen. Jessie was humming to herself, while she was washing the dishes, the pots, and the pans that they had used. Having finished straightening up his kitchen, Rene' stood a bit to the side and watched Jessie wash dishes. He thought he recognized the tune she was humming but couldn't quite place it, and then it clicked.

"Jessie, why are you humming Il est les notres?" He asked curiously.

"What, oh. My French teacher taught it to us to make sure we learned the French words for parts of the body." She placed another dish in the dish rack. "Why?"

Rene' just shook his head laughing. "Do you even know what that song means?"

"Isn't it a song about your body?" Jessie picked up a wine glassed and washed it out.

"Not exactly." Rene' continued shaking his head with mirth. "It's a song about hangovers."

"Oh, speaking of which. What is Viens boire un p'tit...ah...coup a la maison?" Jessie hummed a few bars, so that he would understand which song she spoke of.

"Drop by and have a drink on us." Rene' gave

Jessie as whimsical smile as she kept humming, washing dishes, and shaking her hips to the tune. "Why was your French teacher teaching you guys French drinking songs?"

"Do you know another way to get a bunch of students to learn a language, that they are only taking credit hours for, so that they can graduate?"

"Ah," Rene' nodded in understanding. "Your teacher was a genius." He chuckled. *And you are a surprising person.*

Rene' stood there chuckling to himself and watching her hip movements while she washed the dishes. She was having fun in the most menial of tasks. He wondered how she kept herself entertained during guard duty.

I wonder how our children would endure having her as a mother. Why am I even thinking about her like this? Because we are a man, and she is a woman. There is a reason I live out here alone. People can be tiresome. She's not people. She's one person who enjoys your cooking. She's an accident victim and she's a paying guest, don't forget. Eh. So, what. So...she's...what is it about her? I don't know, but I like her, and Sarah doesn't seem to mind her either.

Rene turned looking over his shoulder at Sarah, his dog. She didn't usually take to quickly to strangers, but Jessie... René stopped looking at Sarah and returned his attention to Jessie. René liked having someone to cook for. Lately, he had been imagining cooking for his future wife. That he would play with their kids, while she washed the dishes, after he'd cook dinner. That they would help their kids with their homework, play some games at family time, and then he and his wife would put the kids to bed. Later, he and she could... René stopped, his fantasy faded, and he realized what he had been thinking...wanting...desiring.

Is this really a good idea? He stayed still for a minute, thinking, contemplating, ogling her hips.

René walked over to where she stood. Jessie's back straightened as she became painfully aware of how close he was to her. Having his presence so close to her awakened something within her.

"Thank you for doing the dishes for me."

"You're welcome. It's the least I can do. Dinner was delicious." She rinsed the soap off another plate and placed it in the dish rack. "Makes me wish I knew how to cook."

"As I said, I will teach you while you are here." He rested his chin on her shoulder and watched her wash the dishes.

"Eh, maybe. I seem to be stuck here for a while."

Jessie lifted her shoulder slightly and shrugged him off.

"So, what were you up to today?" He placed his hands on either side of the sink and trapped her there.

"Well, uh, nothing much…" Jessie rinsed off a plate and became very aware of his closeness. Very aware of him indeed.

"I just realized; we didn't make a dessert." He gently whispered into her ear.

"Dessert?" She squeaked, but then she cleared her throat. She placed the dish down, dried her hands, then placed them on the sink in front of her.

"I'm craving something sweet," He whispered, "Are you?"

"Depends." Jessie shivered when He gently kissed her ear.

René was having trouble holding himself back. *Calm down*, he told himself. "Depends on what?"

"What did you have in mind?" Her words were breathy and forced.

René took her hands and forced her to face him. "If you want to thank me properly," He dwelled on her playful brown eyes. "I will take a kiss."

Jessie stared into his eyes. *They're brown, like mine.* Their bodies were flush against one another.

Jessie could feel him, and she was sure that he could feel her heart beating faster.

"A kiss?" Jessie derided. She tried to push him back, to give herself a little more room, but he would not budge.

"Yes, just one kiss." He then looked past her and into the sink. "Then you can go back to washing the dishes."

"Just one kiss." She told him firmly and her eyes narrowed. *I hardly know him...but he did save my life. Besides its just one kiss.*

René leaned forward and gently kissed her lips. His kiss was so...so...tantalizing and...tasty, that she stopped trying to pull away from him, closed her eyes, and enjoyed his dessert. René kissed her more passionately and Jessie responded to his fervent kiss. René was glad that she was no longer resisting him. He let go of her hands, placed them on the sink behind her, and he pulled his waist closer into hers.

Their lower bodies met, and a spark of fire flashed throughout them both. Jessie's entire body felt flushed and her heartbeat quicker. Ironically, she was actually the one doing the advancing now. Jessie's hands instinctually wrapped themselves around René's neck and she responded to his fervent kiss with equal urgency. But all too soon, René let out a soft moan and pulled back from the kiss.

Just like earlier, neither of them moved. Her Earth brown eyes locked with his caramel ones. Both were struggling to catch their breath and they just looked at each other. They continued staring into each other's eyes for a while before he gave her a quick peck. By then Jessie's senses had returned, she pushed him away and she adjusted her clothes.

"Okay, you've had your dessert." She told him. "Now let me finish the dishes."

A smile quirked at the corner of his lips and René retreated to the living room. Jessie just stood there up to her elbows in soapy dishwater and stared at the water, lost in her own thoughts.

Wow. Jessie licked her lips, she still tasted him on her. Still felt his body pressed against hers. Her heart skipped a beat, and she exhaled a breath.

Why did I let him kiss me? She wondered to herself. *I don't even know this guy. Yeah, he saved my life, but...Jeez, it was just one kiss. Come on, you've been kissed before. So why am I still thinking about it?* Because René had left an impression on her. Jessie was still...she wanted to...*girl, don't you dare let him kiss you again.*

When Jessie had finished the dishes, she made her way upstairs to the library. She slid the two-panel pine finished barn door open and went inside. Here Jessie was amazed by the quiet elegance of the room. It wasn't the student desk and chair and a couple of books that she had been expecting. She ran her hand along the smooth polished surface of the wide executive desk.

"Damn," She muttered circling around to drop into the plush brown leather chair behind it. "I could never have something like this in New York. It's huge."

She looked up to scan the large built-in bookshelf that ran the length of the room on one side. The room was lit by natural light filtering in from the big picture window behind her. She spun in the chair grinning like a silly kid for a moment before she stopped and took in the view. It really was beautiful here. Outside the window there was a picturesque winter scene of artfully tall snowcapped evergreen trees and deep powdery snow-covered woodlands in the evening light. She could sort of see why he liked this place so much.

She got up and ambled across the room. The thick colorful rug protecting her feet from the cold wood floor. She plopped down on the big brown leather couch. She let herself slide down stretching out fully to lazily lie on the soft leather.

"Ahh, wonderful." She sighed contently. There was still space for a whole other person on the couch even with her sprawled out on it.

This was officially her favorite room in the house. She was lazily spread out in a warm patch, of the last of the rays of sunlight, surrounded by the smell of leather, wood, books...and salt. She blinked and wrinkled her nose a little. Salt? There were big carved natural crystal salt lamps on display. René used them as book ends on a few of the shelves that was it. Cozy, that was the word. The large room felt cozy. Jessie absently fished around on the back of the sofa and yanked down a thick blanket to let it fall over her as she curled up under it.

"I should get up. I should be writing. I should email Eric to see if there has been any trouble with rescheduling everything for a few days until I can get back home." Jessie should not have been curled up under a blanket. Feeling warm and happy. Well, moving was clearly out of the question, but she could think. She could use her brain for now. What should her next project be?

"I think it should be set in a big old cabin in the woods. Maybe a horror story?" She muttered to herself, curling even tighter under the blanket. "Nah my fans aren't..." She yawned and thought some more. "Maybe a drama. A family gets stuck in a cabin during trip and learn to be a closer family. Yeah..." She giggled slightly falling deeper into a food induced doze. It wasn't long before she was snoring.

When she woke up, it was dark in the library. The sun had fully set, and the moon was rising. Jessie sat up groggy and sore, but her mind was full of ideas for her project. There were several that had entertained her during her dreaming. She got up and scanned the bookshelves. She ran her hands along the spines of the books. The top and middle shelves were lined with books of classical literature. But René also had books of science fiction, fantasy and folklore, adult fiction and adult non-fiction, mysteries, cooking, tragedy, and horror. Jessie read the spines with interest, and she was surprised to also find books on poetry, satire, and philosophy as well.

"Hm, he didn't strike me as the type." Jessie contemplated, with her hand to her chin. "But then again, what do I really know about him."

René also had travel guides of Canada and its forests. Climbing gear and cold weather catalogs.

"The good old Farmer's Almanac." Jessie snickered. "A must for anyone. What's this?" Jessie picked up the book and read the cover. She was astonished. Looking over the lower shelves, she saw that René also had books that covered a wide range of children's fiction. "He also reads children's fiction? I must say that I am surprised. He seems so serious all the time." Jessie thought about René. "He's handsome, yes. But he's also earnest, genuine, committed..." Jessie snickered. "To cooking." Then she thought about *The Kiss*. "Why did he kiss me? Why did I kiss him back? Why am I even thinking about this, I have a book to write."

Jessie sighed and then looked up at the night sky. There were so many stars out. The milky way in all its brilliance, stood out among them. The stars, so tightly packed together, and all of them so bright, it looked like a river. Jessie smiled to herself. Never in her life had she seen something so beautiful. The inky black sky was a canvas, with stars of white, blue, yellowish orange, and some reds splattered against it. It almost looked like someone was trying to rip the universe open and peer through to another dimension. Jessie could easily pick out Orion, but the other constellations were a little more difficult. There was just too much to see. Not even Time Square in all its glory at Christmas, could rival the wonders of the cosmos.

Jessie didn't move, even when she heard the library door slide open. She was too entranced in the spectacle of the universe. René entered the room and stood beside her.

"Here is where you were. What are you doing?" He looked at her, and then he too looked up at the night sky.

"Stargazing." She replied just as plainly. "It's really amazing. So many stars. You never see this many stars in the city...ever."

"Some stars migrate, just like humans." René told her, as he too looked into the night sky. "They are wintering here too."

Jessie looked at René and gave him a small grin. *So serious and yet he has a wit about him.*

"Do you need anything before I go to bed?" René turned at looked at her. *She has beautiful eyes and a nice smile.*

"Oh, yeah! Can I use your computer?" She

pointed to the computer on the desk. "I'd like to get started on my books and keep in contact with Erik. If he's going to leave me here, I should at least make him regret it a bit."

"Sure." René sank into the chair and looked at home there while he worked.

He could have been a big executive in the city, with a tie and a suit, sitting behind a computer all day. Jessie pondered as she watched him type over the keys and push the mouse around. *And yet he chose to be a park ranger. I wonder why?*

René decided that it would be easiest if he made her a personal account. That way he could always erase it when she left and not bother accidently deleting his stuff. "There you go. Just make a password." He stood up and offered her the chair. "Good night then."

"Good night, René. Thank you." Jessie sat down and watched him head towards the door. Then she pulled the chair closer to the computer and began to work. She opened her emails first. René took one last look at her, as she settled into his leather desk chair and prepared to work. Then he closed the door behind himself.

Chapter 5

Jessie was enjoying her warm bed. It was so soft and warm that it was like being hugged. A very safe, warm, and reassuring hug that you never wanted to leave. But something was poking her, poking her shoulder, and interrupting her sleep. She grunted her displeasure and demanded of herself to stay sleeping. However, the poking only continued and was soon followed by a man's voice.

"Jessie?"

"Ugh."

"Jessie?"

"What?" Jessie groaned, painfully unhappy at being awakened.

"Come on Jessie, get up. The fish will not stay hungry forever." René urged her, as he continued to try and get her up.

"Good for them." Jessie muttered, and she turned away from him. "Now go away."

"No, come on rise and shine." René yanked the blanket off her.

Jessie groaned with annoyance and rolled her sleep-crusted eyes at him. "Are you kidding me?" She complained and rolled over to place her feet on the floor. "It's freezing in here." Jessie rubbed her pajama covered shoulders. She had already been there for a week but waking up to a cold room was something she had yet to get used to. Fortunately, almost all her injuries had healed.

"Then hurry up and take a bath."

Jessie turned her gaze towards the window. Jessie saw that it was still very early in the morning. The darkness was clearly waning, but the sun had still yet to rise over the vista.

"Why in god's name did you get me up this early?" Jessie grumbled and she gently rose to her feet. "You're worse than my drill sergeant."

René buttoned his shirt as he answered her question. "Because we're going fishing." He walked toward her, smiled at her, realized that she was staring at him.

God, he's so good looking. Jessie noted his strong chest and chiseled stomach. His dark brown hair, which hung wet about his shoulders. *That wet hair got me into trouble last time.*

Her lips tingled at the thought, and as if he could sense her thoughts, he glanced down at her lips. She quickly diverted her attention to those perfect toffee eyes of his. René Voclain, forest ranger, protector of the trees. *And an amazing kisser,* she added.

"Come on Jessie, stop gaping and get going," he told her, and shoved her towards the bathroom. "Breakfast will be ready soon, but hurry, we need to leave."

"What's the hurry?" She was enjoying his strong hands against her back.

"If the bears get there first, then there will not be much left for us. Now go." he closed the door on her amid her protests and questions.

René went downstairs and made a light breakfast of cereal, toast, and coffee. Ten minutes later, Jessie fully dressed in one of René's long sleeve flannel shirts, jeans, and a pair of his piney winter work boots.

"Do you own anything other than flannel?" He didn't respond and she sat down to eat, but stopped when she found René smiling at her. "What?"

"My clothes look good on you."

"I hate the fact that we wear the same size. You're way bigger than me."

"Yes, but your hips are so..." He leered at her with playful eyes and mimed with his hands as he pulled them apart.

"You finish that sentence, and the bears will be the least of your worries this morning." She glared, as she finished up the last of her cereal.

René chuckled lightly at her. "Okay, okay. Just leave your bowl in the sink."

"Did you feed Sarah?" Jessie wondered, as she looked around for the dog.

"You do it. I have to get the fishing gear down." René headed out of the kitchen and towards the living room.

"Isn't it in the garage?" She pulled the bag of dog food out of the bottom cabinets.

"Nope, it's on the far wall." He reached up and took two fishing rods from off the wall.

"I thought those were for decoration." Jessie found a large salad bowl and poured the dog food into the bowl.

"They're both." René collected the fishing tackle box and made sure the lures and box were ready to use.

No sooner than the first clink of kibble hit the bowl than Sarah appeared. Jessie finished pouring, put the bag back, and watched as Sarah chowed down her breakfast.

"Ready?" René entered the kitchen. Then he saw

that Sarah was eating out of one of his large salad bowls. "Why are you using my good bowls?"

"I couldn't find hers."

René thought about it a bit. "Oh, I forgot to turn on the dishwasher. Well, come on." René handed her one of the rods.

"Sarah's not done yet." Jessie pointed out and looked towards Sarah.

"She is not going with us." Rene turned on his heels and headed towards the door. "We will have to canoe to the spot."

"It's still dark out, how will we see?" She complained, as she fell into step behind him. She was about to close the door, when Sarah came to the door. She looked like a mother bidding her children goodbye, as she sat upon her hind legs. René put the fishing pole and tackle box down and came over to pet Sarah goodbye.

"Good girl, stay here and mind the fort. I won't be long." René assured Sarah, as he kissed her head and rubbed her ears.

"Bye Sarah." Jessie waved. Sarah barked back.

"Will she be alright all alone?" Jessie asked, curiously.

"Sure, she will. Besides, she has got things to do."

René picked up his gear and headed down to the lake.

"Like what?" Jessie mocked him. "Knitting?"

"Wheel of Fortune and the Westminster Dog show." René joked.

"Seriously?" Jessie raised an eyebrow at him. *There goes that dry wit again.* Jessie looked back inside the window and saw that the dog had curled up in front of the TV. "Whoa." She gasped at a loss for words. "You two are so weird."

"Come on." René called out.

Jessie ran to catch up. The morning air stung her cheeks, and she could hear the crunch of the snow beneath her feet. Jessie shuddered a bit as the brisk morning air settled into her bones. She could see her breath before her turn as white as the snow on the ground. She also heard a lone owl's cry and the screech of a dying field mouse. After that, she heard the birds singing their morning songs. *Do birds have reveille?*

"What are you doing? You are going the wrong way." René called out to her.

Jessie stopped and looked around. René was off to her left, but she was heading deeper into the woods.

"Sorry."

"Quit daydreaming and keep up." He scolded, as he waited for her to catch up.

"I was just listening to the forest wake up." Jessie watched him as he took her rod and placing it into the boat. "Isn't the lake frozen?" She wondered, as she looked up and down the coast.

"No, it's not cold enough yet. The temperature must fall below negative one degree Celsius. In January, I can take you ice fishing."

"Please tell me you're joking."

"No. It is about three degrees Celsius right now. Wait till it gets to negative ten, then it will be cold. Come on, get in."

"Do you do this every day?" Jessie stepped into the canoe and sat down.

René shoved off, got in, and started paddling. "No, about every three days or so."

Jessie picked up an oar and paddled too. "What do you do on your non-fishing days?"

"Hunt."

"You're allowed to hunt here?" Jessie smirked to herself, as her mind filled with images of an elven René dressed in green and hunting elk with a bow and arrow.

"I have special permission and a cap on how many bucks I can have a year." René informed her.

After a few minutes of rowing, Jessie's arms started getting cramps and her joints started to ache. She was now aware of how little physical exercise she really did. She switched sides and paddled on her left for a while, but that was uncomfortable because of her still healing wound and the fact that she was right-handed, so she changed back.

"Are you okay?" René asked, as he led them into the waters of the St. Lawrence River.

"Not really," Jessie panted and her cheeks felt flushed. Beads of sweat had already begun to form.

"Are your arms tired?"

Jessie could hear the teasing tone in his voice. "A little underused maybe, but I'm fine. I'm not weak."

"I never said you were." He taunted her.

I'm not weak. She let out an annoyed sigh. "I bet I could kick your ass." She snapped at him, with an arched eyebrow.

"If I let you." He smirked.

"Shut up." Jessie ignored the pain in her arms and paddled faster.

After about fifteen minutes of rowing, René brought the boat to a stop and dropped anchor.

"This is a good spot." He announced. Then he set about getting ready to fish. "Do you know how to-"

"Bait my own hook?" Jessie interrupted him, with an annoyed tone. "Yes. Have I ever done it? No."

"Do you want me to do it for you?" He offered, reaching for her pole.

She smacked his hand and snatched her pole away from him. "No, but you can teach me."

"Okay Ms. Independent." René took up his pole, pulled out a worm from the tackle box, and proceeded to show her how it was done.

Jessie reached for and took up a worm from his tackle box. She held it up and then raised an eyebrow at him. Then she set her pole between her knees, took her hook in hand, and waited for René's instructions.

"Bien." He picked up his hook and he held up a worm. "You take the worm at one end and shove it firmly onto the hook." Jessie mirrored his instructions. "Now, if you leave too much worm off the hook the fish will just eat this end and be on his way. So, you want to thread the worm over the hook in multiple places. Like this."

Jessie watched René and did as he did. Soon her worm was properly impaled on the hook in three places. She showed it to René, and he smiled at her.

"Good. Now just cast your line into the water, like this." With a flick of his wrist, René cast his line over the side and waited for a bite.

Jessie took a breath and then swung her pole out over the waters. Her line landed in the water a fair distance from the canoe. Jessie smiled.

"I'm fishing." She stated proudly.

"Not quite. You still have to catch something."

Jessie stretched and waited. Occasionally, she would give a small tug on her line like René did his. Five minutes became ten, and then twenty, and then an hour. And still they waited. Then something grabbed René's line. Jessie actually got excited, and her adrenaline surged. René reeled it in and found that it was a Coho salmon.

"Nice." She praised him, as he baited his hook again. "How many do we need to catch?"

"I would say about six should feed us for the week." René cast his line back into the water. "But the idea is to catch as many as we can and then freeze the rest."

Soon, Jessie caught one too.

"Hey now, do not get too excited. Reel him in slowly. Reel him in, and then pull, reel him in and then pull." René instructed her.

Jessie was finally able to get her fish into the

canoe. It was about half the size of René's salmon, but her little perch was a proud achievement. René chuckled and commented about the size of her catch as he put it into their fishing bucket.

"Can I mount him to the wall?"

"We only mount the one's bigger than us," He answered.

Jessie grabbed the plastic bucket that René had filled partially with water earlier. She took off the top and looked inside. "I take it you put them in here to keep them alive and fresh?"

"That and to keep the birds of prey from stealing our catch." René made sure that the lid was back on tight. "Crows, eagles, and gulls will steal your catch if you are not watching them."

Three hours later, René had caught his sixth fish. He had caught bass, trout, perch, and a catfish; and none of them were less than ten pounds. Jessie was determined to catch one bigger and wiggled her pole. She had still only caught the one little perch. The sun was high, and its golden light was shining down on them. Though it was still cold outside, the warm rays of the sun were a welcomed delight. The crystal-clear waters rushed about their boat, but it was only a gentle and rhythmic rocking. When she looked to the trees, she saw not one, but three brown bears: a mother and her two cubs. They were off in the distance chasing after their breakfast. She wondered if she would ever get hers.

"They don't seem to like me much." She frowned and tugged at her line again.

"Maybe it is your wiggle." Rene just stared at her. It brought a smile to his face to imagine her wiggling. *If I were a fish, I'd bite her.* But he squashed those thoughts as he returned to himself. "The fish just don't find you sexy."

"Says you." Jessie sniggered, as the images of a fish "wiggling" for another fish to get its attention shot through her head.

Suddenly, Jessie's pole lurched forward. She got a bite...a big bite. She tried to reel it in, but it fought her all the way.

"Oh no, you don't! You're not getting away!" Jessie shouted at it. She pulled on her pole to the point of it bending. Her line almost snapped, but she had learned from René how to let it run and then reel it in.

"If you can't do it, give me the rod and I'll reel it in." He leaned back and watched, amused.

"I got it, thanks." Jessie turned to him and tightly smiled.

Unexpectedly, the canoe lurched as Jessie fought to reel her fish in. René stopped laughing and fought to keep the boat steady. There was something wrong. No fish around here should have been able to do that.

"Um, Jessie, I think you should let this one go." René warned.

"No way! I'm taking him down and I'm gonna mount him in the living room." Jessie pulled harder and braced her feet on the canoe's bow.

She pulled backwards, almost to the point of laying down and then the canoe lurched again. The fish began swimming side to side in a winding motion, trying to free itself from Jessie's hook. But she had yanked the pole hard. She could see that the hook was embedded in the fish's mouth when its head broke the waters.

"That's a sturgeon!" He gasped. "A big one." He looked on in astonishment as he mentally measured the size of it. "Jessie, let it go! That thing won't even fit into this canoe!"

"Then he'll ride side saddle!" Jessie declared. "I will not be beaten by a fish!"

The canoe started to rock violently and threatened to capsize. René tried the best to counter its movements. Even the already caught fish, in their plastic bucket at the stern, seemed to be moving about in fear.

"Jessie! Let it go!" René demanded. His voice was full of panic, and he was afraid that the canoe would flip.

But Jessie continued to ignore him. She wanted to prove herself to him, that she wasn't weak. Prove that she was just as capable, just as daring as the heroes and heroines that she wrote about. But she had reached the end of her line, there was no more. She had to reel it in or let it go. Before she could choose, the sturgeon ran and took the canoe with it.

"Merde!" René hollered from the bow seat. He was hanging on to the sides of the canoe. "Jessie, laisse tomber le pole!"

"Shut up, I got this!" Jessie insisted. "I just need to outlast him."

"Outlast him? Jessie, he is bigger than you per square inch!" René shouted at her. "He is a heavyweight, you middleweight city girl!"

René's outburst only made Jessie more determined than ever to bring that fish down. But the size of the sturgeon overpowered the size of their canoe. René had to cut the anchor loose to keep it from ripping the canoe in half. The fish was now dragging them further and further into deeper waters at the mouth of Lake Ontario.

"Merde, Jessie! Laisser Aller! René hollered.

Just then, the canoe lurched again. This time it was struck from behind. Jessie fell into René's lap, and she lost her pole. She quickly turned over and looked into the waters.

"What the hell was that?" She asked.

The canoe was bumped again and capsized, sending everything into the waters. The cold and chilling waters of the St. Lawrence seeped into their clothes and made them heavy. Jessie felt like she was swimming with lead weights on. Her muscles struggled to operate in these freezing cold waters, her skin began to pimple, and her hairs stood on end as the cold waters rushed over her. René and Jessie both gasped and sputtered to keep water from going into their mouths.

"Jessie!" René called out, as he clung to the overturned canoe.

"What?" Jessie continued to kick, trying to stay afloat.

"I am going to kill you!" He struggled to turn the canoe back over.

Jessie ignored him and descended below the waters. If her fish had gotten away and was far ahead of them, then what had hit their canoe and capsized it. She fought against the natural buoyancy of her body to stay underwater. She wanted to see what had hit their canoe. She looked around and at the last second, she caught a glimpse of a tail. A monstrous tail. She reached out and touched it. Its scales were hard, thick, and sharp. The swish of the colossal tail was making the waters turbulent. Surprisingly, as the tail disappeared into the deeper waters of Lake Ontario, two hands reached down, pulled her up out of the waters, and dragged her into the canoe.

"Did you see that?!" Jessie asked René, as she wiped the excess water from her face.

"What? A fool ass mermaid?" René scolded her. He was livid and dripping wet.

"No. That fish was huge!"

"I know. I saw it." René's teeth were beginning to chatter. "Are you OK?"

"Yes." Jessie stopped looking around and looked at René. What did she see on his face, was that concern? When René caught her staring at him, he looked away. So did Jessie. "Where are the oars?"

"Davy Jones has them." René frowned and looked over the side. "Our dinner too."

"Hold on." Jessie told him and she dove over the side and back into the waters.

René panicked and tried to grab her before she disappeared. After a minute, she resurfaced and threw the plastic bucket into the boat.

"Good thing you had the lid on tight, or today would have been a waste." She told him. "Be right back." She took a deep breath and went back down.

"Jessie!" He called out to her, but she was gone again. "Oh, pour l'amour de…" All he could do was to wait, and he grumbled to himself. Mostly about her stubbornness and stupidity.

"Here." Jessie came up again and tossed him an oar. She was huffing and struggled to catch her breath. Then before he could say anything, she was gone again. Jessie brought him the other oar, and this time, he grabbed her by the seat of her pants and hauled her back into the canoe. She lay there, looking up at him, and laughing. "I hardly think that this is the time for that." She teased him.

"Of all the stupid…I told you to let it go!" René scolded her, and he put the oars back into their half-circle loops.

"Sorry." Jessie awkwardly shrugged and righted herself, then took one of the oars. "Let's go, before it gets dark."

"How are you able to hold your breath for so long?" René questioned her, as they rowed for home.

"Diving School." Jessie explained. "My mother wanted me to be able to swim and function underwater without the need for air. You know, in case my car ever ran off an embankment and into the water or something. Plus, my dad liked to go reef diving. Sometimes, we'd vacation in Florida."

"Bon sang fille, you scared me." René told her sternly.

"Why?"

"Why?!" René started ranting. He took a deep breath to calm down before he started, "You hooked a sturgeon, which is protected by the way. You would not have been able to keep it."

"You could have mentioned that sooner." She was trying to ignore how utterly cold and freezing she was. Her limbs shivered and her teeth began to chatter as she paddled. "Are you still mad?"

"You capsized the boat!"

"That wasn't my fault." Jessie contended, but René just continued.

"And no sooner than I rescue your ass, you dive right back in." He finished in a huff.

"Well, I was already wet, and we needed the

oars." She told him matter-of-factly. He didn't respond to that, and they rowed in silence the rest of the way.

When they finally made it back to shore, René handed the bucket of fish and the oars to Jessie.

"You forgot my poles." René said flatly.

"No, I didn't." Jessie stood there holding the bucket and oars. "My pole-"

"My pole." René corrected.

"...Got stuck in the mouth of the Sturgeon. And I didn't see where yours went. It's damn dark down there, you're lucky I could feel the fish bucket."

Since the anchor was gone, René pulled the canoe to shore, and turned it over so that it wouldn't float away. René took the bucket of fish from Jessie, but he let her continue to hold the oars. René started to leave, and Jessie just looked at the oars. She wondered if she should bring them or leave them here. But then she remembered that René had taken them from the seat when he turned the canoe over. So, she got on her hands and knees and put the oars back under the seat of the canoe. Then she ran to catch up to René.

The sun was setting now and splashed the darkening blue skies with orange and yellow. But as beautiful as the sunset was, the coming night was bringing stinging cold winds with it. Both she and René were suffering from frozen toes, cramping joints, and stinging fingertips. Jessie shivered with cold and wished she was already back in the house. René was walking ahead of her, and he was muttering to himself in French.

"What are you complaining about?"

"I'm not complaining." He spat out and ground his chattering teeth.

"Liar," She retorted. Now that the temperatures were dropping for the evening, Jessie could feel her soaking wet clothes turning to ice. She slapped her sides for warmth and jumped up and down. "That fish was enormous. How does something so big live here and go unnoticed?"

"Because we don't go fishing for sea monsters," René told her mockingly. "Come on, before we freeze to death."

Sarah greeted them at the door. She barked, happy to see them. René gave her a pat on the head and walked the bucket of fish towards the freezers in the garage. Jessie knelt and petted Sarah.

"Hello Sarah, we're home." Jessie kissed Sarah's head. "And you'll never guess what I saw today."

"Now, don't go telling her your fish stories!" René called, from the garage. "Just stoke the fire back up, will you!"

"Only because you asked so nicely!" Jessie yelled back, "And I know what I saw!"

"Of course, you do. So do all the other Champ chasers!" René was now sneezing uncontrollably.

Sarah sat down on her hind legs and waited as her tail wagged back and forth.

"Sorry, girl." Jessie knelt and put another log on the fire. She stoked it into a good blaze and then she started taking off her wet clothes. "I've got to get out of these wet clothes and take a hot bath."

When René came back from the garage, he saw Jessie's wet clothes hanging up in front of the fireplace. All of them. He groaned, frustrated. René felt himself tighten with want as he stared at Jessie's underwear. Sarah just laid in her bed next to the fireplace and watched him undress.

"Do not give me that look." René took off and hung up his wet socks. "This is all her fault." He took off his pants and hung them up too.

Sarah raised her eyebrows and panted. Then her eyebrows fell, and she gave an exhausted breath. René dashed upstairs, got into dry clothes, and then called out for Jessie.

"Jessie!"

Jessie poked her head out of the guest bedroom. "What?"

René noticed that her shoulders were bare. "Get dressed." He practically demanded.

"In what?" Jessie countered. "I was going to hop into bed."

"Naked?" René's eyebrows shot up.

"I was wearing your clothes, remember." Jessie derided him, as she stayed hidden behind the door.

"Oh." René's brow furrowed. "Wait, there. I'll get you some dry clothes."

"Thank you." Jessie scrunched her nose at him. "Oh, and bellhop if you could bring me a warm drink. That would be great."

René stopped, blew out a breath and shook his head. But he didn't turn around. He just disappeared into his room and got a spare change of clothes for her.

"Here." He shoved the clothes at her. "But if you want a hot drink, you'll have to join me downstairs."

"Gonna put the kettle on, ey?" Jessie teased him.

René growled at her but said nothing. He just marched downstairs.

When Jessie finished dressing, she joined Rene in

the kitchen. He had just finished making tea. The aroma of which delighted Jessie's senses.

"What kind of...?"

"It's spiced apple syrup with clementine and cloves." Rene informed her and handed the large coffee cup to her. Then he poured a second cup for himself. "Come."

Jessie looked at her cup and sniffed her drink. It smelled wonderful and its warmness warmed her cold hands. But then she looked up and saw René was leaving her to stand in the kitchen. "Where are we going?"

"To get warm in the living room. The fire is up, and the blankets are on the couch." René walked into the living room and sat down on the left side of the couch. He motioned for Jessie to join him. She didn't argue, thank god, she just sat down on the far-right side of the couch. It wasn't until they had both wrapped up in the blankets and taken their first sips that René spoke to Jessie again. "Jessie, you can't do such fool hearty things all the time."

"What do you mean all the time?" Jessie looked up from her coffee cup and glared at him.

"Erik says you're reckless."

"I'm fun loving." Jessie objected, as her head, neck, and shoulders objected to his judgement.

"Fun is fine as long as you take care." René warned her. "The wilderness is a dangerous place. And it will kill you if you don't pay attention and respect nature. We both could have died today. The river is deep and in the winter months its freezing. We could have ended up with frostbite or hypothermia."

"If it's so dangerous, why do you live here?" Jessie countered, as she took sips of her hot tea. She couldn't hide her contented smile. The spiced apple syrup was heavenly, warm, comforting, and satisfying.

René took note of her smile, but this was serious. "One, its beautiful out here. It's quiet, serine, and consoling. Two, people are exhausting. They argue, they fight, they don't pay attention, and they are too busy running after money to notice other things are more important."

"Damn, who hurt you?" Jessie asked, her face scrunched in disapproval of his negative view of the world.

This time it was René who bristled at her question. "No one, I just prefer to be by myself. It's simpler."

"You're an introvert." Jessie judged and pointed a finger at him.

"So what?" René sat back and crossed his legs.

"I'm an extrovert." Jessie pointed to herself. Then she ticked off her good points while her index finger circled the rim of her mug. "I love having fun. Meeting new people and learning new things." She dipped her finger into the apple syrup and sucked on it.

René whistled, wantonly, and then looked away. He took a sip of his drink and then asked her. "If you're an extrovert, then why are you a writer?" René asked, with curiosity. "Aren't writers introverts locked in their rooms dreaming of fantastic realities, because they don't like real reality."

"Real Reality." Jessie quipped. She took a sip of her drink and then sighed heavily. "I...I was an orphan. My parents died when I was twelve. It was Sister Amy who encouraged me to write. At first, it was for coping. But then it became for fun. New worlds, new places to explore. I wasn't tied down. I could go anywhere and do anything."

René leaned forward. When he spoke, his voice was serious and sharp. "Escaping into fantasy will get you killed out here. Nature is so beautiful, but if you don't watch out, one misstep could be the last step that you ever take." René admonished her.

In between sips of hot apple cider, Jessie watched René as he spoke about the wilderness, its beauty and all its dangers. She couldn't help but picture him as a night elf. Someone who was one with nature, moved through it, protected it, and taught others of it if they were willing to learn. Something about the way he spoke about the wilderness made her curious.

"Jessie."

"Yes, what?" She blinked.

"See that is just what I mean." René scolded her. "You lack focus, you daydream constantly, and you..."

"Ever stop to think that you might be boring me." Jessie snapped at him.

Rene blew a disgusted breath. "City girl."

For the rest of the night, until their tea was done. They sat in silence and just enjoyed the warmth of the fire. An hour later, while René sat wondering why he allowed this crazy woman to stay in his house, he heard a light snoring sound. He looked over and Jessie was fast asleep.

"Why does this she-devil look so damn innocent while she's asleep?"

René put his mug down on the coffee table.

Walked over to Jessie, scooped her up into his arms, and walked over to the stairs.

"No, mom, five more minutes." Jessie blurted out in her sleep.

René smiled and slowly climbed the stairs. He opened the door to her room with his foot and gently laid her on the bed. He took a soft brown bear motif blanket from the hall closet and covered her up. He kissed her forehead and then closed the door.

Chapter 6

The sky darkened and dark clouds moved in. One by one, the stars turned out their lights. The moon was devoured by the blackness of night. The wind whined thru the trees making them moan and wail. An icy blast of snow and ice hit the house with all the fierceness of a storm at sea. The snow itself didn't fall to the ground, but whipped around and flew past the windows, as if trying to escape the evil wind. The blizzard descended upon René's house and tried to bury it in a barrage of snow.

"It's really howling out there, isn't it?" Jessie came down the stairs one step at a time and watched the snow whip around outside.

"It is." René played tug of war with Sarah and her chew toy. "Good afternoon."

"Afternoon?" Jessie squinted and tried to think. "Saturday?"

"Yes."

"Why did you let me sleep so long?"

"You needed your rest." René petted Sarah behind her ears, and then stood up. "You're still recovering."

"From the car accident or the near drowning?" Jessie quipped.

René smirked at her. "Both."

Suddenly, the wind rattled the windows. Startled, Jessie almost fell down the stairs when she missed the final step. Within seconds, Rene was at her side and held her steady. He looked down at her and she looked up at him.

"Be careful." He warned her with a frown.

She gently pushed him away from her. "I know, keep your eyes open and pay attention."

"Well, you were listening to me yesterday." René grinned at her, took her hand, and guided her into the living room. "You are shaking. Are you scared?"

"Scared?" She thought about it, as she let him guide her towards the couch.

Jessie looked out the window at the raging white storm. It was like living in a snow globe that someone had shaken furiously. She remembered that it was a night like this when she drove her car off the road, tumbled down a hill, and crashed into a tree. And yet, as outrageous as the snowstorm was outside, inside it was peaceful and serene. René's home was well built, solid, strong; the soft crackling of the fireplace dispelled the cold and gave the house a warm glow. The *voice* of the house whispered to her, and she felt safe.

"Yes and no," she told him honestly. An uneasy anxiousness fell upon her, as she continued to stare at the storm. "I did almost die in a storm like this one."

"Luckily for me, you didn't." René chuckled. "Come, time to partake in a time-honored tradition." He walked towards the kitchen, washed his hands, pulled down two glasses, and took a bottle of wine from out of the fridge. He brought all of them into the living room. He poured a glass of red wine and handed it to her. Then he poured himself one.

"What are we doing?" She asked, with a sly grin. "Toasting the storm?"

René smirked at her suggestion. "No. Oh, almost forgot." He headed off towards the record player.

"Forgot what?" She asked, curious as to what he was doing.

She watched him look through his record collection, choose one, and then he put it on. Soon, the sounds of soft smooth ambient jazz filled the room. The soft symbols, a gentle but nimbly played piano, a lightly strummed bass, and a smoky saxophone reminded her of a small rendezvous jazz café in New York city, only a lot less crowded. René sat down in his large brown leather lazy boy. He reached out for her and gently pulled her into his lap.

"What are you doing?" She was surprised, but not unpleasantly so.

René took a drink from his glass and then set it down. "For nights like these we tell stories."

She stopped drinking and looked at him. "Stories?"

"Yes. You're a writer," He mused, "This should be right up your alley."

She timidly relaxed into his lap and leaned back. René put his feet up on the coffee table and they just watched the snow fall together.

"Are you comfortable?"

The sweet concern in his voice, Jessie found strangely comforting. *What is it about him that makes me feel so...safe? Is it his strong hands, his commanding, yet sympathetic voice? Why do I feel so secure with a complete stranger?*

"Yes, but there is a nice couch over there." Jessie waved her left hand towards the couch.

Rene took a sip of his wine. "My mother used to hold me like this when I was afraid of the storms."

Jessie said nothing. She just remembered that

her parents too used to do the same. If the storms lasted all night, she even got to sleep in their bed. Jessie sighed and smiled in fond remembrance. She leaned back against René.

"So did my parents." She sipped her wine and then asked. "How long will the storms last? I'd like to be able to go home someday."

"This storm will most likely last until morning." He informed her. "It's known as the Witch of Winter."

"The Witch of Winter?"

"Or the Witch of November, since this is the month for it." He picked his glass back up and took a sip. "It's the name of the Jet stream storm system that comes screaming across this land every autumn. It is said to create storms at sea that can generate twelve-meter waves with winds as fast as 125 kilometers an hour."

"Wow. That's bad." Jessie released a nervous breath.

"For ships it's deadly. It's one of the reasons why we have so many ghost stories."

"And you're going to tell me these stories?" Jessie ran her index finger around the rim of her wine glass, and René watched the pad of her finger intensely. He took a sip of his wine and forced himself not to think about it.

"Well, not all of them are ghost stories." He looked into her eyes, and then let his sight slowly roll down her body. "This is Indian territory, and they have their own myths and legends."

"Like?" Jessie took another sip and enjoyed the warmth of the fire.

"Well," He started, and placed his glass on the end table to his right. "This land that we are on once belonged to the Iroquois Indians." René wrapped his left arm around her waist. "In the beginning, before there was land upon the earth, the sky people lived on a floating island. There was no war. No sickness. No death, and everyone was happy."

"Sounds like fun." Jessie quipped.

René gave her sides a pinch. "Do you want to hear this or not?"

"Stop, I'm going to spill my wine!" She snickered, and he pulled her closer to him.

"One day, the sky woman realized that she was going to give birth to twins, and her husband was mad."

"Should have used a condom." Jessie whispered trying not to grin.

René tickled her this time. Just as his mother used to do him. Jessie giggled and put her wine glass down. She didn't want to spill wine on his chair or his rugs.

"Stop!" She pushed his hands away.

"Then shush." He gave her a warning finger and then tapped her nose.

Jessie rolled her eyes at him. "Okay fine."

René took a drink and started again. "Anyway, her husband tore out the tree of light by the roots and created a hole in the island. Curious, the woman looked into the hole and fell from the sky."

"That murdering bastard!" Jessie sat bolt upright and looked at him. "He pushed her didn't he and then put the tree back to cover up his crime."

René rolled his eyes and went on. "Before she could fall into the sea and die, the birds gave her a safe landing onto the back of a giant sea turtle. The toads brought mud from the bottom of the sea to create an island on the back of the turtle for her to live on. The island grew so big that it became North America. The sky woman, now on her own, sprinkled the dust of the Earth into the air and created the stars of the heavens. Then she also created the sun and the moon."

"Wait where did the dust come from?"

René placed his hand over her mouth to muffle her talking and continued. "The sky woman had her twins and became the Sky Mother. She named them Sapling, who was kind and gentle, and the creator of all things good; and Flint, who's heart was cold as stone. He filled the Earth with mean and evil things. Sapling created lakes and fish. But it was Flint that put the thorns on roses and bones in fish."

Jessie peeled his hand off her mouth. "I've always wondered why roses have thorns." Jessie pondered, as she listened to his tale.

"One day, Sapling had had enough of his brother's meddling, and they fought each other for control. Sapling won. Now, because his brother was a god too and basically immortal. Sapling imprisoned him in the mountain cave beneath the Earth. And when Flint gets truly angry, his anger is felt in the form of erupting volcanoes."

A great gust of wind hit the windows and Jessie jumped, shifting in René's lap. *Maybe putting her on my lap wasn't a good idea.*

Jessie looked up and saw something fly past the window. "What was that?"

René calmly sipped his wine as he tried to keep

his raging thoughts and growing stubby under control. "That was an action figure."

"What, how?" Jessie asked, a bit confused.

"There is a campground about fifteen minutes from here on the other side of the river, it's a lot of fun during the summer. Some kid probably left it there and the storm picked it up." René re-filled his glass and then hers too. "If you come here during the summer, you can enjoy hiking, boating, fishing, mountain bike riding, etc. Even the boy scouts and the girl scouts sometimes have outings here."

"After seeing and trying to walk in so much snow, I can't imagine anyone having fun here." She commented with a distinct scowl.

"You can't?" René frowned. "Are you not having fun here?"

Again, another gust of angry wind hit the house and Jessie flinched, moving around on his lap. He bit his lip and sharply inhaled, then took a large gulp from his glass and tried to shift her without it having been obvious what was happening.

Down boy! Can't have her thinking we're...

"I bet Flint and the Witch of Winter would get along." Jessie mused. "Have fiery flaming snowballs of fun."

René flicked her in the head with his middle finger. "Don't give them any ideas."

"Ow," She pouted, and stuck her lip out while she rubbed her forehead.

René's gaze dropped down to her lips and he took another large swig from his glass, while Jessie remained blissfully unaware of what she was doing to him.

Jessie smiled and the warmth of the fire cheered her soul. Naught but the roaring winds and the crackling of a good blaze could be heard tonight. In all the world, only them two of them existed.

This is nice, she thought. "What other stories do you know?" Jessie asked and took another sip of her drink.

"Well, there is a story about Old Moss Back."

"Who's that?"

"A fish that a man named Jack Brennan was chasing. Jack was a great fishing guide. As the story goes, Jack had caught a fish on his line that he named "Old Moss Back.""

"Let me guess, he had moss on his back?"

"Is this commentary going to go on all night?" He gave her a small groan.

"Yes." Jessie smiled brightly.

"Anyway, he and old moss back fought each

other for hours and hours. But Jack couldn't reel him in. Jack finally lost him when his line broke. The only thing that Jack had to commemorate the battle was one of the fish's scales. Counting the rings..."

"Fish scales have rings? Like trees?" Jessie pondered. *I did not know that.*

"Yes." He told her. "And just like trees you can tell what the fish has been through by reading his scales. Thickness, density, health..."

"That's really cool."

"I am full of useful knowledge." He smirked at her and then took a sip of wine.

"You're full of something alright," Jessie jested, and gave him a distrusting sideward glance. "Next."

"You want another one?" René repositioned himself a little to a more comfortable position, finally having calmed down.

"Yes." Jessie snuggled closer to him and laid her head in the crook of his neck. "I...I kind of like this."

He smiled as he looked down at her. "So do I." He took a drink, wondered which story to tell her next, and then started another story. "I guess I should tell you about the three sisters then. They are the reason we are alive today."

"The three sisters of fate. Yesterday, today, and

tomorrow?" Jessie guessed. "Maiden, mother, and crone?"

"Beans, Corn, and Squash," René interrupted her historical rantings.

"Beans, Corn, and Squash?" Jessie balked and gave René a questioning look. "Wow, you Canadians are weird."

"This is another Iroquois legend." He took his feet off the coffee table and sat up for a while. His legs were beginning to cramp. "These three sisters are often grown together and benefit greatly from each other's company. Corn provides structure for beans to climb. Beans provide nitrogen for the soil, and squash will grow along the grow and prevent the growth of weeds. These three plants were not only the staple of their diet, but the Indians used them as barter for trade goods."

"OK. Continue, three sisters, healthy and strong." Jessie summarized. "So, what happened?"

"Well, there are many versions to this story, but one of them goes like this." René took a drink and continued. "The three sisters, Bean Green, Corn Yellow, and Squash of the Pale Green Shawl, lived, worked, and played together. The youngest always crawled. The second sister was always running off by herself and of course the eldest sister protected them both. One day, a stranger came to the field of the three sisters. His name was Mohawk boy."

"Mohawk boy?" Jessie gave an unlady like snort of laughter. "Now you're just making stuff up to mess with me." Jessie held her left hand to her mouth to keep from spewing wine, as her sides rippled with laughter. "What kind of name is that? Why not Jack the Giant slayer? He loved beans too."

"Shush, or I'm not feeding you."

"Food?" Jessie instantly perked up. "What are we eating?"

"Beans, Corn, and Squash." René teased her, with a mischievous twinkle in his eyes.

She smacked him on his chest with the back of her right hand. "Just finish the story."

"Well, as you can imagine the youngest sister was the first to come up missing."

"Probably got lost in a snowstorm and was held captive by Mohawk boy for months on end." She quipped.

"Stop it." René smacked her thigh. "The sisters were sad."

"Sad? They should have called the cops on Mohawk boy. He was the last seen at the scene of the crime."

"Good grief, city girl. Take it down a thousand."

"Continue."

"Later, Mohawk boy was seen at the water's edge and the second sister disappeared too."

"That's it, I want Mohawk boy fingerprinted!" Jessie declared vehemently.

René broke out laughing. "Sorry, that had not been invented yet."

"Then get the dogs. No, I forgot. You have nothing but wolves here."

René was chuckling so hard that he found it hard to continue the story. He put his glass back down on the end table. "Will you let me finish?"

"Fine." Jessie sat back and crossed her arms.

"As I was saying, with only one sister left, she tried her best to continue on, but Mohawk boy finally realized the error of his ways when he saw how tired with work and how sad she was from missing her sisters; and he reunited the three."

"And the peasants rejoiced." Jessie giggled.

"Okay. That is enough. Get off my lap." He waited for Jessie to stand up and then got up himself.

"Although, it had a happy ending." Jessie walked towards the kitchen to wash out her glass. "Leave it to a man to break up a happy home."

"Oh, good grief. That's it, no more story time for

you," René scolded playfully. He took both glasses, washed out them out, and put them away.

"Aww," Jessie pouted, leaned against the breakfast bar, and then she asked. "So, what's for dinner tonight?"

"Three sisters Chili." He opened the fridge and started pulling out ingredients.

"You weren't kidding," She eyed him incredulously, "You're making me eat story soup."

"Chili," He corrected. "Vegetarian style."

"Vegetarian?" She balked and wrinkled her nose up at it. "What's the point of that?"

"Quit complaining and start dicing," He instructed, as he handed her a knife.

"You trust me with a knife." Jessie gave him a wicked grin and ran her fingers along the edge of the chef's knife.

"Good point." René rummaged through his kitchen drawers and found her a smaller paring knife. "Try not to cut yourself with it."

"What am I going to do with this?" Jessie joked and looked at the small knife. "Hold up a seven eleven? Give me that real knife back."

"Fine. Take the chef's knife but be careful with it." René took the paring knife back and put it away. "My knives are very sharp." He warned her.

"Good to know." Jessie waved the chef's knife around like she was a ninja.

"OK, if you are just going to play..." René scolded her and reached to take the knife back.

"Fine, I'm dicing I'm dicing." Jessie picked up a yellow onion and started dicing it up as René had taught her.

She and René worked together to cut up and dice cloves of garlic, jalapenos, red bell peppers, tomatoes, and butternut squash. Then he sent her to the pantry to bring him some beans.

Jessie looked to her right and saw the pantry, with a see-through sliding barn door. She walked over and opened the door. She walked around, looking for the can of beans.

"Geez, it's like a supermarket here," She remarked, as she went in and looked around. She took stock of his shelves. René had various types of breads, cereals, and rice. Jams and jellies. Canned fruits and pickled...pickles. "That's a lot of beans." She snickered. "Kidney beans, lima beans, pinto beans." She also saw various types of perishable and non-perishable foods here. He was also keeping four bags of dog food, both wet and dry. "At least, Sarah won't starve either."

While Jessie was looking for cans of kidney beans

and black beans in the pantry. René had pulled out his cooking pot, added two tablespoons of olive oil and started sautéing some of the ingredients. When she came back from the pantry, he added to the vegetable broth, beans, corn, squash, and two tablespoons chili spice to the pot. Jessie sat back at the breakfast counter and watched him simmer the ingredients. He tasted it and looked unhappy.

"Get me some avocados, cilantro, and some sea salt, will you?" He requested.

"OK," Jessie stood up and prepared to go to the refrigerator. "But what's a cilantro?"

"What is a..." René looked at her like she was crazy. "Never mind, I'll get it." He went to the fridge, pulled out two avocados and a leafy green herb, and showed it to her. "This is cilantro."

"That's Parsley." She noted looking at the herb and then at him.

"Parsley?" He looked at the herb and then at her. "This is cilantro, not parsley."

She just raised an eyebrow at him and blew it off. "They look the same to me."

"Well, they are not. They taste quite different. To put it simply, Cilantro is spicy. While parsley has a much milder flavor."

"Oh." She rolled her eyes but continued to watch him cook.

"Just go and grab some bowls." He shook his head and let go a small chuckle. "This will be ready in ten more minutes."

She grabbed three soup bowls and nearly tripped over Sarah when she wandered into the kitchen.

"Watch out Sarah." Jessie did a balancing act to save René's china soup bowls. "I don't want to step on you."

Rene took one of the bowls and gave Sarah some. Jessie just looked at him.

"What?"

"That won't hurt her?" She wondered.

"Nah, it is all natural. She will be fine." René took the next bowl that Jessie handed him and filled it with chili. "Here you go. Straight from the soup kitchen," He joked. Lastly, he filled a bowl for himself, walked to the dining room table, and then sat down next to her. "So, what do you think?"

"This isn't bad," She commented, a bit surprised. "Not bad at all."

"Told you." René smiled at her. "The three sister's chili is good."

"Do you have any rolls?" Jessie requested

"In the pantry. Check the top shelf."

"Thanks."

Sarah barked for some more and René filled her bowl back up again, while he waited for Jessie to return. She found the rolls and brought out the bag. She took two dinner rolls and then passed the bag to René.

"So, how do you like it here?" He asked, as he ate a spoonful of chili.

"What do you mean?" She dunked her dinner roll in the chili.

"Canada? My house? Me?" René asked apprehensively.

"Canada? The weather sucks." Jessie reported with mirth in her voice. "Your house. It's a nice house. I like it. Puts my minimalistic apartment dwelling to shame. As for you," She considered him with questioning eyes. "The jury is still out."

"Why? I am a nice guy?" He insisted and took another spoonful of soup.

"I'm waiting for the second act." Jessie blew on her chili before she ate it.

"What second act?" René broke his roll and buttered it.

"When I try to leave, you poison me with arsenic, and then bury my body in the basement."

"Okay, now that is just sick," He scoffed.

"Either that or you try to kill me with a kitchen knife in the shower." She took another spoonful of chili.

"I promise," He put his hand over his heart. "I will not kill you with kitchen utensils. I need them to cook with and I don't need typhoid running through my kitchen."

She flashed a smile and kept eating.

"How about a game of chess after dinner?" René dipped the second half of his roll into his chili.

"Okay," Jessie accepted. "But I play speed chess."

"Speed chess?" René gave Jessie a quizzical look. "What the hell is that?"

"No thinking for hours on end," she told him. "You see it, you move it." She mimed quickly with her hands. "Each move has a fifteen second time limit."

"That's ridiculous," He snorted, "How can you play chess that way?"

"That's life." She shrugged and then took another spoonful of chili. "Sometimes, you don't have days to make decisions."

"Okay," He agreed. "We will play your way, because this I have got to see."

Chapter 7

Jessie was sitting in the library working on her books, when a bright greenish light caught her eye. She stood up and looked out the window. Streaking across the darkened night sky was a luminescent greenish ribbon of light. To her eyes, it looked like a neon purplish green Chinese Dragon zooming its way across the night sky.

"The aurora borealis," Jessie whispered aloud in awe.

Full of curiosity, Jessie rushed down the stairs. She put on the coat that René was letting her use and her boots. Then she went out of the front door, looked up into the night sky, and followed the ribbon of light. Sarah looked up from watching TV and barked. René turned his head to see what Sarah wanted, just in time to see Jessie dash out the front door.

"Now where is she going?" René wondered.

He turned off the TV, much to Sarah's dismay. Then he put on his coat and boots as well. René locked the front door, as Sarah picked up Jessie's trail, and they followed her deep into the woods.

"Where on earth is she going?" René griped and then he called out to her. "Jessie!"

Jessie stopped and turned. She smiled at him and waved. "Come on, you slow pokes! Get the lead out!" Then she took off again.

"There's an idea," René told Sarah jokingly. "Remind me to put lead weights in her boots." Sarah barked once and took off after Jessie. "Hey! Wait for me!" René had to run hard to catch up to them. He stopped a moment to catch his breath. He looked up to see what Jessie was pursuing. "She's chasing...the aurora borealis? Jessie, wait! stop!"

She didn't stop running until she came to a clearing. It was a field full of flowers and a line of trees. Looking at it was...magical. It was like a fairy tale dark forest leading her on to a waiting adventure.

"Jessie!"

"Come on, I want to see what's at the end of the Borealis." Smiled Jessie.

"Quoi?" René finally caught up to her and caught his breath.

But she didn't wait for him. The fresh fallen snow crunched under her feet. The midnight cantata of crickets and other night fowl filled the air with intrigue. Trees of fir, birch, and pine lay out before her, each like a silent sentry of an enchanted forest. Snow covered the land like a marshmallow rug and only a few patches of grass still showed through. She stopped walking only when she came upon a field of flowers.

"Que faites-vous?" René grabbed her hand.

"What?"

"What are you doing?" He rephrased himself. "Why did you come out here and at this time of night?" He waved a hand up at the moon over head.

"I wanted to see where the Borealis led me and it led me here." Jessie pulled out of his hand and waved her hand towards the field of flowers. "To the secret grove."

He laughed at her. "This is no secret. You can see it plainly in the day."

"Well, that's disappointing." She frowned.

"Well, there is one secret." He revealed to her. "Want to see it?"

"Very much." Jessie's eyes brightened.

"Come this way." René motioned for her to follow, and he and Sarah led the way.

"Whoa." Jessie was in awe. The sight of the flowers in bloom at night took her breath away. "What...?"

"This particular grove blooms only at night," René told her.

"A midnight garden." She beamed and slowly walked forward. "Look at it. It's breathtaking."

Jessie walked around the grove and tried to take in everything. She heard the wind blowing gently through the trees. She felt the crunch of the snow beneath her feet. She touched the trees, their bark's texture felt rough against her hands. She stood still, looked up, and listened to the hooting of the owls. She relished the glow of the moonlight shining down on her. René shook his head. It was like watching a child discover the world; and that gave him an idea.

"Jessie, come look at these." He gestured for her to come to him. "They are called Hylocereus Undatus." He then pointed to a particular patch of ground. "Also known as Night-blooming Cereus and they are a cactus that-"

"Cool." Jessie knelt to take a closer look. "Wait, it's a cactus?" The flower was a bright shade of milky white and glowed like a star in the moonlight. She turned and looked at him. "I thought that cacti only grow in deserts."

"No. They can grow anywhere that the soil is dry, has direct sunlight, and the temperatures are below 10 degrees Celsius." René watched, as Jessie sniffed the blooms.

"They smell wonderful."

"Then you're really going to love those." René pointed to another group of flowers that were sun yellow in appearance. "Those are..."

"Those are daisies," She interrupted him, as she turned to look, and then she stood to turn around.

"But they are a special kind of daisies." René took her by the hand and led her over to them. "These are Berlandiera Lyrata, and they smell like chocolate."

"No way," Jessie chuckled and walked closer to them.

"It's true."

She bent down to sniff them, and René watched her with great interest.

So, child-like, and yet, definitely a beautiful woman. He grinned.

"You weren't kidding. They really do smell like chocolate." She stood and walked back over to him. "Imagine that. You won't find those in the city."

"Well, don't let me catch you sneaking out here to eat the grass." Rene jested, pointing an accusatory finger at her. "I know all about you Americans and your obsession with weed."

Jessie snorted her laughter. "We smoke it. We don't eat it."

"I thought you put it into brownies."

"Those are shrooms." Jessie corrected him.

"Americans." He shook his head and chuckled.

"Crazy Canadians," She countered, and she wrinkled her nose at him.

Then something caught her eye. It was a trail of trees that led deeper into the woods.

"Where does that trail go?" She took a step towards it.

Sarah barked in warning and René grabbed her arm, firmly, but gently.

"Nowhere."

"Nowhere? Come on, all trails lead somewhere." She tried to pull out of his grip, but he held her tight. He wasn't hurting her, she noted. But he did not let go of her either.

"Just to a cave." René hoped that an answer would satisfy her curiosity.

"A cave?" She brightened up and tried to pull away from him. "Let's go explore it."

"Let's not." René still held her arm, but very firmly pulled her way from that trail. "Bears hibernate there."

"Oh bears." Her eyes widened in excitement.

"Nope. Sorry Goldilocks." René picked her up and threw her over his shoulder. "Park is closed for the winter. Come back in the spring."

"I'm marooned here, remember." She rolled her eyes and gave an exhausted sigh. "I've been trying to leave for a while." She furrowed her eyebrows, "What is that?"

"What?"

"Listen."

René listened. "Bats."

"Bats?" Jessie questioned. "I thought bats only lived in South America."

"No, bats live in three fourths of the world. The only place that they don't live is Antarctica."

"Will you put me down," She demanded.

"Alright." René set her back on her feet directly in front of him, but kept his arms wrapped around her waist, thus pulling her closer to him. *Can't have her escaping and getting into trouble.*

"If I can't see the bears, can I see the bats?" Jessie requested, still trying to escape his grasp. "Please! I've never seen a bat before."

He rolled his eyes but conceded. "Fine, follow me." He grabbed her hand, interlocked their fingers, and walked off towards the southern section of the grove. There, giant oak trees reached up into the sky. It's great limbs and branches grew and spread out like a giant Chinese fan; and though its branches may have been bared of leaves, its branches were not empty. Jessie looked up and saw hundreds of bats flying about and snatching bugs right out of the air.

"Do you see the edges of white on some of the bats?" René asked, as he pointed them out. He stepped behind her and encircled her in his arms once more.

Jessie grinned. His warm body against hers and her rising feelings for him kept her warm in this cold winter's air. "Yes."

"Those are silver bats."

"That's so cool."

Jessie kept staring up at the tree, but René soon turned her to face him. Having her so near her, she blushed. He stole a kiss from her, and she let out a quiet, breathy moan, that had him heating up despite the snow. He broke the kiss but continued to stare deep into her eyes.

"Did you know there are over 1200 species of bats. And they come in two groups. Mega," He placed a kiss on her left cheek. "And Micro," And another on her right. She gazed softly at him, completely lost in his clear amaretto eyes. René continued with his bat biology lesson. "Mega are your fruit bats and make up the most species of bats," Jessie was running her hand through his hair, nodding as he spoke. "And uh, vampire bats fall into the Micro group. Fruit bats are actually bigger, stronger, faster, and more intelligent than Vampire bats..." He trailed off. Jessie gently brought his head down towards hers and kissed him. *This is perfect. Two souls alone in the night.* He thought. But she brought them both back.

"Wait, Fruit bats are really stronger? And here I thought that it was always the other way around." Jessie thought about it and then laughed. "Don't tell Blade or Selina. They've been vampires forever and think they're all that."

"What?" He was a bit dazed after the kiss, and really wasn't paying attention to her juvenile utterings.

"Blade and Underworld Movies."

"Oh," René scoffed, as he caught onto her joke. "Right."

"I wonder if they will one day make a movie where a person is bitten by a fruit bat and can beat the crap out of Blade and Selina both?" Jessie wondered and she gently ran her index finger down the side of his face and over his lower lip.

"Well, he or she would definitely have the advantage." Rene released her, back up a bit, and then pointed up at the oak tree. "Fruit bats can also travel during the day."

"Really?"

"Yes."

"Ha." Jessie smiled happily and pointed a thumb to her chest. "Put me down for fruit bats during the zombie apocalypse. Instead of blood banks, I'll be robbing grocery stores."

René chuckled at her. "You're a nut, do you know that?"

"Can I pick my own tree?" Jessie smirked at him, taking another look at the bat filled tree.

"No." René shook his head, but then he heard a howl that sounded in the distance.

"Wolves?" Jessie stiffened, her senses jumping to the alert.

"No, That's just Sarah." Rene looked off into the distance towards home. "She wants us to come home now."

"I thought she was with us." Jessie commented, as she looked around for her.

"No, she went home twenty minutes ago," René chuckled. "It's freezing out here and she knows that there's a roaring fire going to waste."

"Ha, mom is calling her kids inside." Jessie laughed, and then she started walking back toward the house, her hand found his once more. "Wait, how can you tell the difference between her and real wolves?"

René smiled at her as he escorted her back to the house. "I can tell."

Once back at the house, Jessie hurried over to stand in front of the fire and get warm.

"That was fun." She rubbed her arms vigorously. "But exploring Canada, in the middle of the night, during winter, is a bad idea."

"Bonjour, Sarah." René greeted his faithful dog. "Is everything OK?"

Sarah barked happily at him, and he scratched her behind the ears.

"Good night, René. See you in the morning." Jessie called out, as she climbed the stairs.

"Count on it," he told her with a smile. "Because I think I know how to keep you entertained while you are here."

"Oh really?" She turned and looked at him. "How?"

"I'm going to make you a beaver."

"Is that another veterinarian joke?" Jessie raised an eyebrow at him.

He gave her a droll grin. "No, that is the starting point for all Canadian Scouts."

"You're going to make me a Beaver Scout?" She deadpanned.

René walked over to the stairs and looked up at her. "Yes."

"Why?"

"Because you're part beaver already." He grinned at her.

"Well, I am a girl." Jessie sniggered.

"No. I mean...tonight I saw a girl full of curiosity and wonder." René took a hold of her hand and held it in his. "Allow me to teach you all about Canada while you are here."

She thought about it. Then she took a step down to meet him halfway. They were the same height now and she looked him in the eyes. "Well, tonight was kind of fun. Do I get a secret decoder ring?"

"No, but I do have an extra uniform." He offered her. "If you want to earn it."

"Is that a challenge?" Jessie grinned, a twinkle in her eyes.

René grinned back. "Why yes, Miss America. It is."

"I'll look forward to it." She smiled, pulled her

hand out of his, and started back up the stairs. "Goodnight, René."

He walked up after her and pulled her in close for one last kiss. Jessie sighed with contentment as she dragged her lips from his.

"Goodnight, René."

"Goodnight, Jessie, Sleep well." René watched her with longing desire, as she walked up the stairs and disappeared into the guest bedroom. Then he smiled to himself. *Who knows, this could be fun.*

The next morning, René made breakfast. As they ate, he filled her in on all that she had to do to become a Canadian Beaver Scout. After that, he began mixing berries, soap, and cornstarch together.

"What are you doing?" Jessie asked.

"Showing you how to make paint like a true Native American Iroquois."

"What for?" She wondered.

"Well...so far you've survived a nearing drowning and discovered a secret midnight garden filled with fruit bats. I think that merits your exploring scout badge."

"One down and fifteen to go," She cheered.

"Come here and watch." René filled a small pot

with water and set it on the stove. Then he filled one of his glass mixing bowls with strawberries and raspberries.

"Sir, yes sir." Jessie giggled.

"Now, there are three things that you need to make paint. You need a pigment for color. That's the berries. You need a binder for stickiness. That's the eggs. And you need an emulsifier for spreadability. That is the soap. And you need a soap that has no dyes for fragrance already in it."

"Ok. What are the steps?" she asked, as she leaned upon his breakfast bar to watch him.

"Step one is to heat strawberries and raspberries in one cup of water for thirty minutes. Step two is to strain the berries but keep the liquid and reserve the berries for use later. And step three is to grate the bar of soap until you have about a 1/3 cup of soap flakes."

Jessie laughed. "Soap flakes sounds like a breakfast cereal."

"No eating," René chuckled at her. "Erik was right. You will eat just about anything."

"Whatever," Jessie gave him a playful shove.

"Step four, we're going to put the soap flakes into a bowl and pour the ½ cup of boiling water from the strawberries over it and stir the mixture until the flakes dissolve." Then he passed the bowl to her. "Start stirring."

"Yes, sir." She took the mixing spoon and started stirring.

"Now we take another bowl and combine cornstarch with ½ cup of water to make a paste. And then we will stir this paste in with the soap mix that you are making." René reached for the bowl and took it from Jessie. He then poured the soap mixt into the cornstarch bowl. "Now we add the strawberry raspberry that we had and mix it all together until we get the color of red that we want."

"Wow, I didn't think it would be that easy to make paint. Commercials on TV make it look so hard." She commented.

"Now, what tattoo shall I give you?" René stopped stirring and looked up at Jessie.

"Make it something cool." Jessie gave him an arm pump.

René chuckled at her bravado. "You're a beaver. So, I'm going to give you a beaver tattoo." He stirred the bowl again to make sure that the mixture didn't congeal.

"Aww."

"Hey, beavers are very well regarded by all Native American tribes." Rene searched his kitchen drawers until he found what he was looking for, a thick sewing needle. "Beavers are determined, strong willed, builders, protectors, and dreamers." René praised her. "I see all these traits in you."

"What is your animal tattoo? Deer, Elk, or Moose?" Jessie took up stirring the mix, while Rene looked for a needle.

"Elk. An elk has strength, agility, pride..." René stuck out his chest and smiled. "We're majestic..."

"Long winded," She teased.

"...Independent, noble, and sensuous." He leered at Jessie.

"Down boy, your ego is over inflating." They each laughed.

"Alright, here we go. That's a good consistent color."

"Are you going to put it on my face?" Jessie asked, passing him the mixture back. "And does it wash off?"

"No and no." René chuckled. "I am giving you a tattoo, so no it will not wash off. Now, where do you want it?"

Jessie's eyebrows rose. "Seriously?"

"If I could choose," He grinned wickedly. "I'd choose your backside. I'd have a wider canvas to work with."

Jessie narrowed her eyes on him and playfully growled at him. "Watch it, Elk boy."

René just laughed at her. "Where do you want it, petit castor?"

"My forearm." Jessie rolled up her sleeve and present her arm to him.

"Bien." René took a sewing needle, heated it over his stove, and then dipped it into the paint.

"When you started telling me the stories of this island, I was really fascinated by them." Jessie watched with interest, as René inked her. "But now, looking at this tattoo. It's so cool to actually be a part of it."

"A part of what?" René didn't look at her but continued his work.

"The history of this island. To be a part of the legends. To be a part of the past." Jessie gave a small smile, as she was lost in her own little daydream. "And maybe...its future."

René looked at Jessie. Her whimsical smile was lost in thought. *There she goes again. Lost in her own imagination.* René smiled to himself.

"What's the matter?" Jessie returned her attention to René. "You're looking at me funny."

"I'm just glad that I have someone to share my time with. It does get boring sometimes, just me and Sarah all winter long." René sat back and studied his handiwork. "That's good, if I do say so myself. Congratulations, petit castor, welcome to the beaver scouts."

Jessie shook her head and laughed. "Beaver scout." She looked her tattoo over as René cleaned up. "That's pretty good. It's a cute little beaver with a big tail. Hey, wait a minute. What are you implying?"

René just started laughing. "Nothing. Not a thing." He continued to laugh.

"What are the three stars for?"

"Your first night here you were looking up at the stars."

"My first night here I was in a car wreck." She reminded him.

"Again, looking up at the stars." He laughed at her, as he washed the bowls clean and put the needle back into the drawer.

"Oh, you Canadian bas-"

"Tsk, Beaver Scouts don't swear." René wiggled a finger at her.

"Then this is going to take forever to become a Beaver Scout," She laughed, but quickly became serious. "Can I ask you for something?"

"Sure, what do you want." René turned on the

water and poured in some liquid soap to do their breakfast dishes.

"Land." She smiled brightly at him.

"What do you want land for?" René asked, as he began to wash the dishes.

"Just a little. I want to start a garden."

"Why?" René's eyebrows furrowed in confusion. "You do know it's winter?"

"Why not?" She countered, with a mocking grin. "Consider it part of my Creative or Earth Merit badge."

"That would fall under Earth. Since you are a writer, that one counts for your Creative badge." René informed her. "You can use the side of the house next to the fireplace." He smiled at her. "Keep the veggies warm in the winter."

For the next two days, Jessie collected branches and limbs from the surrounding forest. She set up a twelve-foot by twelve-foot grid and used René's climbing ropes for boundaries. She and Sarah dug up ten rows of earth and René helped her plant corn, beans, squash, strawberries, blueberries, blackberries, and raspberries. They also planted tomatoes, potatoes, carrots, and peppers. After

René went in to start dinner, Jessie took some fruits out of her pocket.

"Let's plant him some surprises, ey girl." Jessie told Sarah.

She walked about twenty feet from the house and planted apple seeds, orange seeds, some plum seeds, and peach seeds.

"There we go." Jessie smiled to herself. "One of these, if not all, will bear fruit in about seven years. OK?" Jessie looked at Sarah. Sarah barked and wagged her tail. "Shh, don't tell René. Let it be a surprise."

Then Jessie walked about twelve feet and planted more trees. Every twelve feet, she planted a walnut, a chestnut, and an almond. In time, René would have a lovely grove of nut and fruit bearing trees. But for now, her hands were frozen, and she wanted to get warm.

"Okay, Sarah. I'm done." Jessie called to her. "Let's go in. I'm cold. How about you?"

Sarah barked at her and raced her back to the house. Jessie came inside and took off her coat and boots. She hung them up by the front door and then she went to the fireplace and stood with Sarah, trying to get warm again. It didn't take long. René had a good fire going and his whole house was comfortably warm. Jessie stood in front of the fire to get warm. She listened to the crackle and pop of the fire and its embers. She shook the last of the cold from her as the fire warmed her. Sarah looked up and barked at her. Jessie looked down at her and said...

"Yes, Sarah. I do like it here."

Chapter 8

"Jessie!" René called out loudly, as he brought bags of grocery into the house.

"What?!" Jessie responded in a like manner. She was comfortably sitting in the loft, deeply engrossed in a good book, and did not want to be disturbed.

"Get down here now, femme! We have a party to prepare for!"

"Woman?" Jessie's hackles were roaring. "Who the hell does he think he's talking to?" Jessie put the book down, stood up, and prepared to give him what for. When she came to the balcony stairs, she just leaned on the rail and looked down at him. She watched him bring in bag after bag of food. "What the hell are you doing?"

René stopped long enough to catch his breath and looked up at her. "Shake a Leg, Jessie! I need your help!"

Jessie just continued to lean on the railing and made no move to help him out. "What for?"

"The party tonight. It's Christmas Eve !"

"So."

"So? So! What do you mean, so?" René picked up

his bags and brought them into the kitchen. "Quite being a scrooge. Get down here and help me."

Jessie laughed at him as she slowly descended the stairs. "What do you want me to do? Cook?"

"Oh hell no." He chuckled and began placing food on the counter. "I like my friends too much to kill them."

"Ha-ha-ha," She chuckled at him sarcastically. "Hey, at least your house is still standing."

"Thank God for that," He teased her and placed the drinks in the fridge to chill. "No, I need you to decorate the house and make it festive."

"Festive?" Jessie looked around the room.

"Come on girl, get with the program," René told her and he went about putting the rest of the food away. "Set up the tree, decorate the hall, hang the stockings..."

"Yes, yes, I grasp the concept," Jessie told him, as she stood in the living room and looked around. "Where to start?"

Looking down, Jessie saw that René had left several large boxes out for her. She bent down and opened one of them. It was filled with tinsel and bulbs. The next box held the Christmas stars and icicles. And the box after that...

"René." Jessie called out.

"What? Do you need help already?" He answered from the kitchen.

"No, I was just wondering why you have a fake tree when you live in a forest."

"I am a forest ranger, not a lumberjack."

"Sorry, I forgot that I am living with Smokey the Bear." Jessie sniggered.

Jessie opened the tree box and pulled it out. She found the base and then looked for a good place to set it.

"Where do you want the tree to go?"

"In the corner, next to the window, so people can see it from outside."

"Okay." Jessie nodded and went to work.

René poked his head out of the kitchen, as he tied his apron on. He smiled when he saw that Jessie had indeed started to work on putting the decorations up. So, he went back to the kitchen and started cooking.

The tree was a six-foot tree. Good thing, because Jessie didn't feel like standing on a stool just to reach the top of it. She set the base down, installed the spine or trunk of the fake tree, and then she set about installing the branches. They were color coded for an easy install, but after all these years, some of the colors were beginning to fade. Next, she put on the lights.

"René?"

"Yes, Jessie." He responded. He was busy cutting up vegetables.

"Why are we hosting a Christmas Party?"

René stopped for a second. *She said we.* He smiled and then he continued working. "Because it is my turn."

"And you went out and brought all this food?" Jessie was sitting on the edge of the couch, trying to untangle the tinsel. It was slow going, but at least it was going.

"No, the food was delivered."

"So... we can get food in? But we can't get me out?" She questioned him.

"Well, I suppose you could go and sleep at the airport with everyone else." He laughed at her. "But you will miss one hell of a party."

Jessie put the tinsel down and went to the kitchen. She held her right hand to her ear like she was holding a phone receiver.

"Hello, Canadian Police. This is Jessica Tyler. I'm being held hostage by a forest ranger in a pink apron. Send help, please."

René looked down at his apron. "It is not pink. it's

red. And you're not a hostage. You were abandoned like a cowbird egg."

Cowbird? Jessie was going to complain about the analogy, but it was apt. so she just let it pass. Instead, she looked at his apron and tried to imagine what the original color had been. "Maybe ten years ago it was. How long have you had it?"

Jessie watched him pull a large trout out of the fridge. He then began to dress it. She watched him season it and then he placed it in one of the ovens to his left.

"Fifteen years." He noticed that Jessie was watching him. She wasn't working, but she was holding something. "What is that?"

"An ornament, a popsicle stick polar bear." Jessie smiled and held it up to show him. "I think."

René smiled fondly. "I remember those. My brother Jules made a brown one and my youngest brother Noel made the black one."

Jessie cooed at him and looked the ornament over. "Three bear boys. So, there are three of you?" Jessie picked up a strawberry and ate it.

René raised an eyebrow at her. *Wasn't she supposed to be decorating the living room?* "Yes, my younger brother Jules and my youngest brother Noel."

"What are your brothers like? Are they like you? Do they live in the woods too? Are all of you forest rangers?"

René continued preparing food and was now working on the stuffing. "My brother Jules is a cop and married to a young lady named Shelly. They have two twin boys named Harry and Henry. My brother Noel is a firefighter and married to a young woman named Anna. They have two girls; one is ten and the other is seven."

"So, who's coming?" Jessie picked up another strawberry and quickly gobbled it too. "Mmm, so delicious. So juicy."

René raised an eyebrow at her. "Can you not work and talk at the same time?"

Jessie gave a deep sigh, rolled her eyes at him, and then went back to work in the living room.

"To answer your question," René told her, while he prepared the turkey next. "My family, their wives and their children. My friends Tom, John, Jack, and Lukas, who you will no doubt remember helped me carry your limp body back to the house, and their families."

"That's a lot of people. Will they all fit in here?" Jessie wondered. "And of course, I remember John." She looked around again. The house did have a lot of room, but even she couldn't see that many people in here.

"Oh sure." René laughed. "My brother Noel is a firefighter, and he says that I am rated to hold one hundred people. That and I have three exits: Front door, back door, and the garage. So, I am good."

Jessie was now hanging snowflake decorations around the crown molding of the house. The clock struck 4PM. René looked at the clock and panicked.

"Stop fooling around and get back to work." He ordered. "We only have three hours left before everyone starts arriving."

"Must be nice to have a cop and a firefighter in the family. You just need a doctor and you're all set," Jessie joked, and she hung up the tinsel.

"You forgot about John."

"He's not a doctor, he's a vet." Jessie frowned, as she remembered that it was him and not a proper HUMAN doctor that looked her over.

"Same thing," René snickered.

"No, it isn't," Jessie countered.

"Come here a minute," René requested. "I need your help to hold the bird still."

"I'm not touching your bird," Jessie chuckled.

"You know...I am in a hurry...so I am ignoring you. Just get in here."

"That's what she said." Jessie bowled over with laughter.

"Jessie!"

Jessie stopped laughing and brought it down to a sniggle as she did as she was asked. She put down the decorations, shook her head in jest, and then entered the kitchen. René was up to his elbows in stuffing.

"That's not store-bought stuffing, is it?" Jessie eyeballed the thick and colorful stuffing. It smelled delicious. The onions, bacon, and hazelnuts gave the stuffing an aromatic excellence that Jessie couldn't wait to enjoy.

"No. This is pearl onions, Brussel sprouts, hazelnuts, bacon, and other things," René explained, as he hand-mixed the stuffing.

"Straight from the forest huh?" Jessie inhaled the scent and then gave him a playful grin. "Is that parsley or Cilantro?" She pointed to the leafy green sprig that was sticking up.

René raised an eyebrow at her. "Parsley."

"I was just asking," She teased him, and she stole a quick taste.

"Hey! Hands off the stuffing, use them to brace the bird so that it doesn't slide. Now hold the legs open." René requested seriously, as he scooped up some stuffing.

That statement set Jessie to laughing fit and she couldn't stop, as she stood bracing the bird so that it wouldn't fall and held its legs open. "This feels so wrong somehow."

"If it were any day, but today," René stuffed the turkey and pushed the stuffing all the way to the back of the bird. Jessie saw a bit of stuffing come out of the neck and drop to the pan. René then took another handful and kept stuffing the bird. "I would teach you how I stuff a bird."

"Hard and fast apparently," Jessie laughed at him. "Is that your preferred method?"

"Now is not the time for your innuendos." René tied up the legs and drizzled some brown sugar glaze over the top. "Go and set that oven to 350 degrees, please."

"Yes Chef." Jessie saluted him and went to the oven.

She could now see why he had two wall ovens. She opened the door and then stood aside as René lifted the bird inside. He set the timer and then went about cutting up more vegetables for the next dish.

"Okay. Next is the ham and then the vegetable

side dishes." Then René looked at Jessie who was standing there watching the turkey bake. "Did you finish the decorations?"

"No." She laughed. "Someone asked me to help stuff a bird."

"Retour au travail."

"What?" Jessie laughed at him.

"I said back to work, you yankee." René smacked at her with his dish towel. "Back to work." He pointed toward the living room.

"Yes Master." Jessie chuckled, slurred her words, and dragged her right foot. "Igor do this. Igor do that...ha-ha-ha."

"Igor!" René snapped at her playfully with the dishtowel again.

Jessie just laughed at him more and went back to work on the living room decorations. As she was done with the tree and the room decor, she went to hang up the stockings. There were six stockings. One for each of them. Mom and Dad, René, Jules, Noel, and yes even Sarah had one too. Jessie just looked sadly at the stockings for René's mom and dad. She thought about her own parents and those long-ago forgotten Christmases. Christmas music playing on the radio. A nice fire in the fireplace. Mom and Dad laughing and telling stories of when they were kids opening their presents at Christmas. She would tell her parents of all her wishes for Santa Claus to bring her. Jessie's heart grew heavy now, she frowned, and she felt hollow inside. She hadn't set up for Christmas like this since...Jessie's eyes started to tear up and water. It had been a long time since she celebrated properly. She sniffed back the tears and tried to continue working.

René stopped working on his glazed ham with mustard, brown sugar, and thyme, when he heard Jessie sniffling.

"Are you alright in there?" He called out to her.

"Yes," Jessie answered, but her voice cracked in sorrow to the point where even she didn't believe herself.

René wiped his hands on his dish towel and entered the living room. He stopped, looked at the decorations, and smiled to himself. Jessie did a great job. The room looked Christmassy and jolly. The tree was standing tall and lively decorated with ornaments. The lights blinked in and out, truly making the tree magical. The trim of his home nicely displayed icicles and snowflakes alternately. Making his home look like a winter wonderland indoors. Another sniffle from Jessie brought his attention back around to her. She was standing in front of his fireplace and tried to hang his stockings, but she kept wiping her face to hide her tears. He moved to her side and took her in his arms.

"What's wrong?" He asked her softly.

"Nothing."

"Liar. Come on, what is it?"

"My parents. They died when I was twelve." Jessie tried to blink back her tears. "I haven't really celebrated Christmas since then."

René hugged her tighter. "Didn't you go to parties in New York?"

"Yes, but they were lavish parties thrown by the publishing company. My friends never threw private parties like this because they all wanted to hang out with celebrities. So, they and their families always came to the Publisher's Christmas parties. Having a house party like this one...." Jessie sighed and laid her head back on René's shoulder. "Sharing the holiday with just your family. René...."

He turned her around, looked into her eyes, and softly stroked her back.

"I miss my parents," She wept.

Rene' held her in his arms, as she cried into his shoulder. He gently sways her in his arms to comfort her. After a while, René lifted her head and gave her a bright smile. "I would have loved to have met them. I would have told them…"

"Told them what?"

"You did a great job." René smiled at her and then kissed her lips.

Jessie was enjoying René's sympathy, but then a bell went off. The kiss and the spell were abruptly broken.

"You're timing us?" Jessie joked, with a grin and she wiped her eyes with the sleeve of her shirt.

"No, my eggs. I don't want them too hard," René explained, as he hurried back to the kitchen.

Jessie just shook her head and followed right behind him. "One of these days, I have got to learn to cook."

"Well then, here is your next lesson," René told her. "I need you to start making the hors d'oeuvres."

"Me?" Jessie looked at him like he was crazy.

"Yes, you." René handed her a bowl of strawberries. "Start with the Santas."

Jessie just looked at the bowl. "Umm."

"They're easy." He took up a strawberry. "Cut one third of it off, put a little whipped cream on the two-thirds that is left, put two little chocolate chips for eyes, and then put the one-third that you cut off back on for a top. See, Little Santas. Think you can do that?"

"Sure." Jessie smiled. "I think I can handle that."

"Good. When you're done with that. I will show you how to make candy cane cookies."

Jessie went to work on the Strawberry Santas, and René moved around her. He found it quite fun to work with her. She listened well and didn't complain when he corrected her. Soon his ovens were full, and his coffee table was covered in hors d'oeuvres. His whole house smelled wonderful, with pine, cinnamon, and gingerbread. René was happy beyond words, and he was delighted in having Jessie here with him.

Soon, the clock struck 7PM. Jessie was helping René set the dinner table, when they heard a bullhorn good off.

"What the hell was that?" Jessie put down the last wine glass and looked towards the window.

René whipped off his apron and excitedly ran to the door. "Come on, they're here!"

Jessie followed René. She stood at the window and looked out. She saw several snow mobiles pull up and then one large snow tractor. The tractor was pulling a large shipping container with windows.

"Is that a train?" Jessie asked, with disbelief. She had never seen a shipping container used like that before.

"A makeshift snow train. Yes." René smiled and opened the door to his home for his friends and family. "I am so glad to see you guys."

Jessie continued to stand at the window, out of the way, while René's friends and family filled the room. They shook his hands, gave him kisses, dropped off their coats, and filled the room with much merriment. Jessie looked out of the window and stared at the shipping container. It was a bright yellow shipping container with two large picture windows, one on each side. It even had benches. She could see that much through the window. It also had huge snow treads, much like you would see on a tank.

Now that's just ingenious. Probably holds twenty or more with seating. Maybe even forty if they're all standing up. A Wilderness Metro. Jessie giggled to herself.

Jessie turned around and people were still coming in the front door. They brought smiles, more food, like they needed more with all that she and René had cooked. They also brought presents, lots and lots of them, and they were all piled under the tree. Of course, the kids took to shaking them, but they were shewed away. That's when the wine and champagne bottles were popped open, and the drinks started flowing. Lively instrumental Christmas music from all genres was put on and people took to partying like no tomorrow.

Jessie found it kind of hurt her to watch René greet all his nieces and nephews so warmly. Then they ran off to play with Sarah, who barked happily to see them.

Now where has she been all day? Jessie wondered.

She was finally brought out of her own thoughts when someone took her hand and pulled her towards a group of smiling people. Jessie blinked at the woman.

Who is this? She wondered, as she allowed herself to be pulled along.

"Is this the young lady that you were telling me about?" The woman demanded of René.

He stopped shaking hands and taking hugs and kisses, turned around, and smiled brightly.

"Yes, that's her." René came to stand beside Jessie and wrapped his around her waist. "Ma famille, this is Jessie. Jessie, this is Ma famille."

"Hi," She squeaked out. She cleared her throat and started again. "Hi. It's a pleasure to meet all of you."

"Jessie, this is my ma mère. Denise Voclain." René introduced his mother to her.

The woman gave Jessie a bright motherly smile. "Hello, darling. I'm so glad to finally meet you. René talks about you all the time." Mrs. Voclain greeted Jessie warmly.

"*When?*" Jessie wondered.

Denise Voclain had all the grace and style of Grace Kelly. She was a cropped feather do brunette with smiling soft brown eyes. She also had an angular chin, high cheek bones, and what Jessie was starting to call the Voclain family trait of pointed ears. She was a sweet and motherly type, warm and welcoming. A few lines around her eyes, but they didn't detract from her looks one bit. Denise was a woman of medium height and had a fine body. Not an athlete, but she did take good care of herself. No sooner than Jessie had finished her initial judgment of Mother Voclain, had René continued with introductions by introducing her to his brothers.

"'And these are mes freres, my brothers Jules and Noel."

"Hello." Jessie turned to face them and smiled.

"And leurs épouses. Shelly and Anna."

Jessie shook their hands as they were introduced to her. Shelly was a take charge kind of woman and was the first to shake her hand. Her medium frame was a little overweight, but not fat. Jessie could see Shelly's Irish heritage in her bright red updo hair, brown eyes, and a smile that could be mistaken for a constant smirk if you didn't know better. To Jessie, Shelly seemed cheerful and welcoming.

Anna on the other hand, seemed more submissive when in Shelly's shadow. Anna wore her full and bouncy brown curls with a feathered flip. She had blue eyes and a smaller frame compared to Shelly.

Both men stepped forward and shook Jessie's hand too. Jules squeezed her a bit hard, but Jessie squeezed right back. Jules smiled at her.

"Good. I like a person with a firm handshake."

Jules Voclain, the cop. Strong features, piercing brown eyes and black. His walrus mustache is what caught her attention, like what you'd see on a cop from an 80's tv show.

"One of your parents must have been a cop," Jules said, and smiled at her.

"My father." Jessie nodded to him.

"She's a babe," Noel remarked, looking her over. "Good hips. Where'd you meet her?"

Jessie smiled to herself as she looked upon Noel Voclain. He was an alert and ready to help kind of guy. Noel had black hair with a faded haircut. Brown eyes, a round face and a pencil mustache. He also wasn't as stocky as his big brother Jules.

"Scene of a car accident," René offered.

"Who was in the accident?" Noel gaped.

"Me." Jessie gave a small grin. "René saved my life."

"A woman in distress and you didn't call me?" Noel hit his brother René on the arm.

René rubbed away the pain of the punch. "You said you were busy. What were you doing anyway?"

Noel put his arm around his wife and held her close. "My wife." He laughed heartily.

"Pay them no mind." Mrs. Voclain said. She gently pulled Jessie away from her wayward boys and walked Jessie through the rest of the family introductions.

Mother Voclain kept pointing out people and introducing her to them, but let's face it. She wasn't going to remember them anyway. Mrs. Voclain's grandchildren though were easier to identify. Jules' sons Harry and Henry were twelve-year-old twin boys. They were both redheads like their mother, but they seemed to have their father's build of strong and stocky. With crew cuts and cheerful smiles, they played tag and keep away with the girls.

Noel's girls were not twins. Susan was ten years old, and her little sister Alice was seven years old.

Aunt Patty was a bubbly mystic type. She dressed in wild flamboyant colors with a skirt that flared at the bottom. She kept explaining the importance of astrology to ones being, as she opened more wine bottles.

Uncle Robert was an old jock with a beer gut, and in his glory-days was a hockey player.

People talked and laughed. Children played with Sarah and with each other. They were engaged in slapping game of some kind, that involved identifying playing cards. Couples danced close together as cheerful Christmas Jazz played. This too seemed to give Jessie a pang in her stomach. Everybody was drinking, eating her hors d'oeuvres, and having a great time. The magic of Christmas cheer warmed her heart and yet made her feel more alone than ever. She felt like a fish out of water among all these genuinely happy people. Mrs. Voclain brought her out of her melancholy thoughts when she handed her a glass of wine and guided her to sit down on the couch. But before Mrs. Voclain could say a thing, Jessie was battered with questions, as she sat surrounded by René's friends and family.

"So, tell us young lady," Aunt Patty requested. "What do you do in New York?"

"I'm an author." Jessie grinned, none too easily.

"Really?" Little William asked, as he hung over the arm of the couch to talk to Jessie.

Little William was Tom's son, and despite both his parents being bright and happy people, seemed a little dark and gothic. He wore black slacks, a black dress shirt, and a nice black sweater. He liked to talk about and listen to ghost stories and things that go bump in the night. He had been sneaking up on people and scaring them by pretending to be a spider on their shoulder until his father made him stop. And now he was hanging around her.

"Yes." Jessie nodded, acknowledging his presence.

"Like what?" Cousin Roberta asked. She was a vibrant and boisterous person, who seemed to be enjoying life a great deal. "Are you a published author?"

"Yep." Jessie was deliberately keeping her

answers short and sweet. *Oh, my goodness, I've forgotten how to mingle. I used to party at Angelo's and now...I just want to hide in the library.*

"Come on, don't clam up," Cousin Roberta demanded playfully.

"Promise not to laugh." Jessie was stalling. She was trying to think of her lesser-known works.

"Yes, yes," Mrs. Voclain and the kids promised.

"I don't," Cousin Roberta answered honestly.

Jessie smirked at her. "Nicolas Nevada." She thought that she was safe with that one. It was years old, and it was an adventure comic book for kids.

"Nancy and Nicolas?!" Cousin Roberta exclaimed excitedly. "My son Peter and my daughter Penny both loved those books. They were so sad when that series ended."

"Everyone has to grow up sometime." Jessie chuckled, as she shrugged.

"Wait a minute!" René's mother sat up straight. "That means you're Jessica Tyler. You wrote The Journey and The King of Four."

"Uh, yeah, I did," Jessie blushed.

That's when René's other Cousin, Jennifer, let out an ear-splitting yell of excitement.

"Oh, my goodness. Jenny, don't do that." Mrs.

Voclain scolded her, and she plugged her left ear with her index and middle finger.

Jennifer was a playful and fun-loving type of girl. Her demeanor practically pushed people out of the way and demanded attention. She ignored her aunt and stood to her feet.

"People, People." She tinged her glass with a fork for attention.

"No, please don't," Jessie begged.

"We have a celebrity author in our mists," Jennifer stated with pride.

"Really, don't," Jessie begged again and tried to grab Jennifer's arm.

"This is Jessica Tyler, celebrated New York author, writer of The King of Four and the Nancy and Nicolas adventure stories!"

Jessie shrank in dread, but René's mother pulled her off the couch and guided her to the middle of the room. Everyone was smiling, clapping, and raising their glass to her in toast. Little kids ran up to her and hugged her. But the older kids merely nodded their praise.

"Those were really cool books," Peter declared with a distinguished voice.

Peter was wearing beige slacks and a white dress shirt with a red V-neck sweater. He had his hands in his pockets as he came to stand near her. Spirited brown eyes and a smirk gave him the look of a mischief-maker. He was obviously trying to act older than he really was. Whether by choice or by his mother's behest Jessie couldn't tell.

"Thank you, Peter."

"Please make another one," Penny begged, and she held onto Jessie firmly.

Penny was Peter's younger sister. Her caramel eyes were hidden by her glasses. She reminded Jessie of a very short librarian that was dressed for the holidays. No sooner than Mrs. Voclain had separated Penny from her, Henry stepped up to her.

"Can you write a book about me?" Henry asked, very assertive and full of hope. "I'd make a great character. I could be a ninja."

"Henry, you and your brother are already characters. Now, now kids, let her breath." Mrs. Voclain shewed them away and then held her glass high. "To Jessica Tyler."

"To Jessica!" The room erupted in great cheer.

"Thank you." Jessie graciously accepted their praise and held her glass up. "Thank you for allowing me to celebrate Christmas with you and for treating me like one of the family."

"Cheers!"

"To Jessica!"

René smiled. He was so happy, that he thought he would bust. His whole family seemed happy with her. She had fit in just fine. A hand clamped hard on his shoulder brought him out of his thoughts.

"She's a keeper," Jules told him seriously. "She's smart. She's fun, and if she's anything like her books, then she's adventurous too. That means she won't mind living here, in the woods, with you."

"So, tell me," Noel chuckled, as he ribbed his brother in the stomach. "How is she? Are her hips firm?"

Jules gave his brother an annoyed sideways glance. "What is it with you and girls' hips?"

"Who are you ogling this time, Noel?" Anna stepped over to the little group. She was enjoying the Strawberry Santas that Jessie had made.

"Jessie," Jules told her and he took another drink from his glass.

"Oh, she's nice and very polite," Shelly added with a smile, as she looked over at Jessie and Mrs. Voclain.

"I'm telling you René. You need to marry this girl," Jules practically demanded of him.

"Well, I..." René' began.

Just then, the ovens' bells went off.

"Dinner's ready!" Shelly announced.

Shelly, Anna, and René, all started pulling dishes out of the oven. While Shelly and Anna set the dishes on the breakfast bar, René put the pies in the ovens so that they would be ready after dinner. Jules and his brother Noel also helped by bringing out dish after dish and setting them down on the dinner table. All the family, René's friends, and their kids gathered around the table and sat down. Aunt Patty and Cousin Diane helped to arrange and make room for the vegetable sides and to arrange the dishes brought by the rest of René's friends. The kids fought for a place at the table, furthest from their parents, and the wine glasses were filled to the top.

Jessie tried to help René, but Mrs. Voclain would not let Jessie out of her sight. She sat Jessie at the dinner table next to her and René sat across from his mother. He smiled brightly at Jessie, sitting by his mother. She belonged here.

"May I have your autograph?" Cousin Diane requested sincerely.

Cousin Diane was Aunt Patty's first-born

daughter. She was tall and had an angular face, the Voclain ears, and a pert nose.

"Sure," She nodded agreeably.

"She'll do autographs after dinner," Mrs. Voclain declared with a chuckle, and she shewed Cousin Diane back to her seat. "Let the poor woman eat first."

Everyone sat down. There was more than enough room for all. Food was passed around, drinks were poured, and even Sarah got the Ham bone. Then, all heads bowed, and Mrs. Voclain said the grace.

"Dear Lord, we thank thee for your provision and protection. For the morning and your mercy. For thy rest and shelter that come at night. Thank you for our food and friends, our health, our wealth, and our peace filled lives. And thank you for bringing Jessie to us this year and for saving René. Amen."

The table echoed. "AMEN."

As everyone ate their food and talked among themselves, Jessie leaned over to Mrs. Voclain. "How did I save René? He was the one who pulled me from my crashed car."

"Crashed car?" Cousin Diane repeated in shock. "How did you two meet anyway?"

Jessie told them all the story of how she had come to Canada. Of how René and his friends had saved her life, and of how she was marooned by her editor.

"That's so romantic." Penny gushed happily. "You should write that as a story."

"Sorry, I don't do romance novels. I find them a bit, corny," Jessie replied meekly, but honestly. She cut up and ate her ham, but Penny kept asking questions.

"But wasn't Of Plays and Pals a romance novel?" Penny asked, in between bites of the Broccoli Cauliflower Mac and Cheese.

"That wasn't meant to be a romance novel. It wasn't even supposed to be a novel," Jessie chuckled. "It was just some madcap stuff that my friends and I threw together because we were broke and we were bored. That story was never even meant to be published. In fact, I threw it out one day while I was spring cleaning."

Penny balked at her. "You threw it out? Why would you throw it out? It was funny. I liked it." Then she looked at her questioningly. "If you didn't want it published, then who did it."

"Erik, my personal assistant and editor." Jessie told them with a whimsical shake of her head. "He pulled it out of the trash and sent it into my publisher. Sometimes, I think my publisher is as big a sap as he is."

"You may not be proud of it," Mrs. Voclain smiled at her, and then she sipped her wine. "But it is still very well written. It is lighthearted and funny and full of surprises."

"Thanks, but as I said, it was written in jest. It was just a bunch of silly half-baked daydreams of things that we wish we could do."

"If that book was silly," Wade, one of René's friends from work, began to speak. "Then you made up for it with The King of Four." He smiled at her and held a glass up to give her a small toast of approval. "That was an epic tale and my kids begged me to read it every night. I don't mind telling you that I wanted to read it too."

"Thank you." Jessie smiled. She knew her books were good. They were top grossers and kept her living well. But it was always good to hear praise from your readers.

Dinner continued and then gave way to dessert. There was sticky toffee pudding, apple, cherry, pumpkin, and sweet potato pies. There was even eggnog ice cream. Jessie was delighted with René's ability to cook, and she sampled more than some of his dishes. She couldn't remember a time that she had eaten so much and so well.

Soon it was time for games. Jessie had never laughed so hard in her life. Charades, Marco Polo, Twenty Questions, and Name that Tune were only some of the games that they played. Suddenly, an array of light began to shine outside the windows, and all the kids ran over to them.

"Look!" Little William shouted. "Aliens!"

Now the adults came to the window, and they looked out.

"It's a meteor shower," Aunt Patti announced happily. "Oh my, such colors."

The dark night sky was a glow and full of stars. Reds, yellow, blues, and white filled the night sky like diamonds in a display case. Occasionally, a red or white one would zoom by them and pass on into the unknown.

"Cool!" Peter exclaimed, impressed with amazement.

"I've never seen a meteor shower before," Jessie commented. Soon, just looking out the window wasn't enough for her. She ran outside and René followed her.

Jessie stood out on his lawn and looked up into

the sky. It didn't even matter that her neck was starting to ache. She didn't want to miss a thing. She just stood there staring at God's wonderful jewels of light. There were so many stars here. In the city, she only ever saw just one or two maybe five tops and a planet if they were lucky. But here in the wilderness, the entire sky was full of stars. There was nowhere that she could look that she didn't see one hundred thousand stars staring back at her. She spread her arms out in joy and fell backwards into the snow. A meteor shot by, and she just laid there with the grandeur of the night sky filling her eyes and her imagination. René's mother smiled at her.

"Heh, writers." Wade laughed. He hugged his wife and went back inside.

Everyone laughed at Wade's little joke and then went back inside too. It was a very cold out, but it was a clear night; and the temperature inside was definitely better than the temperature outside. René smiled to himself and then went over to collect Jessie. He knelt beside her.

"You'll catch a cold, laying there like that." He hovered over her.

"Shush." Jessie told him with a smile. "And move, you're blocking my view." She pushed him away.

"Well, that is fine with me." He chuckled at her. "Lay out here in the snow. Get wet and cold. I will just give you another bath."

Jessie grabbed a handful of snow and threw it at him. René laughed and scooped up some snow and dumped it on her. That did it. Now a snowball fight between René and Jessie ensued.

"SNOWBALL FIGHT!!" Henry shouted with glee.

Now, all the kids rushed outside and joined in. Over twenty children ran, and played, and threw snowballs at each other. It was a full blown bloody free for all. Jessie hid behind a tree and let loose with shot after shot that always hit their mark. Alice and Susan took up making snowballs for Jessie; and Jessie flung them with a great arm.

René and the boys all took on Jessie, but Jessie didn't stand there waiting for them to hit her. She nimbly dodged their shots and nailed them with shots of her own. Then three of the cousins joined the fight as well. René was pelted with snowball after snowball by Jessie and his own cousins. It wasn't until Mrs. Voclain got hit in the face with a snowball that she brought the war to an end.

"That's it!" She yelled. "Everybody inside!"

Much complaining and whining began and a lot more grumbling as everyone headed back inside

René's house. Mrs. Voclain punished each one of them with a slap on the butt too as they entered the house. First the kids, then the cousins, and Jessie too.

"Sorry, Mrs. Voclain." Jessie sniggered an apology.

"Oh, I'm sorry dear." Mrs. Voclain apologized to Jessie. "Once I got started..."

Jessie gave Mrs. Voclain a big grin. "No worries, Mrs. Voclain. I'm sure that was for something bad I've done this year."

René was the last to come in. He was laughing and shaking snow off his clothes and out of his hair.

"That was actually fun." René admitted, shaking the snow from his hair.

"I love snowball fighting." Jessie grinned with delight.

"I actually haven't done that since I was a kid. My brothers and I would take on the neighborhood kids. We were awesome." Rene' remembered with bright smile.

"With all this snow and it's been that long?" Jessie wondered about him. "You need more fun in life." Jessie pointed a finger in his face.

He laughed her off, but then his mother called his name.

"René Basile Voclain." Mrs. Voclain began, quite seriously. "I want a word with you."

René didn't get a spanking from his mom, instead, she pulled his ear and hauled him off in the direction of the garage.

Behind her, Jessie heard laughing. It was René's brothers.

"Ha-ha, mom took him to the tool shed." Jules laughed.

"Man, his butt will hurt tomorrow." Noel laughed too.

"She's punishing him for this?" Jessie asked. *That seems a bit excessive.*

Before she got her answer, she was scooped up by Shelly, Anna, Diane, and the kids. They wanted autographs and the inside scoop of any new stories that she was currently writing.

Towards the end of the evening, one last game was played. The Mistletoe Game. There were two hats. Every boy put their name in one hat and the girls of course all put their names in the other one. Now as the game goes, whoever's name is called must come and stand under the mistletoe and give or receive a kiss.

"This is a game?" Jessie asked. "I thought it was

only when someone was caught under it that a kiss was given."

"Trust me, Jessie." Diane laughed. "This is way more entertaining."

"Come on, Jessie, you too." Penny told her. "Put your name in."

"Oh no, not me." Jessie backed out.

"Too late." Jennifer smiled with mischief.

"Oh, you didn't." Jessie feared. "Jenny." Jennifer and Diane both just giggled mischievously at her. "But doesn't that get a bit problematic if the one your kissing is not your spouse?" Jessie was seriously wondering who she would have to kiss, as she looked at the males in the room.

"Nah, it's all in good fun. Kisses are cheek only. Unless you happen to draw your spouse." Diane explained. She took a drink and waited for the fun to start.

"Guess that explains the terms kissing cousins." Jessie chuckled.

"Didn't you ever play this game back home?" Diane asked.

"No. The last time I remember playing, only one cowboy hat was used."

"Now that would get confusing. I can see how that would be very entertaining though." Aunt

Patty snickered. "Is that how they play in New York?"

"No, but if it was, that would explain a lot." Jessie chuckled.

Suddenly, Uncle Robert called her name and held up the piece of paper.

"Go on Jessie, your name was called." Penny told her.

"Me? No, please, not me." Jessie protested.

It was Diane and Aunt Patti that whisked her up and pushed her towards the mistletoe. While she was looking for a way out of this, Uncle Robert called out René's name.

"Looks I got my Christmas wish." René smiled, as he stepped closer to her. He took her hand in his and gave it a light squeeze.

"I want a recount." Jessie joked, while she stood nervously beneath the mistletoe.

"Don't worry, just one innocent peck on the cheek and it's all over." He teased her.

"One small kiss?" Jessie raised an eyebrow at him. "Because I don't trust you."

"S'il vous plaît." René winked at her.

Jessie aimed for the side of his cheek. However, René turned his head and claimed her lips. He wove his arms around her and pulled her closer. The longer the kiss lasted, the less and less Jessie tried to end it.

Why do his kisses always feel so nice?

"Eww." The kids all laughed.

Noel looked at his watch and began to laugh. "Fifteen seconds. thirty seconds." He continued the laugh. "This could go on for a while."

"Ah hem." Jules cleared his throat. "Break it up. Some of us would like to go home."

Jessie pushed René away. "The cops have arrived." She stepped away from him with heated cheeks and looked at the floor. "Bar's closed."

René lifted her head, and his eyes sparkled with laughter, as they stared into each other's eyes. "Can I have one for the road."

God why is his smile so...so.... entrancing, satisfying, and just plain delightful? Jessie shook her head no. Mostly to clear her thoughts. "Nope, might lose my liquor license." *And my underwear.* "Go home." Jessie walked away from René and headed towards the kitchen.

"I am home." It may have sounded like a quip because this was his house, but René genuinely smiled to himself as he watched Jessie walk away from him.

René, Jules, and Noel just watched her. Jessie was

cleaning up plates and storing the leftover food away.

"If you don't marry that girl. I will arrest you for stupidity." Jules threatened his brother. "Boys!" Jules called out to his two sons. "It's time to go."

"Aww." The kids complained. But Sarah escorted them to the door.

"Nice party bro." Noel slapped his brother's back. "Can't wait for next year."

"It's your turn next year." René reminded him, and he pushed his brother's arm off his shoulder.

"Yes, but your house is better. Besides, you'll have a wife and child to show off by then." Noel ribbed him. "Anna, are you ready to leave?"

"Yes, dear." Anna said her goodbyes to the family. "Goodbye mother Voclain. See you tomorrow. "Susan! Alice! Time to go! Put on your hats and gloves, please."

René bid all his guests and their families farewell. The Wilderness Metro was loaded up and they all left. All except Mrs. Voclain.

"That was fun," Mrs. Voclain told Jessie, as she helped her clean up and put dishes in the dishwasher. "I'm glad that you are here."

"So am I." Jessie smiled. Then she remembered something. "Oh, I have to call Erik."

"Go right ahead dear."

Mrs. Voclain finished filling the dishwasher with the first round of dishes and then turned it on. She grabbed a glass of wine and sat down on the couch to rest. René came and sat down beside her, while Baby It's Cold Outside played on the radio.

"So, what do you think, maman?" He asked her, seriously.

"She's nice, intelligent, well-spoken." Mrs. Voclain took a sip of her wine. "I like her."

"Jules, thinks that I should marry her," René' relayed, as Jessie made her phone call. He smiled as he watched her talk to Erik. She was so excited. *Most likely telling him about all the fun she had. And probably worried about her virtual fish.* Rene' grinned to himself. His mother's voice brought him out of his thoughts.

"Maybe He's right," Mrs. Voclain agreed with a nod.

"Noel thinks I should mount her." René chuckled. For some reason, his mind chose to fill his head with images of Noel doing Jessie from behind with his hands on her hips. All the while having told her how great her hips were. René rolled his eyes.

"Noel's a nut.," Mrs. Voclain sighed heavily with great contentment. "I don't know how Anna puts up with him." Mrs. Voclain took another sip of her wine, as they sat and watched Jessie happily talk to Erik on the phone. She was wishing him a Merry Christmas and asking him how things were going at home.

Mrs. Voclain got up, ran her fingers lovingly through her son's hair, and kissed his forehead. "I'm going to bed. Don't stay up too late." She put her glass down and walked off towards the stairs.

"Yes, mom." René smiled. "Sleep well."

Jessie finished her phone call with Erik and then came into the living room. She stood before Rene'. "Did your mom go to bed?"

"Yes." René stood up, took Jessie in his arms, and danced with her. Jessie rolled her eyes at him. René rested his head against hers.

René and Jessie slowly waltzed around the room and for the first time in a very long while, she felt loved. Jessie fell perfectly in step with him, as if they had been together all their lives.

René just smiled at Jessie. He loved having this woman in his arms. His whole body seemed to brighten and become lighter wherever he held this woman in his arms. *This is the one. I **know** she is. I've never felt this way about any woman before. But* *this woman; Jessie is special, and I want to spend my life with her.*

Five minutes later, Jessie was starting to feel fluffy and light, like she was a princess dancing with her prince. Maybe it was the champagne, but dancing with René like this, was intoxicating and made her feel warm all over. Then she noticed all the presents that were still stacked in the corner and under the tree.

"Um...René,"

"Yes, Jessie." He responded. He lifted her forearm to his lips, and he kissed the beaver's tail on her arm.

"Your family forgot their Christmas presents."

"Don't worry, they will be back tomorrow...I mean today at noon." He assured her, as he glanced up at the clock. "They will have lunch first and then everyone will get to open presents."

"Oh joy, round two." Jessie giggled.

René stopped dancing, stood back a bit, and looked at her. "What is the matter? Do you not like ma famille? They like you." René looked a little hurt by her playful outburst.

"Oh no, don't get me wrong." Jessie corrected herself. "I think they're swell."

"Swell?" René gave her a wry grin. "You really are a writer."

"Something wrong with you?" She asked him. "You seem... a little...upset."

"I'm not mad." He assured her.

Jessie pushed him away. "No, but you do seem...bothered." Jessie judged his countenance. "Does your butt still hurt?"

"My butt?" René looked curiously at her, but then he understood. "Oh, you mean...no, no, mom did not spank me. She did give me an earful though."

"May I ask what you guys discussed?" She folded her hands behind her back and waited for his answer.

René took her left hand in his and kissed the back of her hand. "You mostly." Then he pulled her closer and lightly kissed her lips.

"Me?" Jessie looked puzzled and gently pushed René away. "Why?"

Now René really did look worried. He sighed. "Go sit down, there is something that we need to discuss."

"Okay." Jessie wondered what they needed to talk about, that was this earth shattering, that he was being this serious for.

But she went over to the couch, sat down, and

waited. René went to the dining room table. Picked up their glasses, grabbed an almost finished bottle of wine, and then returned to the living room. He was pouring Jessie a glass of wine when she just asked him.

"Are you kicking me out of the scouts?" She joked. The air was too dense with seriousness. She had to break it, or she would choke.

"What?" René nearly spilled the wine all over himself. "Non, no." He put the bottle down and handed her the glass.

She took a sip so that it wouldn't spill and then she sat back. "Oh, good. I was worried for a minute that I would finally be able to get out of here."

René gave her a lopsided grin and then went to pour himself a drink. He drank it down and then poured himself another. Jessie just watched him. His demeanor was serious.

"Look Mohawk boy, release Miss Beans." She ordered him in her best mobster voice. "That or let me go. I got things to do you know."

"What things?" René smiled. That was better. She liked him better when he smiled. "You don't do things. You don't even do the windows."

"I wash dishes," She protested, glancing at him with mirth filled eyes over the rim of her wine.

"Hardly," He laughed.

"Well, someone does keep distracting me." She grinned at him, with playful eyes.

Then he got serious again. "Jessie...do you like me?"

She smiled at him and pretended to think about it. "Hm, sometimes." She took a drink.

Rene' cleared his throat and then began. "There's something that I want to tell you."

"And what is that?" Jessie smirked. "That my cell in the cellar is finally complete and that you will be my one and only patron forever."

"What?!" René panicked and his eyes bulged. "Where the hell does your mind go at night?"

Jessie laughed at him and put her empty wine glass down on the coffee table. "I'm a writer who loves to read books and watch old movies. I'm surprised that you haven't seen that one."

"I did," René just shook his head. "I'm just surprised that you still don't trust me. What did I ever do to you?"

Jessie just sat there and gave him a wicked smile. "Well..." Suddenly, a curious thought hit her. "Did your mom go to bed?"

"Yes." Rene' nodded, finishing up his glass of wine.

"And in whose room is she sleeping?" Jessie asked, with a puzzled look.

René chuckled at her. "Yours."

"Then where am I supposed to sleep?" Jessie complained, as she pointed to herself.

"You could sleep with me, if you'd like." He offered her seriously, as he put his glass down.

"That's forward," Jessie joked. "Did you plan this?" She eyed him with suspicion.

"No." He assured her, as he offered her his hand to help her stand. "Mom always sleeps in the guest room." René put his arm around her, as he guided her upstairs. "You're the party crasher." They stopped in front of the door to his room.

Jessie looked at the door to his room. It was like finally being allowed to see what lay beyond the outer worlds. Jessie reeled in her imagination and turned to looked at Rene' "Well," Jessie smirked at him wickedly. "Well, if I'm upgrading my room, what will I get in return?"

Rene' laughed. "You're already getting free breakfast and free wi-fi."

"How about a full body "spa treatment"?" She traced his face and chin with her right forefinger and stared into cyan eyes. She gently guided his chin towards her and kissed him avidly.

Ready to fulfill her every desire, Rene' broke the kiss, opened the door to his room, and said, "I can arrange that." René chuckled, swept her off her feet, and bridal carried her into his room.

Chapter 9

In the morning, Jessie was taking a hot shower when René decided to join her. Last night, she had thrilled him beyond words, and he wanted to return the favor. He smiled to himself as he undressed, she was completely unaware of him. Removing his underwear, and opening the shower door, René joined her in the shower.

Jessie was in the shower, letting the hot waters run over her. She loved his rainfall shower head. It was like taking a bath outside while standing underneath a waterfall. Suddenly, she heard the shower door open, and she looked over her shoulder. There he stood, as nature intended. He didn't ask to join her, he just did.

René stepped into the shower with her and stood behind her. He moved in close and held her waist gently in his left hand as his right hand took the soap from her. He began with little circle around her stomach; and then the circles slowly got bigger. He washed her chest and her stomach, as he kissed her right shoulder, and spoke to her in French.

"Tue s belle. J'ai envie de toi. Tu m'excites. Permettez-moi de vous avoir."

The tone of his romantic expressions spoke to her very core, and she willingly submitted to his deeds. He pulled her closer to him and soon there was no room between them for the water to run. René gently and purposefully ground his manhood between her buttocks.

"Oh René," Jessie sighed with great contentment. "Ca se sent si bien."

He smiled and whispered into her ear. "I will show you what feels even better."

With that, he moved his hands to her hips, pressed the head of his shaft into her, and she absorbed the fullness of his length within her sheath. The sensation of his intrusion sent maddening molten waves of pleasure through her, as he purposefully penetrated her. Jessie breathlessly panted, relishing the breaching of her defenses, as his rigid and engorged member made puree of her will. His shishna reared hot and hard within her yoni, deliberately delivering delight while her body enclosed around him, and pulled every bit of retas from his body.

René rested his head on the back of her neck as

he reveled in the rush of ecstasy and adrenaline. Jessie felt...euphoric in the aftermath of their heated melding. They both stood in the now cooling waters of the shower, dripping wet, but completely satisfied.

"Veux-tu m'epouser?" He bade her. "Please. Let me be your famille."

Jessie just stood there, stuck between him and the shower wall. She was stuck between staying single and having her freedom or getting married and becoming a wife and mother. The word mother hit her like a ton of bricks.

Am I ready to be a wife and possibly a mother?

"Do you love me that much?" Jessie asked, unsure of how to answer him.

"Yes." He answered her most definitely. "Do you love me?"

Jessie lowered her head and let the cold water run down her back. She just stood there...thinking. "I...I...kind of, sort of...I mean we just met."

"And yet I feel as if I know you." He whispered to her softly.

"You've been reading my books." She quipped.

"Ha!" He snorted and withdrew from her. "Tell me truthfully." He turned her around to face him and rested his forehead to hers. "Do you love me?" He stared deeply into her eyes.

Jessie's heart raced, as did her thoughts as she looked at him. His eyes were so hard and intense, and yet seemed of quicksand as they pulled her into him. She could feel his sincerity and his manhood as it rested against her, seemingly ready to fulfill her every desire yet again. And yet, the question was, did she feel the same?

Do I love him? Could I stay here and spend my life with him? What about my life in New York? "I...I don't know." Jessie looked away from him and lowered her head; she couldn't look him in the eye anymore. "I like you. I like you a lot. But..."

"Then let me convince you to stay." He gently lifted her head and kissed her deeply. Their lips met and she shuddered with a desire to do it all again. The mere touch of his strong hands sliding down her back to give her buttocks a good squeeze, set her insides throbbing and unchained her wild need.

While René was still showering, Jessie had gotten dressed, and now went downstairs for breakfast. She was feeling good, and the feeling got better as the savory scents of a cooking breakfast filled her nose and made her stomach churn with growl. But then it clicked.

Wait a minute, if René is upstairs in the shower, who's cooking breakfast?

Jessie stepped into the kitchen and was shocked to see a matronly woman cooking breakfast. Jessie froze. She was taken aback that she hadn't heard this woman come in. *Ha, what would you have heard over your "grunting"?*

Mrs. Voclain noticed Jessie's questioning face and so she introduced herself, again. "I'm Denise Voclain, René's mother." The woman smiled warmly at her.

"That's right, the Christmas party." Jessie stood dumbfounded and she made her memory recall the Christmas party last night.

Mrs. Voclain was wearing René's pink apron, cooking breakfast, and slipping Sarah bacon strips. Sarah wagged her tail happily. Sarah whimpered for another piece of bacon, but Mrs. Voclain waved her off.

"Now, now, save some for Jessie and René."

Sarah wandered off to the living room to watch TV. Jessie was about to get a plate down from the shelf when Mrs. Voclain giggled at her. Jessie was wearing Rene' pajama top and a pair of his red boxers.

"You might want to have more clothes on. It still a bit chilly outside." Mrs. Voclain plated the bacon up, as she gave Jessie sideways glances.

Jessie looked down at her attire. "Oh crap. Sorry. I'm sorry." Jessie blushed, hard and she tried to pull the long flannel shirt down lower to cover up the boxers and the fact that she was not wearing pants. Her cheeks felt heated, and her heart was pumping fast. "I'm going to go and get dressed."

"Good Idea." Mrs. Voclain's eyes sparkled with mischief, and she gave Jessie a knowing smile.

Jessie fled the kitchen. She was halfway up the stairs, when a fully dressed René came down, looking dapper and fresh.

"Your mom is downstairs," Jessie told him in passing.

René sniffed the air. "That means breakfast is ready." He smiled and ran the rest of the way down the stairs.

"Good morning to you too," Jessie chuckled. *Mamma's boy.*

Ten minutes later, a fully clothed Jessie sat down to breakfast. Rene sat at the breakfast bar stuffing his face with pancakes, while his mother cleaned up the kitchen.

"Well nice of you to join us." Mrs. Voclain snickered, and she poured Jessie a cup of orange juice.

"Taken any longer and you would have missed Ma mère pancakes," René swished his pancakes around in the syrup and then shoved them into his mouth.

Jessie took the last two pancakes and the last three strips of bacon. Then she heard Sarah whimper and she looked over at her.

"Don't look at me like that, you've already had more breakfast than me," Jessie joked. Then she picked up the syrup and poured it over her pancakes. "Is this real maple syrup, fresh from the tree?"

"Speaking of trees," René laughed. He stood up, put on his jacket, and then called Sarah to him. "Come on Sarah, let's go and chase some squirrels."

"René hun, why not let Miss Tyler take Sarah out for a walk. I want to talk to you a bit."

"Umm, yes ma'am." Rene pulled his eyes from his mother. *I wonder what she wants to talk about.* René turned to Jessie. "Do you mind taking Sarah for a walk?"

"Sure, no problem." Jessie licked syrup off her fingers. "Just keep mine warm for me, and I'll eat it later." Then Jessie turned to Sarah. "Come on, girl, Let's go and play."

Both Mrs. Voclain and Rene watched as Jessie bundled up in Rene's coat, ushered Sarah out, and then closed the door behind her. That just left Rene' alone with his mother. Rene' just sat at the breakfast bar, cutting up his pancakes, while Mrs. Voclain stared at him.

"Something you want to tell me?" Mrs. Voclain urged her son.

Uh no. "No, not really." René didn't look at his mother but kept trying to hide his mischievous grin.

His mother only continued to eye him. This made him squirm and he sighed. René wiped his mouth with a napkin, took a deep breath, and began his explanation. "Her name is Jessica Tyler and she's a guest for the winter."

"A guest?" Mrs. Voclain arched an eyebrow at her son. *I don't believe you.* "Do tell."

"Nothing to tell. She crashed her car into a tree when a deer jumped in her path. She had a concussion and John said that she needed the rest.

So, she's staying here for a few weeks. We told you that last night."

Mrs. Voclain smirked at her son. "I remember, I was there. But if she's just a patient, then why was she wearing your flannel **pajama** shirt?" Then she practically laughed at her son. "And **your** red underwear."

"I... uh, we..." Rene' blushed, coughed to clear his throat, and tried to explain. "Well, she only has one set of clothes and I've been..."

"What are your intentions with this girl?" Mrs. Voclain asked, as she cleaned up the kitchen. "Is she a weekend friend or...something more? Because you've had young ladies over here before, but you've never slept with them."

Rene' took up his orange juice, took a swig, and then set the glass down. "Well, she started out a just visitor recovering from a bad accident. But then she ended up..."

"In your bed." Mrs. Voclain chuckled at her son.

"Maman!" Rene's face betrayed his surprise at his mother jibe. "Good grief. I...We...It's just that something about her intrigues me." René faced his mother with a smile.

"Like what?" Mrs. Voclain took a sip of her drink.

René thought about it and then he chuckled. "She's a mystery puzzle box."

"A what?" Mrs. Voclain scoffed at him and then chuckled too.

"She's funny...and surprising...and...just when you think you've figured her out; she pops you another surprise." René's eyes lit up as he spoke about her. "She's...let's just say that once her imagination winds her up, you don't know how she'll pop. She's...she's..."

"An intriguing puzzle." Mrs. Voclain laughed. She took a sip of her orange juice.

René sat back and sighed. "I know I shouldn't even be thinking such a thing. I mean she's going to be going home as soon as her editor says that she can come back."

"Wait, what?" Mrs. Voclain looked at her son and furrowed her brow. "What do you mean when she's allowed to come back? Has she been banished or something?"

"I'm surprised that you didn't see it on the news. Her publisher says that she's been trending since she disappeared and that her books are really selling out. They want her to stay gone in order to milk the masses."

"Ah, yes. Nothing beats have a great marketing

strategy." Mrs. Voclain thought back on her younger days. "A good marketing campaign can make or break a business."

"Anyway, her publisher has abandoned her here for the winter."

"So again, I ask you, what are your intentions?"

"Well, as I said, it started out just a bed and breakfast arrangement." Rene' told his mother.

"But..."

"But I like her." He confessed. He stroked his chin as he thought about her. "Sure, she's loud and noisy sometimes. Sure, she doesn't pay attention and daydreams all day. But she's also a great listener and an avid learner. I'm teaching her to cook and to be a Beaver Scout."

"A Beaver Scout?" scoffed Mrs. Voclain. "What on Earth for?"

"It's just a game. Give the little city girl something to do while she is here."

"I thought she was supposed to be writing, while she's hiding out."

"Come on mom, you know there's more to life than just dreaming your days away." Rene' shook his head and then sighed deeply. "I want her to know and enjoy the real world too."

Mrs. Voclain smiled at her son.

"Besides, I've been thinking about wanting to start a family. This house is just too much for just one person."

"Yes, it was a fine starter house." Mrs. Voclain looked around the room. "You've made some improvements."

"Winter gives me a lot of time to do things." He picked up his orange juice and took a drink.

"Your father and I were very happy here." Mrs. Voclain smiled with remembrance. "But after having three kids and needing to be closer to the school district. We just decided to move."

"Well, I want to start a family and she's the one I want to start a family with."

"Really?" Mrs. Voclain smiled at him. *Finally.* She thought to herself. *First one born, but last one to come to his senses.*

"I know it sounds crazy. I know we just met. Truthfully, she's nothing but trouble. But when I hold her in my arms. It just feels..."

"Right." Mrs. Voclain said, as she stared into her glass.

"Yes. That's it exactly. It just feels right." René nodded in agreement. "I feel... I feel like she's the one that I've been waiting for."

Mrs. Voclain wiped her wet hands on Rene's

apron. "I felt the same when I met your father." Mrs. Voclain ran her fingers lovingly through her son's hair and kissed his forehead.

"Well, besides "pillow talk", Mrs. Voclain chuckled. "Have you discussed any of this with her?"

Just then, Jessie and Sarah came back inside. "Hi, I'm back."

"Nice to have someone to come home to, isn't it?" Mrs. Voclain hinted at Rene'.

"Yes, it is." Rene' smiled.

Chapter 10

The next day, Rene' went looking for Jessie. She wasn't downstairs by the fire, and she wasn't in the kitchen, looking for leftovers to microwave.

"She must be upstairs." Rene' wondered to himself.

He left Sarah warming herself by the fire and went upstairs. He looked in the guest bedroom, but she wasn't there.

"Welp, that just leaves the library." Rene' pulled the wooden door aside and looked inside. There deep in thought and staring at the computer screen was Jessie. *Working on her books, no doubt.*

Jessie didn't hear Rene come in, she just kept typing away on his keyboard. Her nimble fingers gliding over the keys with precision and purpose. He didn't want to disturb her train of thought, so he just reached for a book and sat down on the couch to read. It wasn't until he coughed to clear his throat, that Jessie looked up from her writing.

"When did you come in?" She asked, wondering why she hadn't heard him come in.

"Half an hour ago." He closed the book he was

reading and laid it down on the end table. "You were working. I didn't want to disturb you."

"Disturb me? I didn't even hear you come in." Jessie looked at the door and then at him. "Was there something you wanted? Do you need your computer back?"

"No." He shook his head. "I was just wondering where you were. I haven't really seen you all day."

"Sorry." Jessie sat back and stretched. "Sometimes I get lost in my own world."

"Sometimes?" He snickered at her.

She grinned at him. "What's for dinner?"

"I don't know." He shrugged. "Maybe a fish dish. I still have fish left from our fishing trip."

"That could be delicious." Jessie nodded in agreement. "Do you know how to make Salt & Vinegar Potato Chip Fish Fillets?"

Rene' arched an eyebrow at her. "No."

"No worries, let me just grab the recipe off the internet." Jessie looked down and her fingers started typing again.

"May I ask what book you were working on?" Rene' sat back and rested his arms on the back of the couch.

"Well, since you were telling me about the myths, legends, and folklore of this region, I decided to look more into it. And I found a story that I like." Jessie found the recipe and hit the print button.

"Which one?"

"The one about the ghost ship The Roaming Rouge."

"That all female pirate ship that got stuck in the ice?"

"Yeah, that one." Jessie now turned to face him. "I researched everything I could find on it."

"Why?"

"That's the question." Jessie eyes lit up as she talked about the ship and her crew. "Why did these women take to sea? Why did they become sailors, which can be a hard job even for a man? Why did they become pirates? How did they get stuck in the ice and die?"

"The Wicked Witch of Winter got them and killed them all." Rene crossed his legs and explained. "Some died of starvation, but most died of hypothermia and frostbite. The last time the ship was seen, the crew were still in their beds and some still at the dinner table, table set, but nothing to eat. The captain was still sitting in her captain's chair writing in her log, quill frozen to her hand."

"See that's one hell of a story." Jessie smiled

brightly, but then she frowned and gave him a questioning look. "And what do you mean the last time she was seen?"

"Well, she is a ghost ship." Rene' gave her a small grin and pulled from memory the tales of the Roaming Rouge. "When nights are freezing cold and the fog rolls in, People swear they've seen the ghost ship still sailing the Saint Lawrence River."

"Cool. Wonder if I'll get to see it?" Jessie mused.

"So, what did you write about them?" Rene' asked, as he uncrossed his legs.

"What to hear? Let me read you some." Jessie re-opened her story on the computer and started reading.

Robin was dreaming, or at least she thought she was. She heard a lively sea shanty going through her head, and when she got up to go to the bathroom, she found herself signing it.

~

I used to be a farmer and I made a living fine,
I had a little stretch of land along the C.P. Line.
But times went by, and though I tried, the money wasn't there,
And bankers came and took my land and told me "fair is fair".

*I looked for every kind of job, the answer always
no*
*"Hire you now," they'd always laugh, "we just let
twenty go!"*
*The government, they promised me a measly little
sum.*
*But I've got too much pride to end up just another
bum.*
*Then I thought, who gives a damn if all the jobs
are gone,*
I'm gonna be a pirate on the river Saskatchewan.
*'Cause it's a heave-ho, high-ho, coming down the
Plains*
*Stealing wheat and barley and all the other
grains*
*And it's a ho-hey, high-hey, farmers bar your
doors*
*When you see the Jolly Roger on Regina's mighty
shores*

~

Robin looked out of the bathroom window and saw ghost lights of blue, green, orange, and red. The mysterious orbs of light traveled through the woods, and they all seemed to converge at one spot.

"Where are they going?" Robin wondered.

She washed her hands, left the bathroom, and went downstairs. She donned her boots and her coat and out the door she went. Rebecca woke up when she heard the door open and barked at Robin. Rebecca blew an exhausted breath and walked over to the door. Rebecca sat there and barked and barked. Her barking of course woke Basil up. Basil rolled over, but Robin was not there.

"Robin?"

Hearing Rebecca barking, Basil got up and put on his clothes. He went downstairs and found Rebecca at the front door barking. He flung the front door open and looked outside. He saw Robin's footprints disappearing into the dark forest.

"Not again." Basil groaned and shook his head. He looked down at Rebecca and laughed. "Our inmate has escaped again."

Basil put on his boots and coat and then he and Rebecca chased after Robin. The night was crisp, clean, and cold. There was a full moon shining down and the wind was brisk. It was snowing lightly, and Basil could hear nothing but the sounds of the snow crunching beneath his feet. Suddenly, he started hearing music and signing.

Rebecca and Basil followed Robin's footprints and found her standing in the snow at the banks of the river. She was looking at an enigmatic fog that was rolling in towards them. Fog was supposed to be white. After all, it's only a thick cloud of water droplets that hovers near the earth's surface. But this fog was a ghostly silver blue with some wisps of green flowing through it like *"unseen"* winds. Basil walked up to Robin, and she heard him approach.

"Nice of you to join me." She snickered.

"What are you doing?" He asked angrily.

"You mean besides freezing?" She quipped.

"If you are cold, then stay in the house and come back to bed."

"Aren't you curious?"

"About what?"

"That." Robin pointed and a ghost ship was coming down the river.

Basil's eyes bulged in shock, and he shook his head in disbelief. "What the...?"

"Whose is it?" She asked him, as she pulled the collar of her coat closer to her.

"Why are you asking me?" Basil chuckled at her.

"Because elf boy, you know every Canadian ghost story, remember?"

"What's the name of the ship?" Basil resigned himself to her crazy whims.

"Uhm." Robin looked at the bow. "The Roaming Rouge."

Basil searched his memory for the name. "The Roaming Rouge was a pirate ship that roamed the coasts looking for treasure, supplies, and fun. They would loot any ship that they came across. They would steal gold, jewels, rum, and other supplies. However, while other pirates had their hideouts in warmer waters, The Roaming Rouge hid up North, where they knew that no one would follow them."

"That's rather smart. Cause your Canadian winter weather sucks." Robin giggled. "Hold up all winter, with gold and goods, and set sail next spring to do it all again."

"Yep. Anyway, the legend goes that they buried their treasure while they were gone and dig it up when they got home." Basil explained.

"Who needs a bank and their service fees." Robin laughed.

Basil chuckled at her and continued his story. "But this time, they could not find it."

"I hate that when that happens." Robin snickered.

"What?" Basil blew on his hands to warm them and watched the ship sail down the river towards them.

"Squirreling something away to keep it safe and it's so safe that I can't even find it." Robin quipped.

"Yes, well, the captain had his map, But the terrain had changed. Weather, loggers, etc. His landmarks were gone. He and his shipmates couldn't find their storehouse of treasure, but they kept looking and looking. Unfortunately for them, the weather was getting worse and worse." Basil continued his tale.

"Damn Canadian Winters." Robin giggled.

"The captain vowed that he'd find it…"

"If he had to search all of eternity to do it." Robin finished the story with sadness in her voice. "They probably got lost in a witch of winter snowstorm, ran aground, got frozen in ice, or sank. All hands were lost as they froze to death."

"You got it. The witch of winter froze the ice, trapped the ship, and all hands froze to death. In the spring, when the ice thawed, the ship sailed on. Every winter, when the moon is full and the time is right, you can hear singing, you can see ghost lights, which are the souls of the sailors still searching for their treasure, and you can see the Roaming Rouge still roaming the waters of Canada." Basil finished his tale and adjusted his footing. He wanted to go back inside his safe warm home. He wanted to go back to his warm bed. But Robin... "What's the matter?"

Robin stood there watching the ship sail down the river. Her eyes were sad as they followed the ghost lights on their search.

"I know what it's like to be lost. To have no idea what you're looking for or where to find it. To be sailing in circles with no rudder to guide you or anchor to keep you from drifting endlessly."

Basil walked up to Robin and put his arms around her. "What happened? Did you get lost as a child? Wondered off when they told you to stay put?" He snickered lightly.

"My parents died. Not only did I stop celebrating Christmas, but I also had no idea what to do with myself. I'd just sit in my room at the orphanage staring out of the window. Wishing to be anywhere else but there. I guess that's one reason that I became a writer. I read books to travel earth and have adventures. I made up stories to entertain myself."

"Wait a minute." Rene' held up a hand and interrupted Jessie's story telling.

"What?" Jessie looked over to him. "You don't like it?" Jessie worried.

"No, It's not that." He brought his hand down and waved it toward her. "But you put yourself in the story?"

"Yes, usually do." Jessie sat back in the armchair. "Just bits and pieces to flesh out my characters."

"So, if I read your books, I'll learn all about you."

"You probably could." Jessie nodded.

"Did you have a dog? Because I thought you said you had virtual fish." He snickered.

"I do and Rebecca is Sarah. I'm surprised you didn't get that."

"What?" René rolled his eyes and let out an exhausted breath. "That must mean I'm Basil." He waved a hand to himself.

"Well, your middle name is Basil."

"How do you know that?" He questioned her, taken aback that she knew, without him telling her. *What? Did mom tell her?*

"Some of these books," Jessie waved her hand towards the bookshelf. "Have your name in them."

"I don't remember writing my name in these books." René looked towards the bookshelf.

"Well, if the handwriting is any judge, you were very young." Jessie smirked at him.

"You were raised in an orphanage?" René asked, changing the subject.

"Yes. After my parents died, I had no one to look after me. So, for six years I was a resident of Lang's Lost and Found."

"Lang's lost and found?" René scoffed. "What the hell kind of name is that for an orphanage?"

"Technically," Jessie told him with a mocking grin. "It was called the Lang Foundation. The lost and found is what us kids called it."

René just shook his head incredulously. "So why did you become a writer? Didn't play with the other kids?"

"I didn't like the other kids." Jessie blew out a disgusted sigh.

"Why not?" René crossed his arms.

"Half of them were nice and playful and played with each other, but not with me. The other half of them were mean and played malicious pranks on everyone. They would do nothing but cause trouble and pick on the other kids. But they would all listen when I told Sister Amy my stories. She was the only one who would take the time to listen to me. She seemed amused by my wild ass stories.

She noticed that my stories kept the other kids calm and quiet. So, she set up story time and I could take as long as I wanted to tell my stories. Day after day, my stories would get bigger and longer and more epic. After a while, it got so that I could keep them kids quiet almost all day."

"No wonder I can't get you to shut up." René unfolded his arms and gave her a knowing grin. "You're used to talking all day."

Jessie stuck out her tongue at him. "It was Sister Amy who wanted me to start writing my stories down, so that when I left the orphanage, she could keep telling the stories."

"Now that's a good story." René smiled softly at her. "What happened to Sister Amy?"

"She lived for another thirty-five years and died at the age of seventy-two. She saved thousands of kids like me. Every year until she died, I always sent her my books and others that I picked up from around the world as I traveled. When I became a big-time author, I sent the orphanage the extra money that I made. When she died, I brought the orphanage and named it the Sister Amy's Neverland. There's a statue of Sister Amy with her arms open, and a smile on her face, as she greets all the children who have to come and live there."

"You're a good kid." Rene' gave her a genuine smile.

Jessie noticed that his smile seemed to light his whole face. His smile made him seem less serious and more inviting. The twinkle in his eyes, the puff of his cheeks, his strong chin. He was just so ruggedly handsome and...caring.

"I wanted to thank her for all that she had done for me. The orphans have all that they need, in food and water, rooms and clothes. Toys are only given on their birthdays and at Christmas."

"Did you instill that rule?" René asked her intently.

"No, it's always been that way. The sisters of the orphanage didn't want us becoming entitled. They wanted us to be thankful for what we needed, not be spoiled with what we wanted."

"Do you ever visit them anymore?" René yawned.

"Only to visit Sister Amy's grave. I never go inside, and I never tell them who I am. To them, I'm just an orphan who grew up there."

René smiled to himself, as he listened to her story. *Such a strong willed, wild one, and yet she has a hidden heart of gold. Maybe she does know the true meaning of life. It's not the riches of a man, but the richness of his life.* "Well, back to the pirate story."

Rene' leaned forward and listened intently. "I'd like to hear it."

Jessie sat once again leaned forward and read from her manuscript on the screen.

Suddenly, Rebecca started barking. Basil looked down at her and petted her head.

"What's the matter, girl?"

"The ship has stopped." Robin informed him and she stepped out of his arms. "Look, it's lowering the gang plank."

"Don't even think about it." Basil warned her.

At that moment, all around them, the ghost lights appeared and surround them. The lights dimmed and became human in form. The ghosts of the lost seamen stood waiting to board the ship. Robin looked around and saw their bodies and looking behind her, she saw their faces. They really were emaciated. They really had starved to death. But what really surprised her the most was that they were all female. Females of all color, shapes, and sizes, were skinny, to the point of being boney. But they weren't skeleton women, which is what Robin had expected them to look like. Instead, they looked like famine victims. Robin and Basil just watched in stunned silence

as each sailor stepped forward and waited her turn to board the ship. It was an eerily quiet night, except for the crickets and the owls. Only they dared to speak.

"So, did any of your stories happen to mention that this ship was crewed entirely by women?" Robin asked Basil, with an amused grin.

"Not a word." Basil looked on, with bewilderment.

"That's men for you" Robin quipped. "Mohawk boy strikes again."

Basil scoffed at Robin's gibe but continued to watch the scene play out in silent wonder. Robin watched as the female captain greeted her female crew as they came aboard.

"Welcome back, any luck?"

The captain's voice was barely a whisper, but Robin heard it just the same. It was as clear as if the captain was standing right next to her and whispering into her ear. Robin's heart sank deeper within her as each time she saw the sailors shake their head no. Robin felt sorry for them. It was the same year after year for all eternity. Something had to be done to end their pain.

"Permission to come aboard, Captain?!" Robin requested.

The captain and her crew stood looking over the side of the ship at her.

"Robin, don't." Basil warned her. He tried to hold her back, but Robin slipped out of his grasp and stepped forward.

"It be bad luck to have a woman aboard." The first mate chuckled at the captain.

The captain just looked at her first mate and smiled at her. She knew their whole crew was female. But old wives' tales died hard, and it was still a rule of the sea.

"Well, that would explain why we seemed to be cursed." The captain responded with a half-amused grin, since she was missing part of her jaw.

That got a laugh out of the whole ship and Basil just slapped his forehead.

"Robin." Basil growled at her. "No."

"Oh, hush up. Where is your sense of adventure?" She smiled at him.

"Where is your sense? See, this is why the sky woman fell from the sky. She was noisy."

"She was pushed." Robin insisted with playful smirk.

"Ugh." Basil gave up. "I give up. You are impossible."

This brought more laughter from the ship's crew.

"What's the matter, lubber?" The ship's gunner laughed at him. "Can't control your misses?"

Basil gave an annoyed and exasperated breath. "Who controls a tiger by the tail?" Basil shouted back.

"Captain," Robin called out. "What if I can help you find the treasure?"

Abruptly, all laughter stopped. The night was quiet as the wind gently blew.

"Robin, no! Do you want to disappear and sail for all eternity?" Basil warned her with great concern.

"Then follow me on land and make sure that I don't disappear. And if I do, then at least you can call my family and tell them what happened to me." Robin suggested, matter of factly, as she walked up the gangplank.

"Robin!"

Rebecca barked and barked her warning. She too wanted Robin to come back. Both Basil and Rebecca knew that ghosts were unpredictable.

Nice one minute and deadly the next. There was no telling what those ghosts would do.

Robin boarded the ship and saluted the captain. "Good evening, Captain."

"You're not afraid of us, lass?" The captain's large hallow eye sockets looked Robin over.

Robin looked the captain over. She was five foot nine and looked to have been about forty years old when she...died. She had large hallow eyes, long dark hair, a sunken diamond face, and a tall pear shape. She wore a white linen shirt with a tabot, a long blue camlet coat, long black velvet pants, and black ankle boots. She was...a pirate. In fact, if Captain Hook had been female. He probably would have looked like her.

"Terrified. I have no idea what you are going to do. But I do know that you need help and as a solider, it is my duty to help those who cannot help themselves." Robin told the captain.

Goose bumps practically popped and jumped upon her skin as she stood so very close to the stuff of nightmare.

"That be kind of you." The captain smiled at her. Her face was sunken and her smiled was to be pitied.

"May I see the map?" Robin requested.

The crew prepared to leave. The gangplank was raised, and the sails were unfolded. The signing began again, and René could hear fiddles, accordions, pipes, guitars, and drums.

"Robin!"

Basil ran along the shoreline and tried to follow the ship. It wasn't moving fast. In fact, he found that he could just walk and kept up with the ship just fine. But how long would that last? Once the wind caught the sails, he had no doubt that the ship would pick up speed. Basil knew that he should go and get his snowmobile, but he didn't want to leave Jessie alone with them.

Basil's heart filled with fear as Robin moved away from the ship's railing and deeper into the ship. The captain brought Robin to her cabin and allowed her to see the map. The captain rolled the map out before her.

"Here is where we left it." The captain told her. "Year after year we came back to it."

"How do you know that it's still there?" Robin asked, hesitantly. Pirates could be...aggressive about their treasures. "Someone could have dug it up by now."

The captain looked at her. "You are right; they could have by now. But we hid it well."

"You have *clues* to find it with?" Robin asked, with great interest.

The female captain laughed at her. "We are not so...convoluted. We have the precise locations written down."

"But if the precise location is written on the map..." Robin questioned.

"This map has never left this ship." The captain assured her.

Robin looked into the eyes of the captain. She was serious. Pirates did guard their gold. If anyone else had boarded their ship in the past with goals of stealing their gold, then they would have met with great resistance. Robin studied the captain's map.

"Hey, I've seen this map before."

"Impossible."

"No, not your map." Robin clarified. "But a map like it."

Robin left the captain's cabin and ran to the railing. She looked to see if Basil was still following her.

"Hey Basil!"

Basil looked up and saw Jessie standing at the railing. His heart sored. She was safe and she looked happy.

"Robin!"

"Basil! Go home and get your map of the park off the wall in the loft. I need it."

"For what?"

"I can find the treasure, if I match their map with your map." Robin revealed.

Basil stopped walking and shook his head. "Seriously?"

"Come on Basil, get the lead out."

"Je ne peux pas te croire! Will you just get off that ship and come home?!"

"The faster we find the treasure, the faster you'll get me off this ship." Robin smirked at him.

"Argh!" Basil rolled his eyes and slapped his forehead. "OK, BIEN!" He turned to leave, and Rebecca followed him. "No, girl. You follow Robin and lead me back to her. OK?" Rebecca barked her understanding and stay with the ship. "Good girl. I will be back."

Robin chuckled and looked at the captain. "He's such a good boy."

That brought laughs and chuckled from every woman on the ship. Robin stood on the deck of the ship and looked up into the sky. She could feel the wind gently blowing over her shoulders. Hear the waves of the river's waters. Smell the...well she wasn't sure what that smell was, but it smelled like rotting wood and...yeah dead pirates. But the sensation of sailing, seeking out new worlds, navigating by the stars, and the adventures at sea fueled Robin's imagination. A comic book series about lady pirates might be a good story to tell.

"Maybe I could have been a sailor." Robin mused.

"So, what do you think of it so far?" Jessie asked, impatiently waiting his approval.

Rene' thought about it. He leaned his head to the left and then to the right. He nodded a bit. "Is it for kids?"

"Young adults."

"I can see that they might like it." He nodded in agreement.

"Do **you** like it?" Jessie waited with bated breath for his answer.

"I like being in it." He smirked.

Jessie rolled her eyes at him.

"What happens next?" He asked, with interest.

"I don't know, that's as far as I've gotten so far."

"Do they find the treasure?"

"They will." Jessie nodded, jotting down a few more lines of text. "Everyone loves happy endings."

"And for those who don't?" Rene' sat back and gave a sigh.

"Robin drowns and becomes part of the crew."

"Told you that Canada will kill you, if you don't pay attention." Rene' chuckled.

"Hey, at least she gets to visit Basil every ten years." Jessie smiled and shook her head in amusement. "Question is, does he wait for her?"

Jessie looked up and over at Rene'. Rene' looked directly at her and their eyes met.

"I can see Robin worth waiting for. Even if she is a curious pain in the ass, who doesn't listen."

"Hey!" Jessie threw a crumpled piece of paper at him.

Rene' easily dodged it by moving his head to the side. "So why did your pirates become pirates?"

"Well, Barbara, one of the crew, was an aristocrat at one time. And her father wanted her to marry a man named Adam Mast. Rich landowner or something, but she did not want to. She loved a boy named sailor Jason Travers and they ran away together. But when she told him that she was pregnant and that it was his. He left her. Barbara cried. She was disgraced and couldn't go home.

The captain of the Roaming Rogue took her in. Barbara had her child, left him at the orphanage, and took to the sea. She never looked back...until now."

"That's stupid." Rene' judged. "I don't know any women who would willingly give up their child. Even if they are disgraced." Rene' told Jessie point blank. "She would have taken the child with her. Raised the kid to be a pirate and take revenge on Mr. Travers."

Jessie thought about it. "That could work. But you've obviously never tried to raise a child at sea. There are too many dangers, and the kid would probably fall overboard the first day that it learned to walk."

"Well, whatever you decide to write. I'd like to read it when you're done." Rene' gave her a small smile.

Jessie blushed but nodded yes. "Sure. I could use the feedback."

Chapter 11

It was 8AM and Jessie eased herself from René's bed, showered, and dressed. She went downstairs, but there was no fire going and no breakfast. Wanting to surprise him, Jessie started the fire and stoked it, so that the house would be nice and warm for him when he came down.

Jessie wasn't hungry, so she decided to go to the garage. She had heard about René's snowmobile, but he had also told her that it was broken. She aimed to correct that little problem. Jessie walked the hall behind the kitchen and opened the door to the garage. She was stunned by what she saw.

"Whoa, nice garage. He obviously doesn't use it though. It's too damn clean."

Jessie walked around inside of René's two car garage. It had high arched ceilings, was well insulated against the cold, and four forty-inch bright white LED shop lights hanging down from above. It had sturdy built in wall storage, hanging racks filled with climbing gear. Two ceiling fans, two normal sized windows on the left wall, and a high quality, heavy duty, triple layered custom wood carriage doors.

"Well, if you get locked out this way," Jessie mused. "You're sure not getting back in."

She pressed the green button on the wall. The door pushed some of the snow out of its way as it opened. Jessie pushed the red button to make it stop, and the door closed. The last thing to see here was of course René's vehicles. He owned a Ford Truck, a Polaris Ranger three-seat ATV, and a Polaris Titan Adventure snowmobile. Jessie ran her right hand along the hood and fender of his Ford Truck. She grinned to herself as she thought of her mother.

I should see just how much of my mother is in me and hotwire his truck. Jessie snickered to herself at this thought as she let it pass through her head. Jessie then jumped onto his snowmobile and tried to start it up. She cranked it and cranked it, but it just wouldn't start.

"Yep, it's broken," Jessie sighed heavily, but then she gave a wicked grin. "But I bet I could fix it though." Jessie walked over to the drawers, pulled them open, and one by one she checked their contents. "Bolts, nuts, screws, lures...Lures?" Jessie shook her head and kept looking.

She walked past the snow sleds from yesteryear, the mountain bikes, the camping gear, and the lawnmower. But again, she stopped at the lawnmower.

"Why do you need a lawnmower?" Jessie chuckled. "Just get a couple of goats and your good." Jessie also saw two very large rectangular freezers. "Dead Bodies or Fresh kills?" She laughed to herself and opened one. "Yep. Fish." She closed the lid. "Bins, Racks, and Hooks all in use for storage. "I must say, this is the neatest guy I've ever met. Even Erik isn't this bad."

Jessie gathered the tools she needed and mentally praised René for actually having parts. Even if he didn't know how to use them, he was prepared for every event.

"Good boy scout." Jessie giggled, and then she got to work.

Sarah tried her best to wake René up, but that didn't work. He just groaned at her and rolled over. So, Sarah went to find Jessie. She found her in the garage. She was wearing his flannel shirt and jeans and she was kneeling beside his broken snowmobile. Sarah walked up beside her and wagged her tail. Jessie just reached out and stroked her fur.

"Morning, Sarah. René still not up yet? *He must*

still be sleeping." She mused. *Odd, he's usually always up before me.* "I told you, you have to jump up and down on him. Then he'll wake up." Jessie laughed. But Sarah whimpered at her. Jessie looked at her. "Oh, I see. Time to chase the squirrels."

Jessie put down the tools and got up. She petted Sarah's head, hit the green button for the garage door, and then took Sarah for a good long walk. It was about an hour before they came back. But Jessie was having fun and enjoying the quiet sunny morning. She had watched deer watch her. Viewed birds flying overhead and wished she could fly too. She had played fetch with Sarah and then wondered how her virtual fish were doing. She also saw white foxes, snow rabbits, and a beaver. She chuckled as she remembered her tattoo and looked down at her arm. Then Jessie smiled even harder. She had to. It was just a beautifully sunny winter's day.

"Today is a beautiful day." Jessie spoke aloud. "It's just so damn...peaceful here. Erik was right. I needed to stop and slow down. Maybe I could live here and write books. Whoa, why did I say that? Would I really give up New York? The hustle and bustle. The noise, dirt, and crime. The restaurants and shows. Would I really leave it all behind?" Jessie looked around and saw the trees, the snow, the clear unclogged blue sky. She listened to animals call back and forth to each other. She watched rabbits dart in and out of the trees. She smiled at the feel of the sun on her face. She inhaled deeply and exhaled slowly the fresh, forest air, heavily scented with pine trees. "I don't know, possibly."

Sarah came back, her paws crunching the snow. She looked up and woofed at Jessie, then turned and headed back towards the house.

"Yeah, yeah. I'm coming." Jessie took one last look at the sky.

In the distance, Jessie heard Sarah bark. Then she too headed back towards the house. When they finally got back, René was standing at the garage door, waiting for them.

"You could at least close the door." He glared at her with is arms crossed, like an angry father. "I'm not heating the whole neighborhood."

"Oh yeah, God forbid a bear should wander in here and start wasting water or using your electricity to charge his cellphone." Jessie mocked him.

"Or your houseguest steals your broken snowmobile and your dog." René uncrossed his arms, pointed an accusing finger at her, and pretended to be mad at her.

"Wasn't stealing it." Jessie playfully pushed him out of her way. "I was fixing it."

René's eyes bulged in surprise. "You got it fixed."

"Of course, what are car thief mothers good for?" Jessie picked up René's tools and put them away. "Dad had the fastest and best running police car on the force. They used to joke about the fact that mom had secretly installed NOS tanks on his police car."

René jumped onto his snowmobile and started it up. "It runs!" René jumped off the mobile and hugged Jessie for all she was worth. "Merci beaucoup, Jessie!"

"You're welcome." She smiled at him. René stopped hugging her and started looking round for supplies and then she watched him as he filled up the hard plastic saddlebags with pails and other gear. "Think of it as a belated Christmas present."

René got back on and then held his hand out to her. "Do you want to ride with me?"

"Sure." Jessie took his hand and then climbed on the back of the mobile.

"Watch the house." René told Sarah.

Sarah barked a promise at him and then he and

Jessie took off into the snowy morning. Sarah stood on her hind legs, pushed the red button, and the garage door closed behind them.

It was a beautiful winter's day. The Earth was blanketed in fresh snow, gleaming, pristine, and untouched. The light scent of the pine trees wafted through the air and the sparkling water tickled the air with its rushing trickled. The lightly falling snow only added to the magically majestic landscape of mountain, sky, earth, and water.

"This is so cool!" René gushed happily and the snowmobile glided over the glistening snow. "Do you know how long this mobile has been broken?"

"A long time?" Jessie teased and she wrapped her arms tighter around René.

But she wasn't really paying attention to him. She was too enthralled by the bunny rabbits and the deer that were foraging for breakfast. By birds tending their nests. By the eagles and hawks flying high above them. Soon she realized that they were quite some ways from the house and that they were going uphill.

"Where are we going?" Jessie asked him.

"Some place that I have not been to for a long time."

"And where is that?" Jessie jested. "Civilization?"

"You will see." He laughed.

René took Jessie to a high mountain bluff. The snowy open ground was soon halted by a thick dense forest. René got off the snowmobile and opened the left saddlebag. He pulled out two pails. In the meantime, Jessie had wandered off. She was looking at the winter's landscape that lay before her. From this height, the valley lay sprawled out before her. The bright blue skies with cotton ball clouds. Some trees dotted the landscape below. The crystal-clear river ran right through it, sparkling all the way as the sun reflected off it.

"Man, what a view." Jessie sighed happily. "I've been gone too long. This is starting to look better than 5th Avenue."

Jessie was lost in contemplation. She had traded high-rises for mountains. Honking horns for bird calls. And thousands of pedestrians for not a single soul in sight. But somehow, she didn't feel sad or unhappy. She just watched as God painted the sky. A rainbow had formed, but it wasn't the arched bow that she had always seen. No, this time it was different. This time it was a ribbon of color that ran vertically from red to violet. To her eyes, it was like a door peering into another land. The reds, yellows and oranges reminded her of the volcanoes that created the islands. The greens of the lush trees and grasslands. The blues and indigoes of the oceans, seas, and the violet of the unknown depths that were yet to be explored.

"I want to go there." She heard herself say. "I want to explore that hidden untouched land. I wonder...would I find angels there?"

"What are you muttering about?" René asked, as he came to stand beside her.

"Look." Jessie pointed up towards the rainbow.

"Wow, I have never seen a rainbow like that before." René gave Jessie a playful nudge. "Did you do that?"

Jessie smiled and pushed him back. "I wish. You know, I've seen things here that I never thought that I would get to see. Or wanted to see. I was always so busy looking down and taking care of the daily grind, that I never looked up." Jessie looked up into the sky again. "I've seen the milky way, a meteor shower, and now a rainbow that I swear is a secret entrance into another world. I wonder, if a plane flew through that rainbow right now, would they be there and no longer here?"

"Well, wherever they end up, they would be entitled to a free bowl of Lucky Charms." René laughed. Jessie looked at René and she laughed too. "See, just one more reason for you to stay here with me."

"One more reason?" Jessie raised an eyebrow at him.

"I gave you the library." René counted on his fingers.

"And?" Jessie crossed her arms and waited for him to finish.

"And free room and board."

"Free? Erik's paying you five grand a week to keep me here at winter camp."

René leered at her. "Spa services."

Jessie rolled her eyes at him and gave him a playful grin. "Okay. Enough of that." Then she saw what he was holding. "What are those for?"

"Oh, here." René handed her one of the pails. "This is Maple Mountain, and we are going shopping."

"Shopping?" Jessie's eyebrows shot up.

"You liked the maple syrup, did you not?" René started walking off and Jessie followed.

"Heck yeah." Jessie smiled. "That was the best syrup that I have ever tasted."

"Well, we are here to get some more." René led Jessie over to a group of maple trees and noticed that they were overflowing. "I have not been able to get up here and..." René stopped and looked at the first tree.

"What is it?" Jessie walked over to see what the matter was.

Rene' frowned. "In my absence, it looks like the bears have been helping themselves."

"Did they leave us any?" Jessie laughed, as images of thieving bears in ski masks or bears with stocking over their heads danced through her head.

"Oh yes, there's plenty." René cleaned up his equipment from the first tree and then moved on to the others. "Making syrup is like making moonshine really. You collect it and then you boil it."

Jessie started laughing. "Forest ranger and maple syrup moonshiner."

"Come here and let me show you something." René educated Jessie about Maple trees. "These groups of trees are sugar maples, while that group of trees over there is red maple. Red maples produce a lot of sugar, but the best sugar comes from the sugar maples."

Jessie helped René clean up and fix his taps, while René explained how to collect the sap and the process of turning the sap into syrup. Out of the ten tapped trees, six of them had been raided by the bears. They spent most of the morning cleaning and fixing the equipment. However, four of the tapped trees remained untouched. These were the ones that Jessie and René gathered their maple sap from. René packed the sap into the saddlebag of his mobile and then climbed on.

"Come on Jessie, we have another stop to make."

Jessie came up to him, licking her fingers. "This stuff is sticky."

"That is because it's pure sugar." René smiled at her. "And stop licking your paws, or you're going to get a rush. Come on, Get on."

Jessie got on and they were off again. René drove over the hills and snow and this time they stopped in front of one giant tree.

"Whoa." Jessie gaped in awe and wonder. "Now that's a tree."

"Yep, That's old Mike." René looked up at the tree and began telling Jessie all about it. "Old Mike is a seven-hundred-year-old oak tree. It is one hundred and twenty feet tall and has a circumference of forty feet. The shade that it gives covers sixteen thousand square feet. Just one of its branches from tip to tip is one hundred and eighty feet."

"Looks like a Michelle to me with those knots."

René snorted at her, and he got off the snowmobile. "This tree is the oldest tree in the forest and fathered most of the other trees."

"Why is he male if 'she' mothered the forest?" Jessie asked, looking up at the great tree.

"Because they're seeds." René opened the right saddlebag and he pulled out another pail, a suit, and a pair of spikes. "Hence male. Now if they were eggs. Then yes, we could have named HER old Michelle." René continued laughing.

"Fair enough." Jessie snickered.

"But this tree was named after Old Mike who was a Canadian loyalist." René explained, and he set the gear down. "First sergeant Michael Voclain was an arrogant, but dedicated, and loyal man. Canada hated British rule, but Britain guaranteed the Canadians freedom of language and religion. The Americans would not. So, choosing the lesser of two evils, the Canadians sided with the British before, during, and after the war of 1812."

René continued as he pointed out various sights to her from across the river. "First sergeant Mike and his men disrupted American supply lines, but also defended the towns of Kingston, which was a main British Naval Base. He and his men also stopped raids, defended small villages, and sabotaged American ships. First sergeant Mike was also a trusted messenger and he often carried messages, warnings, and news to British forts up and down the Saint Lawrence River."

"So Old Mike here was a war hero?" Jessie summed up.

"Yes," René continued his tale. "First Sergeant Mike died while trying to defend a First Nation Settlement from an American attack. His men defended it well and all the native Americans escaped, but Mike and his men were slain, and the village was burned to the ground. The Iroquois brought first sergeant Mike here to the top of Lookout Mountain, because that's what it used to be called, since you can clearly see the St. Lawrence River. They buried him here so that he could always see the land that he had honorably defended with his life."

"That was a sad story." Jessie sighed. "But also, a very heroic tale. He challenged the Americans and saved an Indian village."

"If you look over across the way, you can just

barely see the old totem peeking out from the tree line."

"Yeah, I can." Jessie affirmed, as she squinted and looked over the river. "I never would have noticed otherwise."

"Well, that's enough sightseeing. Here," René handed her the pail. "How's your climbing?"

"What?" Jessie balked. "You want me to climb this tree?" Jessie looked up and saw its height.

"Yes."

"What for?" She questioned.

"Honey."

"What?" Jessie looked at René.

René laughed at her. "No, not honey dear. Honey food." He pointed to his mouth.

"Oh, you mean the Winne-the-Pooh stuff."

René smiled at her puerility.

"Sure, I'll do it." She smiled brightly. "I haven't climbed a tree in years though." René helped her put on the suit and attached the spikes to her feet. He hung the pail off her belt, and they walked over to Old Mike. "Now, don't wander off, while I am gone." Jessie commanded him. "If I fall, I will need you to take me to a doctor. A real doctor."

"If you fall from that height, forget the doctor.

You'll need a mortician." René frowned. "Listen, if you don't want to..."

"No. no. I'll be right back." She chuckled. "Just hold my beer."

René watched her with curiosity as she climbed higher and higher. When Jessie finally reached the top...

"My God, what a view." She remarked, as she looked around at the world below.

"What are you doing?" René called out to her. "Just reach inside, get the honey, and come on back down." He told her. "I hate funerals."

"Keep your flannels on." She hollered back.

Jessie reached inside the tree and pulled out a honeycomb. It was dripping with honey and bees. They didn't like her messing with their nest. But with René's suit on, she was well protected. She reached in again and pulled out another one. After placing that one too in her pail, she reached in and pulled out a third.

"That should be enough." Jessie sealed the pail and began her climb down.

René stood back as Jessie came down. Some of the bees were still mad enough to follow her down. After making sure that she was leaving, they returned to their nest.

"Doesn't the stinging hurt?" René asked, as he stood perfectly still.

"Not really. I'm surprised how well this suit protects me. It's not professional grade, but it's really good protection."

Jessie put the pail down and took the suit off. René helped to take the spikes off her feet and put them back into the trunk of the snowmobile.

"Did you have fun up there." René smiled at her.

Jessie scoffed at him, but then thought it over. "Yeah. No problem." She boasted. "If I can repel out of a helicopter, then I can climb a tree." She looked up at it again and smiled. "You'd not believe the view from up there."

"I would. I've made the climb one hundred times and it always takes my breath away. Care to drive back?" He asked her.

"Me?"

"I want to see if you have been paying attention." René climbed onto the back of the snowmobile.

"Listen up elf boy, I was top of my class in Land Nav." Jessie got on up front and started the snowmobile up. "You ready."

René chuckled, as put his arms around her. Jessie smirked to herself and thought about the position of his hands; but then she put the snowmobile in gear and revved the engine.

"Hey! Don't spill the groceries!"

"Yeah, yeah mom. I got it." Jessie grinned and headed for home.

Chapter 12

Today was actually a good day. It was a little warmer than it had been, so tonight instead of snow as usual it was a rainstorm. The wind howled as it blew through the fir trees. The rustling of the tree's branches only added to the howling noise of the storm. The thunder rumbled, as cracks of lightning occasionally lit the dark night sky. The rain fell and bounced off the roof, windows, and snow before finally resting on the ground. The sound reminded Jessie of a thousand fingers typing endlessly upon a keyboard. Jessie shivered as she watched and listened to the storm raging outside.

"Jessie." Rene' called to her.

Jessie turned and looked towards him. He was holding a bottle of Spiced Rum and two glasses.

"Care to join me?" He beckoned to her.

Jessie smiled at him. She walked over to him, took her glass, and sat down upon the couch. Rene' picked up a blanket, sat next to her, and wrapped them both in it. Then he poured the drinks.

"Thanks."

"Je vous en prie." He smiled at her.

"So, what tales shall we tell tonight?" She sniffed her drink and took a sip.

"I'd like to hear more about your parents." He requested, as he sipped his drink. "So far all I know is that they died. I'd like to hear how they lived. You said one was a cop and the other was a...a car thief?"

Jessie curled up her feet and sipped her drink. She stared at the roaring fire and listened to it crackle and burn. She let her mind wonder back to her youth.

"Yep, she was a car thief." Jessie gave her a Cheshire grin. "Care to guess how they met?"Rene' looked at Jessie with astonishment. "Your mother was really a car thief?" *Never would have guess that one in a million years.*"Yep, and a good one too." Jessie said proudly. "My mother was Vina Tyler, and she actually came from a very rich family. They were historians, collectors, and art dealers. My grandparents gave my mother everything she could ever want. Clothes, cars, education, everything. But none of it made her happy. She was raised by a governess, educated by top rated private tutors, and given the finest food from the best cooks in the world. But it wasn't enough or rather it wasn't what she wanted. She wanted her parents love and attention. I mean what kid doesn't. When she started stealing, they started yelling and lecturing her. She finally had their attention. Even if it was only for five minutes, it was her five minutes. Consequently, she started stealing bigger and more expensive things. She was actually kicked out of a private school for stealing the headmaster's car and racing it. She told me that at one time, she was wanted by Interpol for car theft and illegal street racing." Jessie explained rather happily.

"What happened after that?" René sipped his drink and listened Jessie's story, as the thunder continued to roar and boom outside. "How did she end up with..."

"With me?" Jessie smiled harder. "My father Reese Peterson. Mom used to call him Reese's Pieces. He was a small-town boy from nowhere. A good boy scout from a family of civil servants. His family was full of judges, clergymen, clerks, accountants, and soldiers."

"That's very interesting." Rene' stopped drinking and looked at her. "That's something we have in common. I come from a long line of soldiers as well. Family stories say that we fought against the Americans back in the day."

"Well, all my relations on my dad's side are selfless, dutiful, and honorable."

"Wait, so you do have some relatives?" René reasoned. "Why didn't one of them...?"

"Yes and no." Jessie shrugged.

"No?"

"My mom's parents are dead. And my dad's side of the family disowned him when he married my mom, the car thief. My cousins all consider dad a traitor to his family name and me from 'bad stock.'"

"That sucks." René's eyes carried worry in them, but he just sipped his drink and continued to listen.

"I never thought about it before, but I'm the black sheep of the family. I am the family secret." Jessie laughed.

"You and your mysteries." He chuckled.

"Anyway, them shunning me never bothered me because I know my parents loved each other and that they loved me." Jessie smiled with remembrance.

"How did you parents meet anyway?" René asked with mirth. "Police line up or something?"

"Oh, did I forget to tell you about their world wind romance."

"World wind romance?" René scoffed.

"Yeah, dad chased mom all over the planet."

Jessie explained happily. "Oh, I also forgot to mention that dad went from boy scout to become a U.S. Marine to becoming a New York City cop. He first met mom when he went to stop a bank robbery."

"She robbed banks too?" Rene's eyebrows shot up.

"No, she was the getaway driver." Jessie laughed.

"Seriously?" René shook his head. "Are you sure you're not just making this up." He chuckled at her. "Because I can't see Sister Amy sitting still for this one."

Jessie playfully kicked Rene' but continued her story. "Dad chased mom throughout the city and made the fast and furious movie crew look like Sunday school bus drivers. Dad chased mom for five years."

"Five years?"

"Yeah, every time she'd steal a car. He'd chase after her."

"How did you father finally catch her?"

"EMP."

"EMP?"

"Electromagnetic Pulse." Jessie explained. "It shuts down the engine of a car, so that it cannot be driven. Unfortunately for mom, it stopped on some train tracks. She couldn't get out because the windows needed power."

"Didn't the doors work?"

"They were dented in from the chase." Jessie mimed with her hands, as she told the story. "She couldn't get them open."

"What happened next?" Rene' asked, and he poured himself another drink.

"Dad ran to her rescue. He smashed the windows and pulled her out. She still had the scar years later and would always show it to me when she told me the story."

"Every good scar has a story." René teased and lifted his glass in a toast.

"Yeah, come to think of it." Jessie lifted her shirt a bit and showed René her scar from her car accident. "I've got the same kind of scar." Jessie loving ran her fingers across it. "Guess I ended up like my mother after all." Jessie smiled at the thought of that.

"Did your mother ever change?" René asked, as he refilled her glass."She kind of had to." Jessie laughed. "Can't have your wife running around stealing cars, while you're locking everyone else up for it.""So, what happened. How did he get her to settle down?""Well," Jessie gave her a wicked grin.

"It was marriage or jail. Thus, my mother plead her belly and got off. Twice, if my father was telling the truth." Jessie laughed.René snorted and almost shot Rum out of his mouth. "Jessie."Without warning, the lightning crashed, and the thunder gave a great roar. It was so loud and so strong that it shook the house. The lightning crashed again, and a brilliant white light filled the room. Jessie jumped in startled fear closer to René. He put his arms around her and pulled her closer to him. When they could see again, the house was engulfed in darkness. The lights had gone out and the only light in the room was coming from the fireplace. The cabin filled with shadows as the fire's light flickered and danced."Are you OK?" René asked, holding her close to him."Yes," she shuddered. "But that strike was so close to the house.""Don't worry, this house is well built and sits on solid rock. My great grandfather built this house from scratch. Over the years, during the long winters, I've added a few things to it here and there." Rene' kissed Jessie forehead."Did he design it? Was he an architect?" Jessies inquired.

"No, he was a soldier and a builder." René now took his turn to a story. "This is the story of my family. Due to the Napoleonic Wars, Napoleon ordered all ports under his control closed in 1806. The wheat merchants could not trade their goods in Europe and so came to America. And things improved, but only for a little while, because now the British were stopping and searching American ships. They would take men, who they said were British Deserters, and the cargo that they needed or just plain wanted.

The Voclains were wheat merchants, and their ship was finally sunk, when British Admiral Smith sank Emmett's ship for non-compliance of his majesty wishes. Fed up with the war, the Voclains moved to Ontario Canada, but peace was not here either. The Americans were now fighting the British over shipping and land grabbing disputes. As most Canadians, the Voclains were now caught in the middle. They tried to eke out a living by growing and selling wheat. They traded with the British, the Native Americans, and the Americans. But the war brought an end to that as well. American forces killed the Voclains as British sympathizers and burned their homestead to the ground to keep it from supplying British and Indian forces. Only the little girl Neva survived and escaped to the Iroquois Nation. They hid her and cared for her, and when she grew up, she married an Iroquois and they had children."

"So, your people have always been here." Jessie smiled. "That' so cool. To have a home, a land, a people, to know where you come from."

"You don't."

"Not anymore." Jessie sighed. "After I left the orphanage, I joined the Army and traveled from place to place. I'm a writer now and still traveling is in my blood."

René chuckled. "So, you're a Roaming Rogue after all."

Jessie laughed. "Shut up." She sipped her drink and changed the subject. "So how did you parents meet?"

"Well, it's not as exciting as bank robbing." René chuckled. "My mother was a chef, and my father was an army cook. They met at an advanced cooking class given on the weekends. Their "competition" for bragging rights as to who was the best cook led to some interesting interactions between them. As dad tells the story, mom got him drunk on Cherri and Wine, and they ended up in a hotel room together. Mom and dad got married when they found out that she was pregnant."

"No wonder you turned out to be such a good

cook." Jessie laughed. "So how the hell did you get into forest rangerery? Come to think of it, if you're from a family of soldiers and chefs, why are you and your brothers not chefs who own their own restaurants or something?"

"Because one year, mom and dad sent us to career camp."

"Career camp?"

"A camp where you get to try out different careers and see which one you like."

"Too bad we don't have something like that in America." Jessie snuggled closer to him. "That sounds like fun."

"Needless to say, Jules is now a cop and Noel is a firefighter."

"And you are a forest ranger." Jessie sat up straight and looked at René. "Do you realize that you and your brothers all chose careers that help and rescue other people?"

"We did, didn't we?" René gave a small grin and wrapped an arm around her. "Must be in our blood to serve and help others."

Jessie snuggled closer to René. "Thank you for saving my life."

"You are most welcome...Robin." René smirked.

Jessie ribbed him...hard. Rene' just chuckled

some more, refilled their drinks, and enjoyed the warmth of a good fire and great company.

The storm continued to rage all night, but neither of them noticed or cared. They just sat in darkness and watched the fire flicker and dance in fireplace. Rene' was lost in thought when he heard the soft snoring of Jessie. She was sound asleep and still holding her glass. Rene' took the glass from her hand and set it on the table. He put his glass down too, then he gently moved to stand up. He picked her up and bridal carried her up the stairs.

"Do not worry or fear mon petit ange des neiges. I will keep you safe and warm."

Chapter 13

Jessie heard voices. She came down from the loft and noticed that René and his poker buddies were having a game.

"Hey, put up or stop yuh noise." Jack laughed and took a drag from his cigar. "Mi ave a house and three kids to pay for."

Jack was a tall dark skinned, but a little pudgy, Jamaican with medium length light brown hair and hickory brown eyes. He obviously spent his early years in Jamaica because he had a thick accent.

"Notice that he didn't say wife." Tom laughed. He was drinking beer and reshuffling the cards in his hand.

Jessie smiled at seeing Tom again. She had thought that Tom would look more like Jules, but he was the total opposite. He was a smaller man of five foot ten. A lean and dapper Brit with wavy dark brown hair and caramel-colored eyes. He dressed casual in slacks and sweater vests. He talked about computers and computer games. But then even cops must have a tech department.

"You would nae have three kids," John laughed at

Jack. "If you'd quit picking up lonely women that break down on the highway."

Jessie rolled her eyes when she saw John yet again. She chuckled as she thought about him. She didn't even own a pet and yet she saw more of the vet than she did her own doctor back home.

"Hey, mi provide a valuable service to di community." Jack told them with a wolfish grin. "Mi get dem cars off di street and mi provide dem ladies wid a safe ride home. There be nuff wackos out there."

"Your services should come with a free condom." George sniggered. He dealt the next hand and took a swig of beer.

George was also Jamaican, but he was short for a male. At four foot eleven, he was considered a dwarf. His short stature and broad chest gave him the look of a baby bear. And with his cool black curly fade hair and gingerbread brown eyes. He was a cuddly teddy bear and Jessie couldn't help but stare at him. George, unlike Jack, was Jamaican in heritage only. His English was far better than Jack's. So, he must have been educated here in Canada.

A flashback reminded Jessie that René had told her that he and his buddies were having a poker game when they rescued her from her burning car. She was beginning to wonder how George had helped. That made her snicker. However, she hadn't seen them again or had a chance to thank them. René and the boys had set up their card table up in the living room a few feet from the fireplace. Jessie came and stood beside the couch as they played on.

"So, how ist your house guest?" Lukas asked. "Or did she go home?"

Lukas Schmidt was definitely the blond haired sapphire blue-eyed boy of old. He was six feet tall and had a ripped physique. He had a broad chest and shoulders, wide hips, strong arms like trees. He looked like he could snap you in half just by giving you a hug. He was a proud man, a sure of himself kind of guy, and he liked to be the boss. If you couldn't tell by his demeanor, then you could surely tell by his well-tailored clothes.

"Nah, she's still here." René reported and he asked for two cards.

"Really?" Both Lukas and George perked up.

"Yeah, the airport is still closed, and the roads are still impassable." René recounted.

"Dude, if she really wanted to leave," George took

a drink. "She would have hopped out of here on your snowmobile. I saw you riding it the other day."

"I thought you said it vas broken." Lukas addressed René.

"It was," René looked at his cards and furrowed his brow in thought. "But she fixed it."

"Shi fix it?" Jack was stunned by her abilities. "Even mi couldn't get dat damn ting to wuk again, how shi do it?"

"Her mother was a car thief and taught her all the tricks of the trade." René chuckled.

"Seriously?" Tom chortled. "Her father was a cop, and her mother was a thief?"

"Wow, that lassie is stowed o' surprises." John gave a great grin and took a drink of his beer.

Jessie listened to them talk and watched them play. Just then, John looked up from his hand and noticed Jessie watching them.

"Hello, Jessie. How dae ye feel?"

"Clothed, for a change." She chuckled, now walking closer to the group. "How are you?"

"Boys," René got up and introduced her to his friends. "This is Jessie Tyler."

"Hi." They all chimed in.

"Jessie, you know John." René introduced them in

turn. John nodded to her. "Tom and Jack, you met at Christmas."

"Hi guys. Good to see you again." Jessie smiled at them.

"This here is Lukas." René pointed at him. Lukas stood, gave her a curt nod, and looked her over. "And the other one is George." George waved his hello, as René introduced him.

"Hello guys, nice to finally meet you." Jessie said. Then she looked around the table at all of them. "I just wanted to thank you guys for saving my life last month."

"No problem." Tom smiled.

"Glad to do it." Jack beamed.

"How long do you plan on staying?" Lukas asked, with a poisonous smile. "Because maybe next time you should stay at a hotel."

"There better not be a next time." Jessie laughed at him. "I can't afford to keep crashing cars into trees just to pick up men."

"Is she wearing your shirt?" George noted, with a mischievous grin.

René looked at Jessie. "Yes. I haven't been able to take her shopping yet."

"He does nae want her bolting on him once thay reach the highway." John laughed.

"You know," George chuckled and took a drink. "Amazon delivers, and by drone no less."

"Want to play with us, lass?" John offered and he pulled out a chair for her.

"No, thanks. Guys don't like it when I take their money." Jessie joked, with a wicked grin.

"Nah, come on sit down." George prompted. He scooted his chair over and made room for her.

"Have a seat." René told her, as he sat back down.

Jessie sat down and looked around the table. "Why not, I need money for a hotel room and a plane ticket anyway." She laughed, as she looked at Lukas.

"Who's turn is it to deal?" Tom asked, taking a drink.

"What are you guys playing?" Jessie inquired. "Poker, blackjack, or gin?"

"Poker." They all said.

Lukas passed her a beer and gathered the cards to shuffle them.

"Are you guys playing straight or wild?" Jessie asked.

"Straight." George laughed and then pointed to René. "René is the only wild one here."

"Yeah, we all live in the city." Tom chuckled.

That brought a round of laughter from the whole table. René rolled his eyes.

"Ah, shut up." He scolded them.

"So, what's the buy in?" Jessie looked at the pot. It was a modest pot. *These guys obviously aren't high rollers.*

"Twenty dollars." Jack said and put his money into the pot.

"Do you even have any money?" René scoffed at her, with a raised eyebrow.

"Speaking of which, you guys didn't happen to see my wallet anywhere, did you?"

"It wasn't in the car," George replied.

"That melted piece of toast was lying in the snow." Jack relayed. "Burned to a crisp."

"Well," Jessie playfully frowned. "I have no money, no ID, and my two for one coupon from chick-fil-a has gone up in smoke. Bummer."

Tom laughed at her. "Tell you what, for one percent of your salary. I'll give you one hundred dollars to play with. That'll get you started."

Suddenly, Jessie got a wicked idea. "Two percent of my pay and we up the buy-in to fifty dollars."

Now all the guys sat up straight, their jaws dropped open, and they eyed her. René leered at her.

"YOU want to play high stakes poker?" René questioned her, skeptical of her seriousness.

"If you guys agree." Jessie offered. "If not, I'll take Tom's money and we can keep this game friendly."

"Too late for that." Lukas threw his fifty bucks onto the table and gave her a wolfish grin.

"I'm game." John added his money to the pot.

"Me too!" George chuckled.

"Your funeral." René snickered and tossed his money in too.

Jessie chuckled, reached for the cards, and shuffled them like a professional card shark.

"Tom?" Jessie asked, politely.

"I shouldn't." Tom said. "The wife will kill me if I come home and tell her that I lost the house in a card game."

Jessie laughed. "Tom, I wouldn't dare do that to you. What happens here stays here. You guys get your belongings back at the end of the night." Jessie promised. "But your money stays with me." She grinned.

Jack laughed and rolled his cigar between his lips. "Mi like dis gal."

"Mine." René told him with a smile and narrowed his eyes on him.

"Alright." Tom agreed and put his money in the pot. "I'm in too."

"Jack?" Jessie inquired, with a raised eyebrow.

"Definitely." Jack anted up, sat back, and waited for the fun to begin.

"Good." Jessie dealt every man his hand. "Five card draw, nothing wild." Having said this, she looked at René and laughed at him. "OK, who starts."

"George does." René told her. "We go alphabetical. It is faster."

They all looked at their cards.

"Alright, I bid another fifty." George stated, with his best poker face.

"Call." Jack added another fifty also.

"Raise." Jessie smiled.

"With what?" René scoffed and took a drink.

"Damn, gal." Jack laughed at her and knocked the ash from his cigar. "You'd betta pace yuhself. Wi have all night."

Jessie smirked at René. "One hundred dollars." She smiled at them all.

"You're bluffing." Tom considered.

"Who me?" Jessie grinned wickedly and raised an eyebrow at him. "I never bluff."

"Alright." John chuckled. "I'll see yer hundred and raise ye."

"You shouldn't. You're married, remember." Lukas laughed at and mocked John's accent. "I'll raise ye."

"Call." René told them and put in his hundred dollars. He looked around the table but rested his eyes on Jessie.

"Prufen." Lukas happily threw his hundred into the pot.

"I'm gonna regret this." Tom sighed heavily. "Call." And he added his hundred dollars into the pot.

"Alright George." Jessie called out to him. "How many cards do you want?"

"Three." George slid his cards across the table.

"Three for the sir." Jessie dealt him three new cards, took a drink, and then turned to Jack. "Jack?"

"Hm..." He considered his options.

"While he's thinking," George spoke up. "How are you liking Canada Jessie?"

"For what little I've seen of it. It's okay." Jessie smiled. "The people are very nice, but your weather sucks."

John and Tom laughed at her. Lukas took a drink and looked at his cards.

"I'll tek four." Jack finally looked up from his cards and passed them over.

"Four? Wow, you have high hopes." Jessie sniggered.

"He's hoping for a fourth kid." George laughed.

"Not from me he ain't. Let's see." Jessie looked at her cards and placed them down again. "The dealer takes two." She looked over at John. "What about you Johnny?"

"I'll take two as well." John reported and handed her his cards. He took his two new cards and arranged them in his deck. Jessie saw him tilt his head to the side. Maybe this new hand was better. "Sae how's work, George?"

"Work sucks." George griped. "The poachers are back."

"You have poachers here?" Jessie wondered. "I thought that was just in Africa."

"It's all over the vorld." Lukas told her seriously. "Vherever you have rich people just giving money away for exotic pleasures. You vill always have an adventurer, or down on their luck jerks trying to make a buck."

"So, what are they hunting here?" Jessie inquired, with a worried brow. "Eagles eggs?"

"Nope," René told her. "This year its sea minks."

"Sea...minks?" She raised an eyebrow at René. "And those are?"

"Canadian Minks." René enlightened her.

"I thought fur trade was illegal now." Jessie took a drink.

"It is, but now-a-days, it's exotic pets that are all the rage." George added.

"Who's turn it?" Jack asked, to get everyone's attention back onto the game at hand.

"Mine." René looked at his cards and offered up three. "I will take three."

"Three for you." Jessie handed him his cards. "Lukas?"

"Zwei." Lukas requested and held up two fingers.

"And Tom." Jessie smiled at him.

"Just one." He smiled back.

"All or nothing, huh?" Jessie joked with him. "I like you, Tom."

"Thanks." He laughed and arranged his cards. "So does my wife."

"OK, boys." Jessie finished dealing the cards and sat back. "Time to see who's got the gold. George."

"Another fifty." He offered.

Jessie rolled her eyes at him. "You know George, benchwarmers never get anywhere."

This statement set René to laughing...hard. Jessie just looked at him.

"What are you laughing about?" Jessie asked. She didn't get the joke.

This set Lukas and George to sniggering too.

"What's so funny?" Jessie asked, and she raised an eyebrow at Lukas and George.

"Nothing." All three of them answered, still sniggering.

"I'll tell you later." René promised her.

"Stop wid di baseball jokes and let's get back to da poker." Jack told them, as he puffed on his cigar.

"Okay." George tried hard to stop laughing. "I'll make it eighty."

"Raise." Jack said. "Anotha hundred." Then he looked at Jessie, suggestively. "Yuh still wa rump?"

"I call." Jessie grinned right back.

"Ditto." John said and put up another hundred dollars.

"Over to you René." Jessie challenged.

"I am in." He leered at her. "Two hundred, and you do the laundry this week."

"Too rich, I'm out." Tom said and folded with dignity. "I got kids AND a wife to feed."

Jack puffed on his cigar but raised one eyebrow at Tom's slight.

"Alright fellas." Jessie chuckled with delight. "Drop em."

"Two pair!" George announced happily. "Just pass the money this way please."

"Damn!" Jack threw his cards down. George's pair was higher than his pair.

"Nae sae fast." John leaned forward and showed his cards. "I git three o' a kind." He beamed with pride. "That means the pot is mines."

"Think so." Jessie smiled.

"What you got little American?" Lukas asked, with a snide look.

"Full house. Bucks over does." Jessie spread her cards out before them. "Read them and weep. Eights over fours. The money is mine boys."

"Verdammte René, please tell me that you've got a flush or something." Lukas begged.

"Nope, just a straight." René turned his cards over and sighed.

"I think this Yank is a ringer." George laughed.

Jessie collected all the cards, while Lukas went to get more drinks. The pot stayed where it was, and John dealt the next round.

"I've got rotten luck." George complained as he received his cards.

"Luck is a lady, and some am I." Jessie took a

swig of beer and looked over her cards for the next hand. "You'll be broke before me."

"Can wi hurry dis up." Jack complained. "Someone out there may need mi help tonight."

"Another log on the fire, René." Jessie ordered.

"You do it." René grinned, giving her a sideways glance.

"Fine." Jessie stood up and left the table. She walked over to the wood bin and put another log on the fire. She stoked it a bit and then returned to the game.

However, while she was gone. René switched hands with her and gave her all of his junk cards. The other guys just looked at him and then started shaking their heads with mirth and laughter. As Jessie sat down again, she noticed the other guys were laughing at her.

"What?" She asked. "You didn't spike my drink, did you?"

"Now vould we do that?" Lukas asked, with a wicked grin.

Jessie stared at him with narrow eyes. "You might rabbit, you might."

"We didn't." Tom said, with a hearty chuckle. "That's against the law."

"Oh, yeah, I forgot that you were a cop." She

smiled at him and took up her cards. Then she saw what they had been laughing about. Someone had switched her cards. But she was not about to let them get the better of her. So, she smiled and asked. "Who's turn is it?"

"George's." Lukas said, and then asked. "How many?"

"Two." George slid his cards over and received two more.

"Jack?" Lukas called out.

"Four." Jack kept only one card and he kissed it for luck.

"Jessie?" Lukas stared at her and waited for her answer.

"Three." She requested. She took her cards, arranged them in her hand and took a drink.

"Und now John." Lukas waited.

"Two." John sighed deeply and passed his cards over.

"René?"

René scratched his chin and then passed over three cards. "Three."

"OK, und the dealer takes two." Lukas took his two cards and set the deck down. "Alright George, start the bidding und let's get this over vith."

"One hundred dollars." George placed his C-note onto the pile.

"Call." Jack blew smoke rings, while he tapped off his ash into the ashtray.

"Last chance fellas." Jessie gave them an evil grin. "Cause I'm going all in."

The boys all stared at her. René and John both whistled at her bravado. Lukas started growling and George was lost in his imagination. Tom was the only one who seemed in control of himself tonight.

"Whoa." John stopped and considered what was at stake. Question of him was, did he really want to lose everything that he had won tonight. Eh, what the hell, it's only money. John pushed all his winnings onto the pile. "Fine. I'm all in too."

"Merde." René whistled. "I'm not sure I can cover all that."

"Then you'll owe me dinner." Jessie told him.

René huffed at her. "Fine. I will take that bet." He challenged her and pushed all his money into the pot.

"Lukas?" Jessie asked.

"You don't even have to ask." Lukas smirked at her and pushed all his winnings into the ever-growing pile of money. "I'm all in too."

"Tom?"

Everyone looked at Tom. Tom sat stoic and thought about it. Then he just put his cards down and pushed back from the table a bit.

"I'm a married man, with kids to support. I fold." That said, He crossed his arms and waited for the end to come.

Jessie smiled. "Win or Lose, Tom, I'm sending you two percent of my pay."

"But I folded." Tom called out. His back still turned.

"But you're a gentleman, who loves his wife." Jessie told him. Then she turned and addressed the others. "Alright, boys all bets are off. Time to see who gets the gold."

This time everyone laid their hands on the table at the same time. Jessie smiled brightly as she had the highest hand this round.

"You know what time it is boys." She grinned.

Laughter and much complaining ensued, but five guys stood up and placed their hands over their hearts and sang the American National Anthem. Jessie just sat arms folded and looked around the table. She was greatly enjoying the show.

"I must say, you Canadians sure know how to

treat a girl and make her feel at home." Jessie laughed.

"Kiss my ass." René sat back down and gathered the cards to put them away.

"Sore loser." Then she turned to Lukas and chuckled. "You should consider a singing career." After that, she got up and turned to leave. "Well, that was a lot of fun. Thanks guys."

"Where are you going?" René questioned her.

"Laundry duty." Jessie winked at him and headed for the mudroom.

The mudroom slash laundry room had white tiled floors, cedar cabinets with uppers and lowers for maximum storage, a laundry sink, and a cedar wood bench for sitting. The opposite wall had a rail for hanging up clothes from the dryer and hooks for coats. The cedar open shelves on the left wall were for boots and gloves and things.

She started separating clothes to wash.

Lukas and George watched her leave until she closed the laundry door behind her, then both of them hit René.

"What the hell?" René flinched from their rebuke.

"You and I need to talk." Lukas complained.

"Why can't a girl's car ever catch on fire at my place?" George joked, as he sat back down.

"Good night, René." Tom shook his hand and slapped his back. "That was a really interesting game."

"Next game is at your house," René reminded Tom, as he waved goodbye.

"Okay," Tom laughed.

René and Tom both laughed, and Tom left first. He was followed by Jack and John. Lukas stayed to finish his beer and watch TV. But Sarah growled at him when he tried to change the channel. He argued with her about it for a while and then he just ended up watching the Santa Paws. René chuckled at him, as he cleaned up and put away the poker table.

"Did George leave?" René asked Lukas. He didn't see George, but his hat was still there. He picked it up.

"Nah, he vent to say goodbye to Jessie." Lukas told him. Then Lukas looked down at Sarah. "Come on Sarah, can ve at least vatch a K-9 cop show?"

René shook his head at Lukas and then went to find George. He went to the mudroom and found George chatting up Jessie.

"What are you doing?" René asked George with an annoyed looked.

"He was trying to convince me to wash this shirt too." Jessie answered plainly, as she loaded the colored clothes into the washer.

René snickered when he noticed that George's had a black eye. He walked up to George, looked him over, and shoved his hat at him.

"Mine." He told him firmly.

"Hey," George put his hat on, smiled, and then backed up with his hands up in surrender. "It was just a friendly feel."

"Ha!" Jessie laughed, and she looked over the settings on the washer. "That was groping."

"Come on," George slowly backed up more as he beheld René's angry face. "You can't tell me that you haven't been thumping that."

"Go home, George." René told him, and he pushed the button to open the garage door.

"Can I at least get a kiss for the road?" George quipped. "It's cold outside."

Jessie turned, looked at him, and then she smiled brightly as she walked towards him.

"OK, I'll give you a kiss."

René balked, but George puckered up. That's when Jessie grabbed him by his ear and dragged him towards the garage door. She smacked his butt and forced him outside. Then she closed the garage door in his face.

"Goodnight, George." She grinned at him from the other side of the door.

"Ooh love, that was cold." George frowned sadly at her and pretended that his feelings were hurt. But then he turned and walked towards his snowmobile. He started it up and left.

René just watched him leave. Then once he was satisfied that he was gone, he turned back towards Jessie. She nodded at him and then left the mudroom to get ready for bed. René smiled at her, walked over to the washing machine, and turned it on.

He had intended to follow Jessie; however, Sarah was waiting for him at the door of the mudroom. René looked down at her. She didn't look happy. René sighed heavily.

"Oh no, what did Lukas do now?" René chuckled at his dog. Sarah just barked at him. "Fine, come on."

René and Sarah walked through the house back to the living room. René saw Lukas watching a spy movie.

"Sarah's mad at you." René quipped.

"She'll get over it." Lukas said, dismissively. "But I am mad at you."

"Me?" René chortled at him. "What did I do?"

"Vhy is she still here?" Lukas turned off the TV and faced René.

Sarah took the remote from Lukas, turned the TV on, and sat down on the remote. René chuckled and shook his head. But Lukas was angry.

"Vhy isn't she at a hotel or something?" He asked René as he pointed upstairs.

"What crawled up your ass?" René sat down in the chair opposite of Lukas.

"You're not the same." Lukas leaned forward in his seat and addressed René with a furrowed brow.

"What?" René asked, completely confused as to what Lukas was getting at.

"You und me, ve used to hang out. Go fishing, go hunting, go out drinking at Mac's."

"Mac's is closed during the winter; and we can still do all those things." René assured him. "I don't see your problem."

"That American is my problem." Lukas ranted at him. "She moved in, and she took over."

"She didn't take over." René brushed him off with a dismissive wave of his left hand. "She's just stuck here till spring."

"Then she's going home." Lukas asserted, as he pointed an accusing finger at Rene.

"Yes." Then René thought about it. "Maybe."

"I don't believe it." Lukas stood up and looked down at René. "You're in love vith her."

"Ugh, what if I am?" René asked and threw his arm over the back of the couch. "What if I want to marry her?"

"Nein!" Lukas shouted.

"Keep your voice down." René instructed him; worried that Jessie might overhear them.

"You remember vhat happened to Reginald. Ve never saw him again."

René laughed at Lukas. "He moved to America. Got a great job that he loves. And has three kids now. Leave him alone, he's happy."

"Leave him alone!" Lukas growled at René. "He's the one who left us alone."

"Are you jealous?" René asked mockingly, as he looked at Lukas.

"Hell no." Lukas recoiled. "I vas married once. She left me."

"Little wonder, you spent all your time here at my house."

"Sorry for being a friend." Lukas chided.

"She thought you were gay." René laughed at him.

Lukas raged at René. "I'm not gay! Und vomen are the worst!"

"I don't think so." René grinned wickedly.

"That's because she hasn't tried to change you yet." Lukas paced in front of René. "You give them an inch und they take a mile."

"So, you're mad at Jessie because Kari divorced you and took half your money." Judged René, as he watched Lukas' rant.

"She's a voman, so Ja. Ja, I am." Lukas looked at René.

"Go home Lukas."

"Don't make the same mistake that I did." Lukas warned.

René pushed Lukas towards the door. "Goodnight, Lukas." He pushed Lukas out of the door and slammed it in his face.

Lukas just looked at the closed door, growled at it, and then went home. René just shook his head and walked back towards the living room.

"She's not like that." René assured himself. Then he turned to Sarah. "Don't stay up too late."

"Woof." Barked Sarah.

René just chuckled to himself and walked up the stairs to bed.

Chapter 14

A week later, René's pack of friends joined him for New Year's Eve. But this New Year's was different in the fact that his brothers Jules, Noel, and their wives showed up. Needless to say, René was surprised.

"Hey guys, what are you doing here?" René questioned, as he closed the front door. "You don't usually spend New Years' with me."

"Just making sure you don't do anything stupid," Jules told him, as he helped his wife remove her coat and hung it up.

"Hello René, so good to see you again." Shelly greeted him with a kiss.

"Where's Jessie?" Anna looked around, as she shed off her coat and hung it up.

"Where else," René laughed, looking upstairs. "She's in the library."

"You sure you didn't lock her in up there?" Noel laughed and looked up towards the loft.

"No." René rolled his eyes at him.

"Did you ask her?" Jules asked his brother firmly.

René stared his brother down. "Yes."

"Well," Anna demanded, beaming brightly, and expecting a yes. "What did she say?"

"Nothing." René sighed, with a knowing grin.

"Nothing?" wondered Shelly. "She didn't say yes?"

"Yes."

"So, she said no." Noel inquired. He too was now frowning.

"No."

"Ok, she didn't say yes, and she didn't say no, correct?" Jules summed up, as he hung up his own coat.

"Precisely." René quipped, as he ushered his family inside.

"I guess that's fair." Shelly declared, with a less than satisfied sigh. "It is a big decision to leave New York and get married."

"Have you told Lukas?" Noel questioned René, with mischief in his eyes.

"She's already met Lukas." René's confident demeanor fell. "And Lukas...well."

"Well, you know, he's here tonight." Jules reminded him, as he saw Lukas drinking with Maryland. "So, you'll have to tell him." Jules looked at his brother sternly.

"I already did." René looked towards the library. "He wasn't happy about it."

"So?" Jules questioned him. "What are your intentions then?"

René laughed. "My intentions are purely honorable."

"Oh, you men and your honorable intentions." Shelly and Anna both laughed.

René's brothers laughed at him as their wives took to playfully beating him up.

"Ah, so here is vhere the fun is." A thick German accent commented happily. "Guten Tag, mein freunde." Lukas greeted them cheerfully.

"Happy New Year's Mr. Schmidt." Anna and Shelly smiled at him.

Lukas bowed to them and smiled. "Happy New Year's to you as vell, Damen." Then Lukas turned to René. "The decorations are very lovely this year, no?"

"Lukas, allow me to introduce my brothers and their wives." He gestured to his younger brother. "This is my brother Jules and his wife Shelly." Then he turned to his youngest brother. "This is my youngest brother Noel and his wife Anna."

"Hello." They all nodded to Lukas.

"Guten Tag." Lukas bowed to them. "I am very

glad to meet all of you." Then Lukas got serious, and he turned to René. "René, I am hearing rumors that your house guest ist **still** here. Another month?"

"If you will excuse us please Lukas." Shelly gracefully curtsied to him. "We will just mingle. Come along Jules."

Jules and Shelly left first, then Noel and Anna made a similar excuse. They headed towards the window seats, drank their wine, and talked. That just left René and Lukas.

"Ist it true?" Lukas asked him.

"Is what true?" Rene sighed heavily. *Why is he like this? Never mind, I know why he is like this. Why can't he just be happy for me?*

"That even after ve talked about this, that she ist still here."

"Yes." René looked at him.

"What ist her name?" Lukas gave René a cool gaze.

René could tell that Lukas was upset. He was being aloof, for the sake of public correctness.

"Now you want to know her name." René said, in between sips of wine.

Lukas rolled his eyes at René. "I know you told me, but I forgot."

"Jessica Tyler." René reminded him. "How could you forget her?" Rene' then snickered. "You lost money to her too."

Lukas scowled at Rene', but let the jibe go. The name Jessica kept ringing in his head for some reason. "Jessica Tyler, Tyler...vhere have I heard that name before?" Lukas wondered. It was bothering him. *I am sure that I've heard the name before.*

"She is a writer." René told him, as he wondered towards the kitchen. "She is..."

"The missing writer?!" Lukas exclaimed in surprise, and he followed Rene'.

"She is not missing." René retorted, turning around to face Lukas. "She is..."

"Her editor und publisher say she is." Lukas reported, and he took a swig of his beer.

"What?" René was very uncomfortable with Lukas staring at him like that.

"Vhat ist your family doing here?" Lukas asked. "They've never come before."

"They said to keep me from doing something stupid." René told him apprehensively.

"Ha, they do not trust you with the junge frau either." Lukas laughed at René, as his eyes fell on

Rene's oldest brother and his wife, while they chatted with Rene's other friends.

"I guess." René was uncomfortable now and he shifted from his left foot to his right foot.

Lukas noticed. This was serious. René was not his usual jovial self. "Can I see her?"

"Again?" René panicked.

"She is a notable author. I should be able to at least get an autograph, no?"

"Umm, I guess. Wait here and I will go and ask her."

"As you vish." Lukas walked off to go and get another drink.

René watched him leave and then went upstairs. He stopped at the library door, took a deep breath, and then knocked on the door.

"Entrez." Jessie told him.

René entered the library. There he saw Jessie hard at work on his desktop and six empty bottles of his raspberry wine on the desk beside her. He shook his head at her.

"Well, learning the language and having fun I see." He snickered at her.

He picked up three of the empty bottles and put them in the recycle bin. Then he came back and picked up the other two. Jessie grabbed the third bottle, quickly drained it continents, and then handed the empty bottle to René.

"Plus s'il vous plaît." She requested.

René put the three bottles in the bin. "Nope come down and get them yourself." Then he got serious. "My friends want to meet you."

"Who?" Jessie hit the save button. Then she leaned back, sat straight up, and looked at him.

"Come and see." René motioned for her to follow him.

Jessie got up and followed behind René. "Why? Is your mom here?"

"No, but my brothers and their wives are."

"I thought you said Christmas was for family and New Year's was for your friends."

"I did." René confirmed and he led the way to the stairs. "I was not expecting them to show up either."

"What time is the fireworks?" Jessie asked, as they descended the stairs.

"9 PM."

"Can we make it 8 pm?" Jessie asked him, as they came to the bottom step. "I'd like to finish my book this evening."

René escorted Jessie around and introduced her to his friends. All conversations stopped and all eyes were on her. They had heard the rumors and read the papers, but none of them really expected her to be real, or for her to still be here. Let alone the rumor that Rene' was interested in her for his wife. Each of them waited their turn to be introduced. Then they stepped forward and nodded to her a greeting.

"Jessie, this is Wyatt Gone." René smiled.

"Hi." Wyatt grinned and extended a hand.

Jessie shook Wyatt's hand. "Hello, it's a pleasure to meet you."

"Wyatt is a chef at the Sailing Grill Restaurant." René added, and he smiled with pride.

Wyatt was of Welsh descent and had dark caramel hair and pecan eyes. He was overweight, but otherwise in good physical shape. He wore bold colors of a red dress shirt with his sleeves rolled up, well-fitting blue pants that were perfectly creased, and elegant brown suede shoes. Jessie also noticed that his shoes and belt were a perfect match. Wyatt had a debonair look about him. Jessie smiled to herself and wondered if he was wearing yellow socks to match his tie.

"And this is Roman Towne." Rene' happily pointed out his next friend.

"Nice to meet you." Jessie smiled.

"Likewise." Roman frowned at her.

Jessie frowned and whispered to René. "Is he happy to see me, or does he always look that way?"

René chuckled at her. "He always looks that way. He's a security guard at the Bramston mall."

Roman was Polish and had dark olive skin. He was of medium build and had a classic taper dark blond hairstyle with a copstash mustache. Jessie wondered if he was a real bodyguard or just a mall cop. Roman's attire of black slacks, white dress shirt, and black sweater vest gave him the look of an angry butler.

René then introduced Jessie to Everett. "This distinguished gentleman is Everett Pearson." René beamed with pride.

"Hi." Jessie greeted him warmly and held out her hand. Jessie was surprised that Everett turned her hand over and kissed it as a true gentleman would.

"Enchanted, young lady." He smiled at her.

"Everett is a history teacher over at Albert College." Rene' added.

Everett, the British history teacher, was tall, clean shaven, and had cinnamon brown hair with a faded haircut. Jessie snickered to herself as she thought of his students being taught by James Bond. A light blue dress shirt, freshly pressed black single-pleat dress pants, a warm khaki sweater vest with shoes and belt to match. Add spectacles and he would have looked like her eighth-grade math teacher.

"And this troublemaker here is Owen Mooney." René introduced Jessie.

"What's up?" Jessie smiled and gave him a short wave.

"How's it hanging?" Owen smiled and waved back.

Owen was a bike messenger, and he too was also British. He was a short mushy fellow from a lower cast. He had coal black wavy hair and mud brown eyes. At about twenty-two, he was the youngest of the group. And if his clothes, of blue jeans, white tee shirt, and bright red hoodie were any indication, Owen was a bad boy who liked to find his fun in having a scrap.

"Not the sausage party I was expecting this to be in this secluded wooden area." Jessie giggled a whisper to René, as they left the brood of boys. "And these young ladies are..."

"Maria and Maryland here are my friends from grammar school. Maryland is a corporate CEO of Jidong de Games." René led Jessie over to where the girls were standing and enjoying the dessert tray.

"Welcome to the shire." Maryland shook Jessie's hand. "Stay awhile and listen."

Jessie laughed at her gamers' greeting. "I used to be an adventurer like you, but then I took an arrow to the knee." Jessie quipped.

"Oh god." René shook his head with mirth. "Now don't you two geeks get started. The last time she met one of my gamer friends, Maryland turned my home into a mead hall. She and Reggie sang Valhalla drinking songs all night."

"Oh fun." Jessie's eyes lit up. "Remind me to invite you to Angelo's sometime."

Maryland Tian was Chinese, had straight black hair, dark pecan brown eyes, and dressed smartly. She was a banana of a woman, slim, but not lanky. As Noel would say, she needed hips. Her Winona Midi Support was the perfect little black dress for an evening like this. But Jessie could barely stifle a laugh as she looked down at Maryland's choice of shoes. Jessie had expected to see high heels, but instead Maryland was wearing black and white Nikes. Maryland noticed Jessie's squashed giggle.

"What? They are very comfortable." Maryland chuckled.

"I think that I've found my soul sister." Jessie laughed.

Rene just shook his head at them both and then proceed to introduce Maria Ivanov.

"And Maria here is the chief medical examiner of autopsies at Kingston General Hospital."

"Wow, must be exciting work." Jessie scoffed; her cheeks puffy with a wide grin.

"Не совсем, but at least the patients do not complain." Maria smirked at her. "And they don't sue me, if I make a mistake."

Maria had a heavy Russian accent. When she spoke, she reminded Jessie of Natasha from the Rocky and Bullwinkle cartoons of her youth. Maria had light toned skin, was of medium height, and had light brown hair, green eyes, and nice cheekbones, which were highlighted when she smiled. Maria was wearing a forest green vintage style Retro 1940s flared winter dress. It has a pleasant V-neck that was elegant, but also nonrevealing. Jessie stood by René and looked around the room. He had an interesting collection of friends. Already her mind was adding them to her repertoire of characters.

Suddenly, she spotted Lukas walking up to them. He still looked so sullen.

"So, I see that this little hen is still in your coop." Lukas grinned at her like an executioner.

René put on his best smile. "Lukas, knock it off."

"I hear that congratulations are in order." Lukas told her, and he extended his hand to her.

Jessie shook his hand and noticed that Lukas was squeezing her hand. So...she just squeezed right back, all the while looking him in the eye. This was a little hard to do since he was so tall, and he was trying to use his height to intimidate her. But he was about to find out. She wasn't afraid of him at all. Jessie laughed at him and shook his hand up and down...really hard; forcing Lukas to let go of her hand first.

"Thanks. Thanks a lot. Nice to know that I am welcome here among you *He-men*."

"Crazy American," Lukas snuffed her. "René, you're slumming. You are better than this. You are a Beta."

"Excuse you?" Jessie narrowed her eyes on him.

Noel just laughed as he watched their face off. "This is going to be fun."

"She's a New Yorker." Shelly reminded them. "They do not back down from fights."

"Let's hope this fight doesn't get out of hand." Anna worried.

"Don't mind him, Jessica." Chuckled Everette. He's still mad because the U.S. Hockey team beat Germany three to one."

"Oh." Jessie smiled wickedly. "What's the matter, comrade can't take another ass whooping from a Yank?"

"Another?"

"World War II." Jessie reminded him, with a smirk.

"Vatch your mouth, fraulein. Or you'll not be as lucky in var number III." Lukas growled at her.

"Any time, little Swiss miss. I've taken down people bigger than you." Jessie taunted him.

"I seriously doubt it." Said Owen, stepping up to her. "Lukas is a three-time Karate and Grappling champion."

"And I'm a one-time Judo champion of Camp Bear Maw for girls." Jessie crowed in jest. "You can't hurt what you can't hit."

"Owen, hold my beer." Lukas handed his glass over to Owen. "Let's see vhat this little American can do."

"Whoa! Whoa! Calm down. Everybody calm down and take a breath." Wyatt interjected.

Lukas and Jessie continued to face off against each other. It was only when René overhead his friends betting on who'd win that he stepped in and broke up the fight.

"Jessie." Rene called to her, as he gently took her by the arm and intwined it with his.

"He started it." Jessie laughed.

"Jessie, didn't you want more Raspberry Wine?" René prompted and guided her towards the kitchen.

"Yeah, OK." Jessie allowed herself to be pulled away from Lukas. "I've got a book to finish anyway."

"Ja, little frau. Go and drink your fruit punch und then return to your library of books." Lukas mocked her.

Jessie pulled away from René, turned around, and then marched right back up to Lukas and stood in his face. "Keep it up, comrade and I'll be punching some lights out of a sour kruat."

In a flash, Roman stepped between Jessie and Lukas. He stood with his back to Lukas and stared Jessie down. He tried to push her back a bit, but Jessie caught his wrist and twisted it. Roman growled at her, as she made him kneel before her, but he easily broke her grip and then stood up again. Now Jessie and Roman stood off against each other. But each were about the same height and neither broke eye contact. René quickly stepped in again.

"Whoa, whoa Jessie!" René ran to stand between them. He physical put a hand to both of them and separated them. "Roman, knock it off."

"You couldn't take me on your best day, buro mauschen." Lukas taunted her, from behind Roman.

"Name your brew, Angeber." Jessie challenged him.

Lukas moved Roman aside and stared down at Jessie. "I only drink good stout German brews."

"What like Hacker, Snyder, or Kloush?" Jessie smirked at him. He was not going to get the best of her. She wasn't just some armchair writer. She had traveled the world and knew five languages.

"Ah," Lukas smiled, genuinely surprised. "You know our beers?"

"Und I like them too." Jessie mocked him. "I've been to Munich more than once."

"Hmph, tourist." Lukas belittled her. Or at least he tried to.

"Okay. Break it up." Now Jules stepped in. "Return to your corners and no more bickering. This is New Year's Party. Not World War III."

"Great idea Jules," Jessie grinned at Lukas. "Let's

take this outside and we'll settle this." Jessie cracked her knuckles for effect.

"Wow, bro." Noel laughed at his brother and put a hand around René's shoulder. "You sure know how to pick them."

"Now, now, Jessie." Anna and Shelly pulled her away from Lukas. "Jules is right. This is a party. Let's have some music and much dancing. Because I'm NOT taking anyone to the emergency room." Shelly told Jessie.

"No, no. Let's settle this international debate right here and now. Outside pea balls and we'll settle this on the ice." Jessie challenged Lukas.

"Pea balls?" laughed Noel. "Don't you mean pea brain?"

"No." Jessie smirked.

"Jessie don't." warned René. "You already own John money for your last hospital bill."

"I'll send him a check. I'm good for it." Jessie stepped around Shelly and again faced off against Lukas. "If his knickers are in a bunch because an American team beat his sorry German one. Then I, Jessie Tyler, an American hereby challenge Lukas, the crybaby German, to a match on the ice. Winner gets bragging rights, and the loser has to honor one request by the champion, within reason and without question."

"Jessie..." René again tried to reign her in.

Lukas grinned. "I vill mop the ice vith you."

"Learn to cook too and you may make a decent wife someday." Jessie taunted him.

"Ohhh." Wyatt, Everett, and Owen teased Lukas.

"Oh boy." René's shoulders dropped.

"This should be fun." smiled Noel. He was itching for some fun.

"This is stupid." Maryland commented. "Why can't you 'men' ever just settle things with a good card game."

"Because I beat him at that too." Jessie laughed. "I'm trying to give him a chance here."

Lukas just growled angrily at Jessie as he remembered that she had not only beaten him at poker but relived him of about seven hundred dollars too.

"Jessie, what are you doing?" René pulled her to the side.

"Having some fun." Jessie shrugged him off.

"He'll kill you."

Jessie looked into Rene's eyes. He was really worried for her. But she just waved him off. *Really, what is there to worry about.* "So what? It's just a stupid hockey game."

"Hey, we Canadians take hockey very seriously." René told her firmly.

"And the South Americans take their soccer seriously." Jessie quipped and raised an eyebrow at him.

"You mean football." René gave her a small smile as he corrected her.

Jessie gave him a gentle rib to the stomach. "Stop worrying and trust me. Or better yet cheer me on."

Everyone filed out of Rene's front door and out into the snow. It was a quiet evening, but it was still cold. The sun has long since set, but the silver moon was beginning to rise. The low temperatures made their cheeks red, and their breath form white puffs of smoke as they spoke. The girls stood on one side and Rene's male friends formed their own team on the other side. Jules, Noel, and their wives took up standing on Jessie's side. As they stood waiting for the challenge to begin, Owen found two strong tree limbs and a pinecone.

"OK. Here you go." Owen gave both Jessie and Lukas a limb and placed the pinecone between them. "Jules, since you're a cop, you can be the referee. Maria, you're the medic."

"You mean the undertaker." Noel laughed.

"This ought to be good." Wyatt smiled.

"Just make it quick." Maryland complained, slapping her sides to keep warm. "It's cold out here."

"Alright, this game is a three-point game. All rules apply. Especially good sportsmanship." Jules emphasized, looking to Lukas first and then to Jessie.

"Here that Dora Ratjen." Jessie taunted Lukas. "No cheating."

"Why you little..." Lukas growled at her.

"Watch it Lukas, there are girls present." Wyatt chuckled.

"Go!" Jules shouted and ran for the sidelines before he got whacked.

Lukas got the puck pinecone first and hit it to Jessie's left. Jessie had to do a quick off balance turn to try and catch up with him. Lukas laughed as he had a breakaway shot for her goal. But Jessie outran him, body checked him, and took the pinecone puck back. She was heading for his goal when Jules stopped her.

"What the hell?" she complained.

"This is hockey, Jessie. Not football. Use the stick more." Jules explained.

"Damn, I forgot. Come on Jessie, think Stickball, not soccer." She chided herself.

Lukas stepped up to her. "Ha! You know nothing of this honorable sport."

"Ha! Nothing. The old man just needed a free breather." Jessie pushed him away from her.

Lukas' shoulders shot up in anger. "I don't need a breather. Ve've only just started. Let's go."

"Shut up and face off!" Roman demanded.

This time Jessie decked Lukas and backhanded the pinecone full force. The pinecone flew towards the trees.

"Goal!" Jules and Wyatt called out.

"Owen, do you mind getting the pinecone for me." Jules requested of him.

"Lucky shot." Lukas growled at her.

Jessie smiled back. "Don't need luck. I'm an American."

"Heads up!" Owen yelled, as he tossed the pinecone at Jules.

"Way to go Jessie!" René and his sisters cheered her on.

"Come on Lukas!" Roman yelled. "Don't let her beat you. She's just a girl! The wolves' honor is on the line."

The boys cheered for Lukas. "Lukas! Lukas!" And then they began to howl like wolves.

"Shhh." René warned them. "You want to bring the real ones out."

"I can take them." Jessie laughed and flexed her arm.

"Oh yeah, right. Like you did on our fishing trip." René laughed.

"Are you two ready?" Jules asked, as he placed the puck between Jessie and Lukas.

"Ready." said Jessie and she hunkered down.

"Ready." Lukas confirmed.

"Go!" said Jules.

Again, they fought over the pinecone as their friends cheered and taunted them. This time it was Lukas who made the goal and it was Jessie that needed a breather.

"Who's huffing und puffing now, little piggy?" Taunted Lukas.

"You'll remember my name when I win." Jessie quickly tried to catch her breath. She stood up and looked at Lukas thoughtfully. "I think I'll make you blow up a life raft. You should be able to do it with all your hot air."

"And you're going to eat my..."

"Lukas, she said within reason." René reminded him firmly.

"I vas going to say schnitzel." Lukas grinned wickedly.

"Sure you were." René narrowed his eyes on him.

"I could." Jessie told him. "It's probably very small."

"Ohhh." Everette, Wyatt, and Owen laughed at Lukas.

"Frau, when I win this next point..." Lukas growled at her.

"Less talking smack and more smacking sticks!" shouted Maryland. "I'm freezing here!"

"Face off," Jules commanded them. "Go!"

Jules threw the pinecone down and Jessie and Lukas again went at it like two wild dogs over a single bone. This time Jules had to call Jessie out for boarding Lukas, and he called Lukas out for charging Jessie. Both were charged with high-sticking. The game was delayed while Maria had to treat Jessie's eye when Lukas hit Jessie for accidentally kicking him.

"Cheater!" Lukas yelled.

"Accident!" Jessie yelled back. "You were hocking me!"

"Was not!"

"If you two don't stop," Jules threatened them. "I'll end this game right now and it will be a tie."

"No!" Both Lukas and Jessie yelled at Jules.

"Alright then. No more unsportsmanlike conduct!" Jules scolded them both. "The score is now Jessie two and Lukas one."

"What the fuck?!" Lukas growled at Jules, but Jules just stared him down.

"You never hit a woman." Jules yelled at him. "One point penalty for unsportsmanlike conduct!"

Lukas growled but otherwise backed down. It was going to stay that way, but then Jessie spoke up.

"Let it stand one to one. This will be match point. It's cold out here and I've got a book to finish."

"OK." Jules relented. "Now face off!"

"Come on Jessie!" the girls cheered.

"Lukas, Lukas, Lukas!" the boys roared.

"Go!" Jules dropped the pinecone and ran for the sidelines.

"Who do you want to win?" Anna asked René.

"I've got $5 Loonies on Lukas." Said Owen.

"I think it'll be Jessie." René smiled. "She's stronger than she looks."

"She looks pretty...hefty." Everette noticed with a grin.

The game finally ended when Lukas' slap shot the pinecone straight past Jessie's head and into her goal. She could only stand and stare as it went zooming by her.

"Damn, that's some serious power shot." Jessie whistled in awe.

"Yeah!" Lukas cheered with pride. "Take that little American!"

"Lukas! Lukas! Lukas!" The boys cheered and howled in victory.

"Aww, good try Jessie." Shelly consoled her.

"Good game, comrade." Jessie smiled at Lukas and held out her hand in friendship. "I guess you Germans can vin a fair fight."

"Ha! This vas never a contest. I vas always going to vin." Lukas gripped her hand in his. "I am bigger, better, und stronger than you."

Jessie just shook her head and smiled. "But still not any smarter."

"Ok. Ok. Germany wins 2 to 1." Maryland declared. "Can we go inside and get some hot chocolate now?"

"I'm sorry that you lost." René comforted Jessie with a hug and a kiss to the forehead.

"I didn't lose." Jessie said and she hugged Rene, mostly trying to steal his warmth.

"You didn't?"

"Nah, I just let the wookie win." Jessie gave René a big grin. "By the end of this evening, I will be a member of your pack." She nodded at him in a knowing manner.

"Oh, you cunning little..."

"American." Jessie joked.

"Yes, you are." René smiled.

From inside, Lukas' voice called out to Jessie.

"Hey! Loser! Get in here. Your punishment has been decided."

"Oh boy." Jessie sighed and let Rene' go as she turned towards the cabin. "Time to face the real challenge."

"Come on, I'll make sure he keeps it light." René promised, and he escorted her back inside.

"Nope. A deal's a deal and I did say within reason."

"Come on little American!" Lukas happily crowed out.

Once back inside, she noticed that all the boys were gathered around the dining room table.

"Ok. What do you got for me?" Jessie asked, and she stepped up to the table.

"This." Lukas' grin was huge and brought out a beer bottle wrapped in a dead animal.

"What...is that?" Jessie laughed, as she looked at

it. "What did you do? Shove a beer bottle down the throat of a dead squirrel?"

"Yep." Lukas smiled with pride.

"Oh my god," Shelly exclaimed. "What **is** that?"

"That is a Brewdog Limited Edition "End of History" Beer." Everette explained. "Very few were made."

"I can see why." Scoffed Anna. "That's hideous."

"And unsanitary." Scolded Maria.

"Seriously Lukas, what are you trying to do, poison her?" complained Wyatt. "You can't make her drink that."

"Don't vorry, if she dies, then Maria can stuff her." Lukas laughed with great pride. "She'll look good on the vall."

"With a beer bottle shoved in her mouth." Noel chuckled.

"Noel!" Anna hit him.

"Just teasing." Noel continued laughing.

"Only you Germans would put beer in a dead squirrel." Jessie commented, as she looked the bottle over. "Wait, that's a REAL dead squirrel."

"Yes. Und we Germans didn't invent this. The Scotts did. I von this bottle at an axe throwing contest."

"Of course, you did." Jessie continued laughing and rolled her eyes at Lukas.

"Here's a cup." Maria handed her a red plastic party cup.

But Lukas took it from her. "No, she has to drink it from the squirrel." He grinned.

"Years old moonshine and kissing a dead squirrel all the same night." Jessie laughed. "Happy New Year's, you damn howlers." Jessie gripped the bottle, popped the top on the table...

"Hey!" objected René. "Mind the table."

Jessie tossed her head back and poured the beer down her throat.

"Chug, chug, chug." Cheered Wyatt and Owen.

Jessie shivered as she finished the brew and stuck out her tongue. "That's the worst tasting squirrel shit that I've ever drank."

The whole room laughed at her.

"You've drunk squirrel shit before?" René laughed at her.

"Shut up Frenchie." Jessie chuckled and put the beer bottle down. Then she wiped her mouth with her sleeve, and her hand on her shirt. "Eww, yuck." And she shuddered again.

"Come on, Jessie. Let's get you a Cherry Vodka

to get that taste out of your mouth." Maryland offered.

Once again, Jessie allowed herself to be shuttled off by the girls. That's when René's friends walked up to him and questioned him more about her.

"Well, well, well, our little René has found a nice teddy bear to snuggle with." Wyatt's delightful laughter filled the air like sparkling champagne. "Where on Earth did you meet her?"

"Where did she come from and how long is she staying with you?" Roman grilled him unhappily.

René was bombarded with question after question. Lukas was more or less pushed to the side. But he hovered on the rim of their conversation.

"Her name is Jessica Tyler, and she is a writer from New York." René told them.

"The missing writer?" Wyatt asked.

"Pour l'amour de Dieu, she is not missing!" René corrected them swiftly before they got the wrong idea. "Both her editor and her publishing house knows that she's here."

"Hmpf," Everett commented. "That's not the way they are telling it. All the papers say her car was found abandoned after hitting a tree, but that no body was found. She's still missing, but they are praying for her safe return."

"Yeah, notice they are not sending out any search parties." René retorted.

"Well, Lukas," Roman told him sternly, as he stabbed his olive with a toothpick and ate it. "Looks like René might be leaving our pack."

"Not if I can help it!" Lukas declared angrily. "You can't marry this girl." He told René straight out. "She's an American. She's no good for you."

"I don't know," Everett flipped through his cell phone, as he now joined Roman. "Says here that she's well accomplished."

"She's rich too." Owen added with an amused chuckle, while reading over Everett's shoulder. He was rather enjoying Lukas' discomfort.

"She's an interesting woman." Wyatt stated happily, and he looked over to stare at Jessie. "I wouldn't mind her laying low at my house."

"I know right," René beamed with pride. "And she fixed my snowmobile."

"Oh, and handy too." Owen smiled. He gave René a pat on the back. "You go boy."

"Does she cook und clean?" Lukas asked gruffly, rolling his eyes. *I cannot believe their stupidity. Taken in so easily by an American.*

"Oh hell no." René joked. "I gave her something small to do and she nearly burned down my kitchen."

"Ha! Some voman." Lukas laughed mockingly.

"What are you so proud for? Wyatt asked, giving him a haughty look. "You don't cook and clean either."

"René, are you serious about this girl?" Lukas asked him point blank.

"Yes." Rene' told him defiantly.

"You are making a big mistake." Lukas dismissed him.

Jessie watched the boys for a while. She knew that they were discussing her. But that really wasn't what was bothering her. What bothered her was...

"Hey Jessie." Maria called out to her, and then offered her an hors d'oeuvre. "What are you thinking so hard about? Are you planning your revenge?"

"Hm, no. My books. This room is filled with great characters and yet half of them are pow-wowing each other."

Maria squeezed Jessie's arm and Jessie looked at her and grinned.

"Are you testing for freshness?" Jessie snickered.

"Cause I'm not dead yet. And don't you dare stuff me with a beer bottle."

Maria chuckled. "No, I know you're fresh. Cheeky too. The way you put Lukas in check. What are you doing here anyway? Are you on the run or something?"

"No, I'm just trapped here till spring." Jessie chuckled. "Your Canadian winters are arduous."

"Is it true what the papers say?" Maryland asked her, curiously. She was snacking on René's butternut rum bread and listened with great interest.

"I don't know. I haven't seen a newspaper in months." Jessie told her.

Shelly filled her in. "They say you went missing in November when you left the conference. You didn't report home or to work by the next day. They feared the worst and called the police. But you hadn't been gone long enough yet to be considered truly missing. Your editor and publisher called all the hospitals and morgues, but there were no Jane Does either. They did offer a reward for any info leading to your whereabouts."

"And none of you took the bait?" Jessie asked, as she leaned against the breakfast counter. "Get your fifteen minutes of fame for recovering a lost author?"

Both Shelly and Anna looked at Jessie. "No way." Then they both hugged her. "You're ours now." They snickered. "Welcome to the family."

"Wait a minute." Maryland's eyes bulged. "Did René ask you to marry him?"

"Yes." Jessie confessed hesitantly, and she looked at the floor.

"Well, that explains Lukas' behavior tonight." Maryland looked over at Lukas while he talked to Rene'.

"And what did you say?" Maria asked her. Her left eyebrow raised in judgement.

"I said...I don't know." Jessie confessed. She hung her head and stared into her drink.

"Why?" Maria asked sympathetically. "He's a nice guy and he'd make a good husband."

"I'm sure he would." Jessie sighed and shrugged her shoulders. "I'm just not ready to get married. And I don't want kids."

"She's wolf material all right." Maryland laughed and took another hor d'oeuvres.

"Why not?" Shelly asked, in between sips of her Cherry Vodka Limeade.

"You're kidding right." Jessie snickered at her. "What's with this wolf talk anyway?"

"Well, when we were all much younger," Maryland explained. "The boys created a boy's only club."

"You know, like they tend to do." Shelly laughed and looked over at her husband who was standing with his brothers Rene' and Noel.

"They call themselves the Thunder Wolves." Maria added.

"The thunder wolves?" Jessie snickered. "Do they have jackets, hang out on street corners, and have dance fights?"

"Jessie, do not mind anything that Lukas says against you." Maria told her and she poured herself another drink. "He had his heart broken, when his wife left him."

"Why did she leave?" Jessie asked softly.

"You have to understand that Lukas and Rene have been friends since primary school." Maria explained. "Rene was Lukas' best man. But Kari never really got it."

"Or rather she didn't like playing second fiddle." Maryland added. "Lukas spent all his time with Rene."

"Ahh. So, I see. He's trying to protect Rene." Jessie nodded with understanding.

"In his own twisted way." Anna shrugged.

Just then Lukas walked up to her. He lorded over her and spoke harshly to her.

"René tells me that he's made you an honorary beaver."

Jessie shook her head. "Yes, he has." She faced Lukas and gave the scouts salute. "I promise to love God and help take care of the world. A Beaver has fun, works hard, and helps family and friends. And the Beavers motto is Sharing, sharing, sharing." She recited.

Lukas looked her over and studied her. "Vell, she knows our law." He judged.

"And she's earned her badges in exploring, creativity, pet care, and..." René began explaining, while he walked up to their little group.

"Pet care?" Jessie questioned Rene'.

"Sarah." René reminded her.

"Oh yeah." Jessie suddenly remembered Rene's dog. "Where is she?"

"At mom's house."

"Come on Lukas," Everette urged with a chuckle. "I think she's earned her Olympic badge tonight."

"Vell, she did handle the challenge vith the grace of a loser." Lukas smirked.

"I can't believe you made her do that." Maryland scolded him.

"Fine. She's earned her Olympic merit badge." Lukas conceded with a begrudging grin.

"Way to go Jessie!" Noel cheered. "Cheers!"

"Thanks." Jessie smiled hard. "No hard feelings Lukas."

"Not by me." He grinned at her with pride. "I von."

At that moment, the clock struck midnight.

"Hey, it's midnight!" Owen announced. "Happy New Year's everyone."

"A toast to the New Year." Lukas led his pack in the lifting of glasses.

Everyone followed suit and picked up a wine glass.

"To family, To Friends, and to René's new pup." Lukas toasted.

"Pup?" Jessie chuckled. "Is that a step up or down from beaver?"

René chuckled and clinked glasses with her. "Shush. I'll explain later."

"Happy new year's!" Everyone cheered.

Chapter 15

KNOCK-KNOCK.

The distinct sound disturbed the hushed quiet of a winter's morning. Two peaceful sleepers stirred, as their serene slumber was abruptly interrupted.

"Qu'est-ce que c'est?" René asked, as he stretched his left arm out to work out the kinks. "Is someone knocking?"

Jessie groaned her displeasure of being so rudely awakened with questions this early in the morning. But she did cock an ear and listened. *Yep. There's someone knocking at the front door.* Jessie giggled to herself and recited,

"Upon a midday dreamy, while I pondered weak and weary, while I nodded, nearly napping, suddenly came a gentle wrapping, wrapping at my chamber door. Tis the wind and nothing more." Jessie snickered, as she groaned her displeasure of being woken up.

"That's not how that poem goes." René tickled her.

Jessie smacked his hands away. "I think Poe will forgive me."

"Nevermore." Chuckled René. The knocking became quicker and louder.

"They seem insistent, could be important." René got up out of bed and put his pants on.

"Well, it is cold out there." Jessie joked and pulled the blankets closer around her.

"Come on get up. Start the fire and some coffee please." Rene requested of her, and he looked for a shirt to put on.

"Alright, alright, I'm up," Jessie groaned and then rolled over.

"No, you're not." Rene frowned disapprovingly. "You're trying to ignore me."

"Is it working?" She snickered from under the covers.

"Get up or I'll do it," He threatened her playfully.

"Yeah, yeah." Jessie blew him off.

René walked over to the bed, pulled off the covers, and smacked her backside.

Jessie yelped and bolted awake. "Did you just spank me?"

"Better than dumping ice cold water on you like mom used to do to us boys." René laughed and buttoned up his shirt. "Light the fire. Start the coffee, and I'll see who's at the front door."

Jessie started the fire and while she was in the kitchen making breakfast, René opened the front door. He was surprised by what he saw.

"Hello, are you Mr. René Voclain?" She asked.

René kept staring at the beautiful woman with her creamy skin and medium length reddish-brown hair. She wore a light blue blouse with a collar and a women's black business suit with matching vest and blazer. She gave him a warm smile, but he could tell that she meant business.

What a beautiful ginger. René finally snapped out of his gaping gaze and answered her question.

"Yes, my name is René Voclain. Can I help you?"

"Yes. My name is Grace O'Maille. I work for mister Wolfram Howell, and he has expressed interest in buying this island for an outdoor executive retreat resort."

"What?" Rene' blinked. His brains raced to process what she had just told him.

"Did you not get the letter from your superiors?" Grace asked, but then she didn't wait for his answer. With her left hand, she reached into her blazer jacket's pocket and pulled out a copy of the letter. "Here you go. I will save you the trouble of reading it now. It basically says that my boss has spoken to your boss, and I am here to take a tour of your island for its potential. Is this a good time for you?"

"I...Uhhh." Rene' stumbled as he looked for words.

"Hey René, breakfast is ready." Jessie came out of the kitchen, holding a cup of coffee for him, and stood beside René, who was still standing at the front door. "Oh, Hello." Jessie too stared at Miss O'Maille. *Little overdressed for the woods aren't you.*

"Jessie, this is Miss Grace O'Maille." René introduced the young lady.

"Again, Hello." Jessie greeted Grace.

"Miss O'Maille. This is Jessie Tyler."

"Well, Hello." Grace looked Jessie up and down, dismissed her within seconds, and returned to speaking to René.

"If this is an inopportune time, I can come back, but I am on a schedule." Grace told them seriously.

"Well, call back later and make an appointment..." Jessie joked.

"Jessie." René gave her a verbal warning.

"Fine. I'll just tumbler your coffee and wrap your breakfast up for you to go." Jessie walked away. "Do you want a lunchbox or brown paper bag?" Jessie snickered.

"Let me get my coat and I'll be right with you." René told Miss O'Maille.

Later that night, when René came home, he took off his coat and hung it up. He sat down to take off his boots and was surprised to find Jessie now standing before him with a glass of wine for him.

"Thirsty?"

René smirked at her, stood, and accepted the glass. René took a sip and then kissed her forehead. When Sarah barked at him, René then noticed that the fireplace was lit, dinner was on the table, and his house was still standing and in one piece. He smiled harder.

"You finally learned to make a fire and dinner without burning my house down." Rene' walked over to the dinner table and looked at it.

"Would it make you feel better if I told you Sarah did it?" Jessie smirked.

"No." René took another sip and sat his wine glass down on the dinner table. His face betrayed his surprise as he saw what was for dinner. "You made beef stew." He smiled.

Jessie took a seat at the table. "I told you that beef stew is good for chilly nights like this."

"Indeed."

"Speaking of which, how was your day?" Jessie poured herself a glass of wine, while René served himself some stew.

René's face fell into a frown, and he sat down to eat. "Interesting."

"Do tell." Jessie raised an eyebrow at him and wondered what had happened today to make him so...despondent.

Rene' waved her off and gave her a silly grin. "Not now, I'm trying to enjoy a good dinner."

Later, after dinner and dishes, René and Jessie sat on the couch, sharing a bottle of wine, and listening to soft Jazz on the turntable. The weather had turned even worse. The lowering temperatures now brought a sleeting rain with it. Jessie was listening to the soft jazz, but she could also still hear the sleet as it hit the strong tightly sealed windows.

"Want to tell me what happened this morning?" Jessie requested.

Rene' took a deep breath and let it out. "Well, Grace O'Maille is a Harvard Business Graduate, who has worked her way up the corporate chain and now works for the Wyoming's Wild

Corporation. She is scoping out the island for an executive resort retreat."

"Why this island?" Jessie sat up straight and looked over at Rene'. "You live here."

"This island is the best island." René smiled proudly.

"Don't you own this house?"

"Yes and no, it's rented. I'm a Forest Ranger and this is my base. If I ever left this job, I would have to give up the house."

"Didn't you say that your grandfather built this house?" Jessie asked.

"He did. He was part of the construction crew. I didn't mean to mislead you. But this place has never really been mine."

"But you said that your family lived here."

"For as long as my father was here, yes we did. But when he left for the city, the house and the land remained within the Park's dominion. I took the house back when I moved in."

"You returned home." Jessie smiled, but then she frowned, her shoulders dropped, and she sat back. "No, I Just assumed..." Jessie looked around the house. *It's not right. This is his home. His grandfather built it. He belongs here.* "Where will you go?"

"Back to my mother's. Just till I can find a new place to live."

"But you belong here. This is your home." Jessie looked at René sadly. "What's a forest ranger without a forest?"

"Unemployed." René chuckled. But then he too frowned. *I don't like seeing her sad.*

"This isn't fair." Jessie pouted and crossed her arms.

"This is life...real life." René commented sadly. "This isn't one of your fairy tales where a found cave of jewels will appear to save the day."

"Now you see why I write books." Jessie drank her wine. "Real life sucks and I can control what happens."

"And here I thought you were an escapist." Rene' ran his fingers through her hair.

"Not a very good one." Jessie scoffed and put her glass down. "I'm still here."

"Tant mieux pour moi, petit rouge."

"Why Mr. Wolf, are you trying to eat me?" Jessie gave him a sly grin.

"I just might." Rene put his glass down, pulled her closer, and kissed her passionately.

One week later, Rene was trying to teach Jessie

to play chess properly, when there was another knock upon the door.

"Do you usually get this many visitors in winter?" Jessie asked. She didn't like it that the hairs on the back of her neck were standing up.

"Only on Friday nights." René smiled. "You know that. You keep cleaning us out." He chuckled and descended the stairs to open the front door. Needless to say, he was surprised by who was at his door. "Ms. O'Maille?"

"Hello, René. I hope that I haven't caught you at a bad time." Grace smiled at him.

"Uh, no. Do come in." René stepped aside and allowed her inside. He offered to take her black mink coat, but she politely refused him.

"Don't you ever call before visiting unannounced." Jessie came downstairs and stood there with folded arms, a raised eyebrow, and a smirk.

Grace raised an eyebrow at Jessie, turned her nose up to her, and addressed René.

"My, this is a nice lodge." Grace stated, as she admired the décor. "This will make an excellent executive suite for Mr. Howell."

"Mr. Howell?" Jessie echoed. "Mr. Wolfram Howell, III."

"Yes." Grace nodded, removed her gloves, and stowed them in her coat's pocket.

"President and CEO of Wyoming's Wild." Jessie recalled. "The outdoors exploration tycoon."

"The one and the same. Mr. Howell is an outdoorsman like yourself." Grace looked seductively at René, as she appraised his physique. "After years of corporate rat racing, he is looking to retire. However, he also realizes the commercial value of this piece of land, and he has decided to make this place an executive spa and retreat resort."

"And he'd live here...in this house?" Jessie asked firmly, as she eyed Grace suspiciously.

"Yes." Grace again nodded politely.

"What about René?" Jessie pressed.

"Oh, he'd be well compensated in a little cabin of his own." Grace addressed Jessie. Then she looked at René seductively. "Big enough for two." She smiled at him and then she started to walk around and appraised the house.

Jessie snarled at Grace's back but spoke to René. "Watch out René, the Europeans are relocating the Iroquois again."

"Shush." René chuckled at Jessie.

"Something wrong?" Grace challenged Jessie with a glaring look.

"What about his job?" Jessie asked. "He **is** the protector of this forest. This **National** Forest."

"Oh, we're not firing him." Grace assured them, with a warm smile. Especially towards René. "He's much too valuable an asset to let go. He knows these woods well. We'd need him as a guide, groundskeeper, animal control, and winter rescue."

"Animal control?" Jessie narrowed her eyes on her.

"Can't have predators running around unchecked." Grace smirked at Jessie.

"You need predators to keep the herbivores in check." Jessie reminded her, as she stood off against her.

René could only watch his verbal sparring match. Grace, a tall stern business shark with piercing blue eyes. And then there was Jessie, shorter than Grace, but somehow...stronger. Her brazen brown eyes staring daggers at Grace. *It's like watching a giant praying mantis try to better a mama bear.* René snickered to himself.

"Oh, the seasonal hunting trips will keep the herbivores in check." Grace smirked. "And the breeding program will keep the cute ones available for the children's petting zoo."

"You can't do that." Jessie protested.

Please don't hit her. Please don't hit her. René wished with all his might. "Jessie, didn't you need to make a call to Erik about your book." René stepped between the two girls.

Jessie wisely took a breath and then backed down. She unclenched her fists and then looked at René.

"Ok, see you in a minute."

As Jessie left to head towards the kitchen, she overheard Grace ask...

"Is she your wife?"

"No." René said softly, as he watched Jessie walk away.

"Girlfriend?" Grace inquired, as she stepped in front of René. Thus, breaking his line of sight to Jessie.

If I knew she were going to stay, I would say yes. But she still plans to leave in March. "No." René looked at Grace. "She's a house guest for the winter."

"Oh good." Grace cheered up and smiled widely. "Now about dinner, so we can discuss this further."

"What would you like?" René offered and took a step towards his kitchen.

"Oh no, you misunderstand." Grace took out her PDA and made arrangements. "I'm talking to you for dinner."

"What about Jessie?" René asked. He looked over to see Jessie still on the phone and discussing her book with Erik. He gave a very small grin as he caught her slipping glances his way.

"She's a grown woman. She can dog sit for a few hours." Grace finished her notes and put away her PDA. "Besides, she won't go hungry. We'll bring her a doggie bag." Grace flashed him a winning smile.

"Umm, I don't know." René hesitated. "I think I should..."

"Don't you trust her?" Grace asked, and she straighten up Rene's collar.

"Of course, I do."

"Then your dog will be safe with her." Grace put her arm in René's and gently pulled him towards the front door.

"Jessie!" René called out.

"Yeah." Jessie hung up and came to see what René wanted.

"Grace and I are going out for a little while. Would you please look after Sarah for me?"

Jessie raised one eyebrow and looked at Grace. "Sure, not a problem." Then she looked at René and gave him a small wry smile. "Have a nice time."

"Don't wait up." Grace told her, with honey and venom in her voice.

"Jessie." René freed his arm from Grace, and he stood before Jessie.

"Yes." Jessie gave him her full attention.

"I...We...Have a good evening." He finally finished.

Jessie smirked at him and patted his arm. "You too." Then Jessie looked past René over to Grace and gave her a look of disdain and a sarcastic grin. "Good night, Miss O'Maille."

Jessie watched them leave. She then wondered how Grace O'Maille had gotten there. The weather has been obnoxious and had added yet another foot of snow. Jessie stood at the front door and watched with stunned awe as she and René stepped into a horse drawn Cinderella style carriage sled, complete with driver, two horses, and...

"The princess probably has a heater and wi-fi radio." Jessie snarked.

Just then, Jessie felt a presence at her side and nudge at her leg. She looked down and saw Sarah.

Jessie hugged her and gave her a reassuring head rub.

"It's okay to come out now. Cruella has left. Unfortunately, she took René with her." Jessie joked. Sarah lightly growled at Jessie. "Hey, don't growl at me. You have more claim to him than I do. Feel free to bite her at any time."

Sarah sat on her hind legs and looked at Jessie.

"Don't look at me like that."

Sarah gave up and walked off towards the kitchen. Jessie smiled.

"You're right. It's time for dinner." Jessie followed Sarah into the kitchen. "What would you like? Do you want me to make you some story chili?"

Sarah raised her ears at that.

"Eh tu, Sarah?" Jessie chuckled. "I'm not that bad. I can cook small meals. I made beef stew."

Sarah walked over to the cabinet, barked, and pointed at her dry dog food bag.

"Still don't trust me, huh?" Jessie joked, as she poured Sarah's dry food into her bowl and put the bag back in the bottom cupboard. "I swear, set the kitchen on fire once and you're scarred for life." Jessie snickered.

"Okay. Now for my dinner." Jessie commented, as she thought about what she could eat.

Sarah looked up from her bowl.

"Oh, stop it. I'm not going to cook. I'm just going to microwave leftovers. Is that okay with you?"

Sarah went back to eating.

"Who's crazy, me or the dog?" Jessie asked herself. *Well, I'm the one talking to her like she understands, so I guess it must be me.*

Chapter 16

In the following week, Jessie noticed two things. One, the weather had slightly improved. It hadn't snowed in two weeks. The grey clouds that usually hung overhead began to thin and the golden sunshine was melting some of the snow. The other thing that she noticed did not make her feel good. She was sleeping more, she was getting sick in the morning, and her breasts were getting more and more sensitive. This worried her. So, this morning she decided to do some research while René was sleeping. She looked up her symptoms online and she didn't like what she saw.

"No way." Jessie's mouth dropped open. "No, no, no. OK, think, think, think. I can't go to town, not yet. René will notice. Wait a minute, I could call John." *John the vet, you'd call a vet.* Her conscience snickered at her. "No choice." She sighed heavily and erased her browser history.

Jessie searched for René's phone and found it on the dresser, where he always left it. Then she snuck off downstairs to the garage to make a phone call.

"John?"

"Hey, lassie. How ye be doing?" John greeted her happily.

"I'm...I need your help." Jessie paced back and forth while she spoke. "Can you come over after René goes to work? I need you to do me a really really big favor."

"Sure, I can." Now John was worried. Jessie didn't sound her usual upbeat self. "But what is it?"

"Can you..." Jessie hesitated. *I really didn't want to do this. But who else can I trust?* "Can you do a pregnancy test?"

"A what?" John stammered. *Well, that was unexpected.*

"You heard me." Jessie snapped at him and pinched the bridge of her nose. "Can you do one? Yes or No?"

"Of course, I can." John shook his head chuckling. *Completely unexpected and yet...not. The way he was fawning over her at Christmas. I should have expected this sooner or later.* "I'll bring two with me. Okay?"

"Okay," Jessie hesitated again. She wanted to tell him to forget it. But, not knowing for sure would be even worse. "Thank you, John. And please...please, don't say anything to René. It just might be an upset stomach is all."

John smiled to himself. "No problem, lass. It will be our secret."

Jessie finally stopped pacing and gave a little smile. "Thank you."

Then she snuck back upstairs and put the cellphone back onto René's dresser. He was in the shower. She could hear the water running. Having put the phone back, she darted over to the library, sat down, and read a book.

Ten minutes later, René came into the library looking hot and fresh.

"Good morning." He smiled at her.

"Good morning." She gave him a side glance and a smile. "Did you sleep well?"

"Extremely." He walked over to her and kissed her forehead. "I like having someone to sleep next to."

Jessie stopped reading and looked up at him. He was so cheerful that she thought that he would start glowing any minute.

"Going to work?" She put the book down as he pulled her up to him.

"Yes." He took her in his arms and rubbed his nose against hers. "But I should be back by five."

"Alright." She kissed him and made him feel as if he would be missed.

"What would you like for dinner?" He let her go and prepared to leave.

"Um, surprise me." She smiled at him. "I like just about everything you make."

"You got it. How about tacos for a change?"

Jessie's face brightened even more. "Yes, definitely. I haven't had tacos in forever."

René laughed at her. "You haven't been here that long." He kissed her again. "See you later, ma belle reine de neige."

"Au Revoir." Jessie waved him goodbye.

Twenty minutes later, she came downstairs and searched to make sure that he was gone. Then she sat down on the couch to wait. There was no fire in the fireplace today. The outside temperature was actually warm enough not to need one. Jessie turned on the TV and nervously waited for John to arrive.

Another twenty minutes passed, but then the doorbell rang. Jessie leapt off the couch and answered the door. John greeted her with a smile.

"Hello Jessie. How are ye feeling?"

Jessie hung up John's coat. "Tired."

"Really?" John pulled out two pregnancy tests kits. "I stopped by the store and picked these up."

He handed them to her. "Go to the bathroom, pee, and while we wait for the results, I'll give ye an exam."

"OK." Jessie did as she was told and used the downstairs bathroom.

When she returned, John had his stethoscope out and was ready to examine her.

"Well, tell me lass, what has bin going on with ye?" John checked her glands and then her pulse.

"I'm tired. My breasts are tender, and they hurt. And I'm throwing up in the morning." Jessie explained, as she let John examine her. John then put the scope to her chest and listened to her breathing. "I would have thought it was just a stomachache, but René's a good cook. His food would never make me sick."

"Won't argue wit ye on that one." John laughed. Then he leaned down more and moved the stethoscope to her stomach and listened again.

"Really?" Jessie looked down at her stomach. "What are you doing?"

"Believe it or not, a good doctor can hear a wee baby's heartbeat at week three or four."

"Are ye a good doctor?" Jessie quipped.

"I'm a great doctor." John boasted proudly and he stood up. "And yes. Ye are pregnant."

Jessie's eyes widened and her jaw dropped.

"Go and get the pregnancy tests. They should be ready now." John instructed her and he put his stethoscope back into his medical bag.

Jessie got up and purposefully walked towards the bathroom. John just snickered to himself while she was gone.

"Oh my god, the lads gonna be a father." John chuckled and ran his hands through his red hair. "Wait till he hears about this."

When Jessie came back, she did not look happy. The color had drained from her face. John walked over to her and took her by the shoulders.

"What's wrong lass?"

"I'm pregnant." Jessie handed both tests back to John. "I can't be pregnant. I haven't got the time to be pregnant."

John looked at both tests and to verify the results. "Well, there's nea for it now, except for exercise and healthy eating habits." John smiled. "René will be pleased as..."

"NO!" Jessie practically yelled at John. She faced him and narrowed her eyes on him. "You said you'd keep it a secret. Swear to me that you won't tell a living soul. In fact, don't even tell dead ones."

"You're nea going to tell him?" John was now very

concerned about Jessie. "You're nea going to get rid of..."

"No!" Jessie gave him a mean look. "My dad always said that if you're man enough to do the crime, then your man enough to do the time."

John snickered at her. "What do ye think yer parents will say?"

"Nothing," Jessie said, blowing out a long breath. "They're dead."

"I'm so sorry lassie." John pulled her into a hug. "It'll be OK. René will..."

"No." Jessie pushed him away. "Swear to me that you won't say a word, especially to him." Jessie glared at him. "Or I'll rip your guts out and shove them down your throat."

"Easy, love." John stepped back and put his hands slightly up in a gesture of surrender. "Patient confidentiality..."

"Thank you." Jessie's look softened. "I just need time. Time to figure this out." Jessie walked over to the couch and sat down. She put her head in her hands.

John packed up his kit and walked towards the front door. "Was that all that ye needed lass?"

"Yes, John. Thank you."

John looked upon Jessie. She didn't seem at all

like other women when they found out that they were pregnant. Neither Shelly nor Anna or even his own wife acted this depressed when they found out that they were pregnant. Weren't women supposed to be happy about the blessed event. John just shook his head and sighed. He put on his coat, and hat, and opened the door.

"It's ye decision, Jessie. But I think ye should tell him."

"You're right." Jessie agreed, but she didn't even look up. "I should."

John nodded his approval and then closed the door. Jessie looked to her right. The door was closed, and John was gone.

"You're right. I should tell him." Jessie sighed again. "But I'm not going to." *I should have left long before now. I can't trap him in a relationship with me just because I'm pregnant. His life is here, and mine is in New York. And I'm not getting married just because I got knocked up. I screwed up really bad this time.* Then the answer hit her. *Erik! Erik will know what to do, he always does.*"

However, the more she thought of leaving René, the more it hurt her. It hurt more than it should have. She had only known him for two months and yet they had seen so much and done so much together. But whether it was now or in March, the outcome would be the same. She had to go home. Jessie wrote René a note, so that he wouldn't worry and hopefully he wouldn't come looking for her.

Jessie then walked towards the garage. She opened the door, got on René's snowmobile, and took off. She hit the red button on her way out and the garage door closed behind her.

When René got home that night, he called out for Jessie. He took his coat and hat off and hung them up.

"Jessie!" But he got no answer. "Jessie!"

Silence. Sarah ran to find Jessie and barked. But she didn't find her. So, she sniffed around. Her sniffing led her to the garage.

"Where's Jessie?" René asked her.

Sarah ran to the garage door and scratched at it.

"Not again." René chuckled and went to the door. He looked out and worry shot him in the heart. His snowmobile was gone. "No, no, no, no, no, no, no."

René closed the door and ran upstairs to look for her. She searched his room and the guest bedroom. But then again, she had nothing when she arrived, so what would she take with her. René came back downstairs and looked around. Sarah then went to the lamp and barked. René was about to open the front door, when Sarah brought him the note and drew his attention to it. René took the note from her, and he read...

"René, it is with a heavy heart that I must leave you now and return home. Whether now or in March, the results would have been the same. Thank you for saving my life. I will always be grateful. I love you and I will miss you, now and always. Jessica Tyler. P.S. Please say goodbye to Sarah for me."

As he read the note, his chest tightened, and it felt like he couldn't breathe. Dread filled him and his spirit died within him. His knees buckled, as all the strength in them failed, and slumped against the wall.

"She's gone."

Sarah barked and sniffed at the note. René got up and ran to the door. He flung it open, and a blast of cold wind greeted him. It was freezing out tonight, but he didn't care. He ran out into the snow and began to look around and in every direction. Tracks ran from his garage, deep into the woods, in the direction of the main road. He looked up at the black night sky to see a ribbon of bright stars. The Milky Way was out in all its glory and the moon was half full. Therefore, there was plenty of light with which to see.

"Jessie!" René shouted with all his might. He waited but got no reply. "Jessie!" Again, nothing. No owls, no crickets, and no wolves.

René's heart was breaking, and it hurt too much to even think straight. For the first time in his life...he had absolutely no clue what to do. René returned to his house and closed the door.

Sarah barked and nuzzled his right hand. She was worried for him. He had never acted this way before. Not even when he had lost his dad. Sarah whimpered in concern, but René just gave her a pat on the head.

He went to the kitchen and tried to make himself some coffee, but his tears kept clouding his eyes to the point where he couldn't even see what he was doing. He stopped and hung his head. His tears fell like raindrops. He felt hollow inside, like someone had not only ripped his heart out, but poured gasoline on it and set it on fire. He couldn't think. He felt nothing but emptiness. He just wanted to sleep. Sarah nudged him and whimpered at him louder to get his attention. René looked down at her. It was just him and Sarah now. Just like it had always been. But that thought made him weep even more. He knelt to Sarah and then rubbed his forehead against hers.

"She left us." René cried into her nose. "She left me."

Sarah could do nothing for René, except share his pain. So, Sarah howled. She howled long and hard, as if mourning for the dead.

"Why did she leave me?" He whispered.

Chapter 17

Twenty miles away, Jessie had finally made it to Lansdowne where she hotwired and stole Jack's four-wheel drive snow truck from the auto lot and drove all the way home. Although it took her seventeen hours, it didn't seem that long at all. She left the truck at a Jack's sister car rental office in America and walked the rest of the way home.

"Jessie!" Erik exclaimed in great surprise. "What are you doing here?" He asked, as he opened the door for her.

Jessie let out a small smile. God, it's great to see him again. Erik was a confident gentleman, well-groomed and wore nothing but well-tailored clothes. Definitely Michelangelo's David in living form.

"I live here." She chuckled meekly at him. Then she looked around the room. Something was different. It smelled different. Then she saw it. There was another woman's coat hanging up next to hers. "Or at least I did. Do I know her?"

Erik smiled. "Her name is Bianca. She's in advertising."

Jessie snickered. "What's she selling?"

"Behave." Erik playfully scolded her, and then he gave her a big hug. "I did miss you; you know."

"I missed you too." She hugged him back just as hard. "Did I miss anything while I was gone?" She asked, as Erik hung up her coat.

"Only the hottest Christmas party in recent history." Erik told her.

Jessie sat down on her couch, leaned back, relaxed, and tried to listen to his story. But...she was lost in her own thoughts. *I'm home and I'm pregnant. Now what? Should I tell him? Did I make a mistake by leaving?*

Erik noticed her demeanor and sat down on the couch with her.

"What's wrong?" Erik laid a hand on her lap and looked her over. "You look awful."

"Nothing." Jessie droned. Her body relaxed and melded with the couch. But she did notice that it was not as comfortable as René's couch. "I'm just tired."

"Yeah, I bet you are. That was a long drive." Erik felt sorry now that he didn't send a car for her. "Why didn't you tell me you were coming?"

Jessie started to tell him, but she wasn't sure what to say. So, she said nothing. She just sighed heavily and let the silence fall between them.

"Erik darling, I'm home!" A young and excited female voice announced.

"Bianca?" Jessie sat up and gave Erik a smirk.

"Be nice." Erik warned her, as he stood to greet his lady friend. "Bianca, I ..." Erik began.

"Hello." Jessie smiled and waved from the couch.

"Oh. I didn't mean to intrude." Bianca began and she looked Jessie over.

"Bianca, I want you to meet my employer, Jessica Tyler." Erik introduced Bianca to Jessie, as he brought Bianca to stand before her.

Jessie rose to greet her. "Hello, nice to meet you." Jessie extended her hand in friendship.

"Jessie, this is Bianca Wightman. Junior advertising executive of Looking Good, Inc." Erik explained.

Bianca blushed and shook the hand that was offered to her in greeting. "I'm sorry about crashing at your place, but Erik assured me that you'd be gone for the winter."

"I was wintering in Canada but had to cut my trip short due to unforeseen circumstances." Jessie explained, with her best painted-on smile. "But don't let me interrupt your vacation. I'll be quiet as a mouse."

"Don't be silly. This is your home after all. I'll just

pack a few things and stay at the hotel down the street." Bianca turned to Erik and grinned at him. "Help me pack."

"Of course." Erik agreed. Erik watched Bianca disappear into his room and then he looked at Jessie. Jessie just smiled at him like a Cheshire cat. "Stop it." Erik demanded.

"What?" Jessie shrugged, and she laughed at him. "I didn't say anything."

"You were thinking it." Erik waved an accusatory finger in her face.

"Nah, I was just thinking about returning the favor of marooning you someday." Jessie giggled. "How would you and Bianca like to go to Easter Island?"

"Erik darling." Bianca called from the bedroom.

"Erik darling?" Jessie raised an eyebrow and snickered at Erik.

Erik growled at her and then he left to help Bianca pack. Jessie just kept snickering to herself as she got up, walked over to her small kitchen table, and opened her laptop. She checked in on her virtual fish and she waved goodbye to Erik and Bianca as they left. The smile quickly fell from her face though once she was left alone with her thoughts.

Jessie sighed deeply. *I'm Pregnant...*

An hour later, Erik returned...alone.

"Is she ok?" Jessie asked, from behind her laptop.

"She's fine." Erik reported in. "She went home."

"No hotel?" Jessie quipped and gave him a wicked grin. "No late-night boom boom?"

"Jessie don't start. Or I will ask you what unforeseen consequences brought you home so early." Erik countered, as he stood before her.

"Umm..." Jessie hid behind her laptop.

Now Erik was concerned. This was not like her at all. But he let the matter drop, for now. Jessie would tell him in her own time.

"Tell, you what. You go and take a hot shower and I'll go and get you a pizza. That should make you feel better." He smiled at her, as he pulled her away from her laptop and gently pushed her towards her room.

"Can I have an apple and strawberry salad instead." She requested of him, as she made her way towards the bathroom.

Erik balked at her. "Who are you and what have you done to Jessie?" He joked.

Jessie smiled...a little. She loved it when he was excited. His eyes seemed to sparkle. "I was abducted by an alien and probed." She recollected with some sentiment. "Multiple times."

Erik raised one eyebrow at her and gave her a surprised smile. "So...you enjoyed your little vacation."

"Yeah, I did." Jessie sighed with regret. "A little too much."

Erik grinned at her. "Well, you go and take a hot shower and I'll bring back your salad and tea from Panera in two shakes of a polar bear's tail."

Jessie walked over to him and hugged him tightly. "Thank you, Erik. Thank you for everything." She kissed his cheek and then ambled towards the bathroom.

Erik just stood there for a second dazed. Whatever had happened in Canada, it had certainly changed her. That was sure. Erik shook his head, cleared his mind, stopped staring, grabbed his keys, and left to go and get her dinner.

Jessie stood in the shower and let the hot waters run over her head and body. She put her hands against the front wall to brace herself and then remembered René. He had trapped her in the shower against the wall and "intruded in her air space". Jessie relished the memory with great delight. He had lovingly bathed her and then he gave her a deep sense of pleasure as they made love in the shower. Jessie's own body betrayed her as she remembered his strong hands against her soft skin. His firm and hungry body pressed against hers. His endearing words of tenderness. Jessie's chest grew tighter and tighter. Her breathing picked up and she grew angry at herself. Jessie struggled to get that memory out of her head, and she pounded her right fist against the wall. She had hoped that the pain of it would clear her head, but it didn't. She was now lost in a maelstrom of what might have been. What's worse is she knew he was hurting too, and it was her fault.

Images of clear blue skies, sparkling rivers, and crisp white snow invaded her mind. The smell of pine and fir still plagued her nostrils, and she swore she could hear the laughter of children. Her children as they played in the woods among the ancient trees. Fishing trips and long hikes with René and Sarah filled her mind and she began to cry.

"Why did I come back here?"

Because you are an author. Her own consciousness reminded her. *You have dates and deadlines. Interviews and book signings. You had a life here too remember. Liar. I came back because I'm a coward.*

Twenty minutes later, Jessie heard René call her name. No, that was Erik's voice. Jessie finished her shower, left the bathroom, and got dressed. She came back into the living room and sat down at their little dining room table. Jessie looked at it and frowned.

Damn, this is so much smaller than René's table. Even René's chess table is bigger than this.

"Here you go Jessie." Erik handed her a salad and a bottle of Raspberry Tea. Then he looked at her. Her clothes didn't seem to fit her right anymore. "Did you lose weight?"

Jessie looked down at her clothes. They were a bit big on her now.

"René's house is manual. We chopped firewood, fished for dinner, and climbed trees for syrup and honey." She chuckled with fond remembrance.

"Well, you look good." Erik complimented her. He took his own dinner out of the bag too and sat down. He opened his pasta salad and began to eat.

"Thanks, but I don't think I'll stay this thin for long." Jessie opened her tea and took a swig.

"Well, since I didn't expect you back until March,"

Erik took a bite of his pasta salad and then continued. "There is nothing on your calendar until your TV interview. So, you can just relax and take it easy."

"Did you get the manuscripts I sent you?" Jessie took a bite of her salad and then remembered the garden she had planted, as she looked at the strawberries. Her eyes began to tear a bit as she remembered getting her hands dirty, while René taught her about the land. She blinked them away and waited for Erik's answer.

"Yeah, I got all three of them." Erik reported happily. "I didn't expect you to write four books." Erik took a drink of his tea and wiped his mouth with a napkin. Then he looked at Jessie. "I can see you writing a winter survival guide." He laughed. "That should be useful and insightful. I'm also glad that you finally finished Wolf and Me. Samantha has been chomping at the bit for you to turn it in. She must have called me like nine times. She wanted to know where you were and what you were doing. The Roaming Rouges looks interesting."

"That one's not finished yet." Jessie stopped eating and thought about what she had been doing. She gave Erik a knowing grin. She had been writing books and 'doing' René. She went back to eating her dinner, when Erik went back to giving her the details of what he had been up to.

"I sent that one in promptly so Samantha could start on it. But I must ask you. What is Lost in the Snow?"

Jessie stopped eating again and looked over at him. She swallowed and said... "My journal."

"Really?" Erik blinked at her. "You've never kept a journal before. Notes about your books and the characters, yes. But never a journal."

"Yes well, I'm a writer and so many things kept happening to me that I wrote them all down. Wait till you read about the roaming rouges."

"Oh, now this, I want to read." He smiled at her brightly. "What did you do in Canada?"

"You may not want to know." She chuckled at him. "It's not for the faint of heart." With that, she went back to eating. "Just remember the alien probings."

Erik sat up straight and cleared his throat. "Well, as your editor, I will keep an open mind and read it objectively."

"Oh yeah, see how objective you are when you get to chapter six." Jessie finished eating her salad, drained all her tea, and stood up to leave. "I'm going to bed."

"OK." Erik opened his laptop and turned it on.

"Don't stay up too late." Jessie warned him, with a small smile.

"Uh huh." Erik just lowered his eyes and began reading.

Jessie just shook her head and went to her room. She took a deep sigh and then stretched out onto her bed.

"Oh, I've missed you." She mumbled to herself. But as she lay there, she had to admit. *I'd rather be in René's bed more.*

Chapter 18

The next morning, when Jessie woke up, she expected to see René sleeping beside her, but she was alone. She looked around, a bit confused, and then she remembered. She was home now and there was no René, not anymore. That thought hurt her and her chest tightened. She touched the middle of her chest and rubbed the pain away, but then dismissed it. She had things that she needed u to do today.

Still dressed only in her bra and panties, she went to the bathroom, took care of her morning business, washed her hands, donned her favorite blue and white athletic sweats, and then walked into the kitchen. She opened the fridge and pulled out bacon, sausage, two eggs for Erik, and started making breakfast. She also put the digital coffee maker on, so that Erik could get his morning fix. She yawned and was turning the bacon over when she heard a glass break. She jumped and turned. It was Erik. He was stunned. His eyes bulged, his mouth was hanging open, and he was staring at her.

"Erik! Don't do that!" Jessie scolded him, and

then she went back to cooking breakfast. She put toast into the toaster and pushed the button down. "What's wrong with you? You scared the crap out of me."

"Me?" Erik shook his head and blinked his eyes to make sure that he was really seeing what he was looking at. "What's wrong with you?"

"What do you mean, what's wrong with me?" Jessie questioned him, confused by his behavior. "I'm fine."

"Are you?" Erik chuckled. "One, you're making breakfast. I thought that was my job. In all these fifteen years, not once have you ever made breakfast." Erik bent down to pick up the broken pieces of his mug. He put the broken pieces in the trash and reached for the broom to get the rest. "In fact, why are you up so early?"

"I haven't?" Jessie asked, trying to think back. "Really? But you like your eggs over easy, right?"

Just then, the bacon popped. Erik quickly cleaned up what was left of his mug, while Jessie continued to make them breakfast. Ten minutes later, Erik had the table set for two and breakfast ready for the both of them. He buttered his toast, as Jessie served him breakfast.

Erik looked up and smiled at her. "You must have really enjoyed your vacation in Canada?"

Jessie thought about it and then grinned. "It was educational."

"So, I see." Erik snickered. "You're up early. You learned to cook."

"Only simple dishes." Jessie picked up her glass and took a sip of her orange juice. Then she started piling bacon on her bread for a bacon sandwich. "After I accidently set his kitchen on fire, I..."

"You what?!" Erik dropped his fork.

"Don't worry. His house is still standing. His brother Noel is a firefighter." Jessie joked.

"Good grief, Jessie." Erik shook his head but continued eating his eggs.

"I said I was sorry." Jessie pouted and tried to look cute.

Erik just rolled his eyes at her. "Did you learn anything else?"

"Oh yes." Jessie reported happily like a little girl back from summer camp. "I learned to hunt and to fish. How to tap trees for sap and make syrup. How to climb trees and fight bees for fresh honey..."

"Wow," Erik mused playfully. "Jessie the woodsman. You had quite the grand adventure, didn't you?"

"Yeah, I guess I did." She smiled. *Living a real adventure, instead of just writing about them.* Just then, a police car went by, and a Jackhammer started up. Somewhere in the building, feet were running as fast as they could and was calling out for someone to hold the elevator. "Was this place always this noisy?" Jessie asked, a bit annoyed. She looked towards the window and gave it a disapproving look.

Erik was stunned by her new behavior. "You've changed." He judged and he poured himself another cup of coffee.

"Really?" Jessie finished her bacon sandwich and picked up her orange juice.

Erik nodded. "The noise never used to bother you. Or if it did, you never took the time to mention it before."

Jessie sat there listening to New York as it woke up. Her ears were accosted by the sounds of trains running by. People were talking and some yelling for others to move it, or to watch where they were going. Car horns honking at intermittent intervals and the footsteps of thousands all beating upon the city sidewalks. Buses coming and going as they picked people up and dropped people off. School buses blowing their horns for late children and mother yelling at their children to remember their lunches and homework. All this noise, so many sounds. It was sensory overload and it hurt her ears. Not to mention the sound of the wind as it blew through the streets, over and around the buildings, and across city grates.

"I think this room needs some soundproofing." Jessie judged, as she looked around. "We need to redecorate a little too. Remind me to schedule a renovation."

Erik raised his eyebrows at her, but then he picked up her phone and made a note in it. He also put a reminder in his phone, and then he began to eat his sausages.

"What's on the menu for today?" Jessie reached across the table to get more orange juice.

"Nothing. You're still on vacation until March, remember." Then Erik noticed her tattoo. "Where did you get a beaver tattoo and when?"

"Oh, this." Jessie looked at her forearm. She had forgotten about it. "René inked me." Jessie grew a big grin. "I'm an honorary beaver. It's the equivalent of an American cub scout."

Erik started chuckling and shook his head at her story. "You're a Canadian Beaver Scout? Ha-Ha-Ha."

"What?" Jessie was a little shocked that he didn't believe her.

"Um, why?" Erik asked her pointedly.

Jessie shook her head with fond remembrance and her eyes sparkled with mirth. "He did it to keep me from getting bored."

"What, you bored?" Erik laughed at her, and he scrolled thru the morning news on his phone. "With your imagination?"

"Alright, Alright. Just finish your breakfast." Jessie told him and she started to clean up. "Since I'm still on vacation, we have time to play."

"Speaking of playing," Erik smiled, and he put his phone down. "I finished reading Lost in the Snow."

Jessie stopped, turned back towards him, and stared at him. "All in one night?"

"I know." He shrugged at her. "But once I started it, I just couldn't stop reading it."

"And?" Jessie put the orange juice and the butter back into the fridge.

Erik stopped eating and wiped his mouth. "I think...it's great. I'll be your best book yet."

Jessie came back to the table, turned his chair around, and glared at him. "NO."

"Oh, come on, Jessie," Erik crossed his arms, miffed, but they didn't stay crossed for long, because he talked with his hands. "It's really good, and I must say I never thought you'd do romance novel."

"And I'm not about to." Jessie continued to clear the breakfast things away. She put the dishes in the sink and began washing them.

Erik just watched her, disbelief coloring his face. "He really made a domestic out of you, didn't he?" He shook his head and chuckled at her. "Never thought I'd see you with dishpan hands."

Jessie looked at him. "What are you talking about? You act like I don't know how to do any domestic work at all. I did survive quite well before you came along you know. I was in the Army."

"I know." Erik stood up with his empty cup and plate. He brought them to her and tossed them in the water. "It's just that as long as I've been here, I've been the one to do everything."

"You said you wanted to," Jessie informed him, as she continued washing the breakfast dishes. "So, I just let you."

"Hmm." Erik watched her for a while. Then when the silence began to get uncomfortable, he went back to work. "Shall I tell Samantha, that you're home now? She'll want to know."

"Tell her..." Jessie thought about it. She wanted

to be home and working again. That would take her mind off René, but at the same time. She didn't want to start working again. It was nice not having anything to do. She could read or sleep or travel...yeah, maybe I'll travel a bit. Anywhere, but Canada. "I'm home, but on shore leave. Let her know I'm dead until March."

"Will do." Erik reached for his laptop, opened it, and started sending emails.

Jessie finished up the dishes, wiped her hands on the drying towel, and left the kitchen. She walked over to the window and looked out of it. The city streets below were full of activity. People of every shape and size, of every class and ethnicity, all going to work or to school. People of purpose, ambition, and determination. Jessie sighed. Somehow, she wasn't one of them anymore.

Erik looked over his laptop at her. "That reminds me, have you called your friends? Dani and the others. They've been calling and leaving messages for you."

Jessie thought about her friends. Dani, Sofia, Angela, and Brit. They had been her best friends since college. She could always count on them for a good time. They were hardworking, fun loving, and dependable. But they were also superficial, a little pushy, and could be just as silly as she could. Which is why she liked them. They weren't judgmental, but they could be fastidious.

"I'll call them later." Jessie promised. "I don't think I could stand up to them right now."

Erik just shrugged and went back to work. "Alright."

Chapter 19

"What's that noise?" Erik pondered, as he prepared himself a cup of coffee. Erik followed his ears and that brought him to Jessie's door. He knocked. "Jessie? Jessie are you alright? Can I come in?" Erik's only answer was another round of vomiting. *That's doesn't sound good.* "Jessie?"

Erik entered Jessie's room and found her throwing up into her metal trash can. He rushed over to her and gently placed a hand on her back.

"Jessie, are you alright? Was it something that you ate yesterday? Do you want me to call you a doctor?"

Jessie shook her head no. When she sat up, Erik noticed her face. He shivered, stood, and brought her the tissue box.

"Here."

"Thanks." Jessie wiped her mouth and then placed a knuckle to her forehead. She was trying to knead away the headache that was forming. "Aspirin."

"Sure, ok. I'll be right back." Erik moved quickly to comply with her request. He re-entered the room, holding an aspirin bottle and a bottle of water. "Do you know what made you sick?" He held the bottle of aspirin up to her.

"I'm pregnant." Jessie said flatly.

"What?!" Erik pulled back the aspirin bottle.

"I'm pregnant. Just give me the aspirin and I'll tell you later."

"I'll be right back." Erik turned to leave the room. "Let me get you the lose dose version."

Erik returned minutes later and gave Jessie the aspirin. He watched as she took the aspirin, drank the water, and then tried to clean up her room.

"So, you're pregnant." He said, then he smirked. "I'd ask you how that happened, but I've read your book so..."

"I'm so screwed." Jessie picked up tissues and threw them in the trash, then she made her bed.

"Obviously." Erik chuckled.

"Not what I meant." Jessie growled at him. "I don't want Samantha or anyone finding out about this."

"Not an option come your second trimester." Erik informed her. "The only thing you can do now is take care of yourself and see a good doctor."

"I know a good vet." Jessie chuckled, as she thought about John.

"What?" Erik cocked an eyebrow at her.

"Nothing." Jessie waved him off. "Do you know a good doctor with tight lips?"

Erik smiled. "Do I?"

"Not what I meant." Jessie chuckled. Then she bent over in pain and held her right side. "Stop making me laugh."

"Let me call Christine. She's a friend of mine and a pediatrician. She'll sort you out." Erik pulled his cellphone from his pocket and made a phone call.

Jessie just sat on the bed and waited, making mental notes to buy a new trash can and some air freshener.

"Ok. She can come over after her shift tonight." Erik put away his phone and looked at Jessie. "Jessie, how could you be so stupid. Why wasn't he wearing protection or you on your pill?"

"I was in a car accident, and **you** marooned me. My last pill was over two months ago, because obviously I wasn't planning on getting laid in the first place!" Jessie yelled at Erik.

Erik just sighed at her and then said. "Well, since this is your first pregnancy. You're not going to like all the changes that your body is about to put you through. You've obviously hit the mood swings early. Your breasts are going to get bigger, your veins may become visible, and your breasts will also likely get sore or tender. You're also going to be getting tired more often and sleeping later. I wonder what cravings you will have. Although, for right now, we should see about getting you on the BRATT diet."

"Bratt Diet? There's a diet for pregnant women?"

"No, it's a diet to help with the nausea and vomiting. Its call BRATT because its bananas, rice, applesauce, toast, and tea. Things that you can easily swallow and digest. Maybe they will help settle your stomach."

"How in the hell do you know so much about this sort of thing?" Jessie asked him, as she sat on the bed, and looked up at him like a teacher giving a lecture.

"My friend Christine. She's a doctor, and at one time, she was my fiancé."

"Was?"

"It was our mothers' idea." Erik explained. "But we both had ideas of our own. I went into publishing, and she continued on in school to become a doctor."

"So where does Bianca fit into this picture?"

Erik gave her a knowing grin. "She's...entertainment...for now."

"Are you two going to get married?" she asked, gently rubbing her stomach to settle it.

"Who me and Bianca?"

Jessie's shoulders dropped and she rolled her eyes. "No, you and Christine."

"Don't know." Erik shrugged. "We're both very busy people."

"Well, don't let me hold you down." Jessie slowly leaned back upon her bed and rested.

"Did Rene' hold you down?" Erik smirked at her.

"Shut up, Erik!" Jessie turned, grabbed a pillow, and threw it at him.

Erik ducked the pillow and laughed at her. "Well, come on."

"Where are we going?" asked Jessie.

"Out." Erik took her by the hand and guided her up. "Get dressed and we'll take a walk. You need the fresh air..."

"Fresh air...in New York?" Jessie joked.

"Ha-Ha, very funny. Get dressed. You also need the exercise."

"Fine."

"Ok, I'll see you in a bit." Erik took out his cellphone and started making notes. "We'll go shopping and get a few things."

"I don't need baby clothes just yet." Jessie balked at Erik.

"No, but you do need the proper foods." Said Erik, making his list and checking it twice. "My mother is Italian, and my grandmother knows excellent soups."

Jessie watched Erik close the door before she turned towards her closet.

"What have I done?" She sighed heavily. "And what am I going to do?"

The day was sunny and cheerful, but a little chilly. Both Jessie and Erik donned their coats and left their apartment. The wind blew through the city streets and over grates creating low tones. The beeping of car horns and the rumbling clack of the trains filled the air. There were no tweeting birds, only cops blowing whistles as they conducted the traffic flow. There were no animals foraging for food, only the bustle of people going to work and shopping at the hundreds of street side stores. No calls of elks or moose, only the call of police cars and ambulances.

"What's the matter Jessie? Erik asked, as they walked the streets of New York. "You seem melancholy today."

"It doesn't feel right." Jessie shuffled slowly behind Erik, as she looked around the city. She saw the filthy streets and wondered when the street sweepers would come by. Giant glass bricks instead of high rises, a humongous city full of noise and people everywhere, like ants in a colony. "Everything seems so different now."

"What do you mean?" Erik looked at the same things that Jessie did, but he saw nothing different or out of place to him.

"Everything seems so noisy and congested." Jessie pointed to the construction crews, and the taxi cabs, and the New York City traffic. "Not to mention, all of these people. I feel like I'm in a cattle showcase."

"It's New York City." Erik chuckled, deftly stepping between people on the overcrowded sidewalks. "It's always been this way."

"It's small and confining." Jessie's shoulder was bumped when someone walked pass her. "It's...it's...crowded and claustrophobic."

"It's New York City." Erik put his arm around her and kissed her forehead. "Not Canada."

"That's the problem." Jessie sighed, and she watched the other pedestrians talk on their cellphones. She watched them try to hail cabs. She watched them come and go and all of them were looking down. *Just like I used to do.* "I've lived here my whole life. I'm a New Yorker to the bone. There is no better place to live than here. Everything is at your fingertips."

"But..." Erik prompted. He and Jessie stopped walking and stood in front of a street vendor selling dime novels.

"But I feel like I don't belong here anymore." Jessie sighed, and lazily fingered through the books. "I was writing in my blog yesterday and couldn't think of one damn thing to write."

"Writer's block?" Erik questioned, while browsing for a book to read.

"No, I kept daydreaming. I kept thinking about René and Sarah, about fishing the waters of the St. Lawrence, about chopping wood and climbing trees. About staring up at the stars at night. Not just one or three, but a whole sky full." Jessie raised her arm and waved it to the right to indicate the entire sky, then she dropped her arm, and looked over at Erik with a frown. "Tell me to stop it. Tell me to snap out of it. Tell me to..."

"Stop being stubborn and go home to René." Erik playfully smirked at her.

Jessie rolled her eyes at him. "You're no help at all. I forgot I was talking to a hopeless romantic."

Suddenly, there was a great squeal of feminine excitement.

"Jessie!"

Jessie and Eric both looked up and to their left. Four African American women were happily headed towards them. They were sharply dressed and to the nines in their expensive business suits and dresses. Jessie looked at her jeans and loose shirt. She not only felt different from them, but she looked different too. She thought hard about it. Then she remembered. She used to wear black slacks and dress shirts.

"Oh no," Erik let out an exhausted sigh. "It's the fun bunch."

"What is it with you and my friends?" Jessie wrinkled her nose at him.

"It's like getting swarmed by the cast of Waiting to Exhale." Erik chuckled. He picked up a book, read the spine, and then put it back down again. "They're the reason you work yourself to death."

"How?"

"Remember, these are the ones that whisk you off to parties and premieres. They're the ones that believe in play now and let someone else do the work. They're grasshoppers."

Jessie chuckled at the analogy. "They're not that bad. They all have jobs. Brit has ant-like qualities. She's meticulous."

"She's OCD." Erik laughed and handed the bookseller ten dollars for his book.

Jessie laughed. "Stop it."

"Just remember, you've changed. They haven't." Erik took his change from the vender and then looked at Jessie. "You're pregnant and they're not."

Jessie's shoulders slumped. "Oh yeah."

"Jessie!" Dani hugged her best friend tightly.

Dani was as upstanding as an oak tree. She was steadfast, sensible, and dependable. She also had silky curly brown hair, an Amazonian build, with cinnamon skin, and a pointed chin. Her business suit presented her as a trustworthy professional. The kind of person you wanted on your side in a legal battle. Jessie sort of hugged her best friend back and prayed to god that she wouldn't feel her baby bump.

"Hey Dani, how are you guys?" Jessie smiled at her friends.

"Where have you been?" Sofia looked Jessie up and down. Something about her was different, but she couldn't tell what. "You disappeared off the face of the earth."

"No, I didn't." Jessie faced her friend and reacquainted herself with Sofia's image. Had she really just forgotten her friends?

Sofia had deep set eyes the color of coffee. With a come-hither stare that made you want to stop and take a drink. Her jet-black hair was worn in the style that reminded you of a wave upon the waters. She had sun kissed skin, a tapered chin, and small cupped ears. Full and kissable lips and a smile that could melt even the coldest of hearts. Her upbeat demeanor was light, cheerful, and playful.

"I was just up north." Jessie quickly explained.

"Up North? So why didn't you call us back?" Angela asked. "We've been calling you and leaving you messages for months."

Jessie blinked and turned to face Angela. Angela was a dynamic woman with narrow brown eyes. Luxurious, curly, neck length hair the color of coffee and cream. She was dignified, but playful and simple. She had a medium but busty build and a large Nubian nose. Her wardrobe was business black as well, but way more sumptuous, with hints of blue.

Jessie suddenly remembered what happened to

her phone. "Oh yeah, my phone was destroyed in the car accident. I had to get a new one."

"Car accident?" Sofia exclaimed. "What car accident?"

"I swerved to miss hitting a deer. My car skidded off the road and I smashed into a tree."

"Holy smokes!" Dani looked her friend up and down with great concern. "Are you OK?"

"I'm fine." Jessie waved her off, and silently hoped that she wouldn't notice that she was pregnant.

"Hi Erik." Angela greeted him seductively.

Erik politely smiled back. "Hello ladies." Then Erik looked at Jessie. "I'll see you back at home."

"Deserting me again." Jessie teased.

"Sorry Captain." Erik bowed to her. "Mermaids and sirens are your department. Just remember to stuff your ears with cotton. I do." Erik laughed, as he walked away from the group of women. "Don't worry, Jessie. I'll get the groceries and meet you back at home."

"Mmm, Jessie. If I had a man like Erik at home," Angela grinned brightly. "I'd never leave it. And I sure as hell wouldn't leave him all alone for months."

Jessie chuckled at her cougar-ish friend. "A man like Erik, I can trust to be alone for months."

"So where were you, when did you get back, and why when you got your new phone didn't you call us to tell us that you were OK?" Dani asked, a little angry with her friend. "We've been worried sick about you."

"I..."

Jessie pulled her eyes away from Erik's retreating back to face her friends once again. It was great to see them again. Familiar faces that have known her since college. Her best friends that have shared all the major events of her life. Champagne at Reggie's when she signed her first book with Samantha McCarter and the Page Sage. Banners, balloons, and Bacardi after her first book signing. Pirate tattoos when she went for her first book tour in the Caribbean. And mugs of Heineken, when she did her first international book signing at the Word Witch, the Page Sage's sister company in Germany.

Brittney who was a cheerful woman with soft brown eyes, like two drops of sweet chocolate. She had luxurious dark brown hair that reminded you of a lion's mane. She was of medium height but had a lean athletic build. Dark colored skin, with wide feet, and strong hands. She wore an elegant and tasteful business dress. She was sexy, but sensible.

"Jessie! Jessie! Earth to Jessie!" Sofia shook Jessie by the arm.

Jessie snapped out of her thoughts and laughed at them. "Sorry, I was just thinking."

"Well, stop thinking and let's eat." Brit pulled out her phone and started ordering. "There now, it'll be ready by the time we get there." Brit smiled at them.

"Good idea." Angela agreed. "Because I want to hear the whole story. Where you've been, what you were doing, why you crashed, and was your doctor cute." Angela giggled, as she led the way

"Cute doctors?" Jessie thought about John, the Vet. She laughed and shook her head. *There were no cute doctors, no sexy nurses, and no hospital drama. Just a very opinionated Scottish vet.* "Does a Scottish vet count?"

Dani took Jessie's arm and walked with her while Angela and Sofia squealed with delight.

"You had Gerard Butler looking after you?" Sofia exclaimed excitedly. "Oh you, lucky girl, you. Tell me all about him."

"Nothing to tell." Jessie shrugged.

"No wonder you didn't come back." Angela added, her face aglow with glee. "I wouldn't come back either."

"Doctor, I have a fever. I'm burning up." Sofia acted out, as she feigned being sick.

"Don't worry, I've got just the thing for it." Angela laughed. "My injection will fill you up with good medicine."

"Oh my, doctor what a big needle you have." Sofia snickered.

"Eight and a half inches, all the better to cure you with my dear."

Jessie broke out laughing as did Brit and Dani. "Are you done?" Jessie chuckled, and they walked into Panera, as Brit held the door. Sofia and Angela just laughed even more.

"I hate to break it to you guys, but John was married." Jessie informed them. She walked into Panera and looked for a place to sit.

"Oh, John." Angela's eyes lit up. "That's a good strong name with broad shoulders." Angela flexed her arm's biceps in a manly way.

"Oh, stop it." Jessie rolled her eyes.

Dani stepped up to the cashier and announced their names. They picked up their meals, paid, and chose a table. As they sat down to eat...

"Did you see last night's episode?" Dani asked, and she unwrapped her chicken avocado melt sandwich.

"Yeah," Brit answered. She rooted her fork around in her green goddess cobb salad before taking a bite. "It was good, but a little predictable though."

"Episode of what?" Jessie sat there trying to remember the television shows that she used to love to watch.

"What? What do you mean what?" Sofia put down her Napa almond chicken salad sandwich and started at Jessie like she had lost her mind.

"The only show that matters." Angela sipped her plum ginger hibiscus tea.

"And that would be?" Jessie rolled her eyes and stirred her ten-vegetable soup.

"Power." Dani reminded her. Then she pulled a tomato out of her sandwich and ate it. "You used to love that show. You'd come over to my apartment and we'd watch it together because you don't own a TV."

"Why don't you own a TV?" Sofia took a bit of her sandwich and wiped her mouth with her napkin.

"Just one more thing to pack and keep track of." Jessie shrugged and took a spoonful of soup. "My laptop pro is all that I need." *Hey, this isn't half bad. I should tell René about this. You'd call him? Her conscience reminded her. Nah, he probably already knows.*

"What happened to you Jessie, you seem out of it." Brit noticed and tried to put her finger on why Jessie looked different.

"Nothing, it's just that after not watching it for a while, I've kind of gotten out of it." Jessie's senses were in heaven with this soup, and she took another spoonful.

"Ohh, binge party!" Angela announced happily. "Season four is playing now because season five is coming out. That'll catch you up."

"I'll pass." Jessie stirred her soup absentmindedly. Then she noticed that all her friends were looking at her. "What?"

"Something must be wrong with you." Brit judged. She speared a bit of boiled egg with her fork and ate it. "You're passing up a chance to binge watch Power."

Jessie shrugged. "I just don't find it so important anymore." She stirred her soup absentmindedly.

"Not important?" Sofia feigned shock. "Quick, somebody take her temperature." Sofia waved her fork towards Jessie. "She's delirious."

Jessie rolled her eyes at them. "Oh, stop it."

Jessie was hoping to eat her soup in peace for a

while. She really was hungry. Guess that came from being pregnant. But the questions didn't stop and now they were back to question number one.

"Jessie, what were you doing in Canada?" Dani asked her, seriously, as she wiped her mouth.

"I was driving back from a book signing in Syracuse, when I got into a car accident." Jessie put her fork down and sat back. She crossed her arms and answered their questions as succinctly as she could. "I was gone for a while because of the massive snowstorms that they were having."

"Oh yeah, took my dad three days to get back from his business trip. His connecting flight in Toronto was really delayed. Were you there?"

"No. I ended up snowed in on Hanowa Island in Ontario, Canada at René's house." Jessie explained with a bit of a grin.

Angela blew on her Broccoli and Cheddar soup. She was listening, but now that Jessie had mentioned a mysterious man, her curiosity went into overdrive. "Wait, who's René and is he cute?" She directed her gaze squarely on Jessie, rested her chin on her right hand, and waited for Jessie's answer.

"He's a French Canadian forest ranger, who looks

after and protects the Thousand Island Canadian National Parks." Jessie's grin increased.

"Yes, yes. But is he cute?" Angela asked again, as she eyed Jessie mischievously.

"Mmm, this honey mustard dressing is good." Sofia commented, as she ate her chicken salad sandwich. "I should google the recipe so that I can make it at home."

"Do you know how honey is made?" Excitement colored Jessie's eyes, as she leaned forward to explain.

"They just get it from bees and package it." Sofia took another bite of her chicken salad sandwich.

"Actually, honey comes from the nectar of flowers. So, what you're really eating is flower nectar. The bees bring the nectar to the hive and break it into simple sugars. The hexagon shape of their honeycombs and the constant fanning of the bees' wings causes evaporation and turns the sugar into honey." Jessie pointed to the jars of honey that decoratively lined the walls of the restaurant. "It's the nectar that gives honey its color too. If bees collect it from orange blossoms, then it will be light in color. But if they collect it from wildflowers, then it will be a darker color."

"Really?" Brit turned a bit and looked at the

lineup of honey jars. "That's interesting. I've always wondered why there were so many different colors. I just thought that each one was given a different artificial color for marketing purposes."

"René and I collected real honeycombs from a real tree and then he showed me how to cut off the wax caps that the bees make to keep the honey inside from falling out. We then had to spin the honeycomb to force the honey out of the combs." Jessie's hands were busy as she mimed out all their actions that winter.

"Guess I now know why Buzz the honeybee spins his little honey stick to drip his honey onto our cereal." Sofia giggled.

"After that, René showed me how to heat the honey and strain out the remaining wax and other impurities. Then we'd bottle it in mason jars and set them in his pantry." Jessie smiled with fond remembrance.

"Sounds like you learned a lot from this René guy." Dani eyed her friend, and she rested her chin on her folded hands.

"I did actually." Jessie blushed and she sat back. "Do you want to know how to make real maple syrup?"

"Wow Jessie, you've changed." Dani announced and she sat back also.

"Have not." Jessie's back straighten and she objected.

"Yes, you have, and I can prove it." Dani smiled at her.

"How?" Jessie poo-pooed her old friend.

"Come with us to Angelo's and we'll party till dawn like we used to do." Dani invited her and then watched for her reaction.

Jessie flinched. She remembered Angelo's. Angelo's was the hottest themed night club in town. It played on being the crossroads between gamers, comic fans, and anime cosplayers. There were discussion groups, and contests, robotic fights, and movies that played on overhead screens. Epic fantasy music filled the air, as did the food and drinks. Jessie had loved the place and hid there often. Some of the characters in her books were even based on the people she had met there. But now...now just thinking about the place made her cringe. It was crowded, noisy, and...overwhelming. Such a large melting pot of pop culture.

"Umm, I can't." Jessie lied and she went back to eating her soup.

"And why not?" Dani raised an eyebrow at her old friend.

"I have a book to finish." Jessie looked up from her soup and chuckled. "You know how Erik gets when I have work to do. He's worse than a mother hen."

"Speaking of books," Brit held up her cellphone. "Have you guys read this new book called Lost in the Snow by Layla Rahbar."

"Oh no, not another book, by the book boss." Angela snickered and sipped her blood orange lemonade. "You need a man."

Brit rolled her eyes. "And you need to read more, instead of just looking at the pictures in marriage magazines."

"Never mind, you two." Sofia took a sip of her peach tea but gave Brit her full attention. "What is the book about?"

"Lost in Snow is about a girl who crashes her car and is pulled from the burning wreck by a handsome male elf named Leslie, who lives in the forest. She's a city girl who's taught by the country boy the real meaning of living and they fall in love. However, their warring families, one a construction conglomerate and the other an organization of naturalists threaten to tear them apart and they find themselves on opposite sides of the same war. After many adventures, misunderstandings, and hardships, they…"

"They what?" Sofia asked, totally interested.

"Nothing, that's where the book ends." Brit explained, and she put her phone away.

"Seriously? It ends? Just like that?" Angela too had been hanging on to every word. "I've never heard of a book that leaves you hanging like that."

"Me neither." Sofia pulled out her phone and bought a copy of the book, so that she could read it herself. "When is the second book coming out?"

"I don't know. Neither Ms. Rahbar nor the publisher is saying anything." Brit told them and she drank some of her agave lemonade.

"They're just trying to drive up public interest." Dani reasoned and finished up her sandwich.

He sent it in anyway. After I expressly told him not to. Jessie grated her teeth in anger but kept smiling anyway. *At least he sued a pseudo, but I'm still going to kill him.* Jessie reflected.

"That sounds a lot like what happened to you." Dani suggested, and she looked straight at Jessie.

Jessie snapped out of her thoughts and made a face at Dani. "No, it isn't."

"Yes, it does." Dani said. "You wrecked your car.

You were saved by a forest ranger, and you learned a lot from him. Only question is, do you really love him?"

Jessie stared at her with her mouth open. Then she closed her mouth and shook her head. "Lost in Snow is a work of fiction. Any resemblance to actual persons living, dead, or undead, is purely coincidental." Jessie ended with a snicker.

"Too bad you didn't write it." Sofia pondered. "It would have made a great Hallmark channel movie."

"I don't-" Jessie began.

"Do romance novels. They're corny." Her friends finished and they laughed at her.

"You have to admit it." Brit stated, thinking about the premise. "Dani could be right. Those events sound pretty similar to your Canadian holiday."

"No relations." Jessie insisted. She sipped more of her tea.

"Wait a minute, says here that Layla Rahbar is an author that is with the Page Sage." Brit noted. "That's your publisher, isn't it?"

At that moment, Jessie noticed that one of the waitresses was pretending to clean the table next to them. However, Jessie noticed that no table at Panera's ever needed that much cleaning. This was one of the cleanest establishments in the city.

"Hi." Jessie waved to the waitress.

"Oh, hello." The waitress straightened up and came to their table. "Can I get you ladies anything?" She pulled out a pad and pencil and waited patiently.

"No, thanks." Jessie smiled and started to stand up. "We were just leaving."

"We should leave a tip." Sofia realized and began searching her purse for appropriate change.

"Read Lost in the Snow." Brit quipped. "It'll knock your socks off."

"Here." Dani handed Jessie a pen from her purse and a clean napkin from the table next to them.

"What's this for?" Jessie questioned; a bit confused.

"Autograph." Said Dani plainly.

"Oh ok." Jessie leaned on the table and signed the napkin. She then handed it to the waitress and gave the pen back to Dani. "Have a nice day."

The waitress looked at the napkin and her eyes bulged wide. "You're Jessica Tyler?!"

"Yes." Jessie nodded.

"And you wrote Lost in the Snow?" The waitress gawked at her with awe and appreciation.

"No." Jessie lied and shook her head no. "Layla Rahbar wrote it."

"But don't let that stop you from reading the best romance novel ever written." Brit smiled at the waitress and handed her a ten-dollar bill. "Don't worry Sofia. I've got it."

With that, all the girls left. Once outside, Sofia looked at her watch.

"I've got to get back to work. Depositions don't write themselves. Goodbye Jessie, don't be a stranger give me a call sometime and we'll do something." Sofia hopped into the first empty cab that she saw, and she was gone.

"It was really good to see you again, Jessie." Angela hugged her friend goodbye. "Call me when you're ready to marry your handsome forest ranger and I'll give you a good deal on the wedding arrangements." Angela joked.

"I'm never getting married." Jessie assured her, with an amused grin.

"Never say never." Angela laughed, waved goodbye, turned and walked away.

"She's right." Brit looked over at her friend and wiggled a disapproving finger at her. "You never know when you'll meet mister right."

"I've stopped bar hopping and the last time I was in church; half the men are married already." Jessie scoffed, shook her head, and let out a long sigh.

"And the other half were single, right?" Brit assumed.

"No, the other half were the sons of the married men and none of them were of marrying age." Jessie quipped.

"Don't give up Jess." Brit smiled at her. "He's out there."

"I'm not looking." Jessie insisted.

"Well, you should be." Brit told her. "You're not getting any younger."

"Now you sound like Samantha, my publisher." Jessie frowned.

"Stop by the house sometime and I'll make you a delicious meal." Brit offered.

"You and René would get along fine." Jessie chuckled. "Do you know how to make three sisters chill?"

"No." Brit frowned, then she smiled. "But I'll make you some Kataifi or some Loukoumades. They have honey in them." Brit winked at her and then she left.

Jessie waved goodbye to her friend and that left her standing there with Dani. Dani was standing there with folded arms and looked like a disapproving mother.

"So, are you going to tell me the truth now or

are we going to keep playing stupid?" Dani raised a suspicious eyebrow at her.

Jessie looked at Dani. She was giving her that look again.

"I don't know what you mean." Jessie insisted and she turned to walk away.

Dani grabbed her arm and pulled her back to face her. "Don't hogwash me Jessie." Dani looked her dead in her eye. "I'm a polygraph examiner. I know that you're lying."

"Am not!" Jessie protested, again playing the victim.

"Are too!" Dani charged and let go of her friend's arm.

"Am not!" Jessie giggled.

"I'll tell the teacher." Dani laughed.

Jessie just shook her head. "I never could win an argument with you."

"Come on, we'll go to my place. I'll make you some tea and you can tell me the truth. The whole truth and nothing but the truth." Dani took her friend's arm and they walked together back to Dani's townhouse.

"Can I plead the fifth?" Jessie chuckled.

"No." said Dani flatly. "But you can tell me when

and where and why you have a beaver tattoo on your arm."

"How did you know?" Jessie balked in surprise. "I thought this shirt would cover it."

"It did, but you signed that autograph, remember?"

"Bloody hell, you're sneaky."

Dani put her arm in Jessie's, and they walked back to Dani's apartment together. Jessie finally told Dani the whole truth as they shared apple cinnamon tea. But she didn't tell her that she was pregnant. She wasn't going to tell anyone that.

"You were always the giving and imaginative one." Dani chuckled and blew on her tea to cool it.

"And you were always so cynical. You never believed in anything." Jessie reminded her, with a smirk.

"Why are we friends again?" Dani laughed.

"I don't know." Jessie shrugged with mirth. "I think you cross-examined me once."

Both the women laughed and then enjoyed an afternoon of tea and a game of gin rummy.

Chapter 20

Barely a week later, Jessie fell back into her old habits. Seeing them again, Jessie really did miss spending time with her friends. She went to all the plays, night clubs, and parties like she had in the past. Only now, Erik accompanied her.

"You're coming to Angelo's?" Jessie questioned, as she watched Erik don his coat.

"Yes."

"Why? You hate Angelo's."

"To keep you from doing stupid stuff." He smirked at her.

"What stupid stuff?"

"Drinking, smoking...getting laid again without intention." He laughed at her.

"I hate you." She Pffted, shook her head, and locked their apartment door.

Angelo's was a video game themed restaurant that was hugely popular place to play. Its design was modeled after Sheffield Castle in England. But the gamers of New York made it their own. Each section of the castle was inhabited by different sorts of gamers. The North was populated by the Action gamers. The East court belonged to the Role-players. The Southern side belonged to the Sports gamers and the West side was the territory of the card and board gamers.

Angelo's was bustling with activity. Epic gaming instrumental music poured out of the speakers and saturated the atmosphere with a sense of adventure. Jessie couldn't help but smile wide as she recognized her friends and their cosplays of choice. The soldiers and space marines were drinking and telling stories of conquests. The mages, knights, and elves were ordering food from Anime cos-playing maids. The basketball and baseball fans were arguing over whose teams were better; and the football and rugby boys were debating the manliness of gear vs. no gear.

Erik followed Jessie as she meandered from room to room, district to district. Neon menus displayed the specials of the day. Everything from Z-Kaiseki to Seafood Meuniere.

"Jessie!" came a great yell of excitement.

Jessie turned around and saw a troll coming towards her. She smiled.

"Well, hello Joey Joe. Long time no see." Jessie greeted him with an outstretched arm.

Joey gripped her hand and pulled her into a big hug. "Well, if it isn't Lost Linkle, where ya been?"

Before she could answer, Joey grabbed her by the hand and dragged her into the fairy forest RPG section of the castle.

"Hey guys, look who I found!" Joey called out to his friends.

Jessie pushed him away and stuck her chest out with pride. "Oh, you know me. I'm searching and stealing, fighting, and killing, traveling around in circles." Jessie smiled at her long-time gamer acquaintances, Susan, Martha, Peter, and Jerry.

"Ha-Ha, damn girl, you had us worried." Susan lifted a grog in salute to Jessie. "We thought you were dead."

"Who said I was dead?" Jessie questioned, giving Joey a strange look.

"He did." Joey pointed to Erik.

Jessie stared at Erik and growled at him.

"I said no such thing. I said that you were marooned on a desert island and that it would be a miracle if you survived." Erik grinned, as he looked over the menu.

"Well, he didn't lie." Jessie shook her head. "I was maroon on an island in Ontario, Canada. And I survived only because a lone wood elf took me in."

"Seriously," Joey gaped at her.

"Welcome back from tartarus!" the merry group called out in cheer. They raised their glassed to her in a toast.

Joey grabbed a mug from the table and brought it to her. "Sit down and tell us all of your adventures, Linkle."

"Hey listen." Erik admonished, as he pointed a finger at her. The others at the table laughed at the known reference. "No grog."

"Seriously?" Jessie just looked at Erik. "Who died and made you boss?"

"You did...mom." Erik smirked and raised an eyebrow at her.

Jessie growled at him, and then turned and looked at her friends. "Sorry boys, no drinks, doctor's orders."

"Sit a spell and tell us all." Requested Joey.

Jessie didn't sit down, but she pulled out a chair, put her right foot on it and leaned forward. She spread out her hands to hold the attention of all. She narrowed her eyes on them and began her tale.

"It was a dark and stormy night." Jessie mimed her tale as she told it. "The wind blew in great billows. The snow fell in a tumultuous flurry and blanketed the world in snow. The thunder lit the landscape just in time for me to see a 12-point buck dash into the road. I slammed on the brakes and swerved my car. But I had no control. The ice on the road was my master now. The car hit the guard rail and flipped over." Jessie clapped her hands together for effect, and then mimed the rolling of her car with her hands.

"Whoa." Sighed Martha in awe.

"Damn." Hissed Joey. "Man, am I glad that you survived. A crash like that and you could have been killed."

"Then what happened." Asked Jerry. "How did you survive?"

"Well, when I came to. I felt as if I was being carried." Jessie looked around and pretended to be lost and confused. "I was lying over the shoulder of someone. Someone with a furry white coat."

"A white coat? In a snowstorm? After Labor Day?" chuckled Susan.

"Must have been bigfoot." Laughed Peter. "Who else would be out in a snowstorm in Canada?"

"Jessie." Erik chuckled to himself.

Jessie stood up and looked at Erik. She raised an eyebrow at him. "I heard that." She smirked.

Erik just held his right hand up in surrender and feigned innocence.

"Never mind him, what happened next?" requested a newcomer.

Jessie looked towards him and saw that more people had now come over to listen to her tale. She smiled.

"Well, you're not far wrong Peter. Because when I was finally laid down to rest, I saw two of the biggest and hairiest hands that I've ever seen. "

"No way."

"Way. When I woke up next." Jessie looked around and motioned with her right hand for them to draw nearer. "I was lying on a flat steel table and a bright light was shining down from above. It was so bright that I had to squint to see. The table was cold, and my bruises were stinging, almost to the point of itching. I tried to scratch, but that's when I noticed that I was strapped to the table. I heard voices, but I was unable to understand the language." Jessie mimed her tale as she waved her hands or held them close to her side. She looked around the table and kept her audience engaged. "All of a sudden, a man of medium height held out a hand over my body. It was then that my blood ran cold. He had only three fingers."

Erik spit out his drink and looked wide eyed at Jessie.

"What a minute." Susan scoffed and held up a hand for Jessie to stop her tale. "Are you saying that your doctor lost two of his fingers?"

Jessie blew out a bated breath and looked ominously at Susan. "I'm not sure he ever had five to begin with."

Erik could only listen and roll his eyes as Jessie made up the wildest tales of adventure that he had ever heard. Ghost ships, ghost lights, big foot, aliens, and other stories of the Canadian wilds. Jessie had Lon Milk, while her friends engaged in Nuke Cola and Witcher Moonshine. Erik ordered Nebula Salmon Teriyaki for Jessie and himself.

Without warning, a fight burst into the room and brought Jessie's story to an end. It seemed that the Night elves were battling the Space Marines again. Jessie's eyes lit up and she jumped up from her seat. Suddenly, she felt a strong hand on her shoulder.

"Don't even think about it." Erik warned.

"Aw, come on." Jessie's shoulders dropped and a frown spawned upon her face.

"Do you remember what happened the last time you jumped into a fight?"

Jessie's smile was big and bright. "Hell yeah."

"No." Erik warned her sternly. "Sit down or we go home."

"Oh, come on." Jessie sat down and crossed her arms like a disciplined child. "I wanna play."

"Jessie, you can't." Erik admonished her like a discipling father. "You might get hurt."

"So. Scars make great stories." Jessie lifted her shirt and showed off her scar from the car accident. "See."

"Damn, where did you get that scar?" Peter asked. He took a good long look at the scar and gently rubbed his index finger across it.

"Fighting bears and trying to pass the beaver initiation." Jessie smiled.

"Damn, you're worse than Krillin." Laughed Joey.

"Krillin? Really? Can't it be someone cool like Dandy of Space Dandy?" Jessie grimaced.

"Nah, you're more like Hyatt from Excel Saga." Erik laughed.

"I will shoot you." Jessie threatened Erik. "In fact, I owe you a death for Layla."

Erik froze and then he smiled. "Behave or I'll spill the beans...corn and squash."

"First marooning me, now blackmailing me." Jessie chuckled and she pointed a finger at him. "You sir, are no gentleman."

Out of nowhere, more yelling and shouting. Jessie looked over and saw a table flip over, the Orcs and Klingons yelling at each other. Jessie shook her head and pinched her nose.

"Seems they've got their Star Trek in my World of Warcraft. That's it, I'm outta here." Jessie stood up to leave. "Come on Erik."

"We're leaving?" Erik tossed down a C-note to pay for their food and drinks.

"Yeah, I can't take it anymore." Jessie shook her head. "Later Joey!"

Joey turned and saw Jessie leave. "Later Jessie, Have a great night!"

Exiting Angelo's Jessie took a big breath and let it out. She looked up into the night sky. Only three stars were out, but the crescent moon was high.

"I miss the night sky." Jessie mused.

"Calling it a night?" Erik asked, as he stood beside her.

"Alright, I admit it. I'm done." Jessie shook her head and headed for home.

"I did tell you that you'd get tired more easily." Erik reminded her.

"I don't think baby likes New York." Chuckled Jessie. "I feel nauseous, and I'm getting a migraine."

"Then again, maybe it was the four glasses of Lon Milk mixed with Seafood Paella." Erik fell in step beside Jessie.

"No, I'm starting to really miss Canada." Jessie reflected wistfully. "It was so nice and quiet there. You could hear yourself think. People weren't arguing or debating, music wasn't blasting. It was just...quiet, serene, peaceful, and sure."

"Sounds like Rene kept you safe." Mused Erik, as he too occasionally looked up at the night sky.

Jessie sighed. "What do I want?"

Erik looked at her and smiled. "Sounds like you want to go home."

"Come on, cab stand is this way." Jessie pointed to the left.

"But the airport is that." Erik smiled softly and pointed to the right.

Chapter 21

Jessie had tried to return to her old ways, but now-a-days, quiet evenings at home with a good book was the norm for her. She was now in her second trimester and was beginning to show. She also really didn't want to answer all the questions that suddenly being pregnant would bring. It was a warm night with a cool breeze, and New York was as busy as it ever was, with purposeful people doing meaningful things. Unexpectedly, Jessie's phone rang, but Eric answered it.

"Hello, yes. A what?" Eric turned to Jessie. "Do you want to go to a party for Giorgio? He's back in town and he's celebrating another art sale."

Jessie looked up at him from her book. "No."

"I'm sorry." Erik relayed. "Jessie is indisposed tonight. Maybe another time."

"Thanks." Jessie tossed out her grateful reply as she continued reading.

"You're going to have to start explaining to your friends that you're pregnant and can't shake your booty like you used to." Erik went back to typing on his laptop.

"Hell no. Do you remember the baby shower that they threw for Yolanda's first child?" Jessie cringed.

"Yes." Erik chuckled, heartily. Erik stopped typing, turned, and looked at Jessie. "I remember. You came home drunk off your ass and kept ranting all night about a Chippendale dancer at a baby shower."

"Erik, those girls are crazy." Jessie sat up, put her book in her lap, and told him. "It started out as a simple baby shower. But once the drinks started, then there was karaoke, and spin the bottle, and..."

"Wait, were there any men at the baby shower?" Erik raised an eyebrow at her.

"No. Not until the Chippendale showed up. Why?"

"Then who the hell were you girls playing spin the baby bottle with?" Erik was now laughing so hard that he held his stomach. Jessie said nothing. She just hid behind her book as Erik laughed harder. "God, now I wish I had gone with you."

"Good thing you didn't." Jessie chuckled and she turned the page. "We also drew names out of a hat to see who got to change the Chippendale dancer's diaper."

Erik stopped laughing and smiled wickedly as he thought about it. Jessie noticed.

"No Erik. Bad Erik."

"I'm surprised your friends haven't thrown you a baby shower yet." Erik contemplated and he regarded at Jessie's growing stomach.

"They won't. I didn't tell them." Jessie picked up and went back to reading her mystery book.

"Not even Dani?" Erik's eyebrows shot up and betrayed his surprise.

"Dani knows everything." Jessie said, then she corrected herself. "Everything but that."

"Well, that's good." Erik mused happily and he went back to his typing.

"Why?"

"Because you two grew up together at the orphanage." Erik reminded her. "You shouldn't have secrets from her."

"That's what she said." Jessie laughed.

"What does she think about René?" Erik turned to the next page and began typing that one too.

Jessie stopped laughing and sighed. "She thinks I should go back."

"I think that she's right." Erik agreed.

"I can't." Jessie narrowed her eyes on him.

"What are you running away from?" Erik stopped typing, turned, and faced her.

"I'm not running?" Jessie insisted. "I have a life here too you know. And I like it."

"Are you afraid of marriage?" He questioned. He now rested his folded hands against his lips and considered her plight.

Jessie sighed heavily. *Why couldn't people just let things go?* "No."

"Motherhood?" Erik pried and raised one eyebrow at her.

"Wash your mouth out with soap." Jessie snapped at him.

"Ha-ha, what is it with you and kids?" Erik mocked her, as he held his sides with laughter. "Do you like them or not?"

Jessie blew him off and went back to reading. "Not."

"Liar." Eric scoffed. He stood up, walked over to their couch, and stood before her. "I watched you entertain a lost kid once, with a paper puppet for an hour until his mother and a cop showed up to claim him."

"I know what it's like to be lost." Jessie frowned and turned another page. "So, sue me."

"This is about your parents, isn't it?" He crossed his arms and looked at her with sympathy.

Jessie said nothing, but she did start to tear up.

Erik knelt before her, held her arms, and kissed her forehead. She didn't need to say anything. He knew.

"You're afraid to fall in love and then to lose them, aren't you?" Erik sat down on the couch beside her. He scooted close to her and put his arm around the back of the couch.

"Why bother?" Jessie sighed in a depressed manner.

"Why bother?" Erik chuckled. "Is this that same girl that stares up at the stars at night?"

"You mean star." Jessie snickered. "This is New York City after all." Jessie absentmindedly turned the page in her book. "There's too much light pollution here to see the true night sky."

"Why did you really come back here?" Erik asked. "You could just email me the books when your done writing."

Jessie put the book down and stared at their small dining room table. She remembered Rene' huge dining room table and all the family and friends it could hold.

"I'm not ready to be a wife and mother."

"Why not?"

"What do you mean why not?"

"If you love René as much as I know you do, then why are you not ready to spend your life with him?"

"I don't know." Jessie sighed.

"Yes, you do. So did Nicolas." Erik reminded her.

"Nicolas and Nancy had to grow up. All people do." She looked over at Erik. "Every man or woman, once they meet "the one" will leave their family and friends to start on a new adventure. That adventure may take them around the world, or it may take them just next door. But even if they leave, they will always love the ones that they've left behind."

"Then what are you really afraid of Peter." Erik ruffled her hair. "That you won't remember the way back to Neverland. That I won't be your Tinkerbelle anymore."

Jessie gave a snort of laughter. "You're the only man alive that could say that with a straight face." Then Jessie frowned and stared at her tummy. "That I will fail."

Erik laughed at her. "You haven't even tried yet. I swear you'd jump off a cliff without a second thought, but it's marriage that frightens you."

"Hey, one's temporary." Jessie pointed her index finger at him. "The other is permanent."

"It's very temporary, if your chute doesn't open." Erik laughed.

"It's not worth the risk." Jessie sighed and then slipped into slouch.

"It was for your parents."

"That's hitting below the belt." Jessie chided, but she so fondly remembered her parents and the love they had for each other. "They'd face any challenge and they faced it together. Be it in-laws, co-workers, or even criminals."

"And you and René will face life together. Be they bears, beavers, or bees." Erik snickered and he gave her a loving squeeze.

Jessie gave him a sideways glance, her eyes twinkled with mirth, and she ribbed him hard with her elbow. "Stop that."

"Okay, okay, I'll stop." Erik gave her a small grin as he rubbed her stomach. "Are you alright? Do you need anything?"

"No, I'm fine. I just wish..." Jessie sighed. She looked at him and he waited for her to tell him. But she didn't. "Nothing."

"Why don't you just call him?" Erik suggested, again placing his arm on the back of the couch.

"No."

"Email him then." Erik prompted, and he mimed typing with his right hand. "That way you don't have to hear his voice."

"Stop it." Jessie ordered. She just stared at her book. She had read the same sentence now three times.

"Fine." Erik rolled his eyes and gave up.

Jessie kept her eyes focused on the book. She couldn't look at him right now. He was making too much sense. "If love is so great, then why don't you marry Christine?" Jessie shot back at him.

Now Erik sighed. He sat back, leaned his head against the couch, and thought about it. "One, my mother wants me too. Two, I told you she's Roman Catholic like my mother."

"Aren't you Roman Catholic?" Jessie snickered. Now she looked at him.

"Yes, but I'm...unorthodox."

"I'll say." Jessie sniggered; mischief made her eyes twinkle.

Erik smirked at her. "We have two very different outlooks on life, and yet we are both too busy for such things."

"If not Christine, then who?" Jessie asked. Then she remembered Erik's lady friend. "And what are your intentions towards Ms. Wightman?"

"Bianca?" Erik blanched, and then he gave her a wicked smile. "Definitely impure."

Jessie rolled her eyes at him and shook her head with mirth. "Do you have any real candidates?"

Erik thought about it a bit. "There was you. Until you got impregnated on skull island by Peter Pan." Erik laughed at her.

"Me?" Jessie balked and the book dropped from her lap. She left it to lay on the floor.

Erik looked at his employer and smiled. "You're a strong woman, with a great mind, a fine body, and you always go to church."

"You wanted to marry me?" Jessie asked and looked at Erik seriously.

"No, I wanted to work for you." Erik corrected her. "You're my best friend."

Jessie acted shot and wounded. "Aww, I'm in the friend zone."

Erik laughed. "You're serious when you need to be. But you're funny all the time. Life with you is one big adventure." He waved his right hand into the air.

"Careful, Little John. Maid Marian may not measure up to me." Jessie warned him. "And because you're looking at me, you may miss out on an awfully big adventure of your own."

Erik sighed, as he thought about her words. "You're right...for once." He smirked at her. "It looks like neither of us will be getting married anytime soon."

Chapter 22

Jessie has been gone for six months now, but the memory of her still haunted him. So did Lukas. Once he found out that Jessie had left, he made it his mission to cheer René up. But really René just wanted Lukas to leave him alone. Although he never said, 'I told you so', Rene swore that he could hear it in his voice.

But today, René had decided not to let it get him down, as he stood on the front step, took a deep breath, and let the fresh mountain air invigorate him. The summer sun suffused his face in warmth and light. But suddenly, a single cloud covered the sun. René opened his eyes and then he saw why. Miss Grace O'Maille's car pulled up to his front door. His smile faded, but he quickly pasted on a new one. He walked over to her car and opened her door for her. Out stepped Grace O'Maille and she was all smiles.

She's like a shark with rows of teeth. René's conscience told him. But he cleared that thought from his mind as he cleared his throat and said, "Good Afternoon, Miss O'Maille. A pleasure to see you again."

Grace gracefully stepped up to him and gave him a quick peck on his right cheek.

"I assure you, Mr. Voclain, the pleasure is all mine. Mr. Wolfram Howell is giving me a month's vacation here to scope out the place and to get it surveyed for the engineers."

"Engineers?" René panicked a bit but was curious.

"Oh, don't worry hun. They're not touching this house at all. That's firm."

Grace moved to the trunk of her car and René followed. The driver already had her bags sitting on the ground. René looked at all her luggage.

"What's all that?" René asked, with an amused grin.

"My wardrobe."

"You said you were staying a month." René chuckled at her. "Not moving in forever."

"Don't be silly dear. A lady has needs." She giggled at him and gently dabbed her head towards her bags.

Jessie didn't. René thought with a smirk. *She showed up with nothing.* Then René smiled to himself. *Jessie wearing nothing is a much better idea.*

"René darling, you'd better not be undressing me with your eyes." Grace winked at him.

René snapped out of his daydream. "Huh, sorry, no."

"That's good. We hardly know each other." Grace told him. Then she walked up to him, softly touched his shoulder, gave him a playful wink, and then walked toward the front of her car. "Maybe at the end of this month, we'll know each other better, oui."

René picked up her bags and skillfully tucked one under his left arm.

"Thank you, René darling. I'll be inside in a moment. I need to speak with my driver."

It took René four trips to get all her bags into the guest bedroom. René sighed heavily as he brought the last of her bags in and looked around the room. As far as he was concerned, this was Jessie's room and allowing a complete stranger in here felt wrong somehow. Sarah sat in the doorway looking at him.

"Don't look at me like that. Jessie made her choice. She didn't want to stay." René told his faithful dog, as he subconsciously rubbed his deer head tattoo. "Why does it still hurt, Sarah?" He looked at her. "It's been six months."

"Woof. Woof." Sarah barked and then walked off as Grace came upstairs.

"Oh, I forgot that you had a dog." Grace watched her go by. René moved aside and let Grace into the room. "Thank you so much, René honey." Grace looked around the room. "My this is a nice, quaint, little room. Very comfortable. Little Rustic. Just needs a woman's touch."

Again, René thought about Jessie. *Her touch definitely wasn't...gentle. In fact, I can't remember the last woman dared to conquer me. Heh, I was unquestionably on the receiving end of her lovemaking.* René mentally slapped himself. "I've got to take Sarah out for her walk and make my rounds. I'll be back around 5pm to make dinner." René informed her.

"Oh good. That'll give me time to get settled and make some phone calls." Grace smiled happily and began to unpack. "I'm going to enjoy this."

René nodded gentlemanly. "Good afternoon, Miss O'Maille."

"René darling, you can call me Grace."

René tried not to visibly shudder. *Call a smiling crocodile by their first name? Watch out René.* "Thank you, um...Grace. I'll be back later." René spoke to her and then called out for his dog.

"Sarah!" René called, but his dog didn't come. He descended the stairs. "Sarah." Still no answer. "Where is she?" He wondered.

He searched the house and found that Sarah had moved her dog bed to the warmest corner of his garage. Here his faithful dog laid, looking bored out of her mind.

"Oh, come on." René chuckled at her. "She's not that bad." Sarah gave him a mean look. "What's the matter with you?"

Sarah growled and buried her head.

"You know damn well that this is all out of my hands." René told his dog, as he opened the garage door. "I don't own this house."

Sarah raised her head, woofed at him, and then turned away from him again to lay back down.

"Come on." René called to her. "Time to go to work." Sarah didn't move. René shook his head and gave her a wicked grin. "OK, you can stay here...with her." René teased.

Sarah jumped up and ran out of the garage door. René just laughed at her as he closed the garage door.

"I can't believe even my own dog doesn't want to be in the same house with her.

Once outside, René looked over and saw Jessie's Garden.

"Huh, three sisters chili might be good tonight." René considered. Sarah's barking brought him out of his thoughts. "Alright Sarah, I'm coming."

Later that night, René came back to find Grace and two other people in his home. They were gathered around his dining room table with maps of the islands and plans for resort cabins lying about.

"Hello Grace?" René called out.

"Oh, René honey, you're back. Did you have a good day?" Grace greeted him happily.

"Yes." René stepped forward towards Grace, but Sarah moved towards the garage. René noticed but said nothing in front of guests. "Who are your friends?"

"Oh, this is William and his brother Kent." Grace introduced each gentleman. "They are the surveyors and engineers that I told you about." Then Grace turned to them. "Gentlemen, this is René Voclain, our Nature Ranger and host."

Both men turned around to greet him to greet him. "Mr. Voclain."

"Mr. Williams. Mr. Kent." René greeted them with a handshake.

Grace laughed at him. "No honey, those are their first names. Their surname is Fernandes."

"Oh, sorry. You gentlemen make yourselves at home." René told them, then he turned to Grace. "If you'd like to help me outside a moment."

"Outside?" Grace looked at him curiously. "With what?"

"Dinner. I'm going to make three sisters chili and we need ingredients."

"You have a farm?" William asked with interest.

"No, a small garden." René pulled a basket out of the coat closet.

"May we see it?" Kent asked and joined Rene' at the front door.

"Sure." René nodded and led all three of them outside to the left side of the house.

"Wow." William remarked, more than a little stunned.

"I thought you said it was a little garden." Kent laughed, as he looked from left to right and back again.

"This is little." René smiled and started walking towards the section where the beans grew.

"René honey, this is a small grocery store." Grace

chuckled. She didn't move but stayed where she was at the mouth of Rene's Garden. "Don't you think that you overdid it a little."

"Wasn't me." René smiled honestly. "Jessie..."

"Jessie?" Grace frowned. "The snow crash victim?"

"Snow crash victim?" William and Kent balked at each other and then looked to Grace for clarification.

"Yes, gentleman." Grace smiled proudly. "My René is a Bona fide hero. He rescued Jessica from her car when she crashed into a tree this past winter. He even nursed her back to health until she was able to go home."

"That's really impressive, Mr. Voclain." William praised him.

"It's sort of my job." René gave them a weak grin. "I'm a forest ranger."

"What vegetable is this?" Kent asked, pointing the vibrant purple fruit. "I've never seen these before."

"Eggplants." René answered, "And they're actually not a vegetable. They're a fruit. They are also part of the Solanaceae family and because of its purple color people used to believe that it was poisonous, and that if you ate it that you would go insane."

"Oh." Kent reached out and touched one.

"What's the matter boys, never seen real food before." Grace politely hid her laughter behind her hand.

"Not in its natural habitat." William joked, looking around, as he walked carefully among Rene's vegetables.

"Yes, we don't often see our food before it hits our plates." Kent quipped, wiping the dirt from the eggplant onto his pants leg.

"Well, lady and gentlemen, start picking vegetables." René told them.

"You want us to pick vegetables." William questioned.

"Good Book says that if you don't work, then you don't eat." René joked.

"I'm not really dressed for manual labor." Grace graciously bowed out, as she looked around René's amazing garden.

"But we are?" William and Kent joked, looking down at their business casual suits.

"René honey, we'll just leave this to you." Grace sashayed back to the house.

"Fine, but dinner will be delayed thirty minutes." René shrugged, and then knelt to work.

"That's fine." Grace called out. "It will give us a chance to finalize some ideas."

René just laughed at them as the three of them left to go inside. Out from nowhere, Sarah was suddenly at his side.

"Well, look who came out to play." René chuckled.

As René chose and picked vegetables, he couldn't help but remember helping Jessie plant this garden. What he hadn't known was that she had planted him fruit and nut bearing trees as well. He could already see their shoots coming up from the ground. If he cared for them properly, he'd have his own private orchard in seven years. Then he frowned.

"If the princess and her ogres don't level my land for their private resort." He grumbled.

When he had finished gathering his beans and vegetables, René went inside and headed towards the kitchen. Sarah headed back towards the garage.

"Seriously." René shook his head. He placed his basket down, took off his muddy shoes, and then walked towards the kitchen. He spoke to Grace as he passed her. "Would you like to help me cook?" Then he noticed that she was on the phone.

"I'm sorry honey, I can't." Grace placed a hand over the receiver. "I'm on the phone with my boss right now."

Rene' nodded and then asked, "Is he coming over for dinner?"

"Oh, that's an idea." Grace smiled brightly. "Mr. Howell, would you like to join us here for dinner? René is cooking chili. No? you can't. A raincheck is fine, just let me know when." Grace then returned her attention to René. "Go ahead René, dinner for four please."

"Okay." René proceeded into the kitchen. He washed his vegetables, diced them, and then began cooking.

Soon, the whole house smelled delicious. René took a break from his cooking and looked up. Grace was on her laptop, working no doubt, while William and his brother Kent were watching a game on his TV. René shook his head and began to set the table for four people. Then he called them to dinner.

"Grace, gentlemen, dinner is ready. Come and get it." Rene expertly carried four full plates to the table and set them down.

"Oh great, I'm starved." Kent jumped up from the couch and came to the table.

"Thank you, Mr. Voclain." William stated, as he took a seat at the table. "It was good of you to cook for us."

"No problem. I love to cook." René smiled weakly at them.

"You're not joining us?" Grace asked. She took her seat and placed a napkin in her lap.

"Not yet." René told her, as he filled a bowl with chili. "I've got to feed Sarah."

"Oh, that's right. You have a dog. Where is she? I haven't seen her much." Grace blew on her chili and then ate.

"She's in the garage."

"René," Grace frowned. "You didn't have to banish her for my sake. I'm only here for a month."

"She'll be ok." René chuckled. "It's only for a month."

During dinner, Grace talked to Willian and Kent more than she talked to René. René just listened to all their plans. Plans of resorts and lodges for the executives of Wyoming's Wild Corporation. René shook his head, sighed, and he ate his dinner.

*At this rate, I should have eaten in the servants'
quarters with Sarah.* René mused.

"René, dear are you alright?" Grace looked at him
curiously.

"Oh yes, just remembering to walk Sarah after
dinner." He wiped his mouth and then poured
himself a glass of wine.

"Well, what do you think?" Grace asked René.

"About what?" René put down his spoon and gave
her his attention.

"A cottage for two on the east side of this island."
Grace gently wiped her mouth with her napkin.

"That's fine." René smirked. "The bears will love
it."

"Bears?" Grace looked at him, puzzled with
shock.

"Yes, if you mean the east side of the grotto
field with the stream, that's bear territory. They
hibernate there. Might be nice watching bears walk
by in the evenings." René snickered.

"Well, they have to go." Grace took out her PDA
and made notes. "They will have to be relocated.
That spot is too perfect for our future home."

"Relocate them?" René looked at her seriously.
Then he joked. "What kind of low-income housing

do you plan on building for them." Then René's brain caught onto what she had said. "Wait, us?"

This comment set William and Kent to laughing.

"No wonder Goldilocks broke into the house of the three bears and stole their porridge." William laughed.

"Well, it's a dangerous neighborhood." Kent laughed. "I'm surprised children are allowed to roam the streets at night. Who knows what the wolves are planning."

"Good thing this isn't India; or we'd have lions, tigers, and bears to worry about." William chuckled and rested his chin on his folded hands.

"Oh, maybe we should build fairy tale cottages and honeymoon suites." Kent suggested.

"Whoa, whoa, whoa gentlemen. This is going to be a high-class executive resort. Mr. Howell will be living here, and..."

This statement set the gentlemen laughing again.

"Poor bears can't afford this neighborhood." William stated, now holding his sides with laughter.

"We'll have to relocate them to a protected reservation island and give them fish rations." Kent laughed and poured himself another glass of wine.

René just shook his head. *oh my god, these people are crazy.* Then he stood up to leave.

"Where are you going René honey?"

"Dishes." René held up his plate.

"Don't you have a dishwasher?" Grace waved her hand towards his kitchen washer.

"Yes, but I only use it for large dinner parties." René continued to the kitchen. "Small venues like this I can wash by hand."

"OK, but I'd like to talk to you." Grace handed her plate to William, and he placed their plates on René's counter.

"Well, that's our cue." William walked towards René's front door. "Come Kent."

"Thank you for dinner." Kent drained his glass of wine, and then went and donned his coat. "It was delicious."

Grace stood up, and like a gracious host, she saw her guests out.

"Oh, it was no problem. We loved having you. I'll see gentlemen tomorrow at 10am."

"10am. Got it." William affirmed. "Good night, Miss. O'Maille."

"Good night, Mr. Voclain." Said Kant.

Grace closed the door, cleared off the table of the glasses, and brought the glasses to René.

Well, she can work. René mused. "They seem nice." He told her, as he turned on the water.

"They are the best in the business." Grace told him. "But I have plans for you as well."

"Really?" René raised an eyebrow at her. "Plans beyond park ranger and guide?"

Grace O'Maille walked over to René and put her arms around him. She sniffed his neck and then laid her head against the back of his head. René noticed that she was as tall as he was.

"René darling. My plans for you are many." She sighed happily. "I asked my boss for a month's vacation here, so that we could get to know each other better. By the end of this summer, I'm hoping to announce our engagement. I already have plans in place for a September wedding with beautiful fall colors of red and gold."

"Uhh, a month is a bit fast to fall in love, isn't it?" René asked, as he tried to think of how to let her down easy.

"Maybe. But I fell for you the first day that I saw you." Grace held him tighter. "A big strong, studly, handsome man of the forest. A girl would be out of her mind not to fall for a guy like you."

And there you have it, definite proof that Jessie was crazy to leave you. René's mind joked. "That sounds more like lust than love." René told Grace truthfully.

Grace released him and René turned around to look at her.

"What an odd thing to say." Grace's face betrayed her surprise.

"I've seen it before." René gave her a weak smile. "And I've done it myself. Lesson learned."

"Not the snow crash victim?" Grace gave him a look of both shock and concern.

"Who Jessie?" René balked. *Why does she keep calling her the snow crash victim?* "No." René lied. "She wasn't here long enough for me to..."

"Good, because ghosts of former lovers are the hardest to shake."

Tell me about it. René thought.

"I thought that I'd never get over Derrick." Grace sighed and her eyes lowered away from Rene' to the sink full of dishes.

"Derrick?"

"He was a friend once. Turns out he was just using me for my connections. We broke up badly." Grace brought her left knuckle to her lips and bit it. "But I still loved him. Stupid me." She shrugged.

René couldn't help himself. He moved forward and put his arms around her.

What are you doing? René's conscience asked him pointedly. *What? I'm a rescuer. It's in my nature.* René told himself. *Don't worry, I've got this. Keep hugging her like that and you'll wake up to find yourself with a ball and chain.*

Chapter 23

It was still very early, when René snuck into the guest bedroom. He quietly tip toed over to the bed and watched his houseguest sleep.

"Wow, she snores." René chuckled to himself, as he stood watching her sleep. Then he leaned over and gently touched her shoulder. "Grace. Grace. Wake up, Grace."

"Hmm, what is it René dear?" Grace answered him sleepily. "What do you need?"

"For you to come fishing with me." René smiled at her. "The freezer is empty and…"

"Fishing?" Grace rolled over and turned on the owl lamp on the nightstand. "René darling, we can pick up fish at the grocery store on our way back."

"But fresh caught fish that you fish yourself are…"

Grace gave him a stern look and raised an eyebrow at him. "René, I love you, but I'm not getting up to go fishing." Grace yawned, and then stretched her arms up. "What time is it anyway?"

"4am." He told her seriously.

"4am?!" Grace looked over at the clock and then at René, as she flopped back down on the bed.

"René love, go back to sleep. We can go grocery shopping after the meeting."

"What meeting?"

"We have a meeting with the city planners to ensure that we have adequate electricity, natural gas, and water for each lodge." Grace informed him, and she yawned again.

René shook his head disapprovingly. *We should stop this.* His conscience told him sternly. *How?* René asked himself. "What time are "we" attending this meeting?" René asked her.

"10am." Grace mumbled.

"I'll see you then." René said, leaning back. "I'm going fishing."

"Take care." Grace mumbled, pulled the covers up, and then started snoring again.

At 10AM, René came back with a cooler filled with fresh fish. Grace met him at the door and glared at him angrily.

"Where have you been?" Then she got a whiff of him. "Ugh, you stink."

"I told you that I was going fishing." René merely stated, as he walked towards the garage to put away his catch. *I'm a grown man, I can do as I wish.*

"And I told you that we have a meeting at 10am."

Grace scolded him. "I had to rearrange a few things, but they are willing to meet with us at 11AM." Grace opened the door to the garage for him. "I don't like rescheduling meetings. It makes me look incompetent. Please refrain from "going missing" when I need you."

Going missing? René's conscience laughed. Jessie was gone missing for a month and Erik didn't complain this much.

René put the fish in the freezer. Sarah poked her head up and barked happily when she saw him.

"Good morning, Sarah." René chuckled.

Then she saw Grace, shook herself, and turned back towards the wall. Sarah growled at him.

"Jeez, you're still holding a grudge."

Grace looked at her watch as she watched René interact with his dog. *This is ridiculous.* "René, I need you to focus, honey." Grace told him sternly. Grace tried to enhance her calm, but her feelings of agitation with him sent her nerves on fire. "Please go upstairs, shower, shave, dress, and be back down here by 10:20AM please. Because we need to leave."

René turned around and looked at her. His hackles roared, but he only nodded to her, as he left the garage.

"As you wish."

"What made you go fishing anyway?" Grace asked, as she followed him to the stairs. "I told you that we could go grocery shopping after the meeting."

"I always hunt and fish my own food." René told her, as he ascended the stairs. "There's a reason I live out here alone." *That and people tend to annoy me.*

Fifteen minutes later, René came downstairs looking hot and fresh. Grace smiled at him. She stepped forward, inspected him, a brushed a bit lint from his sleeves, and straightened his collar.

"Now that is much much better." She praised him with a great big grin.

"Glad you approve." *Not that I actually care what you think.*

"Are you ready?" Grace helped René into his coat.

"Yes." René said, as he locked the door and prepared himself to face this day.

Later that night, a physically exhausted Grace and a mentally exhausted René came home.

"That was a very productive day." Grace told René, as he opened the door. "I'm going to take a long hot bath."

Surprisingly, Sarah ran into René and barked angrily at him.

René smiled at her. "Hiya girl, did you have a nice day." René knelt to pet her head and stroke her fur.

But Sarah just walked past him and pointed at the door. René stood and moved toward the front door.

"Ok, Sarah. I'm sorry I'm late." Then Rene' turned to Grace and smiled at her. "Go ahead and take a bath, I've got to walk Sarah. I'll make dinner when I get back."

Grace just shook her head. "Oh no, not tonight." She grabbed his arm, before he could leave.

"Let me guess, you have more plans." René chuckled.

"For being such a good sport and a great host," Grace smiled brightly at him with coy and seductive eyes, and she made soft small circles upon his left pectoral. "I'm taking you to dinner."

"Where?" He questioned. He was only half listening to her. His eyes were trying to follow where Sarah had run off to.

"Alo's."

"Alo's?!" René stared at her. "That's all the way on the other side of Lake Ontario."

"I know, but this side of the lake is rather lacking

in stellar eating establishments." Grace removed her coat and hung it up.

"If you want French cuisine, I can cook it for you." René smiled proudly.

Sarah barked at him.

"No, I wouldn't dare ask you to cook today. Not after all that you have done for me today. Please René, honey. Let me reward you." Grace smiled at him.

Sarah barked at René.

"With French food?" René joked. "You do know that I'm French, right."

Sarah barked at him.

"Oh you. Stop being a bad boy." Grace turned on her heels and headed upstairs. "Go and walk your dog, let me freshen up, and then we'll go to dinner."

Sarah barked at René yet again, this time from outside the front door.

"Okay," René sighed, a bit frustrated, watched her head upstairs, and then he walked over to Sarah and took her out.

Summer in Ontario, Canada is nothing like their winters. Their summers are warm. Their skies are clear, and the gentle breezes make them great days for hikers and great nights for campers. Tonight, the setting sun filled the sky with apricot orange and fire yellow, while the coming night filled the twilight sky with shades of cerulean and cobalt. The white and fluffy clouds were now flattening out, as if a heavenly painter was spreading his paintbrush across the sky. So gorgeous was the coming night, that Grace drove with the top down.

Two hours later, Grace and René were enjoying a booth at Alo's Restaurant in Toronto, Canada. The décor was simple, but elegant. Light grey cushioned benches matched the light grey interior walls. A dark grey trimmed out all the windows and doors. Gold cylinder lights hung down like microphones from the ceiling. Tables were made of the finest polished oak. Large dark green plants and young trees lined the corner walls, giving the restaurant a light airy, and forest like feel.

"Oh my, isn't this nice." Grace commented, as she noted the décor. René took her coat for her and then pulled her chair out. "Very chic."

René looked around. To him it was just another restaurant. "It's okay." He shrugged dismissively. "If you like this sort of thing." René took his seat, as the waiter appeared.

"Good evening, my name is Walter, and I will be

your waiter this evening. May I take your drink order."

"I'll have a nice white wine," Grace requested, and she began to look the menu over.

"I'll have a Perfect Caesar," said René.

"I'll return shortly with your drinks." Walter bowed to them.

"Thank you." Grace smiled at the waiter, and then at René. "Are you alright?"

"Hm, yes. I'm fine," René droned, and he read his menu.

"You don't seem fine," Grace noticed his despondency and her smile slipped into a frown. "Is anything wrong?"

"Hm, no. I'm fine." René gave her a weak smile.

Soon the waiter returned with their drinks and then stood at the ready to take their dinner order.

"I'd like to try your east coast scallops." Grace told the waiter, and then handed him the menu.

"And for you sir?" Walter asked René.

René handed Walter his menu. "The veal chop please."

"Very good." Walter nodded. "I will get them both ordered for you."

René took a sip from his drink and nodded pleasantly. "This is really good." Then he noticed that Grace was staring at him with a warm smile. "What?"

"You look very handsome." Grace felt warm, and happy, and...content. "Business casual suits you very nicely. Much better than flannel."

"I clean up well." He chuckled and adjusted his collar with pride. "Besides, flannel is comfortable."

"I'm serious." Grace told him firmly.

There go those crocodile teeth again. René thought.

"You could be an international male model if you had a mind to be." Grace took a sip of her wine, and then looked around at the restaurant's décor.

"Is that to be my next career move?" René took another sip of his drink.

"Is that what you would like to do?" Grace asked him seriously. "Because I can make it happen for you. I do know certain people that could help us."

"I bet you do," René mumbled, and took another drink.

"And that means." Grace raised an eyebrow at him.

"In the days that I've known you, I've discovered that you are a very capable, responsible, and determined woman. Nothing derails you when you've made up your mind."

"Is that not a good thing?" Grace's head leaned to the left and she looked at him.

"For some, yes." René assured her with a nod, and he took another satisfying sip of his drink.

"But not for you?" Grace's smile faded.

"Me?" René cleared his throat and chose his words carefully.

"Yes, what do you like?" Grace gave him her full attention.

"I am a simple man. I like the forest. I like the lessons that it teaches me. Look before you leap. Never underestimate your enemies. Enjoy the day and stop to appreciate the summer fields before the winter snows set in. I am not as "driven" as you are. I am very happy just ...being."

"Just "being" as you call it, is nice," Grace admitted. She saluted René with her glass and then took a sip. "When you're on vacation. But..." Her eyes narrowed on him. "Business is business, and the bills need to be paid. And that means seizing the opportunity when it presents itself."

Yep, she's a shark. René mentally scoffed.

"Are there any other interests that you have that I should know about?" Grace asked him slyly.

"I like to fish." Rene' grinned at her teasingly.

"So, I gathered." Grace sat back and took a sip of

her wine. "But we do have grocery stores for that sort of thing."

"Sarah and I also enjoy hunting." Rene now looked around the restaurant and took in the décor. *This is a nice restaurant, but its...fake. I'd much rather be walking the trails at home among some real trees.*

"Sarah?" Grace questioned, trying to remember where she had heard that name before.

"My dog?"

"Oh yes of course." Grace smiled at René and her cheeks puffed happily.

"The boys and I love playing poker on Friday nights." René took a good long sip from his drink.

"Every Friday night?" Grace asked, wondering how many rowdy men she'd have to put up with.

"No. Some of my friends like John are married. So, we only play twice a month."

"And what does John do?" Grace was listening, but she was also moving the silverware from her right-hand side to her left.

"He's a veterinarian."

"That reminds me. I haven't seen any doctors, dentists, a Starbucks, or any sign of civilization..." Once Grace finished neatly arranging the silverware on her left-hand side, she looked up at Rene'.

"We're a small town and I live on an island." René laughed at her. "The closest civilization is twenty klicks away."

Grace gave him a funny look. "English please." She teased him.

"Twelve miles." *Twelve and half*, he heard Jessie's voice say.

"Well, that's no good. Changes will have to be made." Grace took out her PDA and made notes. "A reliable road for one."

"More changes to the island?" René gulped the rest of his drink in one shot.

Grace noticed and put away her PDA. "Tell me more about yourself René." Grace requested. She folded her hands and listened.

"Well, not much to tell. My grandfather was in construction and built the house that I now live in. My father was an Army cook and my mom was a chef until she retired. I have two younger brothers, Jules and Noel. They are both married to two wonderful ladies, Shelly and Anna. Jules has two sons, Harry and Henry. Noel has two girls, Susan and Alice."

"Will you be wanting two kids as well." Grace

smiled at him. "Something like one boy and one girl to keep the symmetry of your brothers?"

"I had thought about it." René smiled and nodded affirmingly. "And you? What is your family like?"

"I'm a college grad and the last of five kids." Grace told him and took a sip of her wine.

"Five?" René raised his hand for the waiter to bring him another drink.

"Yes. My parents were always driven, and my father wanted his own NBA team."

"Really?" René chuckled and signaled the waiter for another drink.

"He almost made it. I have four brothers." Grace smiled.

"That must have been tough." René said, as he remembered his childhood.

"It was. I had to fight for everything." Grace said seriously. "He let my brothers tease and beat up on me because he wanted me to be strong. He wanted me to be able to survive on my own."

"I'm sorry." René said softly.

"I'm not." Grace sighed heavily. "He was right. I am strong." Grace smiled.

"So, did your father get his NBA team?"

"Nope, my eldest brother Richard is a doctor. Next eldest is Victor and he is a lawyer. Travis is an accountant. Tommy is the civil engineer, and I am the real estate agent."

"You're in real estate?" René looked up from his drink. "I thought you were marketing and sales."

"Nope, Acquisition and sales of real estate." Grace smiled proudly.

"Pardon monsieur and madam, your dinner is ready." The waiter announced, and two servers placed their dishes in front of them and then left. "Is this adequate for you?"

"Yes, it looks delicious." René complemented.

"May I have some more wine?" Grace requested, as she raised her glass.

"Oui madame. I'll be right back." The waiter retrieved the bottle and poured her another glass. René asked him to leave the bottle. The waiter nodded and then said, "Bon Appetit."

"Now this is good food prepared to perfection." Grace commented happily, the aroma of her meal putting a smile on her face, as she placed her napkin in her lap.

René smiled at her and shook his head.

"What's so funny?" she asked him.

"I could have made this at home." He assured her proudly.

"Oh you." Grace lifted her glass and René followed suit. "To us." She smiled.

René didn't seem sure about this statement, but he toasted her anyway.

"To us..."

After a wonderful meal, and a two-hour ride back home, René suggested a midnight walk.

"A midnight walk?" Grace repeated, as she tiredly walked up the stair to Rene's place.

"Yes. It's a beautiful night, full of stars, and the weather is nice and warm." René took Grace into his arms, as they stood on the porch. "What could be more romantic?"

Grace enjoyed his embrace, and she considered his proposal. "Romantic?" And then she yawned. "You might be right, but I'm tired." She looked into his eyes and smiled again. "How about a rain check?"

René let her go. "Okay, A rain check." He opened his front door for her, and Sarah came running out.

"Oops, I'm sorry." Grace frowned with sympathy. "I forgot about your dog."

"You go on inside and I'll walk her." René chuckled.

"Don't be long." Grace winked at him and went inside.

René ran to catch up with Sarah.

"You okay, girl?" A growl was her only response. "I'm sorry. She wanted to go to Alo's. That's on the other side of Lake Ontario." Sarah gave him two angry yips. "No, sorry. No doggie bag this time." Another growl. "Oh, stop it. I said I was sorry."

It was a beautiful summer's night and René took Sarah for a nice long walk. A full moon lit their path. The warm summer's wind gently blew through the trees. The long grass seemed to wave like the rolling waves of an ocean as he walked through it. Crickets sang and fireflies blinked their mating calls.

René sighed, as he thought of Jessie. "She would have loved a night like this."

He wouldn't have had to ask her to join him, he'd be running to keep up with her. She'd be rolling in the grass with Sarah. She'd be looking up into the sky and telling him stories about the constellations.

"Look Sarah, Hercules and Cygnus are out." René pointed.

Sarah barked happily.

"Ha-ha. Knowing Jessie, she'd say it was a man running away from a woman."

She barked again

"No, I'm not calling her. She left me. You see she hasn't called me. She's not looking back, so why should I?"

She whimpered.

"No. Now come on, Grace is waiting for me."

Sarah didn't move. René looked at his dog and crossed his arms.

"Oh, come on. What are you going to do, move out and get your own apartment?"

Sarah walked to her right and pointed.

"Mom's house?!" René rolled his eyes, and his head and shoulders dropped. "Seriously? You really dislike her that much?"

Sarah stated barking and yapping in quick succession, like she was talking.

"Is that all?" René joked, and he crossed his arms.

Sarah whined again.

"She's only going to be here for a month...or two."

Sarah walked off. René groaned, gave in, and followed his dog.

"Sarah! Alright, fine. I'll take you to Mom's tomorrow."

Chapter 24

The next day, René and Sarah arrived at Mrs. Voclain's house.

René's mother's house was a two thousand square foot craftsman style house with four beds and three baths. The blue exterior with white trim gave the home a happy, warm, and inviting look. René climbed the three steps to the house and stood on the porch. He was so proud of the house that his father had built for his mother that his chest swelled with pride. His cheerful smile faded for a moment when he rang the doorbell and remembered why he was here. A smile that returned as his mother opened the door.

"Hi mom."

"Hello René." His mother smiled at him. "Nice to see you." Then she looked at him curiously. "Why are you here?"

"Can't I just want to see my mother?" René entered the house and kissed his mother on her left cheek.

"Oh, is it my birthday." Mrs. Voclain joked. "I'm old dear. Sometimes I forget my dates."

"Ha-ha mom. Very funny." René hung up his jacket and headed into the living room.

Sarah barked happily and circled Mrs. Voclain.

"Hello Sarah, nice to see you too." Mrs. Voclain knelt and rubbed Sarah's ears.

"Can you watch Sarah for me till the end of the month?" René asked, as he looked over the family pictures on the fireplace.

"Sure, but why?" Mrs. Voclain came into the living room, with Sarah trailing behind her.

"Because Sarah doesn't like Grace." René picked up the picture of his father and smiled at it.

Sarah entered the living room, sat on her hind legs, and then Sarah growled at René.

"Oh, shut it." He told her and he put the picture back.

"And who is Grace?" Mrs. Voclain asked, as she stood between René at the fireplace, and Sarah at the couch.

"A real estate developer. Her boss is buying the island and they want to change it into an executive retreat..."

"Where will you live?" she asked with concern.

"Well, if Grace gets her way. We'll be married and living on the east side of the island with the bears." René laughed. He looked not only at his mother's wedding photo, but the wedding photos of his two brothers and their wives. His heart felt a twinge of pain as he wondered if his wedding photo would ever join them.

"I thought you had your heart set on Jessie." Mrs. Voclain reminded him purposely.

René bristled and Mrs. Voclain noticed.

"Jessie said no and then she left me." René almost growled at his mother, and he turned around to face her. "She made her choice."

Mrs. Voclain smiled warmly at her son. "If you love her, call her."

"No." René scowled.

"Why not?" Mrs. Voclain raised an eyebrow at him. "Fine, then invite Grace to dinner." Mrs. Voclain requested. She walked over to the couch and sat down.

"What? Why?"

"Because I want to meet her." Mrs. Voclain sat back against the couch and looked seriously at her son. "I want to get to know the woman who is going to marry my son."

"No, you don't and I'm not marrying her."

"Then what do you intend to do?" Mrs. Voclain asked her son bluntly.

"Nothing I can do." René looked at the floor and

then he began to pace. "I'm a park ranger and assigned to the island right now."

"Then quit."

"I don't want to quit. I like my job." René stopped pacing and sat on the arm of his mother's couch. "But, if she has her way, I could end up an international male model." René quipped.

"What?" Mrs. Voclain gave René a surprised look.

"She thinks I'm cute." René gave his mother his best "Hollywood" smile. "So, will you do it?"

"Do what?" Mrs. Voclain asked her son.

"Look after Sarah until the end of the month."

"Only if you call Jessie." She countered him.

"Mom please." René requested seriously.

"Oh alright." Mrs. Voclain gave up and nodded yes. "Of course, I will."

"Thanks mom." René stood and gave his mom a kiss on her right cheek.

Sarah happily barked her thank you and Mrs. Voclain gave Sarah's ears another good rub.

"Who's a good dog?" She asked happily.

"Not her. She's a traitor." René kidded. "Leaving your post at a time like this." René crossed his arms. "She gets nothing but bread and water."

"Oh, stop it." Mrs. Voclain snapped playfully at her son. "She has more sense than you."

When René got home that night, Grace had another surprise for him. René was stunned. Mr. Howell himself was standing in his home. Mr. Howell was an adventurous older man with wavy salty peppered hair. He was clean shaven and well-groomed from his head to his toes. Militaristic in his bearing but having an air of someone ready to play. He had thin lips, an angular jaw, and dark brown sugar eyes. His business casual attire gave him the look of an eligible bachelor ready to date.

"Look René darling," Grace grabbed René by his arm and guided him over to meet Mr. Howell. "Mr. Howell himself has come to see us."

Mr. Howell rose off René's couch and stood to greet him. "Hello, Mr. Voclain."

"Hello Mr. Howell." René extended his hand. "I'm glad to finally meet you." Then he looked over at Grace and smiled. "I've heard so much about you."

Mr. Howell shook René's hand firmly and smiled at him. "Now I can see why my Gracie wanted a month's vacation."

"Oh Mr. Howell, please." Grace blushed lightly.

"Mr. Voclain, Gracie, here is my right hand. Make sure you treat her well." Mr. Howell smiled brightly.

"Yes, sir. No Problem, sir." René agreed politely.

"Good Man. Now Grace has been showing me around your home and I like it." Mr. Howell commented, again looking around.

"So do I." René joked.

"I really am sorry to kick you out, but I have promised Gracie to build you one just like it and just as strong on the east side of the island."

"But it will be built with more rooms and more bathrooms, won't it Mr. Howell?" Grace reminded him.

"Ah yes," Mr. Howell chuckled heartily. "Room for the children. I won't forget Gracie."

"So, Mr. Voclain, if it's all the same to you. I'd like you to show me around this island tomorrow." Mr. Howell requested.

"Ah, sure."

Suddenly, there was a knock on his front door.

"Who is that?" René wondered. *Who else did this woman invite?*

"I'll get it." Grace announced happily and she bounced towards the door.

When she opened the door and saw four guys standing there.

"Can I help you gentlemen?" She asked curiously.

"Hey René, what happened to the last girl?" George asked rather loudly.

René balked. "Oh my god, I forgot it's Friday."

"So." Mr. Howell chuckled.

"It's poker night." René told him, and then he ran to the door to intercept his friends.

"What do you get a new model every six months or something?" George laughed, as Rene's friends streamed into his home. "Let me glimpse your catalog sometime."

"Shut up, you guys." René rounded them up and pushed them towards the door. "You guys will have to come back next month. I've got company today."

"No, no. Let's meet your friends." Mr. Howell called out happily to René. "Get to know my neighbors as it were."

"Alright," René ushered his friends inside, as Grace closed the door. "Guys, this is Mr. Howell, CEO of Wyoming's Wild. And this is Miss Grace O'Maille, his acquisitions and sales manager." René introduced his friends to them. "Mr. Howell, this bunch of misfits are my poker night buddies. Jack, John, George, and Lukas." Each man nodded to Mr. Howell as his name was called.

"Awright, good tae catch up wit ye." John shook Mr. Howell's hand.

"Likewise." Mr. Howell smiled. Then he turned to René. "Did you say Poker Buddies?"

"Yes, it's my turn to host this month." René explained.

"Do you mind if I join your group tonight?" Mr. Howell asked. "I haven't played a good poker game in quite a while."

"Let us discuss it." Jack told him.

The boys circled up and talked amongst themselves a bit.

"Where is Jessie?" Jack asked.

"The lass went home." John reported unhappily.

"I don't like this." George complained. "It's like he's trying to replace her."

"Have you learned nothing?" Lukas scowled at him. "Quit it."

"Ugh, I thought we were trying to decide whether or not to let Mr. Howell and his millions play poker with us." John chuckled.

The boys all broke out with smiles and turned to face Mr. Howell.

"Mr. Howell," John smiled at him. "Ye money is welcome 'ere."

Mr. Howell chuckled at them with a hearty laugh and followed them to the dining room table. "I thought it would be."

"Let's play." Lukas announced as he sat down. "Come on, René. Get the cards."

"OK." Then René turned to Grace. "Would you like to play with us?"

"No, I think I'll pass." Grace looked around the table and smiled as Mr. Howell sat down to play. "I've got some work to do on my laptop. You gentlemen have fun."

"Alright, you heard the lady." Mr. Howell smiled and placed his wallet on the table. "Pay up and let's play."

Chapter 25

Jessie now spent her days writing, reading, and researching. Since René had told her the myths, legends, and folklore of the Iroquois; she was now very interested in folklore in general. She wondered if she could weave her adventures with René into a new children's series.

She spent her nights, going to parties and visiting clubs. But somehow, these things just didn't thrill her like they used to. They were too noisy and too loud and being pregnant, she couldn't drink anyway. She had gone so far as to have her penthouse condo renovated. She wanted thicker walls with more insulation and more efficient and noise reduction windows. These days, she spent most of her evenings with Erik, or when she was alone, just looking up at the three stars that she could see from her window.

Today was a cold and rainy morning. It was sixty-five degrees, and the rain fell outside, while Erik and Jessie were warm and dry inside. Both of them sat at the little dining room table with their laptops. Erik drinking green tea and Jessie drinking water. It was at this peaceful time of the day when the phone rang. Erik looked over at Jessie. She seemed deep in thought or up to her elbows in plot. He chuckled at her, got up, and answered the phone. He was surprised to hear voices in French on the other end of the line.

"Hello?" He answered questioningly.

"Don't you hello me!" The irate French woman spoke. "Where is Jessie?!"

Erik stared at the phone like it tried to bite him. Then he shook his head and handed the phone to Jessie.

"It's for you."

Jessie didn't even look up. She just took the phone handed to her and balanced it on her shoulder as she continued typing.

"Hello."

Jessie nearly dropped the phone when the infuriated woman started yelling at her in French. Jessie scrambled to catch the phone before it hit the floor. Then she put it to her ear. Her full attention now on the caller who was yelling at her. Jessie listened and tried her best to understand what the woman was saying.

"What's wrong?" Erik asked her concerned.

"It's René's mother." Jessie informed him. "She's

yelling obscenities at me in French. That much I know." She giggled.

She stopped giggling though when she heard René's mother mention hospital and bear.

"Whoa, whoa, Slow down. My French is rusty. Who's in the hospital?"

"René is in the hospital." Mrs. Voclain informed her, angrily. "You broke his heart you...you...Femme sans cœur!"

"I didn't mean to, but I told you that I wasn't staying." Jessie answered her honestly. "What about the bear?"

"He was almost killed by a bear when some woman wanted to set up a cabin for two on the east side of the island. She was looking around for the perfect spot when they ran into a bear."

Jessie's brow was furrowed with worry and her fear and concern seeped into her voice. "Is he okay?"

"He'll be fine thank God," Mrs. Voclain's voice expressed her relief. But then she got accusatory. "He has another scar though."

"Cool, another story to tell." Jessie quipped; her worry melted at hearing that Rene' was ok.

"Pas cool!" Mrs. Voclain scolded her. "Do you know Grace O'Maille?"

"Unfortunately, yes." Jessie groaned.

"Eh bien, que. Faites Vous à ce sujet?"

"What do you mean, what am I going to do about it?" Jessie nerves tightened up. "He's a grown man. He'll figure it out."

"Do you realize that she wants to buy the island and change it into an executive retreat?" Mrs. Voclain informed her, more miffed about the situation than at Jessie.

"Yes." Jessie sighed heavily and twisted pang, like a nail, hit her chest. *That beautiful home occupied by someone who was not Rene'.*

"And?"

"And what?" Jessie snapped back to reality, and she shrugged. "What do you expect me to do about it?"

"If you hadn't left, then he wouldn't be losing his home." Mrs. Voclain accused her.

"If I had stayed, we'd both be out on the street." Jessie countered.

"If you love my son, you will fix this mess." Mrs. Voclain demanded, and she slammed the receiver down.

"What...?" Jessie began to ask, but she was cut off.

The line went dead.

"Something wrong?" Erik asked, his curiosity was piqued.

"She hung up on me." Jessie placed the phone on the table.

"What does she want you to do?"

"To save her son from a barracuda."

"What?" Erik chuckled lightly.

Jessie explained the situation to Erik. Then she watched as Erik stroked his chin in thought.

"Is there still time for a counteroffer to be placed?" Erik stared at the table.

"I don't know." Jessie shrugged. "The way she was talking, it was a done deal." Jessie sat in silence, but she watched Erik think. She knew that his mind was reasoning, plotting, and offering solutions. That was one of the things that she loved about him. He always seemed to know the answer.

"Well, If I were you, I'd call and see; and then I would start a bidding war." Erik laid out his plan for her to hear. "That will hang things up enough to delay the tear down and who knows, you may win the bid and then the Island will be yours."

"You want me to buy the island?" Jessie balked at him.

"No." Erik snickered, looking at her with bright and mischievous eyes. "Mrs. Voclain does."

Jessie frowned and she thought about it. "Maybe." Then she smiled. "All good pirates have a private island for hoarding treasure. Yeah, this Roaming Rouge needs a Northern home base."

Erik gawked at her. "What?"

But before he could ask her any more questions, the phone rang again. This time it was a fuming Italian woman.

"Hello?" Jessie answered it. She was expecting another round of ranting from René's mother.

"Don't you hello me, you...you Babylonian whore!"

"Come again?" Jessie was taken aback, and she stared at the phone. She held the receiver out and away from her ear.

"Now what?" Erik asked.

"Now, your mom's chewing me out." Jessie reported.

"What?" Erik grabbed the phone from Jessie and spoke to his mother in Italian. "No mamma. Si, mamma. But mom. NO! Ugh! Mom, mom, mom..." Erik finally gave up and handed the phone back. "She wants to talk to you."

"You mean she wants to yell at me." Jessie snickered. She took the phone back from Erik, put it on speaker, and braced herself for another tongue lashing. "Ciao."

"You...you...Delilah!"

"Delilah?" Jessie chuckled.

"Delilah?" Erik mouthed silently, as he too listened to the conversation.

"Could have been worse." Jessie whispered to him. "She could have said Jezebel." She and Erik both laughed. But Erik's mother continued berating her until Jessie finally had to ask her. "Mrs. Champlain, what am I supposed to have done?"

"You stole him from her!" Mrs. Champlain accused angrily.

"Stole who from whom?" Jessie asked, completely confused.

"CHRISTINE!"

Jessie looked at Erik. "Who's Christine?"

"My mother's choice for a wife." Erik confessed. He rolled his eyes and shook his head. "Your pediatrician, remember."

"Oh." Jessie's light came on. "And she wants a man-child no doubt." Jessie continued to laugh at him.

"This is not funny! You HARLOT!" Erik's mother ranted. "He was a good boy until he met you!"

Jessie put her hand over the speaker. "Does she know about Ms. Wightman?"

Erik shook his head. "No and don't you dare." He narrowed his eyes on her.

Jessie snickered at him. "She's still pushing you to get married and have kids?"

"We're roman catholic." Erik shrugged. "It's what we do."

"Do you like her?" Jessie asked, as she crossed her arms.

"You've met her. What do you think?"

Jessie gave him a wicked grin. "I could get used to her."

"But she's Roman Catholic like my mother." Erik leaned back in his chair. "I'd be in hell."

"You will go to hell, if you don't stop hanging out with that... that... WOMAN!"

Jessie's eyebrows both went up and she laughed silently, hiding her laugh behind her right hand.

"Erik, you need to come home and settle down." Erik's mother implored him. "Christine is a nice girl, and she will make you a very good wife. You may not love her now, but in time you will, and you will have many happy years together with your children."

"Mom," Erik butted in. "I'm happy here in New York. I have a great job. A generous employer..."

Jessie smiled and nodded to him. "Thank you."

And that set off another round of ranting from Erik's mother about Jessie.

"Is your mother first generation or second-generation Italian?" Jessie asked, as she continued listening to her rant.

"Second. Ninety percent of the time, she speaks English." Erik told her. "She only speaks Italian when she's really upset or visiting my grandparents."

"Look, Mrs. Champlain, you tell Christine to meet me at Roberto's Restaurant." Jessie suggested. "She and I will have a nice talk and we'll sort this out."

"Meet you...meet you? Over my dead body..."

"Now, now, no need to go that far, I'm sure we can come to an agreement." Jessie offered with a smirk.

"What agreement? The only agreement I will accept is YOU, OUT of the picture!"

"How about a timeshare? I get him during the day, and she can have him at night."

"Che Cosa???"

"Give me that phone." Erik joked. "Momma, calm down. She was only kidding."

Jessie just gave Erik a playful wink.

"No momma. Yes, momma. Look, just tell Christine that we want to talk to her."

But Jessie was growing tired of this endless yelling from another irate woman and took the phone back from Erik.

"Mrs. Champlain, with all due respect, sta 'zitto! And tell Christine, Roberto's Friday night at 6pm."

With that Jessie hung up the phone before Mrs. Champlain could object again.

"Sheesh, what the hell is it with these emotional women?!" Jessie shook her head, trying to clear her mind from all the drama, and threw her hands up in defeat. Jessie started to say something, but the phone rang again. She answered it harshly. "What do you want now?" She yelled in French.

"Sorry, Jessie. I don't speak French. Try English." A cheerful female voice on the other end laughed.

"Oh, sorry Sam." Jessie apologized, and her temper receded. "I've been having a weird morning."

"Well, this should make you happy. You're being given an award for best new author of a romance novel! Isn't that wonderful?!" Samantha relayed the news excitedly.

"What?" Jessie exclaimed. She couldn't believe what she was hearing. "Why?"

"That Lost in the Snow book that you turned in a two months ago. The one you wrote under the name of Layla Rahbar. That was brilliant, by the way. Not putting it under your own name." Sam told her.

"Erik!!" Jessie growled at him.

"Now, don't get mad." He told her, as he stood up and started backing away from her.

"Too late." Jessie stalked him, angrily.

"Plays and Pals was inspired but Lost in the Snow was genius. It was so...moving...and thrilling...and romantic...and heartbreaking."

"I'll break you in half." Jessie threatened. "What will happen to me if people find out that I wrote that book! I'll be ruined!"

"You'd be rich." Sam interjected over the phone.

"I'm already rich." Jessie yelled at Sam. "And respected. I'd rather be respected."

"Come on Jessie," Erik pleaded, as he dashed out of Jessie's reach and tried to keep the couch between them. "I had to send it in. That was a beautiful romance story."

"That wasn't romance!" Jessie yelled at him. "That was borderline sexual harassment!"

"It's not, if you're asking him to thrust deeper and harder." Sam laughed.

"That's it! I'm going to kill you!" Jessie jumped over the couch and ran after Erik.

Erik ran from her and that was when the doorbell rang. Erik ran for the door, opened it, and in walked Samantha McCarter. Samantha McCarter was the executive publisher of The Page Sage. She was ruthless and ambitious, but wise. She was only five foot four, but she commanded attention. She had tawny brown eyes and raven soft hair. She ran her business like the commander of an army, but she cared for the soldiers under her command. Even her black pant suits gave her the look of a general in uniform.

She walked right up to Jessie and hugged her, so that she couldn't go after Erik. As Samantha hugged her, Jessie realized something.

"Why did you call me from right outside my own door?"

Samantha stopped hugging Jessie and took off her coat. Erik took it from her and hung it up. He offered her some water, but she refused. Samantha just took Jessie by the hand and led her over to the couch and sat her down.

"First of all, I wanted to see what type of mood you were in. And given how...steamy that book was, I thought that Erik would need me to run interference for him."

"Well, you have to go home sometime." Jessie eyed Erik evilly.

"Stop threatening him." Samantha ordered. "He's the best thing that ever happened to you."

Jessie stopped ranting long enough to think about that statement. All the years that they had been together. All the times that he had edited her work, kept her on track, and reminded her of important events. All the times that he had looked after her when she was sick and kept her out of trouble and a million and one other things that he had done for her. Jessie's gruff face broke out into a soft smile.

"Yes, he is." Jessie agreed, with a grin.

"Good, I'm glad you agree." Samantha smiled at her. "Now sign this." She held up a pen.

"What's this?" Jessie took up the paper and read it.

"I'm signing Layla Rahbar."

"Why?" Jessie put the paper back down on the table. "I already work for you."

"Paperwork." Samantha answered, as she sat back. "Two, I need a second novel. That will establish you as a totally separate entity and your precious reputation will be spared."

"Oh, hell no!" Jessie protested, as she sat back, and her arms folded. "I'm not writing another book. I don't do romance."

"Well, Layla Rahbar does." Samantha giggled at her. "What's the matter Jessie, out of material? You could always go back to Canada for a visit."

"Bite me!" Jessie growled at her.

"Wow, she is in a bad mood today." Samantha started with surprise. "She's never swore at me before."

"Be lucky it wasn't in French." Erik teased, standing a safe distance away from Jessie.

"What?"

"René's mother chewed her out and then my mother chewed her out." Erik explained. "All in French and Italian. And now, she must come and have dinner with Christine, my mother's choice for a wife."

"You're engaged?" Samantha asked, with excitement.

"No." But then Erik thought about it. "Not exactly."

"Do you want to be?" Samantha asked him from the couch. She motioned for him to come and sit down beside her. Samantha scooted over, forcing Jessie to scoot over and make room for them. "Not all arranged marriages are...bad ones, because you both are going into the marriage with your eyes wide open, so to speak."

Samantha patted Erik's hand as she talked to him. Jessie got annoyed at being ignored and went back to her laptop at the dinner table.

"Do you know the girl?" Samantha inquired. "Have you met her?"

"Yes." Erik nodded and leaned back. "Christine's a good woman and a pediatrician."

"Then why haven't you married before now?"

"We practically grew up together. We're not related or anything, but still... And then there is the fact that she is a doctor. Right now, our careers keep us busy. We just don't have the time."

"Aren't you and Jessie married?" Samantha snickered.

This caused both Jessie and Erik to look at her in shock. "What?" They asked.

"You've been together for fifteen years. That's

eight years longer than necessary." Samantha told them, highly pleased with herself.

"You're forgetting one thing." Jessie told her.

"What?" Samantha asked, looking over at Jessie.

"Common law marriage isn't recognized in New York." Erik sighed, with a smirk. "I'm not entitled to any of her money."

"Only twenty percent." Jessie snickered.

"That still makes him a millionaire." Samantha reminded him. "More than enough to get married on."

"Well, it would get my mother off my back." Erik considered. "A marriage of convenience in name only. Could work."

"You'd have to move out." Jessie told him, as she typed away on her laptop.

"Are you firing me?" Erik panicked and looked over at her.

"No, but do you think your mother would let you continue living here with this Babylonian whore once you're married?" Jessie snickered, as Mrs. Champlain's words came back to haunt her.

"What?" Samantha asked, as shocked amusement colored her face.

"Like I said, my mother was screaming at her this morning." Erik explained.

"In Italian." Jessie added, with an amused grin. "Sheesh, with René's mother yelling at me in French and Erik's mother yelling at me in Italian, all I need is Lukas' mother yelling at me in German, and I'd need an U.N. Arbiter to straighten out this mess."

"Who's Lukas?" Erik asked, a bit confused himself.

"Look, just sign these papers." Samantha collected them from the table and brought them to Jessie for her to sign. "I'll..."

"Fine." Jessie told her with a sideways glance. Then she leaned forward took the paper and signed her name.

"Good, good, good. Now I can make arrangements." Samantha took the papers back. "Now about your second book..."

"Yeah, yeah. I'll get on it." Jessie relented. "I just got an idea for a plot, and I was just jotting down some notes."

"That's great! Let's the three of us have dinner tonight and we'll discuss how this is to go." Samantha stood up and started to leave. Erik went to get her coat. However, Samantha turned and asked Jessie. "Oh, I almost forgot to ask. Why am

I sending two percent of your pay this month to a cop in Canada named Tom?"

"I lost a bet." Jessie simply said and she kept typing.

Samantha looked at Erik, but he just shrugged at her. Then Erik remembered something.

"Jessie, don't you have a favor to ask of Samantha?"

"I do?" Jessie looked up from her laptop.

"You can have her bid on the island for you, if you don't want René to know that you're helping him."

Jessie's eyebrows shot up and then she smiled. "I take back what I said about you. You're a genius."

"I know." Erik smirked and stuck out his chest with pride.

So, Jessie explained her situation to Samantha and begged for her help. Samantha said that she'd investigate it for her, but she wanted a second book as steamy as the first.

"Fine. I'll do my best."

"Good. Then I'll buy the island for you if I can." Samantha promised.

"It could be their honeymoon present." Erik laughed at Jessie.

"Erik, I will kill you and bury you on that island." Jessie threatened him.

Samantha just chuckled at their banter as she donned her coat. Erik opened the door for her, and Samantha left to go and buy an island.

Chapter 26

New York in July is beautiful. Especially in central park. Warm sunny days, cool breezes, temperatures in the seventies. Dog walkers, joggers, and just plain out and abouters were all outside. But Jessie was now six months pregnant and stayed indoors. Today she was working on her children's adventure novel when the phone rang. Jessie instinctively looked for Erik, but he wasn't home. Jessie got up, after a bit of effort, and answered the phone.

"Hello? Mrs. Voclain?" Jessie was surprised to hear her voice.

"What are you doing to stop this?" The French matron inquired sternly.

"I'm working on it." Jessie assured her, although she really didn't know what Samantha was doing.

"Work harder." Mrs. Voclain demanded. "They are going to break ground in late July."

Jessie rolled her eyes. "I'm not a magician, you know."

"No, you're a beaver scout." Mrs. Voclain reminded her with a chuckled in her voice. "Do something Civic."

"Scouts? Scouts. Hm." Jessie thought about it and then an idea hit her. "Don't worry, Mrs. Voclain. I think I have an idea." Jessie assured her.

"Good. I'll tell René."

"I wouldn't." Jessie warned her. "My idea may not work. I'll talk to you later."

"Goodbye Jessie."

"Goodbye Mrs. Voclain." Jessie smiled, as she remembered Mrs. Voclain motherly visage and her wonderful pancake breakfast. Then Jessie called one of her longtime friends. "Angela."

"Yes." Angela answered, and she shuffled the papers on her desk into a folder. "Oh, hello Jessie. What's up?"

"I have a favor to ask."

"Make it quick, I'm in the middle of planning an event." Angela straightened up her desk a little to give it a neat and tidy appearance. "The client should be arriving soon."

"Are you still friends with Darrin the Scout Master and help play den mother to the girl scouts during the summer months?"

"Yes, if they are going somewhere nice, like Spain." Angela giggled. "Why?"

"Can you call Darrin and get them to hold their

jamboree in Ontario, Canada?" Jessie requested and paused her typing to talk to her friend.

"Canada?" Angela looked at the phone like it was a three headed monster. "Why Canada?"

"They can earn their nature, community, adventure, outdoor art badges and I'm sure quite a bit more. There's lots to do at the Thousand Island campgrounds."

Angela took a moment to consider Jessie's request. "Hm, I guess I can suggest it to him."

"Tell you what, make it happen and I'll let you give me a makeover sometime." *I'm going to regret that.*

"This must be important." Angela chuckled, immediately thinking about all the styles that she wanted to try on Jessie. "You'd told me that you'd rather die."

"I did not." Jessie jested.

"Oh, yes you did." Angela looked up and she spied her clients coming. Angela's clients entered the room and sat down in the seats opposite of her desk. "I've got to go Jessie. My clients have arrived."

"OK, thanks for your help, Angela. Bye." Jessie hung up the phone and went back to writing her children's book.

After the client meeting, Angela remembered her promised and decided to call her friend Darrin before she forgot. So, Angela called Darrin. Darrin called Miguel in South America, and Miguel called Pamela in Canada. And in mid-July, René and Grace got a jarring wake up call. A bugle's call blared loudly in the fresh morning air. The trumpet's notes were clear, loud, and strong.

"OH, my lord, what is that noise?!" Grace tired on her robe and ran to find René.

René was in his room, standing at his window, and looking out to see his island covered in scout tents.

"René, what in the hell is going on?! What is that noise?!" Grace questioned him, as she joined him at the window.

"That is called reveille." René explained. "It's how the military and the scouts rouse their troops."

"Troops?" Grace questioned. Her mind began to dash. "Are we being invaded?"

"Looks like it." René pointed out the window. "Those tents belong to the boy scouts of Mexico. Those tents over there belong to the boy and girl scouts of England, France, and Germany, and those tents way over there are the Americans."

Grace's eyes grew wide as she looked out and saw hundreds of scout tents. "They can't stay here!"

"Why not?" Rene' looked over at her.

"Because I've got diggers and over levelers coming this week to start building out the foundations for our executive resort cabins." Grace told him, and she made her way over to his phone on the dresser. "May I use your phone?"

"Yes." Rene' turned and went back to looking out the window. "Guess your levelers will have to reschedule."

"No, I was here first." Grace insisted with an angry glare. "They'll just have to find somewhere else to camp."

"Not likely." Rene' scoffed. "Scouts usually get first consideration."

"Why didn't you tell me about this." She asked him, as she dialed. "I could have scheduled them somewhere else."

"Like where?" René teased her.

"Iceland! They could visit Santa's Workshop!" Grace practically growled at him.

René couldn't help but smile. *Thank God the Calvary is here.* He chuckled to himself.

"Guess I'm going to have to start work early

today." He said, as he turned from the window. He entered his closet, pulled out his scout uniform, and began to get dressed.

"Where are you going?" Grace's panicked voice asked, as she spied him putting on his scout uniform.

"I'm a tour guide and forest ranger. It's my job to greet them and show them around. Some of them may even be here to earn their badges. I'll probably be getting home late this month." He explained and buttoned up his shirt.

"They're here for a month?!" Grace exclaimed with disbelief.

"Yeah, sometimes two." Rene' tried his best not to smile, he just sat on the edge of his bed and but on his boots.

"No, No, NO! This simply cannot happen." Grace started to pace as the call that she was making was connected. "Calm down Grace and think."

"I'll see you later tonight." René called out to her, as he stood up and headed towards the door.

"Mr. Howell, I'm sorry to wake you this early, but we have a problem." Grace looked out the window again as she spoke to him. "I've been invaded by the International boy and girl scouts. They've covered the island with their tents. The work crews won't be able to get in here."

René shook his head at her and left.

It was very late in the evening before René returned. Grace was waiting for him on his couch, and she rose to greet him.

"Where have you been?" she asked pointedly.

"Hiking, canoeing, and archery." René told her succinctly and moved towards the kitchen.

"Those...those..."

"Scouts." Offered René, trying to fend off a more colorful expletive.

"Children." She growled at him. "Have completely ruined my plans. Mr. Howell is a little miffed, but he was a scout himself when he was young, and he said that he is willing to wait. He's even sending one of his sales reps up here to see if the scouts need any gear."

"I doubt it." René chuckled and he washed his hands. "They're supposed to be ready for anything."

"Why are they here? Google says they were supposed to be in South America this year." Grace checked her phone.

"Did Google also say that South America is experiencing civil unrest right now. Or that the

USA and Italy are underwater due to severe flooding. Or that all of Australia is on fire. Canada is the only safe place this year." Rene' explained, as he opened the fridge, pulled out pork chops, and then some vegetables.

"I had to do some serious rescheduling and now they won't be able to start breaking ground until next year." Grace pinched her nose in frustration, as she complained to René.

René just ignored her and prepared to make dinner.

"How long do these scouts plan on staying?" Grace asked him, as she watched him prepare for dinner.

"Three months."

"Three months!"

"Yes, a jamboree is usually about 50,000 strong. There are scouts camping on every island in the thousand islands." René explained.

"Who authorized this?" Just then, Grace's phone rang. "We'll talk about this later. I must take this call, it's Mr. Howell. Good evening, sir."

René shrugged and continued making dinner.

Later that night, as they ate a candle lit dinner,

René noticed Grace's worried brow and pencil thin frown.

"What's wrong? You really don't look happy." René commented, as he filled her wine glass.

"One, is the heat." She told him pointedly.

"The windows are open." René reminded her and pointed to his right.

"That's just more hot air blowing around." She complained and took a sip of her wine. Then she sighed deeply. "Then there is the singing."

René chuckled. "They have assured me that lights out is at 9PM. They promised to be quiet." René cut up his pork chops and took a bite. "That can't be it. What's really bothering you?"

"Three, there's another buyer."

"What?" René dropped his fork. "Sorry. What do you mean there's another buyer? I thought that this was a done deal."

"Yes, so did I." Grace sighed again. "But it seems that someone has caught wind of our endeavors, decided that it was a good idea, and now has put in their own bid. My boss is in a bidding war, and our plans are on hold until full rights can be obtained."

"Who is the second bidder?" René asked.

"We don't know. All we could find out is that it's an overseas buyer." Grace folded her hands and rested her chin upon them. She sighed again and just stared at her food.

René just watched her sulk, and his heart went out to her. *Yeah, she's pushy and driven, but she is doing her best.* "Is there anything that I can do for you?" he asked her softly.

Grace gave him a weak smile. "No. It's a waiting game now. With Mr. Howell's permission, I put in a higher bid this morning. Now we wait to see if they counter."

Chapter 27

Jessie was waiting for Christine at Roberto's. She was sitting in the lobby enjoying their fish tank full of exotic fishes. She was lost in thought and remembering a time when she and René went fishing. She remembered with amused glee hooking a sturgeon. One so big, that it pulled their canoe into deeper waters. She started to laugh to herself as she remembered René shouting at her to let it go. It was such an adrenaline rush. She remembered the canoe being struck twice by something incredibly large and then they were tossed into the lake as the boat overturned.

"That was a fun fishing trip." Jessie told herself.

Suddenly, a strong slap across her left cheek brought Jessie screaming out of her daydreams and back into the real world.

"What the Hell?!" Jessie jumped to her feet and came face to face with Christine's mother, and apparently, she was angry with her. "Who are you?" Jessie asked perplexed.

"I'm sorry." Christine apologized humbly. "Mother, calm down. That was uncalled for. You don't even know this woman."

"I don't want to know this woman." The Italian woman glared at Jessie.

Jessie looked past the angry Italian woman and looked at Christine. Christine was a tall woman, but only compared to her mother who stood a few inches shorter than her. Christine was a petite pear of a woman. She had light brown hair and soft brown eyes. Small hips, that made Jessie giggle as she thought of Noel, and sensible shoes. Christine had the look of a doe about her.

Jessie gave a small inward smile. *That gentle demeanor must make for a great bed-side manner with children.*

"Don't apologize to this...this..." The short angry woman yelled at Jessie.

"We're in a restaurant." Jessie reminded the angry woman, with a mocking grin.

"Woman!"

Jessie just chuckled at her. "Nice to see you too, Mrs. ..."

"This is my mother." Christine introduced Jessie to her. "Mrs. Rosa Gentil."

"Gentil?" Jessie laughed, as she rubbed her cheek. "The hell she is." Rosa Gentil was a medium height heavyset woman, with greying black hair, and brown eyes. Jessie couldn't help but laugh. This gentle rose of an Italian woman was giving her the evil eye and yelling at her, in the middle of a restaurant. Jessie turned to Christine. "She's not having dinner with us, is she?"

"No," Mrs. Gentil said loudly. "I would not break bread with the likes of you."

"OK, fine." Jessie shrugged at Mrs. Gentil. "Buona Sera la Signora Gentil." Jessie hoped that she would take the hint.

"Buona Notte." Mrs. Gentil threw back and she stormed out of the restaurant.

Jessie and Christine just watched her leave. Again, Jessie chuckled and rubbed her cheek. "Well, that was interesting."

Christine turned to face Jessie. "I'm so sorry about that." Christine blushed and lowered her gaze. "She's just so..."

"Overprotective, no doubt." Jessie smiled at her. "No worries. People like her make life interesting."

"You mean troublesome." Christine frown.

Just then, Roberto of Roberto's Restaurant came and asked Jessie if everything was alright.

"Are you OK?" Roberto asked, his face full of concern and his brow furrowed with worry.

"Oh, sure." Jessie smiled and waved off his fretfulness. "My cheek hurts though." Jessie chuckled and she rubbed the pain away some more.

"May I ask what that was all about?" Roberto picked up menus for them from the hostess stand.

"Oh, some mothers can be as bad as angry fathers with shotguns, when their children are dating people that they do not approve of."

Roberto gave Jessie a queer look and then pointed to her, Christine, and back to her. "You and Miss Christine?"

Christine blushed bright red at that suggestion and her back stiffened. "No."

Jessie just broke out laughing and doubled over with giggles.

"I am sorry. I just assumed." Roberto apologized over and over. "I've never seen you with anyone, but Erik and he works for you. Then you tell me a story of an angry mothers while standing here with this lovely young woman." Roberto was now flustered with embarrassment and stumbled over his words, as Jessie kept laughing at him. "What was I to think? I am sorry if I embarrassed you Miss." Roberto apologized to Christine.

"Jessie." Christine called to her lightly. "Jessie, please stop laughing. People are staring at us already."

Jessie wiped the tears from her eyes as she looked around. Then she patted Roberto's back. "That's why I like you, Roberto. You always fill me with great ideas." Jessie took a deep breath and got serious. "Your best table please, Roberto. Miss Christine and I need sustenance and conversation."

Roberto smiled at her. "Then right this way please, Miss Tyler. I will give you a private table."

"Not to private." Jessie joked. "Or people will wonder what we're doing in there."

Christine rolled her eyes at Jessie's suggestive jib and quickly hurried to sit down at the table that Roberto showed them.

At that moment, Jillane walked up to them. "Hello Jessica, causing trouble again, are you?" Jillian smiled brightly at her.

"Who me?" Jessie rested a hand to her chest, shook her head, and tried to look innocent. "Nah."

"That's too bad," Jillane frowned a bit. "My column has been a little dry lately. Are you gaining weight?"

"You have a column?" Christine asked. She looked at Jillane with great interest.

"I'm sorry," Jessie apologized to Christine. "Christine, this is Roberto of Roberto's Restaurant. He's a good friend and an even better chef."

"Buena Noches, Senorita." Roberto bowed to her. "You ladies have a good meal." Roberto smiled, excused himself, and then left.

"And this is Jillane Stevenson of the Daily Life. She's the best metropolitan reporter on all things eclectic."

"Hello, Christine." Jillane reached out to shake her hand. "I am very pleased to meet you." Then she looked at Jessie. "May I ask, and I have to," Jillane giggled. "Why did that woman slap you at the door?"

"You saw that?" Jessie flinched. She really didn't want this to be in the About Town section of tomorrow's paper. *Famed author slapped by angry mother of the bride.* Jessie groaned and tried to think of what to tell her. "It was nothing."

Jillane's eyes sparkled with mischief. "Didn't look like nothing."

"Jillane." Jessie growled a warning at her.

"OK OK." Jillane shrugged and turned to leave. "I'll just go and chat up Roberto."

"Oh, for the love of..." Jessie griped. "It was nothing."

"Me thinks the lady doth protest too much." Jillane laughed at her.

Jessie rolled her eyes and gave up. "She was angry that I'm having dinner with Christine."

"And that matters because." Jillane questioned, with a quizzical look on her face.

"She wants her having dinner with Eric." Jessie explained. *Hopefully, she'll buy this explanation and I can sit down and eat in peace.*

"Oh." Jillane gave Jessie a mischievous giggle, a playful wink, and walked away.

Jessie watched her leave. *And she's still going to chat up Roberto. I better not be reading about this tomorrow.* Jessie shook her head and picked up her menu. "I'm surrounded by nuts."

"Does that include me?" Christine asked her softly, from behind her menu.

Jessie looked up from her menu and stared at her like she had just appeared out of thin air.

"I'm sorry." Jessie apologized. "I forgot about you."

"Yes. I seem to have that effect on people." Christine looked the menu over. Roberto's was an Old-World Spanish Restaurant and its dishes ranged from traditional to exotic.

"Don't tell me, they've been planning your wedding since you and René were born." Jessie surmised.

"Yes." Christine smiled lightly. "We were betrothed right after we were christened."

"Wow, a world wind romance you two." Jessie chuckled. "So, let me ask you, like I asked Erik." Jessie put down her menu and looked at Christine. "Do you want to marry him?"

"Yes...maybe." Christine hesitated, but then corrected herself. "In my own time. Please ignore my mother. I try to."

Jessie sighed heavily. *This...mouse is supposed to be my new doctor? I think I prefer John, the vet. In fact, I know I do. But this baby needs a real doctor, and she is René's friend.* "Look, who you and Erik date is none of my business. Whether or not you two decide to get married is none of my business. And if I were to act as his "wingman", I'd tell you all the great things about him, encourage you to marry him, and be happy for you."

"Why do I feel a but coming on?" Christine asked, and she gave Jessie her full attention.

"I need him."

"Are you going to marry him?" Christine was taken aback and her face now serious.

"What? No." Jessie waved her off. "We just best friends. We're more brother and sister, than friends with benefits. You have nothing to worry about. I'm not after your man."

"Well, that's good to hear." Christine gave her a small chuckle.

The waiter brought them silverware, filled their glasses with fresh water, and then asked them what they wanted to drink.

"Fresh squeezed Lemonade, if you please." Jessie requested of him.

"Of course. And for you Miss?"

Christine took up the menu and looked the drink list over. There was just so much to choose from. Juices, teas, sodas, and liquors.

"Hm, I can't decide." Christine confessed. "They all sound so delicious."

"Take your time." Jessie told her. She sat back, rested her arms on the back of the booth, and relaxed. "We have all night."

"Oh, this looks good." Christine smiled brightly. "A strawberry and raspberry mojito."

"But Miss, that is..." the waiter began.

"An enjoyable choice. I love those." Jessie interrupted him, with a chuckle. "Vamos, vamos, the senoritas are sediento."

The waiter nodded his understanding and then left.

"Now Miss Tyler..." Christine began seriously, and she folded her hands in her lap. "Enough about Erik and me. Erik tells me that you need a doctor."

"Not so loud." Jessie motioned for her to lower her voice. "I don't want the world to know."

Christine moved one of her wayward strands of hair out of her face and smiled at Jessie. "Jessie, you are in your second trimester, I'm surprised that no one's guessed yet."

"Ugh, my second trimester." Jessie put her arms down and slowly rubbed her belly with her left hand. "Just one more to go. Luckily for me, people just think that I'm getting fat."

"Have you been taking the vitamins that I prescribed for you?" Christine chuckled at Jessie's summation.

"Yes, but I'm all out now." Jessie leaned back and readjusted her seat. "I've been meaning to come in and get another prescription, but I've been busy."

Christine rummaged through her purse and pulled out a prescription pad. "You need to make more appointments. You can't keep avoiding the issue." She handed Jessie her prescription. "I'll glad you made this dinner call, but we really should be doing this at my office."

Jessie took the piece of paper, sat back, and

chuckled. "Yeah, I know. Erik keeps nagging me about it. And this dinner was supposed to be about you and him. Not me and you."

The waiter showed up with the drinks and passed them out. "Lemonade, freshly squeezed for Miss Tyler. And a strawberry and raspberry mojito for Miss…"

"Mrs. Champlain." Jessie gave a wicked grin.

Christine's eyebrows shot up. "Gentil." She corrected Jessie.

"Of course," Jessie quipped. "My mistake. Miss Gentil." Jessie introduced her to the waiter.

"Miss Gentil," The waiter smiled and set her drink down. "Please enjoy your drinks."

"Thank you." Christine smiled back at the waiter. He left and Christine spoke to Jessie. "My mother was right about you. You're a very bad person." Christine jested.

"And about to get worse." Jessie grinned. "How's your drink?"

Christine took a long sip and then began to sputter and cough. "What is that?" She put the drink down and looked at it. The brightly colored drink looked harmless but had the back bite of a snake.

"A mojito." Jessie explained and took a sip of her

Lemonade. "It has strawberries, raspberries, limes, mint leaves, club soda, and..."

"And?" Christine keenly waited for the next ingredient. "And what?"

"Rum." Jessie said, with a wicked grin.

"Rum?!" Christine blanched and then looked at the drink like it was an eel with three heads.

"I take it that you've never had a drink before?"

"No." Christine looked at the drink and set it aside. "I'm a doctor."

Jessie laughed at her. "Damn it, Jim. I've a doctor not a drunk."

Christine rolled her eyes and wrinkled her nose at Jessie. And then got serious again. "Have you felt the baby move? Have you had any contractions? How are you sleeping?"

"Yes. No, I don't think so, and I think this kid is going to be a night owl." Jessie sipped her lemonade and her eyebrows shot up in surprise. "This lemonade is really good."

"How have you been feeling mentally and emotionally?" Christine asked.

"Stressed out."

Christine narrowed her eyes on Jessie. "Why? Stress is not good for you or the baby."

"I'm a writer. I have deadlines and interviews."

Jessie reminded her and took another sip of her drink.

Christine looked up at her. "Stop."

"What do you mean stop?" Jessie bristled and asked her point blank.

"I mean stop writing." Christine laid it our plainly for her. "Stop doing interviews. Stop stressing out about work. Calm women have calm children. Do you want your kid anxious and hyperactive?"

Jessie sat there and thought about it. For fifteen whole minutes, she said nothing, as she thought about it. Christine didn't push her, and she didn't say a word. She just waited. Jessie took another sip of her lemonade and finally answered her.

"OK, fine."

"You should take a vacation." Christine sipped her mojito. "You need complete rest."

Jessie shot straight up. "I'm not going back to Canada." she insisted.

"I didn't say Canada. Go where you like." Christine questioned her and she put her drink down. "Why don't you like Canada? What's in Canada?"

Jessie looked away and her temperature rose. "Nothing." She lied.

Christine then took out her phone, brought up

her hospital's app, and begin making appointments in it for Jessie.

Jessie noticed. "May I ask what you're doing?"

"I'm making appointments for you at the lab. Get bloodwork and a urine test." Christine advised. Jessie watched her as she continued to scroll through the lists. "Have you started taking Lamaze or infant CPR classes?"

"What? No?" Jessie's whole body stiffened up at the mire suggestion of it.

Christine sighed heavily. "You need to stop worrying about your reputation and start learning how to properly take care of yourself and your baby. The Lamaze classes will prepare you for childbirth."

"Ugh, I'm going to kill Rene' for this." Jessie mumbled.

"Who's René?" Christine stopped scrolling through her phone and now looked at Jessie.

"A guy I met last winter while on vacation in Canada." Jessie confessed.

"Oh?" Christine was about to resume scrolling through her phone when she remembered something. "Wait, I thought you were missing. Your publisher offered a reward and everything. But you were just on vacation? Did you go AWOL or something?"

"Long story short, I got lost in a blizzard." Jessie chuckled with fond remembrance.

"I guess you were, if you ended up in Canada." Christine took another sip of her mojito. "Well, back to business. I wonder if Erik will...?"

"If Erik will what?" He asked, now standing before them.

"Marry me?" quipped Jessie, now sniggering to herself.

Christine rolled her eyes at Jessie, but then looked up at Erik. "Hello Erik? Nice to see you again." Then she pointed at Jessie. "Are you sure she's ready to be a mother? She's a bit childish."

"Takes one to know one." Erik chuckled and he sat down next to Christine.

"What are you doing here?" Jessie asked. She was a bit shocked too. "We haven't even had dinner yet."

Erik ignored Jessies question and looked at what Christine was drinking. "That looks good. May I?" Christine nodded and Erik picked up her glass. He took a sip, and his eye flew open. "I love these. These are delicious."

"That's what she said." Christine waved a hand towards Jessie.

Jessie just broke up laughing again. "So, the doctor does have jokes."

"What?" Christine asked

"Never mind her." Erik put her drink down, motioned for the waiter, and ordered one of his own. Then he looked at Jessie. "Guess our mothers were right. I leave you alone with her for one night and she's drinking rum."

Jessie just continued chortling. "Is that why you're here?"

"Yes. I'm at home minding my own business when there is this thunderous banging at our door. It's our mothers." Erik looked at Christine.

"Our mothers?" Christiane sighed and rolled her eyes. "What did they want now?"

"For me to come down here and rescue you from her evil clutches." Erik joked, and he put an arm around Christine.

Now Jessie was holding her stomach and tears were rolling down her face. "Stop making me laugh."

The waiter showed up with Erik's drink and then he asked them if they were ready to order. However, when he saw Jessie snickering to herself and wiping tears from her eyes, she asked, "Is she ok? Do you need more time?"

"No, we're fine." Erik assured him with a warm smile. "Jessie is just being Jessie. Her imagination runs away from her every day, and it takes her hours to catch it again."

"Jessie!" Christine scolded her. "Get a hold of yourself."

Jessie stopped laughing and snickering and settled down. She cleared her throat, picked up her menu and Erik looked at Christine, as if seeing her for the very first time.

"That's the first time, I've ever heard you raise your voice...to anyone." Erik smiled at her. "Hello, my name is Erik. Erik Champlain."

"Look just because I don't yell at people..." Christine sipped her mojito, and then she asked Erik. "Why haven't you been making Jessie to go to her appointments or take Lamaze classes?"

"Ugh," Erik's shoulders dropped. "Because she's being childish."

"I am not." Jessie objected and sat in a huff.

"You are too. This is your second appointment with Christine and we're at dinner." Erik scolded her with a scouring look.

"Hey even doctors need to eat." Jessie joked.

"See what I have to put up with." Erik griped.

"Do you mind lowering your voice." Jessie hushed

him. "Jillane is here." Jessie now looked around the restaurant and wondered where she had gone. "I don't need to end up in the style section."

"Well, I can do house calls, but I charge double." Christine held her hand up to the waiter to refill her glass.

"Charge her then, she can afford it, and then she can keep her precious reputation." Erik smirked at Jessie.

"Again, you Erik are no gentleman." Jessie pointed a finger at him.

"No, he's your warden. Erik for the next three months, she's off duty. No more writing, interviews, late nights, or anything. I want her to relax and concentrate on the baby. I've ordered lab tests, and ultrasounds. Make sure she keeps her appointments and get her enrolled in Lamaze classes."

"Warden? You're imprisoning me?" Jessie asked, with annoyance in her voice.

"If you really want to punish her, we can offer her up to our mothers." Erik laughed. "They'll get her ready."

Christine broke out into a snorted laugh and covered her mouth with her hand. "Erik, what are you trying to do. Kill her?"

"From being marooned, to imprisonment, and now banishment? I hate you two." Jessie threw her arms up in defeat and then crossed them in a brooding manner.

Just then, their dinner arrived. Roberto and three of his waiters brought their meals to the table and set them down before them. Roberto smiled at them and said,

"Buen Provecho!"

Immediately, everyone cheered up. The food looked elegant and smelled heavily. Jessie's mouth began to water, and she felt the baby kick.

Wait your turn. Its coming. Jessie picked up her fork and began to eat.

Erik and Christine watched Jessie enjoy her meal, they smiled at her, and then they dug into their meals. The rest of the night Erik and Christine spoke of the future. Jessie only listened and would occasionally interject a joke or some sort of short story of adventure.

"If you really want to entertain her." Erik teased Jessie. "Tell her about Rene."

"No." Jessie blushed and got quiet.

"Now I'm curious." Christine finished her mojito. "What happened?"

Jillane had finished talking to Roberto and the waiter. She now sat at her own table, enjoying a great meal, and taking occasional glances at Jessie's table. Their faces were happy, but Jessie's seemed to be glowing.

"Something's up with her." She mused. "But I'm not sure what." Then she smiled to herself. "Maybe, I should find out."

Chapter 28

Nine months came and went, and Jessie stayed holed up in their apartment. When her second book to Lost in the Snow came out. Cabin Fever was a bigger success than her first book. There were new fantasy characters, a love triangle, angry in-laws, and a world war brewing between reality and fantasy that threatened to tear them apart. And because of the real war raging between the environmentalists and the corporations in the New York headlines, no one cared that Jessie was in the hospital about to deliver her baby on the autumn equinox of September the 24th.

The room was bright white, with clinical instruments everywhere. The smell of lemon pine sol invaded Jessie's nose and she wondered who had used the room before her and how long ago. The sound of the electrocardiograph measuring her heart rate, the sounds of human movement and the shuffling of feet, and the voices of her attendants were only some of the sounds that she could hear. She also heard codes being given over the loudspeakers while wheelchairs, gurneys, and hospital carts rolled down the hall.

"Son of a bitch!"

Jessie was in the worst amount of pain that she had ever experienced in her life. Not even the most violent episode of constipation felt like this. She was in a spread-eagle position with a doctor and two nurses buzzing around her. The doctor was in the middle of delivering her baby, while the nurses monitored her vital signs, relayed valuable information to the doctor, and informed Jessie of her progress. Erik and Christine, both attended her, by holding her hands and relaying instructions to her.

"Breathe, Jessie, Breathe." Christine would try to soothe her. "Remember your lamaze lessons."

"Christine," Erik complained. He tried peeling Jessie's hand off his, but she held him tightly. "When did she get this strong? She's crushing the bones in my hand. I'll never type again."

"I'm going to murder René for this." Jessie vowed angrily, in between breaths.

"Forget him, Jessie. Just concentrate on pushing." Christine instructed her.

"Come now Miss Tyler, just one more push and we'll have him." The doctor instructed her.

Jessie gritted her teeth and pushed hard. By the expression of strain on her face you would have thought that she was about to explode. But soon the precious sounds of a baby's cry told her that she could relax, and she collapsed upon the bed. Relief, complete and utter relief, drained through her entire body. Her muscles relaxed and the pain in her lower regions were now outmatched by the pain in her head, neck, and shoulders.

"Thank god," Erik commented with a great sigh of relief, as Jessie finally let go of his hand. "Can I get an x-ray?" He quipped to one of the female nurses, as she checked on Jessie's IV drip.

The nurse just smiled at him and moved on to do her business. Christine just looked at him from across Jessie's bed.

"Quit being a baby. You'll be fine." She chuckled at him. "I just hope you don't act this way when it's our turn?"

"Our turn?" Erik blanched. "You want one?"

"Our mothers expect one." Christine gently placed Jessie's hand across her chest and patted her on the shoulder. "Good work Jessie. You can relax now."

"I never want to do that again." Jessie griped, as she lay there breathing in and out and trying to calm down.

"Let them get their own." Erik scoffed at Christine.

"They had us remember." Christine quipped with a grin.

"Remind me to tell my mom that she's my hero." Erik laughed.

"It's a boy." The doctor announced and he cut the umbilical cord.

The nurse took the child and cleaned him up. Then she wrapped him in a warm blanket and handed him to Jessie.

"Congratulations, Miss Tyler." She smiled at her.

Jessie took her son and held him close. "Hello, you." She smiled.

Erik leaned in close and looked at him. The little boy was light olive skinned, had a little tuft of brown hair, and had brown eyes.

"So that's what René looks like." Erik quipped with an immense grin.

Jessie held him up and looked at him in the light. "Yeah, He does, doesn't he?"

"He's so cute." Christine gushed happily. "What are you going to name him?"

"I'm not going to. His father is." Jessie told them. "Erik, you and Christine prepare for a trip to Canada."

"Me too?" Christine asked, with great surprise.

"Ever been?" Jessie asked her, as she rocked her son.

"No."

"Then, now's the time." Jessie declared.

"Well, I guess I can take a little time off." Christine put a hand to her chin and thought about it.

"Don't worry." Erik told her, as he kissed Jessie's forehead. "I'll take care of everything." And with that he and Christine prepared to leave the room. "Can't have you sneaking across the border like you did last time."

As Jessie lay there resting, one of the nurses took the baby's vitals, weighed him, and filled out his birth certificate. The other one cleaned Jessie up and then cleaned up the room too. Jessie just lay there listening to the heart monitor's beep and she thought about René.

"I hope you're ready, elf boy. You are about to get exactly what you asked for." *It's time to go home.*

Chapter 29

Two months later, after work schedules and passports were finally worked out. Jessie returned to Canada.

It was eleven O'clock at night when Jessie returned to René's home in the blue mountains. Jessie, Erik, and Christine got out of the car and Jessie carried her son up to the house. Christine turned aside when she noticed that there was a beautiful garden growing just beside the house.

"What a lovely garden." She commented.

Jessie looked and smiled softly. "He's been taking care of it."

"Did you plant that?" Erik asked, a little surprised.

"Yes."

"You can't cook, but you have a green thumb." He joked.

"You know, you're as bad as he is." Jessie gave him a mean look.

"Well, at least our kitchen still stands." Erik laughed.

"Do you want to walk home?" Jessie asked, mockingly. "Come on."

Jessie handed Christine her baby and she knelt to pick the lock on René's door.

"Writer by day. Sneak thief by night." Erik joked.

"Shush you." Jessie snickered quietly.

Jessie easily got the front door open. She opened it wide and let Christine and Erik enter first. Then she entered the room. It was like...well it was like coming home. The house looked the same. Still strong and sturdy, neat and well kept. Jessie took a deep breath and let it out slowly. It smelled like fir and cedar, not car exhausts and sewer lines. Jessie listened and relished the silence. Not a soul to be heard, except the ones that she had brought with her.

Sarah heard Jessie and came to the door to greet her. She was excited to see her again and began to paw at Jessie. Jessie shushed her and gave her a big hug.

"Hello, girl. How are you? Did you miss me? Have you been looking after your boy for me?" Jessie asked in a hushed voice, as she played with her and petted her.

Sarah barked quietly in response to her questions. Then Jessie introduced Erik and Christine and René's son to her. Sarah sniffed each of them, but then stopped and looked at René's son. She cocked her head to the side.

"Yep." Jessie told her. "This is René Jr. and you're going to watch over him, right?"

Sarah sniffed him and then she licked him. This licking tickled the boy and he giggled. Then she yipped, as if agreeing.

"That's a good girl." Jessie smiled at her.

Erik set up the crib a few feet from the fireplace, while Christine brought the other baby things up from the car. Jessie placed her son in the completed crib and Erik went to help Christine put the baby food away in the kitchen and the pampers in the pantry.

Suddenly, a light came on upstairs and everyone stopped. Sarah happily ran up the stairs and barked at René.

"What's all the excitement girl?" René asked.

Sarah didn't say anything of course, she only bolted down the stairs forcing him to follow her out of curiosity. When he got to the foot of the stairs, he saw what all the excitement was about. Jessie was standing there, in front of his fireplace, like she had never left. He said nothing to her, he just stared at her. It was almost like someone had turned on the sunlight and let him out of solitary confinement. Jessie also just stood there looking at him. He was just the same as before, nothing had changed. Just as handsome, just as welcoming. Jessie took a deep breath and let it out. Seeing René again hurt more than she ever thought it could. She just wanted...

"What are you doing up?" She asked him, nervously. "You're usually a sound sleeper."

"I was, but my chest tattoo kept itching. I scratched it and then noticed the sound of scampering feet."

Jessie looked at her beaver tattoo and remembered with fondness that René had inked her with real Iroquois paint.

Suddenly, the room began to glow with a greenish light, and everyone looked up. Through the windows and skylights, they saw the Aurora Borealis overhead.

"Oh, my goodness!" Christine gushed with wondrous awe. "That's so beautiful."

René purposefully walked up to Jessie. He cupped Jessie's face with his right hand and stared deeply into her eyes. He gave her a loving smile and Jessie's heart began to flutter like a horde of butterflies in the summer sun. Big ones that wore combat boots.

"I've missed you." René rested his forehead against hers.

"Believe it or not, I've missed you too." Then Jessie took him by the hand. *I've missed this big strong rough hands. I've missed the feel of them.*

Rene' looked down at her hand in his. *These dry coarse hands, with writers callouses. They feel strong...alive...ready for their next adventure. But this is where they belong. Here with me and I'm not letting go of them again.*

Jessie led him to the crib. "Come here, there is someone that I want to introduce you to."

"Who?" René saw the crib and his eyes went wide with elation.

"Your son." Jessie stood back a bit to let him see.

"My...son." René stood flabbergasted, as he stared into the crib.

Two happy little brown eyes stared back at him. The baby boy giggled at him and wiggled to move. René reached in to touch him. To verify that he was real and not a dream.

"What's his name?" René asked Jessie.

"I don't know. That's why we're here." Jessie told him. *Calm down Jessie, why is my heart beating so fast. Why am I so nervous and excited at the same time?* "As the father of the child, it's your job to name him."

"We?" René looked back at Jessie. "Who else is here?"

Jessie pointed to the kitchen, where Erik and Christine were putting away things and watching the little drama between Jessie and René unfold. They waved their hellos at René.

"My minions, Erik who you've spoken to over the phone and his fiancé Christine, my pediatrician." Then Jessie held up a package full of papers and handed them to René. "These papers are for you to register him as an American citizen AND a Canadian citizen, as soon as you name him. I have given him the middle name of René and the last name of...Voclain." René looked at her, but Jessie continued. "Name him, sign the papers, and then make sure that you register him. I've already signed them...as his...mother."

"Yes, but..." René looked at the papers in his hands, but then back up at Jessie.

"But what?" Jessie wanted nothing more than to be gone already. *But...oh why must everything take so long. What more could he want to know?*

"Is this way you left me without saying goodbye?" He angrily growled at her. René put the papers down and stared at her straight in the eyes. "Why were you trying to sneak in here and sneak by out again without even talking to me?" His eyes were burning with fire. And Jessie could sware that they were staring straight through her. Then he remembered something. "How did you even get in here; the door was locked?"

"René Jr.'s grandmother was a car thief, remember?" Jessie informed him. "There's very few locks that I can't break into or out of."

"That's some resume." René's snapped at her. "You must be really proud."

"What's the attitude for?" Jessie narrowed her eyes on him. "I thought you'd be happy to have a son."

"I am!" He shouted at her and then lowered his voice as to not awaken his son. "I am angry with you."

"What for this time?" She snapped back at him.

"What for?" René snapped back. His shoulders straightened, his back stiffened, and then he unloaded both barrels. "You not only left me without a goodbye, you didn't even call me later to explain yourself, tell me you're pregnant, or even invite me to his birth!"

"Hey! I was...I was..."

"Scared and confused." René offered in a mocking tone.

"Well yeah!" Jessie agreed angrily and then she pointed her finger at him. "I never wanted to be pregnant, a wife, or a mother! How could you do that to me?! So yeah, I went home. I needed Erik to help me. To tell me what to do and to help me get through this!"

"Get through it. It's a child not a passage in a book. You marry his handsome father and together your raise the child in a loving and caring home." René argued. He couldn't look at her anymore and paced the floor. "I know that you're childish and foolhardy, but this is a new low for you." *What in the hell is it about her that excites and infuriates me so much? Why am I so drawn to her? Because she's a thief and she has stolen your heart.*

"Look here Mr. Righteous Indignation, I am my own person. I do what i want when I want and that includes you." *What am I talking about?* "I told you that when you asked me to marry you the first time! I really don't see the problem here."

René turned and looked at her. His leering and wicked grin gave Jessie pause. He rushed forward, grabbed Jessie by her face, and he kissed her. This time passionately.

Jessie, though angry and confused by his actions, was enthralled by his kiss and all thoughts became superfluous. A burning and long unsatisfied need started to grow within them both. Her blood was now humming in her veins, as his brazen hands moved from the sides of her face to down to her squeezable backside. As adjacent as they were, Jessie swore she could feel his erection growing against her. Remembering the warm, wet, vortex of sensations that he could fill her with, it was minutes later before either of them came up for air.

"I..." But Jessie found it hard to find words. Her brain wasn't functioning; she was still under his charismatic spell.

"I, what?" He asked her seriously.

"I couldn't tell you; you'd just ask me to marry you again."

"And what's wrong with that?" He released her and stepped back to talk to her. "It's what people do. Fall in love, get married, have kids. It's the Canadian way." He chuckled.

"But it's not my way." Jessie hung her head. She couldn't look at him. His very image gave her feelings of torment and passion. *He is the one I want, but...* "You wanted children. I never did. You wanted to get married; and I've never even given marriage a second thought." She looked up at him and that was a mistake. *Damn it, why am I in love with him. I just...can't. I have a life. A life in New York that I like just as much. I'm not ready to give that up yet. Are you sure?* "I was just going to come here, drop him off with his father, and then leave again. I'm not staying."

René took a deep breath and let it go. He purposefully stepped forward, picked her up, and threw her over his shoulder like a sack of spuds.

"Hey!" Jessie protested. "What the hell?"

"Sarah," René called out. "Watch over my son." Then he turned to Erik and Christine who were still in the kitchen and trying to give Jessie and René some privacy. "Nice to meet you both. Make yourselves at home."

"What are you doing?!" Jessie yelled at him and beat against his back with her fists. "Put me down, you Neanderthal!"

"I heard about sweeping a girl off her feet?" Christine quipped; her eyes sparkled with mirth. "But I never thought that I would see it done."

René carried Jessie up the stairs, two at a time. Jessie kept trying to fight him off and get him to put her down, but it was no use.

"We might as well get comfortable." Erik told her,

and he took a beer from the fridge. "We won't see them again until morning."

"Seriously?" Christine followed Erik into the living room.

"Well, if they follow the script." Erik opened his beer and took a sip. "First, there's yelling and screaming."

Christine's attention flew to upstairs as she heard raised voices. The argument was heated and long.

"Then comes the throwing of furniture and the fighting." Erik continued commenting and he turned on the TV.

Christine flinched as she heard something hit the wall and brake as it landed on the floor. *That sounded expensive.* There was more foot stomping, furniture scrapping, ceramic breaking, and then there was a loud and heavy thud.

"What was that?" She asked Erik, as she sat down beside him on the couch.

"Either someone's dead." Erik took another swig of beer. "Or that was the bed hitting the wall."

"Erik!" Christine blushed, as she sniggered. "Really."

"Give it five minutes, if no one rushes down here

asking for an ambulance, then we will be here all night." He grinned with mischief.

Christine looked over at Erik as he drank his beer and channel surfed. She shrugged, snuggled next to him, and waited. Ten minutes later, there was a commercial break.

"Well, it's been over five minutes. So, what do we do now?" Christine asked, as she yawned.

Erik looked up at the loft and then down at her. "If you would like to, we could take this time to follow their example."

Christine looked at Erik. He was serious. "You mean here...now? What about little René Jr.?"

Erik looked over at the crib. Sarah was sitting in front of it and looking at the child. The little boy would giggle at her, and she would lightly woof at him.

"He's fine. Sarah is watching him." Erik chuckled.

He put his beer down and took Christine into his arms and kissed her lips.

"That was nice." She smiled at him.

He gave her a wicked grin. "I think you can do better. You just need to practice."

With that, the gentle persuasion of his kiss took her breath away. Christine was startled by his intimacy, but she quietly brewed in his long liquid kiss. Dragging his lips from hers, he then whispered sinuously in her ear.

"Christine Gentil, will you marry me?"

Christine smiled as her chest tightened and her whole body warmed. She wrapped her arms around him and whispered right back. "Yes, Erik. I think it's time we did."

Meanwhile, upstairs...

While René drew Jessie into the maelstrom and beguiled her with his touch, Jessie asked him about what he would name their child.

"Romeo." He kissed her lips hungrily.

"You." Jessie kissed him softly. "Can't" She kissed him deeply. "Name him." Their languid kisses rushed lust through them both. "That."

"Why not?" René pulled away and chuckled at her.

"Romeo?" She questioned angrily, as she lay powerless beneath him. "He'll get beat up in school."

"Every child in our family has a literary name." René slowly withdrew, allowing her to anguish in his leaving, and then once again thrust forward his raw physical desire. His passionate tide overtook her and ignited her own hunger.

Jessie wrapped her legs around his body and clamped her knees to his naked hips. *I've missed the feel of Rene's body.* Jessie lost her senses as she mapped his body with hers. She matched his rhythm, in a push and pull of passion, and they rode the molten waves of sensual bliss.

"Ohhh." Jessie ached with need, moaned with satisfaction, and rose to meet him. "Then name him...Ohhh yess. Oliver, Charlie, or Max." Jessie suggested, as René kissed her tummy. "William, Buck, or Athos." More names poured from her lips; each time René embedded himself within her.

"He is a Voclain, and you are a Tyler. He will be named Romeo, my fair Capulet."

Just before the sun came up, Jessie woke up. She yawned, sat up on her elbows, and then rolled her eyes. Again...again, she was completely naked in his bed.

Damn him. Why is he so much fun to chiavare? Why is he so hard to quit? I gotta stop doing this.

Jessie went to get up, but she found that a rope had been tied to her left foot. She looked down at it and then over at René. She chuckled.

"Nice try. But we Rouges aren't so easily caught."

Balancing only on one foot, she freed herself. Once free, Jessie stood there for a bit, just watching Rene' sleep.

Why do I love you so much? Why, every time I see you, does it get harder and harder to leave? Why do I want to stay here? Why can't I just forget you and get on with my life? Why are you running? I'm not running, I just want my freedom, to come and go as I please. I'm a rouge, not a wife, not a mother. Well, if you don't pull yourself together soon, he'll wake up.

Jessie made her decision, quietly got dressed, and tiptoed towards the stairs. She went downstairs to check on her son. The fire had kept him warm, but not dry. She put another log on the fire and stoked it a bit to keep the house nice and warm. Then she picked up her son and went to change him on the dining room table. Sarah followed her. The little boy began to cry as Jessie took off his diaper.

"Shhh. You wake up your father and there'll be no breakfast for you." She chuckled at him.

After putting him on a fresh diaper, she opened her shirt up and fed him. She sat down in one of the dining room chairs and watched her son feed. He was so small and so helpless. His nose was so cute and wrinkled as he suckled. His tiny hand wrapped around her thumb, and she kissed his hand.

"I do love you little man. I really do." She kissed little Romeo's forehead. "But I'm a roaming rouge. We go where the wind takes us. You'll be safe here with your father. He's a good man. A strong, honest, ...protector. He'll see to it that you have a good life. So be good for him and don't give him any trouble. Because if I ever come back to Canada again...I may never leave."

When the boy finished, she burped him, and then laid him back down to sleep. Jessie then looked over at Erik and Christine. She smiled at them and then she woke them up.

"Come on crewmen, time to go." She gently shook them awake.

As they prepared to leave, Sarah ran to the door. Jessie quieted her with another hug and a kiss goodbye. Erik and Christine rode in the back of the car together. While Jessie got into the driver's seat.

"Okay, kids. Where to now?" She asked, as she started the car and drove away.

"I don't know." Erik said. "Because of the baby, you're free until the Oktoberfest Party at The Word Witch, in Germany."

"Hmm," Jessie grinned wickedly, and then she turned to Christine. "Where do you want to go?"

"Go?" Christine questioned, as she held onto Erik's arm and snuggled against him.

"Yeah, if you could go anywhere in the world and money was no object, where would you go?"

"Well, I've always wanted to see...the Vatnajökull: Iceland, or the Salar de Uyuni: Daniel Campos, Bolivia, or even the Ashikaga Flower Park in Ashikaga, Japan." Christine started naming sights.

"Then we'll see them all." Jessie announced happily. "Let Erik and I show you the world."

"I would love to but," Christine addressed Jessie. "I have a practice to get back to." Then she smiled at Erik. "Beside it'd be a little awkward with you on our honeymoon?"

Jessie grinned into the review mirror. "So, you two are finally going to do it?"

"Yes." Erik beamed, and kissed Christine's forehead. "If that's alright with you Captain?"

"Alright?" Jessie snickered and put on her signal light to turn right. "Hell, I'll even pay for it, Mr. Smee."

"That's right, a captain can marry us at sea, can't they?" Christine remembered.

Erik smiled at Christine, intertwined his hand in

hers, and kissed her hand. "Welcome to the crew, Tiger Lily."

René woke up with a start when he heard barking. The first thing that he noticed was that Jessie was not there. He pulled at the rope and found that she had untied herself.

"Damn it, and that was the best sailor's knot I knew." He groaned. Then he chuckled. "I guess a few knots won't stop her. I should have opted for the ball and chain." He rolled his eyes and laughed. "She would have picked the lock."

Then he remembered his son. René grabbed his jeans, jumped into them, and ran downstairs. Sarah was still dutifully on guard duty and the boy...well he was awake now and rolling around in his crib chewing on his blanket. René petted Sarah on the head.

"Good girl." And then he picked up his son. He held him at arm's length and looked at him. "You're a Voclain alright. You have my eyes and my ears. I guess she was right. They are a family trait. You have her nose and chin though." And then, the little boy yawned at him. "And her attention span apparently." He chuckled to himself as he held his son close to him in his arms. "Well, my little Romeo, our Capulet has fled again. What is wrong with her? What is wrong with me? What am I going to do with you?" The little boy just spat bubbles at him, and René chuckled. "Good Idea. I'll call my brother Jules. Shelly has two boys; she'll know what to do."

Chapter 30

Grace sternly hung up her coat. She sat down on the bench by the front door and removed her shoes. She rubbed her sore and tired feet.

"I can't believe this. First, the boy scouts, then a second buyer. What else can go wrong?"

Then Grace heard René's voice.

"Eat up little man, you're going to need to be strong enough to fight bears."

Curious as to who he was talking to, Grace stood and walked over to the dining room table. Her jaw dropped when she saw René holding a baby.

"Who is that and what are you doing?"

Looking up, René smiled at her. "This is Romeo and I'm feeding him his lunch. How are you doing? And what are you doing back here?"

"I'm miffed, frustrated, and don't change the subject." Grace eyed him suspiciously and then stared at the baby. "We have unfinished business."

"We do?" Rene' gave Romeo another spoonful of baby food.

"The acquisition of this island is currently on hold, and until I have obtained this island and staked my claim, I'm not going anywhere." Grace told him succinctly. "Now back to him." She pointed at the baby.

Suddenly, Anna came out from the guest bathroom from behind the kitchen. She saw Grace and smiled at her.

"Oh hello,"

"Uh, hello." Grace answered in kind, as she looked her over.

"René," Anna prompted René.

"Anna, this is Grace O'Maille. Ms. O'Maille, this is Anna..." René introduced them to each other.

"Another houseguest?" Grace asked, as she raised an eyebrow at René.

"Sister-n-law." René said, and he wiped pureed peas from Romeo's face with his bib. "She is my brother Noel's wife, and they are helping me with Romeo."

"Is the child...yours?" Grace asked Anna.

Anna's eyes fell away from her, and she looked embarrassed. Then she looked to René and reached for Romeo.

"René, give me Romeo and we'll go upstairs. You and Grace have a lot to discuss."

Now Grace's countenance fell. *This doesn't bode well.*

René handed little Romeo over to Anna. "Be a good boy for your Auntie."

Romeo just gurgled and spit little bubbles at him. Grace couldn't help feeling kindly toward the little fella. He was cute, and those cute little puffy cheeks. They were so squeezable. Grace was still lost in thought when René addressed her.

"Grace please sit down and let me get you a glass of wine."

"Thank you and bring the bottle." Grace walked over to the table and sat down. "It's been that kind of day for me."

René nodded and went to get the glasses. He poured her glass first and then sat down at the table to pour one of his own. René waited until Grace had taken her first sips and seemed satisfied before he began speaking.

"Grace, there is something important I must tell you." René began.

"Is it about...Romeo, you called him?" Grace crossed her legs, sat back, and took another sip of wine.

"Yes." René smiled softly.

"Overly dramatic or symbolic?" Grace asked, with a slight smirk.

"Everyone in my family has a literary name." René smiled proudly.

Grace's eyebrows shot up in surprise, but then names started running through her mind.

"And you couldn't name him something less flashy like Tom, Richard, or Harry?"

René laughed. "I already have a nephew named Harry. And Jessie said the same thing."

Grace's already sullen face turned into a snarl and her back stiffened. "Jessie? She was here."

René nodded and desperately tried to keep his composure. But just the thought of Jessie leaving him again caused his lip to curl. "She dropped him off and left again." He growled.

Grace uncrossed her legs and sat forward. "I think you'd better start at the beginning before I get very cross with you." Grace then reached for the wine bottle and poured herself a very large drink.

"Um." René scratched the back of his head and wondered where to start. He then took the bottle, poured himself a drink, and then took a deep breath. "Well, it all started back last November when Jessie crashed her car into a tree and I...uh...nursed her back to health."

"I remember." Grace eyed him angrily. "You two

seemed very...close. She even made you a bagged breakfast if I remember rightly."

"Well...yeah. Anyway, due to the bad weather that we had last year, she was stuck here till spring. And in that time, we grew close." René explained, as he unconsciously balled up a fist with his right hand.

"How close?" Grace demanded. "I mean beyond having a child close."

"I asked her to marry me close." René said, and he cleared his throat. "And yes, we did sleep together. But I thought that was the end of things when she left the first time."

As he spoke, Grace noticed that his voice changed in tone. It was no longer cool and even, but angry and a bit hostile. However, Grace said nothing and let him continue explaining.

"I asked her to marry me, and she said no. Not once, not twice, but three times." René told her firmly.

"And that's why you impregnated her?" Grace asked. *I'm starting to doubt his mental faculties. I know he's been a little hesitant in our relationship, but now I feel like I don't really know him at all.*

"What?!" René balked and sat back in shock. *How could she think that?* "No! It wasn't like that at all."

René's eyebrows shot up in surprise and he waved his hands in front of him. "I didn't...we...I thought she loved me." René's voice and tone dropped sharply and became softer and more romantic. "It was a..." He stopped himself and cleared his throat. "We spent the night together and I was happy to share my life with her." Then René's shoulders dropped in sadness. "Three weeks later, she left me. She left me without a word, just a short note telling me that it was time for her to go home." René's voice changed again, and again, he seemed angry. "I thought we had something special and then she just royally dumped me. Had a lovely time, cheer-ro." Finished, René sat back and crossed his arms. He stewed.

Grace snickered at him and shook her head.

"What's so funny?" He asked her, with a raised eyebrow.

"I don't think her note was that short and sweet." Grace chuckled. "If you had left her, then yes the note would have been short. When girls leave a guy, she always has her reasons. The last guy that I had to let down got a three-page document stating the reasons that we could no longer be together." Grace waved her hand dismissively.

"If she had reasons, she didn't tell me what they

were." René huffed at her and gulped down his wine. "But enough about that, how was your trip?"

"Oh no, you haven't finished this story yet." Grace took the bottle from him and poured herself another glass. "When did you find out that she was pregnant with your child?"

"Two days ago." He confessed begrudgingly.

"Two days?!" Grace barely avoided spilling her drink on herself.

"Yep." René took a drink. "Two days ago, she broke into my house in the middle of the night and..."

"Wait, she broke into your house?" Grace couldn't believe the story that she was hearing. *He's making this up. He's got to be. And yet, I know that he's telling me the truth.*

"Yes, if it wasn't for Sarah. I never would have known she was there."

Grace shook her head and took another drink. "Continue."

"Anyway, I demanded an explanation."

"I would." Grace scoffed.

"She told me that she left me because she found out that she was pregnant. And that she was only coming back to drop off my kid to me."

"So...she abandoned him."

"Well..." René worried. *I hope not.*

Grace took a deep breath and sat up straight. "Well, I can't say I approve."

"I..."

Grace held up a finger for him to be silent. "But..."

Just then, Noel came back from walking Sarah.

"Hey guys, I'm back." Noel called out happily.

René shook his head at this brother's upbeat and thoughtless manner. "Hey Noel." Then he looked at Grace. "That's my brother Noel, Anna's husband."

"Oh hello." Noel spoke to Grace happily. He walked forward and reached out to shake her hand. Sarah pulled away from him, sniffed around, and then went upstairs to find Romeo. "It's nice to meet you."

"Noel, this is Grace O'Maille." Rene' introduced them and then took a drink of his wine.

"A pleasure to meet you Mr. Voclain." Grace nodded happily toward him, and politely shook his hand.

"Bonjour." Noel looked Grace over and gave a small smile. "Your hips are..."

"Noel!" René interrupted his brother with a disapproving growl. "Anna's upstairs with Romeo. Why don't you go and join her?"

Noel smirked at his brother. "Alright, I'm going." He smiled at Grace and gave her a quick gentlemanly bow. "Nice to have met you." Noel took the hint and turned to go upstairs.

"Now, as I was going to say," Grace began again. "I still love you and want to marry you." René was going to say something, but she stopped him again. "I would have liked our first child to have been mine, but as Jessie has abandoned her child and the boy will still need a mother..."

"Grace, I...I..." René struggled to find the right words.

"René Voclain, will you marry me?" Grace proposed to René.

"What?! I..." René's eyebrows shot up in surprise. *Did she just ask me to marry her?*

"I assure you this merger would be most beneficial to the both of us."

Merger? René hung his head. "No...I...can't."

"What?" Grace narrowed her eyes on him. "But I thought..."

"Look, I appreciate your feelings for me. I really do. But...I'm not in love with you."

Grace lowered her head and spoke softly. "You could be. We could learn to grow..."

"No." Rene' shook his head. "I'm sorry." Then he

gulped down the rest of his drink. *I need another drink, preferably one stronger than this, but I need my wits about me.*

Grace looked at René and studied his face. "You still love her." Grace declared. Tears were beginning to form, but she blinked them away, and sat back. "I told you René, I won't compete with a ghost."

René sighed heavily. "She's not a ghost." And then he shook his head. *I told you that you shouldn't have led her on.* His conscience reminded him. "I've tried to forget her and move on. I really thought that I had."

"Until two days ago...when you saw her again." Grace steeled her voice. *I know where this is going, and I don't like it. But don't beg Grace. Never beg!* Grace took a deep breath and asked again. "Will you reconsider my offer?"

René shook his head, and his voice was soft and sad. "No."

Grace sat back and took a deep breath. She then took her phone from her pocket and started typing.

"I was looking forward to a long and happy life with you René." She continued typing on her phone. "But I can see now that that has become impossible." Grace then stood up.

"Would you like to make us dinner before you leave?" René offered kindly and he stood up.

Grace leaned across the table and slapped him. "So quick to get rid of me?"

René jumped back and shock colored his face. "No, I just..."

"Then ask me how my day was." She demanded, as she looked down on him.

René sat back and looked up at her. "How was your day?"

Grace sat back down at the table and crossed her legs. She looked René in the eye.

"Number One, Mr. Howell lost the bidding war." Grace informed him.

"Wait what?! How?!" René looked confused. "I thought..."

"Mr. Howell will no longer try to buy this island. Which is a shame. It really is a very beautiful place."

René tried to hide his cheerfulness. "That's awful. But I thought that it was a done deal."

Grace just raised an eyebrow at him. "Two, these islands have been granted historical and cultural significance and must remain as they are."

"Wait, what?" René sat up straighter.

"Don't you know?"

"No one tells me anything." René complained and crossed his arms in anger.

"Apparently." Grace smirked at him. Then she took her phone out again and showed him a news clipping. It was an article about the secretary of parks and recreation accepting the historical society award. "Due to those boy scouts and their culture heritage essay paper, these islands are now recognized as being part of Native American Cultural Heritage."

"Wow." René sat impressed.

"Thirdly, I have lost the only thing that mattered to me, even more than securing this deal for Mr. Howell."

"What was that?" René asked, seriously.

Anna just shook her head. "Oh my God, he is dense." Then she looked down at baby Romeo. "Your father is a bonehead."

"Did he really just ask her that?" Noel asked Anna, as he facepalmed himself.

"Yes. Your brother has all the brains of a brick. Now shush, I'm trying to listen."

Grace shook her head at René. "You. You meant

more to me than this deal. I wanted this deal for my boss, but I wanted it so much more for us. I wanted us to be happy here in a little cabin for two...or more." Grace smiled internally. Then she frowned. "But you still want her and now that she has given you a son, I have lost you for good."

"I'm sorry that it turned out this way." Rene' went to reach for her hand, but...suddenly, a car horn blew from outside.

"My ride's here." Grace dried her eyes with a napkin, stood up, straightened her back and her suit, and then addressed Rene'. "Goodbye Mr. Voclain."

René jumped up and escorted her to the door. She stopped only for a moment to put her shoes back on. René helped her into her coat, and she opened the door. Then she looked back at him, one last time. René lowered his gaze.

"I did not intend for things to turn out this way." René looked her in the eyes.

Grace acknowledged him with a nod and then kissed his cheek. "Goodbye René."

Then Grace turned and walked away. She got into the car. She glanced one more time at René and then the car drove away. René watched until the car was gone. He sighed heavily and then closed the door.

Chapter 31

It was fall now. The leaves were turning glorious shades of red, golden yellow, and soft browns. The nip in the air chilled the neck and signaled the coming of winter. The moon was half gone, but all the stars turned out in fall fashion. Such was the night when the Voclains came to see their newest addition to the family, Little Romeo.

Harry, Henry, Susan, and Alice played by the fireplace with Sarah. While Shelly and Anna fawned over baby Romeo at the dining room table.

"Oh, he's so cute." Gushed Anna.

"Such a good baby. You are." Shelly smiled brightly and tickled him.

"René, why didn't you tell me that you fathered a child." Mrs. Voclain scolded René, as they stood in the kitchen discussing the issue.

"Because until four days ago, I didn't know a thing about it." René countered back.

"Congrats." Noel slapped him on his back and rested his hand on his brother's shoulder.

René smacked Noel's hand off his shoulder.

Jules slapped the back of his brother's head

angrily. "Didn't father tell us to use protection until properly married."

"Ow!" René growled at his brother Jules. "Yes, and I had every intention of marrying her. She's the one that said no to me and left me cold!"

"Entrapment is not a very nice way to propose. No wonder she left you." Jules scoffed, and he crossed his arms in judgement as he leaned against the counter.

"It wasn't like that!" René shouted at his brother Jules. *I don't appreciate them ganging up on me like this. This isn't my fault...exactly.*

Suddenly, the doorbell rang.

"I'll get it." René pushed past his brother Noel and glared at them. He marched to the front door and opened it. "Hello."

Just then, a fist flew in the door and knocked René to the floor.

"What the hell?!" Jules unfolded his arms, walked up to the figure, and showed him his police badge from his pocket. "Explain yourself before I arrest you for assault."

"My name is Mr. Wolfram Howell and I'm here to gain satisfaction for my secretary Ms. O'Maille. Mr. Voclain here broke her heart."

Hearing the name O'Maille, Mrs. Voclain walked up to Mr. Howell and greeted him.

"Good evening, Mr. Howell. My name is Denise Voclain. I am René's Mother."

Mr. Howell gave her a gentlemanly bow. "I'm sorry that you had to see that Mrs. Voclain." He apologized sincerely.

"From what I'm hearing, my son deserved it." Mrs. Voclain looked from Mr. Howell to her son René, who was sitting on the floor and holding his nose. "Boys, pick up your brother."

"Yes, ma'am." Both Noel and Jules helped René to stand up and dragged him over to the dining room table.

Sarah's ears perked up when she saw her Rene' lying on the floor. She barked at the children and then walked away. The children obediently followed as Sarah led them upstairs and out of the way of harm. Susan and Alice followed quietly, but the boys Harry and Henry whispered to each other about missing a good fight.

René sat down, still holding his nose. His brother Jules brought him a bag of ice. While his brother Noel poured a small tumble of crown royal and brought it to Mr. Howell. Mrs. Voclain invited Mr. Howell inside and escorted him over to the couch.

She sat down beside Mr. Howell and Noel handed him the drink. Mrs. Voclain waited until Mr. Howell had finished it before speaking.

"Now Mr. Howell, I believe you are owed an explanation."

"I would like one. My Gracie hasn't been the same since she visited here. She mopes. Her sales figures are slipping." Mr. Howell angrily counted upon his fingers. "I ask her what happened, but she refuses to talk to me. She only keeps apologizing about letting me down. I don't like seeing her like this. It hurts me that I can't help her. And the only thing I can conclude it that **he** had something to do with it." Mr. Howell pointed an accusing finger at René.

Mrs. Voclain called her son René. "Would you care to explain yourself?"

"He broke my nose." René complained, with a nasally noise, as he held the bag of ice to his face.

Anne left Romeo at the table with Shelly and came to stand before Mrs. Voclain and Mr. Howell.

"If I may explain." She offered politely.

"Mr. Howell, this is Anna. Noel's wife." Mrs. Voclain waved towards Anna as she introduced her. Then she asked her. "Do you know what happened?"

"Yes, Ma'am. My various sources have provided me with a nice complete puzzle of events." Anna nodded.

Mrs. Voclain sat back and waited. "Do tell."

"Well, as you know," Anna looked at Mrs. Voclain. "Or may not know." She looked at Mr. Howell. "This story began with a snow crash victim named Jessica Tyler."

Anna told them the whole story. She told them about Jessie finding out that she was pregnant, and about going home, all the way to Grace's entrance, extensive plans, and prompt exit.

"She hit René too when he turned down her offer the second time."

"Second time?" Mr. Howell was on the edge of his seat and paid attention to Anna's every word.

"Yes. Though surprised by his "love child", Grace did offer to be Romeo's mother. But René said no. Personally, I think he still subconsciously believes that Jessie will come back to him." Anna finished her explanation.

Mr. Howell sighed and then grew angry. "Mrs. Voclain, I'm going to hit him again." Mr. Howell hastily stood up.

Anna hastily retreated to the table and stood near her husband.

Mrs. Voclain quickly stood and placed a gentle but firm hand upon his shoulder. "Mr. Howell, while you are well within your rights. I assure you that I will punish my son most strongly for his sins."

"What?!" René complained, still holding onto the bag of ice.

Mr. Howell frowned but relented. "Alright, madam. I defer this matter to you. And don't be gentle with the whip."

Noel appeared before Mr. Howell with another small tumbler of crown royal.

"Another drink?" Noel asked.

"No, thank you." Mr. Howell waved off the show of kindness. Mr. Howell's face and neck were red with anger and his scowl made it more pronounced. But he softened a bit as he politely refused the second drink. "I'm driving."

"You drove all the way here?" Mrs. Voclain asked, more than a bit surprised. *Imagine that he drove all the way here.*

"Yes. Miss Grace O'Maille is my right arm. She's a damn good Sales and Acquisition officer. Seeing her so melancholy...unsettles me."

Mrs. Voclain narrowed her eyes on Mr. Howell and studied him. *He's a good man, to care for his employee in such a manner.* Then she turned and spoke to her son Jules.

"Jules."

"Yes, mother." Jules reported to his mother and stood before her.

"Take René to the woodshed and beat him for me."

"Uh, yes ma'am." Jules nodded and then turned towards René.

"Can I join in?" Noel chuckled.

Mrs. Voclain rolled her eyes and pinched the bridge of her nose. "Anna."

"Yes Mrs. Voclain." Anna smiled and then she struck Noel's chest with the back of her hand. "Behave yourself Noel."

Jules stood before his brother René. "Come on." Jules picked his brother up by his arm.

"But mom..." René complained and pulled out of his brother's grasp. "I didn't do..." He slammed the bag of ice down on the table.

"But nothing." Mrs. Voclain walked up to and scolded her son. "You should have worn protection. You should have called Jessie after she left. You shouldn't have let Ms. O'Maille get her hopes up. You should have explained yourself and your intentions or lack thereof to her. So, to the shed Now!"

"But...but..." Rene' growled at his mother, trying to get a word in.

"Come on, don't make it worse." Jules grabbed his brother's arm and pulled him towards the garage.

"BUT I AM A GROWN MAN!" shouted at his mother.

"And I am still your mother!" Mrs. Voclain stared down her son with ferocious eyes. "No matter how old you get!"

Mr. Howell watched the heated exchanged. He nodded with Mrs. Voclain's point of view, and he straightened his blazer. "I'll not disturb you anymore." said Mr. Howell and he walked towards the door.

Mrs. Voclain gracefully turned on her heels and escorted Mr. Howell to the door. "I'm sorry about all this Mr. Howell."

"So am I." Mr. Howell shook his head. "Good night, Mrs. Voclain."

"Good night, Mr. Howell. Drive Safely."

That's when they heard the first crack of the belt against flesh. René screamed in pain and yelled at his brother.

"That hurt!"

"It's supposed to." Jules chided.

"This is ridiculous." René complained. "I didn't do anything!"

"Not according to the witnesses." Jules told him seriously. "Now shut up and take it like a man."

Just then Jules hit him again. Even hiding upstairs in the loft, the kids flinched as they heard each strike. Noel drank the crown royal that he was holding and then rejoined his wife at the table. Mr. Howell looked to the left from which the sound had come, he nodded with satisfaction and the hint of a smile, and then he nodded to Mrs. Voclain and took his leave. Mrs. Voclain solemnly closed the door. Then she walked to the table, smiled at little Romeo, and tickled his tummy.

"Anna, you and Noel take the children to the movies." Mrs. Voclain insisted.

"Yes, mom." Noel answered dutifully. He stood and called out to the kids. "Line up guys and let's go."

With that everybody came down from the loft sitting area, reached for their hats and coats, and followed Anna and Noel out the door.

"Shelly?" Mrs. Voclain looked on her kindly and gave her a small smile.

"Yes, ma'am."

"Do you mind Babysitting little Romeo for a bit."

"No ma'am." Shelly smiled and hugged little Romeo.

"Thank you." Mrs. Voclain turned and walked towards the garage. "I need to have a word with my son."

Chapter 32

Jessie was doing a book signing in New York. It was the biggest one that she had ever done. Because it was a Christmas weekend, and everybody was in town for the celebration. The Page Sage run by Samantha McCarter, Jessie's publisher, was the sister publishing company of The Word Witch in Germany; and it was their turn to host the holiday party this year.

The Book Nook was brightly decorated in red, green, and gold, with blue and purple highlights. Two tall white Christmas light angels stood at the front door and trumpeted the arrival of patrons. White Christmas lights decorated every border, while neon lights of blue and purple lit the ceilings. The joyous Christmas Carols played on the speakers and filled the heart with cheer. The delightful aromas of nutmeg and gingerbread filled the store because the little coffee store annex had all its Christmas bakery on display. Even the employees were vivaciously dressed in Nutcracker uniforms. Blue jackets and red skirts for women, while the men wore red jackets and black pants. Jessie had her own version of the Nutcracker uniform with dark green pants, a white dress shirt, and a light green jacket.

A red carpet lined with red VIP ropes led to a sturdy black panel computer desk, which had been set up for the signing. Several copies of all her books were laid out for view and thousands of her books were either on the shelves or in the back storage room.

Erik and Christine were both there, but they were enjoying their secret corner, as they watched the groves of people, who had come to get their books signed by Jessica Tyler. Jessie's fans ranged in all ages from five years old to one hundred and five years old. And although she had a fan base that was both male and female, her fans were still about seventy percent female.

Jillane was also there. She was reporting on all the events that were happening this weekend for her newspaper, and to her great joy, that included her friend Jessie. While Jessie signed books, Jillane would ask her questions about each book, take notes, and make jokes with her. Suddenly, a dashing gentleman stepped up. He was wearing pressed black slacks, white dress shirt with a blue pinstriped tie, and a blue casual slim fit pullover sweater. He put a comic book in front of her.

"Who do you want this made out to?" Jessie asked. She pulled the comic book to her and looked at it. It was "The Roaming Rouges" comic book, volume one, her latest feature.

"Make it out to Romeo." The man said.

Jessie froze and her blood ran cold. "What did you say?" She stammered and looked up at the man, who was holding his two-month-old son.

"Romeo René Voclain." René smiled at her. "He wanted to see his mother."

Jessie's jaw dropped and she stared at René standing there with their son. Jessie's eyes widened and she froze with fear, and yet seeing him again also ignited a spark within her and her heart skipped a beat.

"What are you doing here?" She asked, surprise etched on her face.

"Jr. wanted to see his mother." René looked at her. His gaze was focused as he remembered her every feature both in bed and out of it. He smiled at her. *This is my woman, and she belongs by my side.*

"Why?" Jessie choked up a little.

"Because we miss you." René smirked at her.

"Is that really your kid?" Jillane asked with a wicked grin.

Remembering that her friend was also a

reporter, Jessie grimaced. "Jillian, don't you dare!" Jessie demanded.

"I'm not the one you have to worry about." Jillane laughed.

Without warning, a song started playing over the loudspeakers.

"I really can't stay,

Baby it's cold outside.

I gotta go away,

Baby it's cold outside

This evening has been,

Been hoping that you'd dropped in,

So very nice

I'll hold your hands they're just like ice,

My mother will start to worry,

Beautiful what's your hurry?

My father will be pacing the floor,

Listen to the fireplace roar,

So really, I'd better scurry

Beautiful please don't hurry

Well maybe just a half a drink more,

I'll put some records on while I pour."

"No, no, no. Don't do this to me. Not here.

Please." Jessie begged, humiliation and fear filled her like a pond in the rain.

Jessie's eyes went wide in panic. The digital displays that usually displayed upcoming books and book trailers, now displayed as photos of the Canadian winter wonderland. Winter photos of Maple hill and Old Mike surrounded her, as did photos of the St. Lawrence River flashed upon the walls. Apprehension filled her like molasses, and she looked out over the crowds of people that stared back at her. Disbelief colored their faces, followed by smiles, as well as the pointing and whispering. Jessie face palmed herself.

"Oh my god. Why me?" She groaned.

Jillian spoke to Romeo. "Hello cutie."

"Can you say hello to the nice young lady?" Rene' smiled at his son.

"What's your name?" Jillane asked nicely. "Who's your mommy?"

"My name is Romeo René Voclain." René answered for him in a young boy's voice. "And Jessica Vidia Tyler is my mommy." René smiled at Jillane.

"Your middle name is Vidia?" Jillane giggled at Jessie.

"Shut up." Jessie growled at Jillane lightly. Then

she looked at René. "René, why did you bring him here, and why didn't you call, and why..."

"Hey, you didn't call me." René gave her wolfish stare. "You just broke into my house, dropped him off, and left me...again."

"Did you really?" Jillane looked up from talking to Romeo and smirked at Jessie.

"Not what you're thinking." Jessie told her quickly.

"It's exactly what you're thinking." René spoke to Jillane and chuckled lightly.

"And what am I thinking?" Jillane looked at Jessie and smiled brightly.

"This is not news." Jessie gave her old friend a warning wiggle of her index finger.

"You must be kidding." Jillane burst out laughing. "First, you have a son that no one knew about. That is big news." Jillane threw her hands up in the air in a "surprise" fashion. "And then I find out that you broke into his father's house," She pointed to Rene'. "After which you abandoned him." She pointed an accusatory finger at Jessie.

"I didn't abandon him." Jessie insisted and stressed the fact with a light growl. "I left him with his father." She waved her hands towards Rene'. "No one accuses penguins of abandoning their chicks when the mother leaves him with his father to go out fishing."

"Hmm." Jillane just raised an eyebrow at her and put a hand on her chin. "Never thought of you as a mother penguin. But then again, I've never thought of you as a mother. Looks like I was wrong."

Someone sneezed and Jessie's attention was brought back to the people waiting for their books to be signed. They were all watching this little drama unfold with great interest. Some of them were already tweeting the news about her "surprise" child. While others were recording everything on their cellphones.

"Look, can we talk about this later." Jessie requested. "I've got to finish this."

"Have dinner with me?" René requested.

"Yes, ok, just go." Jessie begged. "Next."

"Promise, mommy?" René asked in a childish voice, pretending to be Romeo.

Jessie smiled at her son, and she ran her fingers through his hair. "I promise."

René gave her a kiss and Jessie kissed him back. She heard the clicking of cellphones and cameras, but she didn't care. René stopped kissing her and rested his head against hers.

"Oh," René gave her a wicked grin. "There's one more thing that I think I should tell you."

Jessie groaned and her shoulders dropped. "And what is that?" Then she snickered at him. "The rabbits ran off with all your veggies."

"No, that my mother is still mad at you." René cradled Romeo with his right arm. Romeo smiled angelically at his mother.

"Don't tell me," Jessie rolled her eyes. "She came to slap me too?"

"No, she came to bring you back with us." René pointed to his mother who was standing there with her hands behind her back. "And she brought back-up."

René's mother pulled out a shotgun and cocked it.

"She brought a shotgun?!" Jessie's eyes bulged.

"Nah, that's just a super soaker. Looks real though, don't it?" René told her.

"How did you sneak that across the border?" Jessie asked with a chuckle.

"She also brought my brothers." René grinned with mischief.

The crowds stepped aside, while Jules in his cop uniform and Noel in his fireman's uniform walked up the aisle to stand beside their mother.

"Why are they wearing their uniforms?" Jessie asked. She shook her head and pinched the bridge of her nose. *This is like being attacked by the village people.*

"So, it's official." Jules walked up to her.

"What's official?" Jessie asked warily. *Oh lord, what am I in for now?*

"Miss Jessica Vidia Tyler, I am placing you under arrest." Jules pulled out his handcuffs, turned Jessie around, and handcuffed her. Then he read her, her rights. "You have the right to remain silent. Anything you say can and will be used against you in a court of law."

Jillane started laughing at her. "I've never known that to stop her before."

"Jillane." Jessie growled at her, with her hands cuffed behind her back. "And if you print any of this..."

But Jillane ignored her threats and kept laughing at her.

"You have the right to an attorney. If you cannot afford an attorney, then one will be appointed for you." Jules continued.

"Jillane stop laughing and call Samantha." Jessie stamped her foot. *I believe this charade.*

"As you wish." Jillane pulled out her phone and

she made two phone calls. One was to Samantha telling her to get down here fast, and the other was to her editor telling him to send a news crew even faster. "Done and Done. Anything else you need? Because you have two wishes left. Do you wish for a lawyer?" Jillane snickered at her. "I can call Sofia, if you like."

"No!" Jessie declared vehemently. "The last thing I need is for my friends to find out about this."

"Seriously?" Jillane scoffed at her. "That's what you're worried about. Honey, by tonight this will be all over New York. Ha, forget that. It'll be all over America."

Then Noel stepped up and threw Jessica over his shoulder into a fireman's carry position.

There's bound to be talk tomorrow,
Think of my lifelong sorrow!
At least there will be plenty implied,
If you caught pneumonia and died!
I really can't stay,
Get over that old out.
Baby it's cold.
Baby it's cold outside

That's when Erik and Christine stepped up. As

hilarious as it was to see Jessie in such a position, she did still have a book signing to do.

"May I ask you what the charges are?" Erik requested.

"Whatever he tells you Erik." Jessie tried to say, from over Noel's shoulder. "I didn't do it."

"Really?" Jules took out his police notebook and let the pages full to the floor. "Let's see now."

Jessie just started laughing. "Seriously? Charges as long as your arm, huh?"

Now cellphones were taking pictures of everything. Social media servers were all experiencing server overloads. Jessie could only hang there like a sack of potatoes and endure the humiliation.

"There's the little matter of an illegal border crossing." Jules began.

"I got lost in the blizzard and crashed my car into a tree." Jessie protested.

"Non-payment of your hospital bill." Jules was really trying to keep a straight face. But even he found that a bit hard to do with Jessie hanging over his brother's shoulder like a rack of lamb.

"What bill? John didn't give me a bill and he's not even a real doctor. He's a vet! I should sue him for malpractice." Jessie laughed, as she remembered waking up naked...twice.

"You were looked over by a vet?" Jillane laughed and she made more notes in her notebook. "You never told me that."

"Then there was destruction of property." Jules continued reading.

"Whose?" Jessie demanded, with curiosity.

"René's kitchen." Jules told her.

"I said I was sorry." Jessie razzed. "Jeez, he just won't let it go."

"Running an illegal chop shop." Jules resumed.

"What?" Jessie exclaimed. "I fixed that hunk of junk."

"Grand theft auto." Jules snickered.

"I left Jack's truck where he could find it." Jessie snickered. "Noel, put me down."

"Grand larceny."

"Grand larceny?!" Jessie balked. "Of what?"

"You stole my brother's heart and then you broke it." Noel spoke with great merriment. "Butterfingers."

"That would be destruction of private property, charge number two." Jules licked his pencil and wrote it up.

"Ugh. You're bringing that up now." Jessie

groaned, as she just hung there listening to the absurdity. "Is that it?"

"How about breaking and entering?" Erik suggested with a wicked grin.

"Erik?! Whose side are you on?" Jessie asked him, with an amused laugh.

"Oh yeah," Jules wrote it down. "My brother was almost eaten by a bear because of you, and then there was breaking and entering."

"That wasn't me." Jessie hollered. "That was Grace, and you know it. And I wasn't stealing! In fact, I was making a deposit."

"Wow, Jessie." Jillane laughed at her. "How can you say that your life is boring?"

"Oh, that reminds me." Jules added yet another charge. "Child abandonment."

"WHAT?!!" Jessie shouted. "I didn't abandon him. I just left him with his father. You people are making sound like I'm a horrible person."

Now more and more people were coming into the store as the news of Jessica Tyler's personal life spread through town like a wild brush fire. Even her four best friends, Dani, Brit, Angela, and Sofia were now standing in the Book Nook, and watching all that happened. Jillane's paper was streaming the

Breaking News Story. And Jessie's four friends were watching with great amusement.

"Are you morons insane?! Put me down!" Jessie demanded.

"You're Layla Rahbar!" Someone in the crowd shouted with elation.

Jessie stopped. Then she saw the light of realization fire up in all her readers.

"You wrote Lost in the Snow!" The female voice shouted again.

"And it isn't a fairy tale! It's based on a true story!" Added another, with great excitement.

The squeal of feminine excitement was so loud that you would have thought that they were being overrun by mice. That or someone had the worse brakes in the world.

"Oh my god, no." Jessie's heart sank, and her world unraveled, out of her control. "I did not!" She lied. "Layla Rahbar wrote it. Layla is the author."

"You're Taras and Leslie!" Another fan figured out.

"People please. Layla Rahbar wrote that book." Jessie looked at Jillane. "Help me out here. Tell them Layla wrote that book. You interviewed her."

"I interviewed somebody." Jillane now stood there thinking about it with her pen to her chin.

"It's a pseudonym!" A male of about forty-five reasoned. "You used a pseudo to hide your name."

"Too late." Jillane giggled.

"Oh my god, oh my god, oh my god!" A woman of about twenty-five shouted with exhilaration. She pointed at René, and then Erik, and then, yes even little Romeo. "You're Taras, and you're Leslie, and you're little Emilio, Naida's bastard son."

Now that really set the crowd off. There was giggling, and whispering, and texting and everything. Jessie groaned her displeasure. Even her four friends were beginning to see the truth of things. Sure, Dani already knew everything, but Shelly, Brit, and Angela were only now realizing that Jessie, their best friend had lied to them.

"You know." Jillane told Jessie, as she hung from Noel's shoulder. "You'll have to tell me the whole story now, just to set the record straight."

"I'm gonna die." Jessie flushed from embarrassment. "Damn it, Noel. Put me down." Jessie squirmed and squirmed trying to wiggle lose.

"And have you run off again." Noel scoffed at her. "Not bloody likely."

"Can I bury you in Canada?" René asked with a smirk.

"How long is she going away for?" Samantha McCarter asked, as she came up the aisle.

People parted for Samantha McCarter, like the waters of the red sea. Samantha commanded attention when she walked because she always walked with confidence and pride. She looked like a Nubian goddess Diana but dominated like the goddess Hera. Layla Rahbar, the person that hey hired to be Jessie's proxy, followed behind her like a lieutenant marching off to war.

"And you are madam?" Jules asked her politely.

"I am Samantha McCarter, her publisher, Owner of The Page Sage." Samantha told him.

"Well ma'am, this is a life sentence." Jules told her. "and our mother is the bailiff. Bailiff, take her away."

Mrs. Voclain smiled at Jessie. "Right this way, Miss Tyler." Mrs. Voclain began to walk away, and her son Noel followed with Jessie still other his shoulder.

But Samantha stood her ground. "Where are you taking her?" Samantha asked, in a concerned, but highly amused tone.

"To a shotgun wedding." Mrs. Voclain chuckled, as she faced off against Samantha.

"A shotgun wedding?" Erik was now laughing so hard that he had to cover his mouth.

"Only fair." Christine snorted. "Our mothers gave us one. Now it's her turn."

"I forfeit my turn!" Jessie shouted, still hanging off Noel's shoulder.

"Sorry, Jessie." Christine mocked her, as she stood aside and let Noel carry her off. "Tick Tock always catches Captain Hook."

"Not funny, Christine." Then Jessie turned the best she could and yelled at Noel. "Damn it, Noel! Put me down or else!"

"Don't you listen to her Noel." Mrs. Voclain told her son. "We have an appointment with Pastor Jones at 4pm."

"NO!" Jessie shouted in panic. "Wait!"

Mrs. Voclain nodded respectfully at Samantha, as she stepped around her, and walked towards the front door. Samantha could only watch in stunned silence and amusement. *Jessie? Married? Oh, my god, that poor man.*

"Nothing doing." René told her, as he fell in step behind his mother and brothers. "I've waited for you for far too long. If people want your books, then they will have to buy them on the Internet."

"Oh no." Jessie feared. "Move it or lose it." She

warned him. "You knucklehead, look what you did!" Jessie snapped at René. "You started a stampede!" Then she turned to Layla. "Layla!"

"Yes, Jessie." Layla was highly amused by this turn of events. She sat on Jessie's book signing table and tried to stay out of the way of the stampede. She had never known that Jessie's life was so ludicrous or fantastical. Yeah, that was a better word for it fantastical.

"Can you finish the book signing for me?" Jessie requested.

"And who's name would you like me to sign?" Layla giggled, as she sat down to take Jessie's place. "Yours or Mine?"

René turned and looked at Layla. "Mrs. Jessica Voclain." He smiled brightly.

"Damn you, Canadians! Put me down!" Jessie kept objecting, as Noel carried her out of the bookstore's front doors.

Front doors that were being held open by Jessie's four best friends. Jessie could only hang her head as she hung over Noel's shoulder. She had lied to them for a year. Dani just raised an eyebrow at her. Brit, Sofia, and Angela were trying to be mad at her for lying to them, but they just couldn't. This event was just too...hilarious and ironic. They just smiled at her and waved goodbye to her as she passed by them.

"Et tu, guys." Jessie shook her head.

Brit stepped forward and addressed Jessie. "Paul Beatty once said, if all the world's a stage, then I want to operate the trap door. And this Jessie, is your trap door." Brit smiled at her.

"You should have told me that you were getting married." Angela cocked her head to the side, as she spoke to Jessie. "I would have given you a grand send off."

"Does this look like I planned for this to happen?" Jessie snapped at her.

"This is New York." Sofia laughed at her. "Anything and everything is possible here."

As Jessie was carried out, and her friends waved goodbye, more and more people kept coming in to buys books. The cops had to be called to get law and order back inside the bookstore. The fire department blocked off the streets about the bookstore and between Samantha and Jillane, they brought the Christmas party to a joyous and profitable ending. TV cameras covered the events, people were interviewed, and Layla and her children were having the time of their lives as Jessie's representatives. When people asked where

Jessie was, no one knew. She had been spirited away by her Canadian in-laws. After that, her books were sold out everywhere. People snatched up every novel, comic book, and novella that Jessie ever wrote. Especially Lost in the Snow and Cabin Fever.

Chapter 33

Twelve days later, on January sixth, Jessie and René were married at St. Michael's Church in Lansdowne, Ontario. Erik's mother and Christine's mother both enthusiastically approved of the date, since it was also the Roman Catholic Holy Day Solemnity of the Epiphany, which celebrated the wise kings that visited the Christ Child. They smiled to each other as they relished in the irony.

The church was full and was standing room only. On one side of the church, were all of René's friends and family. Mrs. Voclain sat happily smiling with her newest grandson Romeo in her arms. Jules was the best man. Noel, Erik, John, Wyatt, and Tom and groom's men. Dani was the maid of honor. Christine, Brit, Shelly, Jillane, and Layla, were bridesmaids.

On the other side of the church, were Jessie's literary friends, co-workers, and fans. Erik and Christine's families were there too. Erik's mother Maria and his father Francis, who everyone called Frank. His sister Esmerelda, her husband Marshall, and their two kids Carlos and Carol were there as well. Christine's mother Rosa and her father

Andrea and Christine's sister Elizabeth, her husband Peter, and their three kids Mary, James, and John were there as well.

Not only were their friends and family in good spirits, but so was the weather. It was sunny, but cold, and yet stunningly spectacular. The clear and brilliant blue skies. The clean white snow as it covered the ground. The evergreen and heady smell of pine trees filled the air. The crisp sparkle of excitement in the air reflected René's own eagerness. He could only wait in excited anticipation, as the music started, and his wedding began.

First, came Jules and Dani as best man and maid of honor. The classic navy-blue tuxedo for him and a burgundy A-line V-neck asymmetrical winter bridesmaid dress for her. Then came Susan and Alice, Noel's daughters as flower girls; and René's dog Sarah, walked up the aisle next, as the ring bearer. They were followed by the groomsmen and bridesmaids.

"Why are our parents here?" Erik asked Christine with an amused chuckle, as he escorted her down the aisle to their appointed places. "I thought they hated her."

"One, to thank her for paying for our wedding

and to show her their respects. My family never could have afforded it. And two, to make sure that we are finally free of the "devil women's" clutches." Christine snickered.

"You've got nice hips." Noel told Layla with a wolfish smile, as he escorted her down the aisle.

"I'm married, Mr. Voclain." Layla warned him, with a forced grin.

"So am I." He laughed at her and pointed out his wife and kids in their seats. "I was just making polite conversation."

After everyone had taken their places, Jules looked over at his brother Rene'. He was so happy that he swore he would break into song and float away. As he looked down the aisle to see what Rene' was looking at. He could see what his brother was happy.

Jessie was wearing an elegant white princess ball gown dress with flowing chapel train of sparkle tulle and horsehair. In her hands, she carried a bouquet of burgundy ranunculus, rich black barraca roses, and white and navy-blue anemones, all tied together with a burgundy and blue ribbon. Here comes the bride played by violins, trumpets, and a harp filled the church with heavenly music as Jessie walked down the aisle.

Since Jessie's parents had long since passed away, it was Samantha, her publisher, that gave her away.

"I'm only loaning her to you." Samantha told René. "I want her back at work."

"Don't worry ma'am." René nodded. "She'll be just across the lake."

"I don't believe this." Jessie groaned, with trepidation. "Why am I in a wedding dress?"

"Because the tux wouldn't fit you?" Noel chortled.

"Don't worry, my fairy princess." René beamed at her, as he took her hand in his. "We'll live happily ever after."

Jessie didn't say anything to him, she just smiled and tried not to think about it. Her stomach hurt and was tied in knots. Dread filled her soul, and her hands began to sweat.

Me? Getting married? Jessie feared. Buck up Jessie, her conscience told her. It's just the beginning of a new year and a new adventure. Look at him. It could be worse. Jessie giggled and looked at René. Yeah, what am I worried about. I get to wake up, in a Canadian mountain retreat, to my sexy forest ranger. How bad can it be? To live in this reality. With someone that I love and who emphatically loves me. Whoa, where did that come from. Jessie jumped out of her contemplations when the priest spoke to them.

The priest looked to René and asked him. "René Basil Voclain, voulez-vous prendre Jessica Vidia Tyler comme épouse? Et promettez-vous de rester fidèle à elle, Dans le bonheur ou dans les épreuves, Dans la santé et dans la maladie, pour l'aimer tous les jours de votre vie?"

"Oui." René smiled at Jessie.

Then the priest looked at Jessie and asked her.

"Jessica Vidia Tyler, do you want to take René Basil Voclain as your husband? And do you promise to remain faithful to him, in happiness or trials, in health and sickness, to love him all the days of your life?"

Jessie shook her head and laughed. "Yeah, I do."

"Rings Please." The priest asked.

René took the box with the rings off the pillow tied to Sarah's head and handed them to the priest.

René patted Sarah's head. "Good girl."

"René, place the ring on her finger." The priest told him.

"Avec mon corps, je tiens le culte. Avec mon cœur, je chéris. Tout ce que je suis, je vous le donne. Tout ce que j'ai, je le partage avec vous. De ce jour jusqu'à la fin de la vie. Avec cette bague, je me tiens."

"Jessica, please do likewise." The priest instructed her.

"With my body, I thee worship. With my heart, I thee cherish." Jessie smiled to herself as she spoke the words. For some reason, they filled her heart with joy. "Would all that I am, I give unto you. Would all that I have, I share with you. From this day until forever is done."

"Then by the power vested in me, by God, and the providence of Ontario. I now pronounce you man and wife." The priest smiled. "You may kiss the bride."

René smiled at Jessie, pulled her close, and kissed her well. Noel looked at his watch. Jules just rolled his eyes and cleared his throat. "Time's up. Save some for the honeymoon."

The reception was at René's home and Jessie's friend Angela had done it up right. As the best wedding planner in all of New York, René's home was now a chalet of love. Instead of the pictures of nature that had lined his walls before, now pictures of he and Jessie having fun in the wilds of Canada lined the walls. Pure burgundy silk and gold satin banners hung from his rafters, and they were lit with tiny LED lights that gave a soft glow. Angela used the bold colors of burgundy, gold, and navy blue to elegantly contrast René's rustic home, the beautiful frozen river, and snow laden forest that surrounded it. It gave off an air of a simply perfect winter wedding.

Wyatt called in a few favors and got his company to cater the event. He and his co-workers deftly adapted and decorated the tables with navy tablecloths, burgundy napkins, and golden fine china dinnerware. Each name place card was blue with gold edges and lettering. A few more favors later and René surprised Jessie with Roberto and he and Wyatt created and unbelievable menu for her reception luncheon.

"Jessie!" Jessie's friends screamed with delight.

Jessie rolled her eyes and shook her head. *They'll never change. What can I say? Grasshoppers love a good party.*

"Girl, I can't believe it." Sofia squealed with delight. "You finally did it. You got married." She hugged Jessie for all that she was worth.

"Yah, feel free to shoot me now." Jessie laughed. "I said I'd never do it, but I did."

"About time." Brit chuckled at her. "I was

beginning to wonder if you would. But I'm mad at you too." Brit crossed her arms and frowned at her.

"What?" Jessie was taken aback. "Why?"

"Because you had a child and didn't tell any of us." Brit accused; her index finger sternly pointed at Jessie.

"Yeah, what was up with that." Dani glowered at her. "I thought you swore to tell me the truth."

"Since when is NOT saying anything the same as lying?" Jessie quipped.

"He's a cute kid." Angela snickered.

"He is." Jessie smiled with pride. Then she looked around the room and spied her son in the arms of his grandmother, Mrs. Voclain. "Try freeing him from his grandmother though."

"But not as cute as my designs." Angela interjected, looking up to draw their gaze upwards.

The girls all laughed at Angela. "Yes, yes Angela. The decorations are lovely." Dani chuckled at her and waved a dismissive hand upwards.

"The decorations are amazing." Jessie praised Angela. "Thank you. You truly are the most amazing and best wedding planner ever."

"You know we're going to have to throw you a bleated baby shower." Danni gave her a wicked grin.

"Don't you dare!" Jessie joked. "I'm still having flashbacks from the last one."

"Hey girls, can I borrow Jessie for a while?" René asked. He was smiling so brightly that Dani swore he could light the room all by himself.

"Oh, handsome and dashing." Sofia looked René over. "Hello, big boy."

"Mine." Jessie snickered and she gave René a hug.

"No way." Brit chuckled and pulled Jessie out of his arms. "You get to have her for a lifetime."

"Unless you have some brothers." Angela grinned.

"Sorry girls. They're all married already. I was the last one." René smiled brightly.

"Marriage is like wall street, girls." Angela chuckled. "Timing is everything."

"Hey Jessie!" John greeted her happily, as he and his wife Michelle came over to her. "Crakin' to see you again lassie."

"Hey John." Jessie greeted John with a friendly hug. "Girls, introductions. This is Dr. John." Jessie smiled brightly.

"Well, hello doctor." Jessie's friends greeted him warmly and with much laughter.

Later that night, René schooled Jessie some more in ways of the Iroquois.

"In Iroquois tradition, it is the females that rule. So, when a man marries, he becomes part of his wife's clan. That is why when Romeo is old enough, he'll be getting a beaver tattoo instead of an Elk like mine."

Jessie just listened to René's explanation, as she happily laid naked upon his bare chest.

"René?"

"Oui, ma reine."

"I love you."

"Oui, ma reine, je sais." René sighed contentedly and smile at her. "I love you too." René placed a loving hand on Jessie's backside and gave it a good squeeze. "Shall we give Romeo a sibling?"

Jessie heaved a sigh of utter happiness. "Oui." She grinned.

Receipes

Try these delicious meals at home. All recipes are from an internet website called The Spruce. They are not my recipes, but they are very delicious recipes.

If you are interested in more recipes, then just go to https://www.thespruce.com

Have fun.

Fluffy Eggs

Ingredients

8 eggs

½ cup whole milk

2 tablespoons whole butter

Salt and ground white pepper, to taste

How to Make It

Crack the eggs into a glass mixing bowl and beat them until they turn a pale yellow color.

Heat a heavy-bottomed nonstick sauté pan over medium-low heat. Add the butter and let it melt.

Add the milk to the eggs and season to taste with salt and white pepper. Then, grab your whisk and whisk like crazy. You're going to want to work up a sweat here. If you're not up for that, you can use an electric beater or stand mixer with the whisk attachment. Whatever device you use; you're trying to beat as much air as possible into the eggs.

When the butter in the pan is hot enough to make a drop of water hiss, pour in the eggs. Don't stir! Let the eggs cook for up to a minute or until the bottom starts to set.

With a heat-resistant rubber spatula, gently push one edge of the egg into the center of the pan, while tilting the pan to allow the still liquid egg to flow in underneath. Repeat with the other edges, until there's no liquid left.

Turn off the heat and continue gently stirring and turning the egg until all the uncooked parts become firm. Don't break up the egg, though. Try to keep the curds as large as possible. If you're adding any other ingredients, now's the time to do it.

Transfer to a plate when the eggs are set but still moist and soft. Eggs are delicate, so they'll continue to cook for a few moments after they're on the plate.

Mix-Ins for Your Scrambled Eggs

Some ingredients you could add include, if you choose to:

Chopped fresh herbs

Grated cheese

Diced and sautéed onion (sauté the onion separately and then add)

Chopped, cooked bacon

Diced ham

Pancakes

Ingredients

1 cup all-purpose flour

2 tablespoons sugar

2 teaspoons baking powder

1/2 teaspoon salt

1 large egg, slightly beaten

2 tablespoons vegetable oil

How to Make It

Combine the flour, sugar, baking powder, and salt. Whisk or stir to blend thoroughly.

Stir in egg, oil, and enough milk for the batter to pour easily. Mix lightly, just enough to blend.

Cook pancakes on a hot, well-greased griddle. Flip the pancakes when you see bubbles breaking all over the tops, and then continue cooking until the underside is browned.

This recipe makes 2 to 3 servings.

Tips and Variations

The sugar can be adjusted to suit your taste and your diet, or use an equivalent sugar substitute.

If you use a 1/4-cup measuring cup to scoop the batter, your pancakes will be uniform in size.

Add about 3/4 cup of fresh cleaned blueberries to the pancake batter.

Fold about 1/3 cup of chopped pecans into the batter.

For fluffier pancakes, separate the eggs and beat them to stiff peaks in a separate bowl. Fold the egg whites into the batter after adding milk.

Buttermilk Pancakes – Decrease the baking powder to 1 teaspoon and add 1 teaspoon of baking soda. Add about 1 cup of buttermilk, or enough to make a thick but pourable batter.

Chocolate Chip Pancakes – Add about 1/4 cup of miniature semisweet chocolate morsels to the batter.

Fresh Strawberry Sauce – Combine 1 1/2 cups of sliced fresh strawberries with 2 tablespoons of granulated sugar and let stand for 1 hour or refrigerate for 2 hours. Pour the juices from the strawberries into a measuring cup and add enough water or orange juice to make 3/4 cup. Pour the juice into a saucepan and stir in 1 teaspoon of cornstarch until the mixture is smooth. Bring the mixture to a boil over medium heat and continue cooking, stirring, for 2 minutes. Remove from the heat and stir in the sliced strawberries. Serve over pancakes or use it as a dessert sauce.

Fresh Blueberry Sauce – Wash and crush 2 cups of fresh blueberries. Put the blueberries in a saucepan with 1/3 cup of sugar, 1 tablespoon of lemon juice, and a pinch of salt. Bring to a boil over medium heat and continue cooking, stirring, for 1 to 2 minutes. Chill and serve over pancakes or use as a dessert sauce.

Barbequed Round Steak Strips over Rice

Ingredients

2 pounds boneless beef round steak (1 inch thick), cut into strips

2 tablespoons canola oil

1/2 cup tomato juice

1/2 cup ketchup

1/4 cup water

1/4 cup cider vinegar

2 tablespoons Worcestershire sauce

2 tablespoons brown sugar

2 teaspoons paprika

1 teaspoon salt

1 teaspoon ground mustard

1 garlic clove, minced

1/4 teaspoon chili powder

1/4 teaspoon pepper

4 teaspoons cornstarch

2 tablespoons cold water

Hot cooked rice, optional

How to Make It

In a large skillet, brown beef in oil over medium-high heat; drain. In a small bowl, combine the tomato juice, ketchup, water, vinegar, Worcestershire sauce, brown sugar and seasonings; pour over the beef. Bring to a boil. Reduce heat; cover and simmer for 1-1/2 to 2 hours or until the meat is tender.

Combine cornstarch and cold water until smooth; stir into meat mixture. Bring to a boil; cook and stir for 1-2 minutes or until thickened. Serve with rice if desired. Yield: 6-8 servings.

Beef Stew

Ingredients

2 pounds lean chuck stewing beef or a chuck roast

2 to 3 teaspoons vegetable oil

1/2 teaspoon seasoned salt

1 cup chopped onions

1 can (approx. 10 1/2 ounces) condensed beef broth or concentrated rich beef stock

hot water

3 cups diced potatoes

2 cups diced carrots

2 ribs celery, cut into 1/2-inch pieces

2 tablespoons all-purpose flour

1/3 cup cold water

black pepper and seasoned salt to taste

How to Make It

Cut the beef into small, bite-sized cubes.

Heat the vegetable oil in a Dutch oven or large kettle; add the beef, seasoned salt, and chopped onions. Cook, turning frequently, over medium heat for about 10 to 15 minutes, until the meat is browned on all sides and chopped onions are tender. Drain off excess fat if necessary.

Add the beef broth and hot water to the pot until the liquid level is about 1 inch above the beef. Cover and reduce heat to low. Cover and simmer for 1 1/2 to 2 hours or until the meat is tender.

Add the potatoes, carrots, and celery. Cover and cook, stirring occasionally, for 20 to 30 minutes longer, until vegetables are tender.

To thicken the stew, combine the flour with 1/3 cup cold water; stir until smooth. Gently stir flour mixture into the pot a little at a time, using as much as needed to make the stew as thick as you like it.

Add pepper and taste for seasonings, adding more seasoned salt if necessary.

Expert Tips

For a hearty, stick-to-your-ribs meal, add a few tablespoons of barley about 45 minutes before the stew is done.

Add about 1/4 to 1/2 cup of dry red wine along with the water for some extra flavor.

Three Sisters' Vegetarian Chili

Ingredients

2 tablespoons olive oil

2 (6 to 8 inch) corn tortillas, cut into 2-inch strips

2 medium onions, chopped

1 large red bell pepper, chopped

4 cloves garlic, chopped

1 (15 ounce) can corn, undrained

2 pounds of butternut squash, peeled, seeds removed, chopped into ½ inch pieces

2 tablespoons chili powder

1 1/2 teaspoons dried oregano

1 1/2 teaspoons ground cumin

1/4-1/2 teaspoon cayenne pepper

1 (15 ounce) can black beans, drained

1 (15 ounce) can kidney beans, drained

1 (16 ounce) can tomato sauce

4 cups of vegetable broth

Salt and pepper, to taste

1/4 cup shredded Monterey Jack cheese or Jalapeno Jack cheese (optional for serving)

2 green onions, chopped (optional, for serving)

1/4 cup sour cream (optional, for serving)

2 tablespoons fresh cilantro, chopped (optional for serving)

How to Make It

First, heat half the oil (one tablespoon) in a large saucepan over medium-high heat. Add the cut tortillas and lightly brown. Remove to a paper-towel-lined plate; let drain. These tortilla strips will top your chili and give it a fantastically crunchy finishing touch.

Next, heat the remaining oil (one tablespoon) in the same large saucepan. Add the onion, red pepper, garlic, and corn.

Then stir in the chili powder, oregano, cumin and cayenne pepper. Allow to cook for four minutes, stirring often.

Next, add the beans, butternut squash, and tomatoes, vegetable broth, whole beans. Season with a bit of salt and pepper to taste. Allow to simmer over medium-low heat for 30 minutes. Bring to a boil, then reduce heat to medium-low and simmer, stirring occasionally, until squash it tender.

Serve your black bean and corn chili topped with

tortilla strips, cheese, green onions, sour cream, and cilantro.

Turkey and Stuffing

Ingredients

1 (5 to 7 pound) turkey breast, bone in, skin on
Salt and pepper to taste
1/2 cup butter
3/4 cup chopped celery
1 onion, chopped
4 cups wheat or white bread cubes, dried in the oven
1/2 cup dried cranberries
1/2 teaspoon dried sage leaves
1/2 teaspoon dried thyme leaves
1 teaspoon salt
1/4 teaspoon pepper
1/4 to 1/3 cup chicken stock
Melted butter for basting

How to Make It

Preheat the oven to 350°F. Sprinkle the turkey with salt and pepper to taste and set aside.

In a large skillet, melt 1/2 cup butter and cook the celery and onion over medium heat until tender. In a large bowl, combine the remaining ingredients except the butter for basting.

Pour the cooked celery mixture over the ingredients in the bowl. Toss gently with two spoons to coat. Add the chicken stock and toss until lightly moistened.

There are two ways to 'stuff' the breast.

Place some of the stuffing in between the two halves of the breast. The breast comes folded up, so just pry it apart a little bit and add stuffing; don't pack. Then use kitchen string to loosely tie the breast closed. Place on a roasting pan, add 1/2 cup chicken stock to the bottom of the pan, rub the turkey with some butter, and roast. Place remaining stuffing in a casserole dish, cover, and refrigerate. Add to the oven and bake, uncovered, for the last 45 minutes of the turkey roasting time.

Or you can just place the turkey, skin side down, on a cutting board. Gently pull the two halves apart. Then turn the turkey over and press down on the breastbone so the breast is more opened up. Then put the stuffing in a foil-lined roasting pan and place the breast, skin-side-up, on top. With this method, whenever you baste the turkey, pour some chicken broth or water on the stuffing not covered by the turkey and stir it gently. This way the stuffing doesn't burn and just keeps getting better!

Whichever method you choose, coat the turkey with the melted butter, and roast the turkey and stuffing for 2 to 2-1/2 hours or until an instant-read meat thermometer inserted into the meat reads 165°F. Baste the once or twice during roasting with the pan drippings.

Sticky Toffee Pudding Pie

Ingredients

For the Pie Crust:

1-1/2 cups of flour

1/4 teaspoon

baking powder

1/2 teaspoon salt

1 teaspoon sugar

1/4 cup cold butter cut into small pieces

1/2 cup of refrigerated Crisco® shortening

For the Apple Filling:

Five medium to large Michigan Cortland, Ida Red Apples, peeled, thinly sliced, diced

1 cup brown sugar

3 Tablespoons flour

4 Tablespoons melted butter

2 teaspoons cinnamon

1 teaspoon lemon juice

1/4 teaspoon salt

For the Sticky Toffee Pudding Filling:
1/2 cup praline pecans
1 stick of butter softened
1/2 cup brown sugar
2 tablespoons heavy cream
1 tablespoon lemon juice
1 egg – beaten
1/2 cup
self-rising flour

For the Crumb topping:
3/4 cup of flour
1 cup sugar
1/4 teaspoon salt
1 stick of butter softened

For the Homemade Caramel:
1 (14-ounce) can sweetened condensed milk
1 cup light corn syrup
1 cup sugar
1/2 cup brown sugar
1/2 stick (1/4 cup) butter
1 tablespoon real vanilla extract

For the Praline Pecans:
1 cup of chopped pecans

2 tablespoons butter

2 tablespoons brown sugar

How to Make It

Make the pie crust: Mix all of the crust ingredients in a Kitchen Aid style mixer on medium speed swiftly until crust appears "pea-like." Carefully sprinkle water in crust mix until it starts to become moistened and gathers together. Pat into a disc, wrap and refrigerate for at least one half hour. Roll out onto a floured surface and make and crimp the crust. Freeze until ready to use.

Make the apple filling: Cook the apple filling ingredients in a large pan on medium heat until cooked halfway. Stir in 3/4 cup homemade caramel (see directions below) until melted.

Make the sticky toffee pudding filling: Mix above ingredients just until blended.

Make the crumb topping: Mix all together all crumb topping ingredient by hand or a pastry blender until fine and crumbly.

Make the homemade caramel: In heavy 3-quart saucepan, combine all ingredients, but the vanilla. Cook over medium heat, stirring constantly, covering all parts of the bottom of the pan with a wire whisk to avoid scorching. Stir until mixture comes to a boil. Reduce heat to low and continue stirring until caramel reaches 244F on a candy thermometer or firm-ball stage. Pour in a glass container. Cool to use.

Make the Praline Pecans: Melt butter in small pan on medium-low heat until melted. Add pecans and sugar and stir ingredients until you start smelling the nuts roasting. Take off heat and cool. Crumble.

Assemble the pie: Spread sticky toffee pudding mixture on bottom of crust. Put apple mixture over pudding mixture. Sprinkle with crumb topping. Bake in preheated 400-degree oven for one hour or until the knife easily slides into the center of pie with no resistance. If the pie becomes too brown before done, turn down oven to 350 degrees to finish baking and cover with foil completely. Top with a generous amount of homemade caramel and praline.

9 781949 252378